TALES FROM THE
FORBIDDEN ZONE

Also Available from Titan Books

Dawn of the Planet of the Apes: Firestorm
by Greg Keyes

Dawn of the Planet of the Apes: The Official Movie Novelization
by Alex Irvine

Planet of the Apes: The Evolution of the Legend
by Joe Fordham and Jeff Bond

*Rise of the Planet of the Apes and Dawn of the Planet of the Apes:
The Art of the Films*
by Matt Hurwitz, Sharon Gosling, and Adam Newell

War for the Planet of the Apes: The Official Prequel Novel
by Greg Keyes (June 2017)

War for the Planet of the Apes: The Official Movie Novelization
by Greg Cox (July 2017)

PLANET OF THE APES

TALES FROM THE
FORBIDDEN ZONE

EDITED BY RICH HANDLEY AND JIM BEARD

TITAN BOOKS

PLANET OF THE APES ™: TALES FROM THE FORBIDDEN ZONE
Print edition ISBN: 9781785652684
E-book edition ISBN: 9781785652691

Published by Titan Books
A division of Titan Publishing Group Ltd
144 Southwark Street, London SE1 0UP

First edition: January 2017
10 9 8 7 6 5 4 3 2 1

A CIP catalogue record for this title is available from the British Library.

Printed and bound in the United States.

Did you enjoy this book?

We love to hear from our readers. Please email us at readerfeedback@ titanemail.com or write to us at Reader Feedback at the above address.

TITANBOOKS.COM

CONTENTS

WE FINALLY REALLY DID IT
AN INTRODUCTION

by

RICH HANDLEY

Let me tell you a story about apes.

First, though, let me tell you a story or two *about* a story about apes.

Twenty years ago and change, I found a copy of French author Pierre Boulle's 1963 novel *La Planète des Singes* while perusing the shelves of a dusty bookstore in Canada. My wife Jill and I had driven to Toronto to celebrate our anniversary, and when I saw what I recognized as the novel upon which one of my all-time favorite films, *Planet of the Apes*, had been based, I had to read it. Thankfully, this copy was printed in English, as I don't speak French... or ape, for that matter.[1]

The title had been translated as *Monkey Planet*, which struck me as an amusing misnomer—not only because no monkeys appeared in the novel, but because in the films, apes found the term "monkeys" highly offensive. (I have to wonder, though, who would ever call them that, since they had no contact with other species capable of speech. But I digress.)

I was fascinated by the similarities, and the stark differences, between novel and film. Like the movie, the book featured a

---

[1] Yes, the apes speak English in the films, but in Boulle's novel, they speak their own language.

human space traveler stranded on a world populated by highly intelligent apes, and offered thoughtful social commentary about religious dogmatism, bigotry, the misuse of science and technology, and how the weaknesses of the human species could bring about man's own undoing. Unlike the film, however, it took place in a far more advanced simian society, and was set on (spoiler alert!) another planet, not Earth. It's a brilliant read, and if you've never picked it up before, then you owe it to yourself, as a self-respecting *Apes* fan, to do so... after you've finished reading *this* book, naturally.

I first discovered *Planet of the Apes* and its four sequels as a child, thanks to *The 4:30 Movie*, a daily film showcase that aired on our local New York ABC affiliate in the late 1970s. *The 4:30 Movie* introduced me to Charlton Heston's non-*Apes* films, along with *Godzilla*, the *Pink Panther* movies, *Fantastic Voyage*, *Westworld* (and its sequel, *Future World*), and many other classics, some of which now inhabit my home-video library. But none of it compared to the Apes. When "*Planet of the Apes* Week" arrived each year, nothing else mattered.

Having been born in 1968, the same year in which the first *Apes* film hit theaters, I had never seen any of the movies before Channel 7 propelled me to that upside-down world through the 13-inch, black-and-white Hasslein curve that was our family television. I was hooked, and have been ever since. That final image of Taylor kneeling on the shore, damning mankind to Hell after finding the Statue of Liberty's upper half buried in the sand, shocked ten-year-old me, as it did countless viewers—and a lot of future filmmakers as well, it would seem. *The Empire Strikes Back*, *The Crying Game*, *The Usual Suspects*, *The Sixth Sense*, *Fight Club*, *Memento*... so many films made since then owe a lot to that now-iconic twist ending, which itself owed much to *Apes* co-writer Rod Serling's prior work on *The Twilight Zone*.

Of course, as a fan of the Apes, you already know that. You also know that the 1968 classic spawned not only those four sequels, but four additional films to date, starting in 2001. And you probably know that there were two television series as well—a live-action version set a thousand years before the original film, about three friends on the run from gorilla soldiers (basically, *Apes* meets *The Fugitive*), and an animated series, *Return to the Planet of the Apes*, that bizarrely featured alternate versions of characters from both the films and the prior TV show, in a technologically advanced Ape City similar to the setting of Boulle's novel.

What you might *not* know is that the story didn't end there, with what happened on the big and small screens. An expanded universe of licensed fiction, set before, between, during, and after the apes' filmed and televised exploits, has helped to flesh out the mythos. All of it proudly lines my shelves, alongside my now-dusted copy of Boulle's novel.

These ancillary tales have mostly been told in comic books—nearly 200 issues to date and counting. Yet, when it comes to prose, *Apes* fans have been limited to only Boulle's book, a dozen or so novelizations, and six original novels in the past five decades. As for short fiction? Well, other than a few brief tales published decades ago in a trio of largely forgotten British children's books, licensed *Apes* short stories have been entirely nonexistent.

Until now, that is.

In 2015, Jim Beard and I proposed a project to Titan Books editor Steve Saffel that would be a first (though hopefully not the last) for *Planet of the Apes*: an anthology of prose stories covering the classic era of the franchise, written by popular and respected authors from multiple genres. With a landscape spanning thousands of years, we reasoned, the possibilities for new adventures were infinite. Our intent was to draw upon each writer's unique individual strengths, background, and enthusiasm to craft entertaining tales of the sort that readers might not normally experience.

Titan expressed strong interest in the anthology—which we called *Visions from the Planet of the Apes*—provisionally accepting our proposal provided that the author lineup satisfied both the publisher and Fox. We already had several writers in mind when pitching the book, but we needed to add more if we were to tip the scales in our (and fans') favor.

Jim and I began reaching out to numerous high-profile authors, with the goal of featuring a wide range of stories told with different voices and styles, set throughout the *Planet of the Apes* timeline and spotlighting characters both existing and new. Especially exciting was that we'd be allowed to include characters and settings from both the live-action and animated TV series, branches of the *Apes* family tree that are often overlooked but have loyal fans nonetheless.

After a great deal of footwork, exchanged e-mails, and outreaches to novelists, screenwriters, and comic book professionals, we finalized our lineup. The enthusiastic responses we received to our invitations made it clear that we'd chosen a team of *Planet of the Apes* aficionados—a few of whom had written *Apes* novels or comics in the past, so we were excited to bring them back into the fold. We compiled a list of the pitches we received, then waited with fingers, toes, and eyes crossed as Titan and Fox considered the full proposal. Amazingly, every single pitch was approved... except for one.

Mine.

Somehow, I'd come up with a story that Fox felt was too close to the concept of the latest film, this year's *War for the Planet of the Apes*, which was then still in production. How did I manage to do *that*, you ask, despite having had no knowledge of what the film would be about? Perhaps my years of living amid the radioactive ruins of a once-thriving civilization had awakened a latent talent for telepathy, enabling me to subconsciously read the filmmakers' minds. Maybe I was stuck in a causality time loop, in which future events shaped those of the past and back again, causing me to watch the entire movie before any filming had even begun.

Or, more likely, it was just an unbelievable coincidence.

Thankfully, my precognitive powers proved temporary, as my alternate story idea received a thumbs-up. With the project approved, the authors all happily got to work.

Other large franchises have spawned countless novels and short stories, but not *Planet of the Apes*. This meant that the authors, when conceiving their stories, pretty much had *carte blanche*. We encouraged them to think outside the box, and not to limit themselves to proposing only tales about the most popular characters and settings from the films. After all, while an entire anthology about Zira and Cornelius alternatively bickering and then rubbing their noses together in Ape City could be fun for fans of the chimp couple (titled *Zira Loves Cornelius*, perhaps), it would provide a rather limited and redundant scope for everyone else.

This all paid off, as we ended up with stories from all over the timeline, exploring not only the chimpanzees, gorillas, orangutans, mutants, and mute humans you'd expect to see in *Planet of the Apes*, but also gibbons, baboons, and other surprises along the way. It also meant that in addition to new adventures for Taylor, Nova, Caesar, Milo, Virdon, Burke, Galen, Urko (both versions), Zaius (all three versions), and other fan favorites (Zira and Cornelius among them, don't worry), we'd also be able to introduce more than a hundred new characters to the *Apes* pantheon—not only from Ape City, Central City, and the Forbidden Zone, but from areas across and even outside North America.

Plus, we got to answer a few nagging questions along the way that fans have been asking for decades. Which ones? Ah, but that would spoil the fun.

A few authors proposed stories that could only be written unconstrained by existing onscreen or published continuity, and to shake things up a bit, we let them have at it. While most of the tales fit snugly into established *Apes* lore, two authors contributed stories set years after the first film, ignoring Earth's destruction in *Beneath the Planet of the Apes*, while a third crafted a tale about a certain group of hairy-faced space travelers that differed from other licensed accounts—but is no less exciting. Another writer, meanwhile, turned in a story combining elements of not only the films and the live-action TV show, but the cartoon as well, creating a sort of "Crisis on Infinite Planets," so to speak.

In *Escape from the Planet of the Apes*, scientist Otto Hasslein described time as a highway with infinite lanes leading from the past to the future. Orangutan philosopher Virgil, in *Battle for the Planet of the Apes*, called time "an endless motorway," noting, "It's a blind choice, but you *can* change lanes." In essence, the *Apes* films support the many-worlds interpretation of quantum mechanics, allowing for multiple timelines and realities. Viewed from that perspective, the "what if?"-style entries in this anthology follow the rules of physics as laid down by both Virgil and Doctor Hasslein.

As I sat down to write my own contribution—an historic meeting between Ape City's leadership and those living in the Forbidden City, twenty years after the events of *Battle for the Planet of the Apes* (the extended edition, of course)—I had much to consider:

How might both societies have logically evolved during the decades since the war with Governor Kolp's forces? Which characters from *Battle* would need to be incorporated, and what roles would they play? What aspects of mutant society established in *Beneath* should be present at this early point in history? Was there any other licensed lore from this era to take into account—and were there any contradictions, plot holes, or unanswered questions that I could address? Ultimately, how could I make sure it felt like a sequel to the fifth movie, while setting the stage for the world Taylor would find 2,000 years from now?

Each author, in approaching his or her own unique vision of the planet of the apes, had similar questions to consider. As anyone who has written licensed books or comics could attest to, the greatest challenge, when playing in someone else's sandbox, is to find the right voice for every character and for the story as a whole. It's all well and good to have a great idea involving Doctor Zaius, but if you give him uncharacteristic dialogue ("Howdy, Ursus!") or have him take actions ill-fitting to his onscreen persona (playing Texas hold'em with Taylor and Brent, for instance[2]), it won't ring true and readers *will* notice.

Given how adeptly each story in *Tales from the Forbidden Zone* captures the tones of the movies and TV shows, this was clearly on the mind of every author. The end result is a collection of sixteen stories that I think do the apes proud. I hope you'll agree. I feel honored and privileged that Jim and I are able to present fans with original *Planet of the Apes* short fiction by an immensely talented group of writers, expanding a mythos that began when Pierre Boulle welcomed us to his planet long ago. If the Lawgiver allows, we hope to do so again in the near future.

So let me… let each of us… tell you a story about apes. Unlike Taylor, I'm certain *you'll* like what you find.

RICH HANDLEY
March 2016

---

[2] I would absolutely read a story about Zaius playing Texas hold'em with Brent and Taylor.

Dan Abnett's "Unfired," set several decades before the events of the original *Planet of the Apes* film, delves deep into the radioactive ruins left behind by the great cataclysm of the 1990s to bring those who dwell among them up and into a new light...

UNFIRED

by

DAN ABNETT

No one from the west went to see God anymore.

The journey had always been hard. A long track, fraught with hazards, wearying to mind and body, without certainty of deliverance. But that was how a track ought to be. A pilgrim should not get to see God easily.

The track was a test. Its trials and tribulations were a process of suffering that proved a pilgrim worthy. The journey prepared them for the presence of the divine. The elders of the west said the act of walking the ancient track was itself a part of meeting with God. If you endured it and prevailed, then God had looked upon you favorably. It was not the last step of the way that brought you to God. It was *every* step of the way, alpha step to omega.

But times had changed. Though the track still existed, its demanding route recorded and passed down from one generation to the next, it had fallen out of use. It had become too dangerous to attempt the journey since the Third Race had arisen.

It had become too dangerous since the apes had claimed the territory as their domain.

•

There had been seven of them at the start: Taul and the six pilgrims.

Silat had turned back after the first month, hobbled by feet that had worn bloody and sore. She was slowing them down, and Taul knew she would never make it the whole of the way.

Silat knew she had become a burden. In other ages, the pilgrims would have borne her up and carried her with them, taking on her trial as part of their own. Children helped each other and, by united effort, uprose in the sight of God.

But when Silat went lame, all of them knew their journey would be compromised if they slowed to her rate or carried her. This journey was special. They weren't walking the track for personal deliverance. It wasn't about them. It was about the relic Calio carried in his satchel.

They had stopped to confer, face to face. Silat had nodded to them, the truth unspoken, and had turned to limp back the way they had come. The last Taul had seen of her was a distant figure, receding into the west as evening fell violet across the desert.

The next day, Garig had disappeared from the fireside. They knew that he had gone back to find Silat and guide her home to the west.

Taul doubted they would be seen alive again. Two of them, one crippled, alone, without him to protect them. The desert would eat them.

Pardel died about a month later.

They had been crossing a canyon that split the wasteland, its sides as sheer as cathedral walls. They had made it down one cliff, an arduous descent that had taken a whole day, rested for the night, then picked their way across the cool shadows of the canyon floor. The next day, and the day after that, they had trekked along, looking for a way back up. Taul had been able to taste their anxiety. There seemed to be no way out, no way up. It had been a long time since pilgrims had followed the track. Wind, the heave of the earth, and the scorch-rains of winter had crumbled the route markers away.

Taul had been resolved. He had found a way eventually.

It was precarious. The ascent was slow. They were flushed with fear at every step, every scrabbled-for handhold. They had been forced to rest halfway up the cliff when night fell, perched like roosting birds on ledges no wider than their hips, waiting for daybreak when they could safely climb again.

Taul made it to the top well ahead of the others. He knelt down, saying a little prayer to thank God for his success, even though he knew that he was unfired, and that God was no longer listening. He raised the rifle, its worn wooden stock couched in his armpit, and surveyed the landscape to see what other trials might be waiting for them.

But there was nothing. The land beyond was empty waste. Taul slung his rifle across his shoulder and turned to help the others up the last of the way.

Calio made it first, sweating and exhausted, but fired by the spirit that made him special. Then they pulled Arnia up onto the cliff head. She laughed and sang to the God that had brought her through.

Kotte was next. Quiet, grim—stubborn, in Taul's opinion—Kotte shook off their outstretched hands and refused their assistance. He was going to make it to the top without help.

And he did. Then he lay on his back on the ground in the sun, panting.

Pardel was the oldest of the travelers. He was a long way behind, clawing his way inch by inch.

"You can do it, old soul!" Taul yelled down.

The others were calling, too, shouting encouragement, but not with their voices, so Taul couldn't hear them.

Ten meters from the top, Pardel stopped for breath and looked up at them. He grinned, as if to say, "See? Not so old after all!"

Then his hand fumbled, and a rock tore loose. Pardel tried to grip, but it was too late. They watched him fall, a bundle of rags and spindly limbs in a cascade of dust and clattering stones.

Pardel did not fall all the way to the bottom of the canyon. He lodged, halfway down, caught on an outcrop of rock. They heard him weeping, and moaning in pain.

The others started to talk. Taul saw them look at each other, eyes wide.

"Aloud," he reminded them. "With voices."

"Sorry, Taul," Calio said. "I forget."

"What do we do?" Arnia asked, sadness wobbling her voice.

"We leave him," Kotte said. "We can't help him. He will be broken—"

"We can't leave him!" Arnia exclaimed.

"We left Silat," Kotte said. "A weak link—"

"She turned back," Arnia said. "She turned back. We didn't leave her."

"Same thing," Kotte said. He shrugged, then smoothed his mask where the sweat was making it lift loose.

Calio looked at Taul, who sighed.

"Okay," he said, reluctant. He took the rifle off his shoulder and held it out to Kotte. Kotte looked at the weapon with some alarm, but didn't take it.

"Just hold it for me," Taul said. "I can climb faster without it."

Kotte took the rifle and held it gingerly, as if the violence of its purpose might somehow infect him.

Taul climbed down to Pardel. It took a while. It was much harder going down than up. End-time heat, the blink of God, had transmuted the rock, and the face of the cliff was weak like powder.

Taul heard the old man calling to him. Felt it, too. Unfired for his purpose by the scalpels of the elders, his mind was dull and his inmost self was mute. But a vestige of his inmost remained, and the old man's distress was so great, Taul could feel the pressure of it in his head—a throb, a surge, a heat like fire behind a closed door.

Pardel's legs were broken. An arm, too, from the unnatural twist of it. Blood stained his filthy robes and trickled down the rock face, drying in the hard sunlight. His mask had torn away during the fall, shredding to reveal his inmost self. Taul saw the pale, puckered beauty of Pardel's true face.

That was an indignity. A transgression. To die, so intimately and cruelly exposed. A man chose to show his true face to God. To have his mask stripped away, and to be left in death with his inmost self open to the sky and the carrion-eaters— that was wrong.

"I'll get a rope," Taul said. "I'll hoist you up."

"No," Pardel replied. It was just a sigh. Injury had robbed him of the strength to speak in more than a whisper, though the throb of Pardel's inner fire in Taul's head let Taul know the old man was actually screaming.

"Then what?" Taul asked.

"Peace," Pardel whispered. "And when you come to the place, remember my name to God."

Taul nodded. Gently, he sloughed Pardel's torn mask off the old man's head, averting his eyes. The carefully molded latex of the mask was beyond repair.

He took his own mask off. Taul wasn't sure why he had continued to wear it after the elders rendered him unfired. It meant nothing, because Taul had no inmost self anymore, and his true face thus had no significance.

He fitted his mask onto the old man. Dignity in death.

"How will you do it?" Pardel asked.

Taul was strong. His build and physical power were among the reasons the elders had chosen him. He got his hands under Pardel, and moved him until the old man was sitting up on the ledge. Pardel shuddered as his broken bones ground against each other.

Taul took out his knife and laid it on the ledge. The old man had looked at it, considering the instrument of his death, knowing Taul would make it swift.

When the old man's eyes lingered on the knife, Taul reached out quickly with his right hand and snapped Pardel's neck. It broke like a twig, and he was gone in a moment.

Taul tidied the old man up, tucking his robes around the body to stop them flapping in the canyon wind. Then he said goodbye and climbed back up the cliff to rejoin the others.

Calio, Arnia, and Kotte looked at him cautiously when he reached the top and stood up beside them. Kotte handed back the rifle.

"Pardel went quiet," Calio said.

"He's gone," Taul said. "His track has ended. Omega."

"Alpha and omega," they all chanted.

"Where is your face?" Kotte asked.

"I didn't need it anymore," Taul said. "But Pardel did."

Arnia stared at him.

"I had forgotten how beautiful you are," she said.

They spent two weeks following the track through the craterland. By night, wild dogs barked in the distance, and Taul kept his rifle close. They skirted the rims of wide craters in the heat. The sun made the air buzz and click. Chemical lakes had formed in the basins of the craters, some vivid turquoise or blood-red. The wind stank of sulfur. Occasionally, they could see shapes down in the lakes: rusted, twisted, blackened masses half submerged, buckled metal leering at the sky, vague in the mists that lay across the toxic pools.

They first saw the valley about three days later. The track

had taken them down from the craterland across blast-heath where the air was parched dry, and into a place of blind tombs. The tombs were so old, so compressed by heat and pressure, they almost looked like natural rock formations, but Taul could see the spaces where windows had been, the holes of doorways, the gaps of skylights. There were fragile pipes of green metal that had once been gutters and downpipes. Corroded by time and acid, they flaked into papery ash at the merest touch. Between the tombs, the ground gleamed. Sand, transmuted by God into iridescent glass.

Or, Taul considered, the glass that had once filled the window-gaps of the tombs, blown out in one immense instant of wrath, turning to rain, to fall and flow and fuse.

"We'll shelter here," he told the others.

"We're low on water," Kotte said.

Food, too, Taul thought, though he didn't say it.

"That's why we'll shelter here," Taul said. "Night soon. We'll shelter here, then rise early, moving before dawn while it's still cool."

They entered the ground floor of one of the tombs, and made camp in a blackened room. The light was dim enough for them to remove their tinted goggles.

Everything was dust, except for a distorted metal bowl that Taul thought might once have been a cooking pan. Calio led prayers, then they ate, trying not to notice how little remained in the ration bags. Then Kotte slept, while Calio sat in a corner. He took the relic from his satchel and turned through the holy pages, puzzling over passages in which the leaves were incomplete, or age had faded the laminated paper white.

Abandoning his mask had been a mistake, Taul realized less than a day after they had left Pardel at the cliff. The bare skin of his scalp, his nose, his cheeks, and the tops of his ears had burned raw in the sun. They carried salves and oils to treat skin outbreaks, and they all shared them with him willingly when they saw him start to crack and blister, but the supply was limited.

They were all used to living beneath, in the caves and tunnels of the sect's home underground. Daylight and open air were strangers to them. The elders had warned that surface exposure was one of the foremost struggles of a pilgrim's track.

Arnia, sifting through the dust, found a doll's head. It was bald and eyeless, and the plastic, which Taul assumed had once been flesh-colored, had bleached bone-white. The plastic was cruder than the stuff their masks were made of, hard and brittle, not supple at all. Even so, Taul saw Arnia look inside it, through the neck hole, to see if it had an inmost self.

Taul took his rifle and went up onto the roof of the tomb. There were stairwells, and the fragile remains of stairs. He trod carefully, testing the safety of each step. Where the steps failed, they fell away in showers of dust and debris.

When he reached the roof, the sun was setting, whirring like an angry beetle as it slipped below the horizon. Its bloated red disk seemed to melt into a bar of light where it met the limit of the landscape.

He looked out across the tombs. The walls still facing the sun were washed with peach light, and those at an angle a darker mauve. The shadows were blue, then purple, then soot-black.

Taul looked east, trying to spot the markers of the track. In the very last of the daylight, he saw an outcrop of dark green foliage where the valley began.

They set out before dawn. Taul had told them about the green to lift their spirits. From the tombs, they crossed a mile or two of barrens, and then reached coarse grasses that hissed and swished as they waded through them.

The air had changed. The dryness had gone. There was a scent of something wet and organic.

"Trees," Arnia said, delighted.

Taul nodded.

There were trees. As the valley opened below them, they saw more than trees. There was a forest, deep and thick, tangled, a place of emerald canopies and dense shadow.

There was so much life, more than any of them had ever seen. There was so much life it felt obscene.

Taul led them in, rifle ready. They entered dappled shade and thickets where the sunlight speared in through the leaves. The ground was moist and dark. The fresh air smelled ripe with resin and sap. Small insects chirred and buzzed, and the sight of each small bug droning past made them marvel and laugh, even Kotte.

Taul felt his tension rising. The forest was noisy. Leaves hissed and whispered, stirred by the breeze. Branches creaked. There was the occasional odd crack, or stranger sounds of knocking or tapping. Taul presumed these were the sounds of insects, burrowing and building, or even birds, which he had heard about but never seen.

The noises made it hard for him to maintain alertness. He jumped at sounds. He wished the forest would fall silent so that he could hear the sounds that really mattered.

The sounds of threat approaching.

For the forest would be dangerous. The elders had told him this. A forest was a place of life, and thus resources. Food, wood, soil, water. All three races would frequent the forest to draw on its bounty. The chance of encounter here was higher than anywhere else.

"Go slowly," he told his pilgrims. "Go slowly and watch my lead."

He checked the action and clip of his rifle. He'd done it every day since they had left the west, but now he did it knowing it was likely to be more than just a routine precaution.

They walked in silence for an hour. Then Arnia said, "I hear talking."

They stopped and listened. They all heard a distant babble, but could discern no clear words.

"Wait here," Taul said.

Rifle raised to his shoulder, he advanced, using the trees as cover. He followed the sound of the talking. A voice, or voices—it was hard to tell.

Then he realized it wasn't voices. It was the ripple of running water.

The stream was broad and fast-flowing. It coursed down the hillside under the trees and emptied into a wide pool. The pool was calm. Large, flat rocks stood in the water like islands, sunlit. The trees surrounded the pool, but their bowing canopy did not extend entirely across its width, and the sunlight was bright. Taul saw insects flitting through the light, darting across the surface of the water. He heard splashes and saw slowly expanding circles of ripples on the green mirror of the water.

He knelt at the edge of the pool, pulled off one leather glove, and cupped his hand.

The water was cold and bitter. He tasted minerals and weeds. But it was clean and fresh.

He made his way back to get the others.

They filled their water flasks, washing out the dregs of stale residue. Arnia hummed a hymn as she stooped, praising God for his kindness, alpha and omega. Calio took off his gloves and bathed his sore hands, then turned his back on them so he could remove his mask and baptize his true face. Kotte found berries and some nuts that looked edible, and began to fill his knapsack.

Taul kept watch.

"Someone's coming," Arnia said.

She was suddenly standing beside him. Taul frowned at her. She touched her forehead. "Felt them," she said.

"Warn the others," he said. She used her inmost fire to alert Calio and Kotte without words. All four of them hurried back into the cover of the trees and huddled down. Fear had returned.

Calio was breathing hard, anxiously. He had been in the middle of his ablutions, and had withdrawn in haste. He was still trying to fit his mask back on to preserve his dignity. His hands were wet, and the cuffs of his robe were dripping.

Figures appeared through the trees on the far side of the pool. Wild humans, dirty and ragged in animal pelts. None of them had seen humans much during their lives in the west. Here, humans were said to be more numerous. They were creatures of the First Race, the first makers who had lost their way. From their lineage had sprung the Second Race, to which Taul and his brethren all belonged—those who had come after, who knew and remembered, who had retained thought, and had gained the gift of fire and, through that, inmost selves that were beautiful to God.

The humans came to the pool. Three males and a female. They carried spears, just poles with sharpened ends. They did not speak, neither inmost nor outmost, for they could not. They were mute. The stream had more voice than they did.

They came out along the bank furtively, and then two of the males hopped and leapt out onto the flat rocks in the water, where they stood, staring down into the pool.

"What are they doing?" Arnia whispered.

Taul shrugged.

"Should I drive them off?" Kotte asked. Taul knew what he meant. Those of the First Race were highly susceptible to raptures. With a focus of his fire, Kotte could make them see a pillar of flame or a flash of lightning, or worse. Taul knew

Kotte had quite an imagination. He could conjure a vision with his inmost fire that would terrify the primitives and set them to flight.

"Wait," Taul said.

One of the humans lunged with his pole into the water, and brought it out with something silver flapping on the end. He had speared a fish. His companions showed their approval with squeals and clapping hands.

"They're hunting," Calio said.

"Can you eat fish?" Arnia asked, disgusted.

"I think so," Taul said. "*They* can."

Patiently, the humans scanned the pool, silent and still. Another sudden thrust brought out a second fish. The third male and the female, who had remained on the bank, were moving around the edge of the pool, gathering berries and fruit. The female cried out. She had found something. The male went over to her. The two spearmen on the rock dropped into the water and waded to her side of the pool, inquisitive.

"Oh, no," Calio murmured. "Oh, God, forgive me."

Taul saw what the female had found. In his hurry to withdraw, busy with his mask, Calio had left his satchel on the rocks beside the pool. His satchel. The relic.

"Oh, Calio!" Arnia whispered.

"Now we scare them," Kotte said.

"And make them flee?" Taul said. "With the book?"

Taul rose. He took aim. He felt sick, but a clean shot would drop the female and the book, and the sound of it would send the others running. He was a good shot. The elders in the west had given him four whole clips of ammunition with which to practice before the party had set out. Taul had used them to train, to become proficient with the rifle, so that he could fulfill his duty as one unfired, his hands and eyes trained to kill, his mind surgically neutered to free him from the prohibitions against killing. That was the sacrifice he had made in order to serve God: to be made unholy and invisible to God, to have his fire put out so that he could serve God more selflessly than any before him.

He took aim. He had the female's head lined up in his iron sights, and adjusted slightly for the drop as he had learned to do. His nausea grew worse. He had killed before. He had killed Pardel. But that had been a mercy. This was murder.

And the humans... unfired as he was, with no inmost self, wasn't he more like the First Race than the Second now? These were his own, more kin to him than Calio, Kotte, and Arnia.

Taul steadied. He reminded himself that murder was the defining trait of the First Race. Killing was their mortal flaw. Their capacity to murder had made the world the way it was now. Their gleeful relish in killing had shaped the planet, and had caused the Second Race to be. It had made God, and God was beautiful because God was the First Race's capacity for murder on an absolute scale, yet held in check. Ultimate potential, yet gloriously and eternally restrained as a demonstration of strength and love.

The relic was the greatest proof of that doctrine. It was holy scripture.

The sickness subsided. Taul felt righteous anger. The First Race had loosed murder on the world. They deserved to have murder visited upon them for that sacrilege.

His finger tightened on the trigger.

A shot rang out, incredibly loud in the wooded basin of the pool. One of the human males jerked like a cracked whipcord. The side of his head vanished in a red drizzle. He crashed over into the water.

Eyes wide, Taul lowered his rifle. He had not fired.

Three riders burst into the clearing. Their horses were at full gallop as they rode into the pool, sheeting up water from their hooves.

They were soldiers of the Third Race.

They were apes.

The soldiers were massive, dark brutes, their hair as black as the polished leather hauberks they wore. They were draped in heavy bandoliers, and one carried a rifle, the butt resting on his thigh. He howled orders through a snarling mouth that revealed fangs like daggers. His outriders brandished long riot sticks.

The humans broke and ran. One of the males tried to flee across the pool, but an outrider ran him down and felled him with a vicious smash of his baton. His head split open, the male cartwheeled in a spray of water.

The female had fled with the satchel.

"Stay here!" Taul told the others.

"You can't—" Arnia began.

"Stay the hell here!" Taul snapped. He turned to move, but froze. The ape with the rifle had turned his horse, and was walking it back along the shallows in their direction. Its hooves sloshed the water. The ape was staring at the thickets where they were hiding, as if he had heard their voices. The ape's eyes narrowed, and his brow creased.

He was huge. The power in him, the bulk of his arms and shoulders. The blunt aggression of his brow. Taul had never seen an ape before, not in the flesh. The Third Race was very rare in the bleak wastes of the west. Their kind were the last-comers, those that had arisen last of all, the least of the three races and the closest to animals, yet the most powerful.

Peering through the leaves, Taul found himself fascinated by the threat of the rider. The purple uniform. The well-made leather war gear. The gauntlets and the munition webbing. The bridle and the saddle. The beads of water glittering like sequins in the horse's mane and the ape's hair.

The rifle in the ape's fist. The rifle most of all.

It was almost identical to the one Taul carried. When they gave Taul his rifle, the elders told him they had recovered the weapon and the ammunition from a corpse found in the wasteland. How else? How else could you take a rifle from a monster that powerful unless it was already dead?

Apparently satisfied, the ape thrashed his mount's neck with his reins, back and forth, and swung the animal around. He galloped off across the pool after the others, kicking up a wake of spray.

Taul got up and began to move through the trees, keeping low, running. He could hear the whoop and crash of the hunt close by, the thunder of hooves, the barking call-and-response of the riders. He heard a shot crack out. The Third Race hunted the First. The elders had told him that. They hunted the wild humans to keep them as slaves or kill them as vermin. Vermin most of all.

The Third Race hunted everything.

Taul realized Kotte was with him. "Go back!" he snapped.

"No," Kotte said. "You'll never find the female without me."

"I—"

"In this?" Kotte asked, gesturing to the dense woodland.

Taul knew he was right. Without the gift of fire, he could hardly locate the bright, feral mind of the human female.

"This way!" Kotte cried.

Taul grabbed him and pulled him down into cover. An ape galloped past in full chase. Kotte was forgetting himself. The Third Race had no fire. Their minds were dark, all but invisible to the inmost selves of the Second Race. Kotte could not spot them or warn of them as easily. They had to listen for movement, the thrashing of hooves.

They ran on again. Kotte led the way, focusing his mind.

"She went in this direction!"

They heard hooves, and apes shouting nearby. There were more than three hunters. A whole pack of them. Taul and Kotte reached another clearing, and huddled down again. Two soldier apes rode past, one trailing a heavy rope net.

They heard screams. Animal screams. Kotte winced, sharing a wave of pain and terror.

"She's too far away," he gasped. "She's on the far side of—"

He pointed ahead.

"Does she still have it? The satchel?"

Kotte shrugged. He was struggling.

"I'll bring her to us," he said.

"What?"

"It's the only way."

Kotte tensed. Taul felt pressure in his temples. Kotte had let out his fire. He had projected it. God alone knew what rapture he had cast.

Taul heard a wail. It rang through the woodland. The female was coming back in their direction, running in abject terror, driven by whatever image Kotte had painted in her simple mind.

She ran into view, screaming. The satchel was still wrapped to her, the strap twisted and tangled. Kotte stopped her dead with another spearing thought, and she fell down in a stupor. The desperate force of his fire had probably made her weak brain stroke out. Kotte ran to her and began to untangle the satchel.

"Help me!" he yelled.

Taul hurried to join him. An ape with a rifle ploughed out of the thickets, horse at full leap, showering twigs and torn leaves behind him. He roared at the sight of them.

Taul did not flinch. He stood his ground and raised the rifle to his shoulder. According to scripture, apes were not animals, so the prohibition against killing extended to them, too.

Taul was unfired. He was no longer bound by scripture.

The charging ape reined up hard, his horse rearing. A human? A human in clothes with a gun? Taul, with the beauty of his true face unmasked, wasn't sure what kind of human the ape thought he was, but the shock of him had checked the brute's charge.

The shock was fleeting. With another savage growl, the ape raised his rifle.

Taul fired.

Center-mass, as he had been taught. The shot punched through the ape's torso and snapped him back in the saddle, but didn't unhorse him. Swaying drunkenly, the ape gazed down at the blood squirting out of the hole in his chest.

Taul fired again.

Head-shot. The ape rocked sideways off his horse, the sudden swing of balance bringing the beast down with him. The horse rolled, squealing, kicking at the air, then got up and fled. It dragged the slack, heavy mass of the ape's corpse for a few meters until the stirrup snapped.

Taul ran to the ape and looked down at his kill. The ape lay on his back, staring at the sky, eyes dull but expressing surprise, one pupil blown.

Taul bent down and began to wrench off the ape's bandolier. The ape was so damn heavy.

"Taul!"

He turned. Kotte had risen from the mind-burned female, satchel in hand, but two more riders had entered the clearing. Kotte was out in the open between them and Taul. The apes were charging, batons raised.

Afterward, Taul suspected that Kotte had tried to use his fire against them. Even animals responded to rapture. Taul wasn't sure what kind of deterrent Kotte had employed because his unfired mind was blind to it. Sonic or visual, one or the other, used in haste. Traumatic deterrent was futile, for the minds of the Third Race were impervious to such techniques.

But the charging horses baulked hard and reared in terror. Both apes howled, and one was thrown.

Taul ran forward, shooting from the chest. The thrown ape was getting up, and a bullet knocked him flat again. The other ape was regaining control of his spooked horse, and yanking it around to attack. Taul fired again, and the shot tore through the horse's neck. It fell hard, its legs just giving out, and the ape spilled violently out of the saddle.

Taul felt sorry for the horse. He had been aiming at the rider. But an animal was just an animal. As scripture taught, *"IN THE EVENT OF AN EMERGENCY, DO NOT STOP TO SAVE ANIMALS OR PETS."*

The ape got up. Furiously, he wrenched his rifle from the saddle-scabbard of his shuddering, dying mount. Taul didn't wait for the soldier to pull the weapon free. He put two rounds through the ape's broad body, and a third through his face as he toppled backward.

Something hit Taul hard and knocked him down. Pain lanced through his ribcage and right arm. He lost his grip on the rifle. He had only winged the first of the two apes. The soldier had got up, baton in hand, and struck him down. The ape struck again, savage, trying to mash Taul's head into the ground. Blood from the bullet wound in the ape's shoulder soaked his sleeve and gauntlet, flecking off his fist with every blow. Taul rolled to evade, but the baton smashed across his warding forearms and he cried in pain.

"Leave him!"

The ape turned sharply and found Kotte facing him. Kotte was clutching the satchel against his chest with both arms.

"Leave him be, beast!" Kotte cried.

"You... speak...?" the ape growled.

"I speak with the voice of God," Kotte replied, "and you are—"

The ape brought the baton down on Kotte's head, double-handed, like a woodsman splitting logs.

Taul watched Kotte collapse. He hurled himself at the ape. Winded, the ape staggered. They grappled. Taul was strong. His strength and fury surprised the ape. His fist cracked the ape's jaw sideways and tore his lower lip.

But the strength of the Third Race was of another order entirely. The sheer mass and density of the ape's muscle and bone was terrifying. He was so solid, so powerful. He smacked Taul away from him with the heel of one palm and Taul fell on his back.

The ape took a step forward, hefting his baton.

Then the ape paused and looked down at the handle of Taul's dagger. It was jutting out of his chest. Taul had been obliged to get in tight to ram it home.

The ape dropped the baton. He thumped to his knees. He groped at the dagger's handle, but he could not pull it free. His hands came away bloody. He glared at Taul and exposed his fangs in a grimace. Taul saw murder in the ape's expression. The primal urge to kill.

The ape lunged. Taul rolled aside hard. The ape lay still on the forest floor, face down, one massive arm draped across Taul's back. Taul heard the ape's last breaths rasp out of him. A gurgle. Silence.

Taul hauled himself out from under the weight of the dead ape's arm. He rose.

He could hear the hunt, moving away. The clearing was quiet and littered with dead. Three apes, the horse. The other two mounts had run off, riderless.

Taul was wheezing. The sound of his own breathing seemed to fill the air. His arms and ribs throbbed with pain.

The human female was alive, but her mind was gone. She lay shivering on the ground, sprawled just as she had fallen. Taul doubted she would ever get up again.

Kotte was dead. The ape's baton had crushed the top of his skull. Blood was leaking out of the eyes and mouth of his misaligned mask.

In pain, Taul bent down and picked up the satchel.

He made his way back to the pool. It took a while. Obedient, Arnia and Calio were exactly where he had left them. They emerged from the thickets to help him as he limped up.

"You're hurt!" Arnia cried.

Taul nodded.

"Where's Kotte?" Calio asked as he took the satchel.

Taul didn't answer.

Avoiding patrols, they hid in the fringe of the forest for another week until Taul was well enough to move again. Even then, the progress was slow. Taul had broken ribs, and his breathing was impaired. Regular rest stops were needed.

Calio said very little. He knew that Kotte's fate and Taul's wounds were ultimately his fault. Arnia, always optimistic, tried to cheer up Taul by reminding him that the trials and hardships of the track were all part of the progress a pilgrim made as he drew closer to God.

Taul reminded her that he wasn't a pilgrim. He was unfired, so deliverance to the grace of God was not a reward reserved for him. God was not waiting for him at the end of the track.

After that, Arnia said little either.

Another week, and the woods of the valley gave way to open grassland, where they dared travel only at dawn and dusk for fear of being seen. From time to time, they saw packs of riders crossing the flats in the distance.

After another week, the grasslands petered out, and the landscape became arid again. This jumbled, rocky waste, they knew, was the last stage—a zone shunned by all but the Second Race.

In a place of ravines and deep crags, where the wasteland winds whined and moaned, they found the entrance and went beneath. The place, and its approach, was marked by stacks of stones that only the initiated might distinguish from natural rubble. They had been taught these coded signs by the elders in the west.

To be beneath again felt like a blessing. The tunnels and galleries, old places dug by the First Race, were dank and gloomy. Ground water dripped from the cavernous ceilings. Echoes mocked their footsteps. It reminded all three of them of home, of the sect fastness they had left behind. They took off their tinted goggles, and their eyes, accustomed since birth to the poor light of subground life, quickly and comfortably adjusted. They would not have to suffer the fierce light of the surface again.

They passed through vaults where the ruins and detritus of the Old Life lay scattered, pale ghosts of the world as it had once been. There were inscriptions on the walls that spoke of times and destinations that had passed into God. The words meant little to them, except that they reminded them of the grace which had brought their race from the fire, and bestowed on them their beauty, and taught them to survive.

When at last they passed through the gates and entered the buried city of God, the elders of the Children living there came out to meet them in the silent streets.

The elders were robed and silent. Their masks were impassive. They looked on Taul with what seemed disdain and turned their attention to Calio and Arnia. Taul felt his head swim and pulse.

"Speak aloud," he said. "I have come a long way. I have brought these pilgrims here. I would at least hear what is said now."

"You are pilgrims?" one of the elders asked, turning to look at Taul.

"Yes," Taul said.

"From the west," Calio added.

"Pilgrims have not come for many generations," another of the elders said. "Once many came, but not in our lifetimes."

"The way has become too treacherous," Calio said. "Even for the devoted and the determined."

"Yet you have come," the first elder said.

Calio held out the satchel. "Because of this," he said. "It is scripture. The word of God. And it belongs here."

They were taken into a hall and allowed to sit at a long table of polished wood. Crystal chandeliers hung from the painted ceiling above. The air smelled of candle smoke and incense. Elders gathered to sit with them, perhaps fifteen of them in all, and robed servants brought food and water. The servants washed the hands and feet of Arnia and Calio and, with veils raised for dignity, took off their masks and anointed their hands and true faces with balm and holy oils.

No one went near Taul. He sat at the end of the table, caked with the dust and blood of his track. His rifle lay on the tabletop beside a pitcher of water and a dish of food.

Arnia and Calio replaced their masks, and the servants lowered the veils and stepped away. Calio took out the relic and passed it to the leader of the Children. The leader opened the cover with reverence and started to turn the pages.

Calio nodded.

"You're talking again," Taul said. "Do it out loud."

The leader looked down the table at him.

"Taul is our friend," Arnia said. "Our guardian. He sacrificed the greatest of all things so that he could fulfill that duty. We would not be here alive except for him. So please, Mendez. Let him share in this."

The leader stared at Taul. He nodded.

"I am Mendez XXI," he said.

"Taul," Taul said.

"You come to us unmasked, Taul," Mendez said, "your true face revealed."

"The beauty of your inmost self is very great, Taul," another of the elders said.

"I have no inmost self," Taul said. "I have no true face. This is just… my face."

Mendez frowned slightly.

"You have no inmost fire, Taul," he said. "I reach, but I do not find. My mind touches nothing. And you hear only words when they are spoken."

"This is so," Taul said.

"Were you born this way?" another of the elders asked. It was a woman.

"No," Taul said.

The elders glanced at each other. Taul saw wrinkles of dismay.

"Explain," Mendez said.

"The old track from the west has become too dangerous for pilgrims to pass along it without protection," Taul said. "Far more dangerous than it was in past years."

"The rise of the Third Race has made it so," the woman said.

"It has," Taul agreed. "The apes are very strong."

"Your sect, though?" Mendez asked. "It yet endures?"

"Yes, Mendez," Calio said. "It survives, as do many others, dotted throughout the western wastes, and into the mountains, too. We live beneath, as you do, in the safety of the earth."

"It was of the highest importance that we made this track," Arnia said. "Our elders decided it to be so."

"This was discovered," Calio said, gesturing to the relic, "in a ruin beneath the ground out in the west. This was a year or two ago. Our elders studied it, and saw it to be scripture. It was decided unanimously that it must be brought here."

"Despite the danger of the track?" Mendez asked.

"Despite that," Calio said, "even despite that. The track long abandoned had to be followed again. It was too important to communicate the word of God. Thus, it was decided we needed protection. And Taul stepped forward."

Mendez turned his gaze back to Taul.

"Why you?"

Taul shrugged. He was easily the biggest and most robust figure in the room. The shrug let them see the breadth of his shoulders and the size of his arms.

"I volunteered. Scripture prohibits killing."

"It does," Mendez agreed.

"But survival requires an ability to kill. To defend. To fight. To fight with more than inmost fire, which is weak against the Third Race. I had to be able to fight with these—"

He raised his hands.

"And this—"

He set his left hand on the rifle at his side.

"And with blades, and other means."

"You have killed, Taul?" the woman asked.

"I have. It was necessary, so that we could make the track. And in order to be able to kill, I consented to a procedure. I said goodbye to God, and turned my true face away from him, so that he would not be offended when I broke scripture. I gave up my inmost self."

"In what way?" Mendez asked.

Taul turned his head, and showed them the surgical scars that ran parallel down the base of his bald scalp. "The elders of the west operated. They made me unfired so I could do what God would not permit."

There was a long silence.

"You are a blasphemy," Mendez said. He sounded impressed.

"I take that as a compliment, Mendez," Taul said.

Mendez looked down at the relic. He turned a few more of the laminated pages that the folder contained.

"All for this?" he asked.

"Yes," Calio began.

"It is scripture," Taul said. "The holiest scripture. God is here, in this place. The essence of God is absolute murder, the murder from which we all were born. We have the power of death over life, but only in our resolute determination never to unleash that power do we define ourselves and witness God's love. We celebrate God's wrath, for it brought us into being, and the summit of that celebration is that we *possess* that wrath, yet choose steadfast never to unleash it again."

The elders nodded.

"Except," Taul said, "that is only faith. Faith alone. We firmly foreswear the unleashing of God's wrath. We are proud of that forbearance. In truth, however, we could not, even if we wanted to."

He paused.

"Until now."

Mendez peered at the pages of the relic, tracing words with his fingertips.

"This is…" he began. "This says… 'arming codes'…"

"It is the Book of All Books," Calio said. "The holiest of scripture."

"It is named 'Activation and Ignition Codes and Arming Sequence, US Defense Department Administration,'" Taul said.

"'Us'?" Mendez echoed.

"The language is archaic," Calio said. "I think that means 'our.'"

"That book," Taul said. "It strengthens our belief and binds us to God. Our faith rests on our conviction not to fire God. Now that choice has meaning, because we *can*."

"Proof denies faith," Mendez began.

Calio shook his head.

"Proof fortifies faith," he said, "for without arming codes, we are nothing."

Mendez closed the book.

"You have done a great thing," he said. The elders nodded.

"You have brought us closer to God," the woman said.

Taul rose to his feet.

"Taul?" Mendez asked.

"I will go now," he said.

"Go?"

"I have no place here," Taul said. "I am not of your kind. I knew that when I made my choice and set out to come here. I am an aberration, unfit to live amongst the fires of God's house with God's Children. I see that I make you uncomfortable, the way you look at me." He smiled sadly, and picked up the rifle. "The way you look at this."

"Taul? Where will you go?" Arnia asked. She was genuinely upset.

"I don't know," Taul said. "I don't know of a place where the unfired might live. I will… go and look. I will make a new track."

"You will not be forgotten," Mendez XXI said. He had risen to his feet.

"I should be," Taul said. "I am unfired and unfit."

He turned to leave, then paused. "Bold of me, but may I ask one favor before I go?"

"Ask it," Mendez said.

"I would like to look upon the face of God."

Mendez paused. He glanced at the other elders, then nodded. He raised his hand and gestured for Taul to follow him.

"You may," he said. He placed a hand on Taul's shoulder and led him through into the cathedral.

"I want little," Taul said. "I only want to remember a man's name to him. Pardel. That's the name."

"Very well," Mendez said, "but God will not be able to see you."

"Of course not," Taul said.

In Nancy Collins' "More Than Human, Less Than Ape," we travel alongside a younger Cornelius on one of his first expeditions into the unknown, a quest for truth that will reveal much more to the studious, bright-eyed chimpanzee than he ever bargained for...

MORE THAN HUMAN, LESS THAN APE

by

NANCY A. COLLINS

"I'm going to miss you."

She shyly dropped her gaze as he spoke, then flashed him a glance. It was the same look she'd given him from across the lecture room on the first day of Doctor Orson's comparative zoology class. The one that told him she was the only female who would ever matter to him.

"Not as much as I'm going to miss *you*," Zira replied with an impish smile. "Do you really have to go?"

"It's a great honor to be invited on one of Professor Tarquin's expeditions. And if he's right about the Southern Valley being the original Garden described in the Sacred Scrolls—the very cradle of ape civilization—it will look very good on my résumé when the time comes."

"That's what you said when he claimed to have found the burial vault of Caesar—but that turned out to be a lot of nothing."

"Archeology may be a science, my dear—but it is far from a 'sure bet.' You should know that by now.

"There's no need to worry," he said, placing a reassuring hand atop her own.

"What are you waiting for? Kiss your sweetheart goodbye and saddle up! The others are waiting for us at the city gate."

Cornelius puffed out his cheeks in consternation, glancing toward Professor Tarquin. The elder chimpanzee was on the other side of the low adobe fence that marked the boundary of Zira's family home, seated upon a roan stallion outfitted with heavy saddlebags and a bedroll. Beside the professor stood Cornelius' own mount, a chestnut mare identically outfitted, waiting patiently for its rider.

"You heard the professor," Zira said, taking her lover's chin in her hands and pressing her muzzle against his. They stood there for a long moment, brows touching, eyes closed, inhaling one another's scent a final time.

"Don't worry, Zira," Cornelius whispered as he broke their embrace. "I'll stay safe—I promise."

"I hope you realize you're a lucky young chimp," Professor Tarquin remarked. "Zira's a fine female—beautiful, smart, and from an excellent family, if I do say so myself."

"Oh, yes, sir," Cornelius replied as he swung himself into the saddle. "There is no ape happier than I am when I'm with her."

As the duo proceeded to head down the cobbled streets toward the gates of Ape City, Zira ran to the end of the walk and shouted: "You better bring him back in one piece. You hear me, Uncle Tarquin?"

The elder chimpanzee barked a laugh that swelled his throat sac, and then raised a hand in farewell without turning about in his saddle.

Twelve days' ride later...

"Hurry, Cornelius!" Fausto yelled. "It's gaining on us!"

Cornelius did not have to look over his shoulder to know that his fellow student was telling the truth. He could hear the creature's angry squeals and the sound of its massive body crashing through the underbrush behind him.

Barely twenty-four hours earlier, the expedition had crested the final foothill to find a fertile, heavily forested valley spread before them, bisected by a gleaming ribbon of river fed by the waterfalls that poured down from the surrounding mountains. At the time, Cornelius had thought it was the most beautiful place in the world. However, although the Southern Valley, with its deep glens and natural groves, did not suffer the blight of the Forbidden Zone, that did not mean it was without danger, as he and his fellow student Fausto quickly learned during their trip to the river to bring fresh water to the camp.

Spurred on by sheer terror, Cornelius instinctively dropped his shoulders and began to knuckle-run, doubling his speed. There was a large palm tree ahead of him, its wide bole rising from the jungle floor at a sloping angle. Without thinking twice, he scampered up the trunk, praying that it was sturdy enough to take not only his weight, but that of Fausto as well.

"Up here!" he shouted. However, as Cornelius turned to see if his friend was following, he saw him trip and fall to the ground. Without thinking, Cornelius slid back down the tree trunk to try to help the young chimpanzee to safety, only to have the creature pursuing them charge out of the surrounding foliage, screaming at the top of its lungs.

Cornelius had seen pigs before on the farms that ringed Ape City, but they were a different breed from the feral beast before him. Covered in coarse, matted fur, it was more than eight feet long and weighed nearly a thousand pounds, making it a match for even the strongest gorilla. Its small, beady eyes glittering with blood-lust, the monster slashed at Fausto's prone body with the seven-inch tusks jutting from its slavering jaws. The terrified student's screams launched a covey of brightly colored birds into the jungle sky.

He lunged forward, grabbing at Fausto in a desperate attempt to drag him free, but it was no use. Then, with a brutal lashing of its huge head, the wild boar turned the chimpanzee's panicked screams into a wet gurgle. Cornelius stared in mute shock at the blood gushing from his friend's throat, momentarily paralyzed. He had never seen a fellow ape die before. As he met the creature's murderous gaze, the only thing he could think of was Zira, and how he would never hold her in his arms again.

Suddenly, a silvery blur leapt from the surrounding overgrowth, putting itself between Cornelius and the wild boar. There was an angry scream of pain as a wooden spear punctured the beast's throat and then pierced its chest. The feral hog staggered backward, gore spurting from its wounds, and then dropped onto its knees. The spear struck a third and final time, driving deep into the beast's left eye socket.

Within seconds of its final, high-pitched squeal, a strange figure unlike any ape Cornelius had ever seen before leapt onto the vanquished boar's back, lifting his bloody weapon above his head and shaking it at the sky, as if to stab the sun, while issuing a series of sharp, guttural calls and displaying a pair of large, curving fangs that made Cornelius' heart lurch.

Although powerfully built, the stranger was short and covered in silvery gray hair, which was thickest about his shoulders and back, framing the long, squarish muzzle that jutted from the middle of his face like a loaf of bread. On either side of this prodigious snout, as well as across an equally prominent brow ridge, were smears of paint, the colors of which mimicked the bright flowers of the surrounding foliage. His only other adornments were a necklace fashioned from bones and teeth and a leather loincloth cinched about his narrow waist. However, it wasn't until Cornelius spied the two-foot-long tail dangling between his strange savior's bowed legs that he realized his true nature.

"You're a baboon!" he exclaimed in amazement.

"I am *Baako*," the baboon replied, thumping his chest for

emphasis. His voice was little more than a grunt, as though the very act of making words was painful to him.

"And you speak ape language!"

"I speak *our* words," Baako replied gruffly as he hopped down off the dead boar.

The implications of his discovery were enough to make Cornelius stammer. "B-but, you're supposed to be extinct!"

Baako frowned, causing his paint-daubed brows to draw down even further. "What is 'extinct'?"

"It means dead—like poor Fausto over there," Cornelius explained, gesturing to the torn remains of his fellow ape. "Thank you for saving my life, by the way. My name is Cornelius."

"I am sorry about your brother," Baako said, making a circular gesture on his chest with his fist. "But it is dangerous to enter the battle pigs' territory during the rut season..."

"My brother—?" Cornelius blinked in confusion for a second, before realizing what the other meant. "No, Fausto was not my brother."

"Sister?"

"No, he wasn't *that*, either. He was my friend."

"Friend?" Now it was Baako's turn to look baffled. "We have no such things in the band. Only brothers and sisters, fathers and mothers."

"Sounds very... cozy," Cornelius replied diplomatically.

"This is not a good place for apes," Baako said matter-of-factly. He put aside his spear and removed a flint knife from a sheath attached to his loincloth, then dropped down onto his haunches and began slicing into his kill. "Leave. Before Shaka and the others return. They are away on a hunt, but will be back soon."

"Who is this Shaka?"

"He has the largest harem. The most young."

"He's your leader, then?"

"He is Shaka," Baako repeated, as if that explained

47

everything. "And he does not like apes."

Cornelius nodded and turned his attention back to Fausto's torn and trampled body. "I can't just leave my friend here. Will you help me take him back to my camp?"

Baako heaved a large sigh as he halted his butchering. "Are you *sure* he is not your brother?"

The camp was set up in a clearing a quarter-mile from the river. There were three canvas tents, one each for Professor Tarquin and his associate, Doctor Atticus, and one shared by the students. The horses and pack animals quietly grazed on the lush grass, grateful for the rest after days spent trekking through the high mountain passes.

Doctor Atticus, a distinguished ape of letters and an esteemed primatologist, sat on a folding camp chair, cleaning his rifle, while a young orangutan named Ovid and a chimpanzee called Quintus busied themselves with preparing the afternoon meal.

"I wonder what's keeping Cornelius and Fausto?" Ovid asked. "We can't start cooking until we get some water."

"Maybe they got lost?" Quintus suggested, less than helpfully. He turned to look at Doctor Atticus. "Should we go look for them?"

The older chimpanzee tilted back his head and squinted at the steadily rising sun. "Damn it, I was hoping we could go twenty-four hours without a student disappearing on us. If they're not back within the hour, we'll send out a party."

Ovid gave an abrupt hoot of surprise. "There he is!" he exclaimed, pointing to the edge of the clearing. "There's Cornelius!"

Doctor Atticus turned in the direction Ovid indicated to see the young chimp emerge from the surrounding jungle, dragging a travois fashioned from palm fronds and tree branches. Walking behind him was a short, hideously ugly creature, naked save for a loincloth and covered in silver-gray hair.

Doctor Atticus leapt to his feet so quickly he sent the camp chair flying. "In the Lawgiver's name—what is that thing with you?" he shouted as he raised his rifle.

"Don't shoot!" Cornelius yelled back. "It's all right! He's friendly! Moreover, he isn't a *thing*, Doctor Atticus. He's a baboon—one who saved my life."

"What's all this noise about?" Professor Tarquin barked as he emerged from his tent. "Atticus! Put that gun away before you shoot yourself in the foot!"

The primatologist grudgingly lowered his weapon, but did not take his eyes off Baako. "What happened to Fausto? What did that savage do to him?"

"He didn't do *anything* to him," Cornelius replied, trying to control the growing exasperation in his voice. "We were attacked by a wild animal while getting water from the river. Baako managed to save me, but it was too late for Fausto. In fact, Baako helped me make this litter so I could bring the body back. He was also good enough to escort me to camp—otherwise, I'd still be wandering around in the jungle."

"Ovid! Quintus! Don't just stand there gawking! Help Cornelius with poor Fausto!" Professor Tarquin ordered. As the two students scampered forward to relieve Cornelius of the travois and its grim burden, the archeologist clapped a hand on his prize pupil's shoulder. "My boy, do you realize what this means? You've managed to prove my theory without us having to turn a single spade! The Southern Valley *is* the Garden! It *is* the birthplace of the ape, monkey, and human species alike! It wasn't destroyed after all—and neither were the baboons! My young chimp, they're going to chisel your name in marble when we get back!"

Professor Tarquin's praise made Cornelius swell with pride. From this day forward, he would be in the history scrolls, his name taught to every generation of ape who followed him.

The reality of it was dizzying, if all too short-lived.

Baako's painted brows bunched in confusion. "Ape and man have *never* been in this valley, only baboon. The band escaped to this place long after the great fires scorched the earth and made it Forbidden. It is our home now, but it is not the Garden."

The look of elation dropped from Professor Tarquin's face, to be replaced by one of annoyance. "What do you mean, 'escaped'?"

Baako ignored the question and instead sniffed the air. "You must leave," the baboon said in an urgent voice. *"Now."*

"Who are you to tell *us* what to do, monkey?" Doctor Atticus snorted in derision. "Do you have any idea who you're talking t—" Before Atticus could finish his sentence, a spear struck him in the chest, piercing his sternum. The impaled chimpanzee stared at it in confusion for a long moment before dropping to the ground like a sack of wet laundry.

"Run!" Baako cried as he grabbed Cornelius by the arm. "Shaka is here!" The baboon dragged the chimpanzee back toward the tree line and away from the center of the camp, hiding him behind a fallen log.

Suddenly, the air was filled by a flight of spears, accompanied by a crazed shrieking that seemed to come from everywhere and nowhere—as if the valley itself was screaming. The screams were echoed by Ovid and Quintus as they were struck multiple times by the deadly projectiles.

Cornelius looked up from behind the log in time to see Professor Tarquin running toward the horses at the far end of the clearing. One of the packhorses rose up onto its hind legs, slashing at the air with its hooves as it whinnied in terror, only to catch spears to its flank, throat, and exposed belly. As the mortally wounded animal crashed to the ground, Professor Tarquin leapt onto the back of his unbridled stallion. The roan wheeled about and plunged into the underbrush,

Tarquin clinging to its neck for dear life. Within seconds, both horse and rider were lost from sight, as though the jungle had swallowed them whole.

Cornelius turned his attention back to the camp as a troop of two dozen baboons entered the blood-soaked clearing. They were all, more or less, identical to Baako, in terms of appearance and adornment, save for some who were armed with wooden spear-throwers, which explained the deadly velocity and accuracy of their attack. At the forefront was a large male whose thick mantle of silver-gray hair instilled a palpable aura of command. Cornelius had no doubts that he was looking at none other than the fabled Shaka. The baboon chieftain walked over to where Doctor Atticus' body lay sprawled on the ground and snatched the carbine rifle from the chimpanzee's cooling hands, inspecting the loaded weapon by first sniffing it, and then peering down the barrel.

One of the other baboons made an urgent grunting noise and gestured to something on the ground. Shaka cast aside the unfired rifle and turned to look where his subordinate was pointing. To his horror, Cornelius saw his fellow student, Ovid, lying in the trampled grass. Although Quintus had been killed instantly during the attack, the orangutan had not been so lucky, moaning in agony as he clutched at the javelin jutting from his side. Shaka grunted and nodded his head. The other baboon gave a blood-curdling scream of aggression and charged forward, brandishing a wooden stick with a large rock lashed to one end. Ovid shrieked in panic and raised a blood-smeared hand in a feeble attempt to fend off his attacker. The baboon warrior peeled back his upper lip and brought the club down on the wounded ape's skull, smashing it like a ripe melon.

Upon a signal from Shaka, the rest of the troop began to ransack the camp, hooting and screeching in unison. Cornelius watched helplessly as Professor Tarquin's journals were shredded, the pages tossed into the air like so much confetti, medical supplies were scattered about, and the crates containing Doctor Atticus' scientific equipment were smashed open as if they were eggs.

"Run into the woods," Baako whispered. "Do it before they see you."

However, before Cornelius could move, Shaka turned around and bellowed, "*Baako!* Bring me the ape!"

The younger baboon flinched and glanced down, locking eyes with Cornelius. "No, Shaka!" Baako said with a defiant shake of his head. "This ape is no danger to the band!"

Shaka's upper lip curled back in an angry sneer, revealing a pair of two-inch-long fangs. "This one and the others came looking for us! They want to take us back in chains, like they did before!"

"That's not true!" Cornelius said as he stood up, knocking the dirt from his olive-colored tunic. "We had no idea baboons still existed, much less were living in this valley! We came here on a scientific expedition to locate the cradle of ape civiliza—"

"*Liar!*" Shaka bellowed as he advanced on Cornelius. "You came here to bring us back! That is why no ape can leave this valley!"

"No! The ape speaks the truth!" Baako barked, putting himself between Cornelius and Shaka. "Apes think we are dead! There is no point in hiding from them! No point in the Law!"

"*Blasphemer!*" Shaka shrieked, launching himself at Baako. The younger baboon did not back down, but instead hurled himself forward, screeching at the top of his lungs. The other members of the troop crowded in close, adding their own screams and yells to the horrendous cacophony.

The two baboons punched and clawed at one another, tearing out clumps of hair as they grappled for position. Cornelius had heard of humans fighting to the death over access to food or females, but he had never seen anything resembling an ape engage in such violence. He was both frightened and appalled by the naked savagery on display, even though he knew his own life was in the balance.

With a high-pitched shriek, Shaka hurled Baako to the ground hard enough to stun him. Cornelius' stomach tied itself into a cold knot as the baboon chieftain fixed his bloodshot eyes on him. It was too late to run—and there was nowhere to go, if he did. Assuming Shaka didn't bring him down before he could take two strides, the rest of the troop would run him to ground and tear him limb from limb. Zira's face abruptly filled his mind's eye, and Cornelius wished he had never left her side.

"Apes are not our brothers," Shaka growled, spittle dripping from his exposed fangs. "They have no place among us." However, as he took his first step toward Cornelius, Baako suddenly rose up from the ground and plunged his flint knife into the elder baboon's inner thigh, slicing through the femoral artery with a single, brutal cut.

Shaka screamed yet again, this time in genuine agony, his life gushing forth with every beat of his heart. Baako struggled to his feet and limped over to the rifle Shaka had casually tossed aside only moments ago. As the baboon chieftain fell to his knees, Baako picked up the gun, holding it by the barrel.

"No!" Cornelius shouted. "There's no need to do that now!"

Baako gave no sign of hearing him as he swung the carbine about, bringing the wooden stock down on Shaka's head as hard as he could. Cornelius grimaced and quickly looked away as Baako struck repeatedly, reducing his opponent's skull to a bloody pulp. Although Shaka was responsible for the deaths of his friends and had every intention of killing him as well, Cornelius was still a civilized ape, unaccustomed to such brutality, and took no pleasure in the demise of his enemy. Indeed, the very idea of murder was anathema to apekind and their greatest taboo.

The screams and hoots of the remaining baboons were instantly silenced as Shaka's blood splashed across the clearing. The troop exchanged uneasy glances with one another and grunted in consternation as they rocked back and forth. Baako turned to face them, holding the bloodied rifle over his head, and placed one foot on their fallen leader's body.

"The ape is under my protection!" he barked, pointing at Cornelius. "Understood?" The assembled baboons grunted and nodded their heads, conceding to the new chieftain's wishes. "Kojo! Chuka! Take Father's body back to the village for burial."

"Why would you kill your own father to save me?" Cornelius gasped.

"He was the old way," Baako replied as he watched his brothers lift Shaka's corpse by its arms and legs. "*I* am the new way."

The baboon village was ten miles from the clearing, and if he had not been escorted there by its inhabitants, Cornelius seriously doubted he would have ever spotted it on his own. Unlike the earth-bound stucco and adobe constructs of Ape City, the baboons lived in the canopy of the jungle in an intricate network of covered platforms interconnected by rope bridges and braided ladder ways. The overall appearance of the treetop community was somewhere between a bird's nest and a spider's web perched fifty feet above the jungle floor. By sleeping in the trees, they were safe from not only the battle-pigs that called the valley home, but also the cave bears that lived in the nearby mountains and came down to feed on the fish in the river.

Upon their arrival, Baako's usurping of Shaka's role as leader was accepted by his new subjects without argument.

The new chieftain was greeted by his predecessor's harem, which gathered about him and methodically groomed him in full view of the entire village in what was the most intimate public display Cornelius had ever seen.

As the much smaller females, whose hair was dark brown as opposed to the silver-gray of the male baboons, plucked the nits from their new chieftain's mantle, Cornelius blushed and quickly looked away. In Ape City, every species hid their body hair, while the baboons walked around almost fully exposed, doing nothing to hide their bright red butt-cheeks. Instead of stimulating him, all it did was turn his mind once more to Zira. Whereas before he had simply missed her terribly, now he was truly fearful he might never see her again. He could only offer prayers that Professor Tarquin had succeeded in escaping the valley and was on his way back to civilization. However, the Southern Valley was at the farthest extreme of ape territory, a good four days' ride from the nearest garrison. Assuming Tarquin did make it out of the valley, it could be some time before anyone came looking for him.

As night fell upon the valley, the baboon called Kojo took Cornelius to a small platform outfitted with a hammock and a low table laden with ripe fruit, neatly folded palm leaves stuffed with roasted grubs, and a hollow gourd filled with palm wine. At the sight of the repast laid before him, Cornelius' belly rumbled, reminding him that he had not eaten since the night before. While he feasted on succulent papaya and sweet mangoes, he was joined by Baako, who now wore the ivory pectoral that once belonged to Shaka.

"Is our food to your liking?"

"Yes, thank you," Cornelius replied. "But what I would like even more is to return to Ape City."

Baako shifted about uneasily and scratched at his ear. "Shaka's old lieutenants, my uncles and brothers, have accepted me as chieftain. They also accept that you are not to be harmed. Shaka was the old way. I am the new. I have changed many things today, but if I allow you to leave the valley, I risk revolt."

"Why do baboons live in such fear of apes? Shaka mentioned something about your ancestors fleeing my kind. What did he mean by that? There is no history of animosity between your species and mine that I'm aware of."

Baako sighed and picked up a piece of fruit from the platter, turning it around in his hands. "Apes are the reason we are in this valley. They are the reason your friends were killed today. They are the reason I have my brothers hunting for the chimpanzee who escaped on the horse, the one who thought this place was the Garden.

"He was not entirely wrong, you know. Long ago, back in the Garden, apes, baboons, and humans lived side by side in harmony. Then, one day, the humans set fire to the Garden and laid it to waste. The world beyond the Garden was far harsher and more dangerous than anything they had known before. Because of this, your kind declared that since baboons were monkeys, we were more than human, but *less* than ape. That meant it was our place to *serve* apes, not rule alongside them."

"You were made *slaves*?" Cornelius gasped, aghast at the very suggestion.

"They *tried*," Baako said, with more than a trace of pride in his voice. "But baboons are not easily tamed. We rose up against the apes. There was fire and blood, and many, many baboons were put to the sword for daring to rebel. When the apes realized they could not break us, they chose to destroy us. Those who survived the uprising and the purge that followed fled beyond the mountains, until we found this valley. We have been here ever since, living in peace, yet fearing the day when the apes would drag us back to their city in chains. That is why we made the Law. Today I changed the Law, but I dare not break it. That is why you cannot return home."

"Baako, I'm deeply sorry for what my ancestors did to yours, but I assure you that such things would never happen now. Apekind has evolved beyond those early, primitive days. We're far more enlightened now, thanks to the teachings of the Lawgiver. And while I understand why you feel like you have to do this, the simple fact is that I do not belong here!" Cornelius protested. "I appreciate everything you have done for me, but I *must* return home. I have someone waiting for me—someone who means *everything* to me."

"A mate?"

"Yes—I mean, no. Not yet, anyway."

"Your sister?"

"Damn it, stop asking me that!" Cornelius said, rolling his eyes.

It took Cornelius a moment to recognize the noise Baako was making was laughter. He smiled and joined in. It felt good to share a joke with a friend.

In the days that followed, Cornelius found himself in the unique position of being both an honored guest and a prisoner. Although he was allowed to wander about wherever he liked, he was keenly aware of being constantly under watch. No matter where he went or what he did, one of Baako's sub-lieutenants was always hovering around somewhere in the background.

At first, he was frustrated by the constant surveillance, but as the days went by, he realized that, as an archeologist, he was in a unique position to learn about a civilization long believed to be extinct. Instead of digging up the fossilized remains of their culture, he could observe it in real time, without any of the messy guesswork as to what their day-to-day habits actually were.

To his surprise, he discovered, despite the occasional alarming outburst, that the baboons were an extremely close-knit and cooperative society, working tirelessly for the betterment of the band, as opposed to the glorification of the individual. Although they practiced neither agriculture nor animal husbandry, their adopted home provided them with ample bounty. During the day, the adult females and juveniles of both sexes foraged for fruits, nuts, and whatever vegetables could be found, while the adult males would go on hunts for wild game that often took them to the farthest reaches of the valley. Come nightfall, they would regroup in their village, where they spent the evenings bonding by swapping stories, grooming one another and playing with their children. Most importantly, perhaps because they were all of the same species, they did not engage in the constant ethnic infighting that characterized ape culture. In many ways, Cornelius envied them their simple lives.

At the end of his first week among the baboons, whatever hopes Cornelius had of being delivered from his predicament disappeared when one of the hunting parties returned with what remained of Professor Tarquin's horse. Although there was no sign of the rider, the roan stallion had clearly fallen prey to a cave bear. As the days stretched on, the band gradually lost their initial hesitancy concerning the chimpanzee in their midst and came to accept him, as much as they ever could, even to the point of allowing Cornelius to play with their children. Each night, Baako would come to visit and drink palm wine and ask him questions about Ape City and the world beyond the Southern Valley. Cornelius soon learned that his new friend was quite intelligent, despite his lack of formal education, and was genuinely concerned as to the welfare of his subjects. As leaders went, Cornelius decided that the baboons of the Southern Valley could have done far worse.

Six weeks into Baako's rule, Cornelius was accompanying a group of foragers as they combed one of the groves for that evening's meal. It was a beautiful, sunny day, with a sky as blue as a parrot's wing. The female baboons, who lacked the males' thick, cape-like layer of hair about the shoulders, were contentedly chattering among themselves, gathering fresh fruits and nuts in wickerwork baskets. The young baboons who were able to walk helped with the foraging, while the infants were carried on their mothers' back in slings woven from the same palm fibers used to make the adults' hammocks.

As Cornelius studied the idyllic scene before him, he wished Zira could be there with him to see it, and wondered what she would have to say about it all. In many ways, the only thing that made his life with Baako's tribe unpleasant was his separation from the only female he had truly cared about. So focused was he on thoughts of his far-away love, Cornelius did not notice the rustling sound behind him until a palm was clamped over his muzzle and he was yanked into the underbrush. Cornelius struggled against his unseen kidnapper, biting at the hand covering his mouth.

"Ow! Damn it, Cornelius! Stop! I'm trying to save you!"

"Professor Tarquin?" The young chimpanzee stopped his wild flailing and turned to stare in amazement at his mentor, who was now considerably thinner and had a fresh scar bisecting his brow ridge, but was otherwise in one piece. "You're supposed to be dead!"

"It's not from a lack of trying," Tarquin replied, pointing to the wound on his forehead. "I was attacked by a cave bear while trying to escape the valley. Luckily, it preferred the taste of horsemeat. I had to make my way through the mountain pass on foot, but somehow I made my way down. A farmer found me wandering through his field, delirious with fever, and nursed me back to health. After that, it was still a three-day walk to the nearest garrison. It took some time to convince them that I wasn't simply a raving lunatic—"

Cornelius' eyes widened in alarm. *"Garrison?"*

From somewhere in the near distance, there came the call

of a hunting horn. The baboons foraging in the grove raised their heads as one upon hearing the unfamiliar sound, trying to locate its source.

"Oh, no! *No!*" Cornelius moaned, his heart sinking like a stone.

The gorilla cavalry burst from the surrounding woods in an explosion of leaves and flying sod, sabers and guns at the ready, trampling a dozen baboons under the hooves of their horses before they even knew they were under attack.

As Cornelius watched in horror, tears pouring down his face, the red-garbed gorillas hacked at the fleeing baboons with their swords, riding down mothers and babies as if they were nothing more than human vermin in a corn field. Within moments, the bucolic grove was transformed into an abattoir, the screams of the terrified females and children echoing across the valley. Even worse, it was only a matter of minutes before the males would come running to the rescue. However, there was no way a few dozen baboons armed with clubs and throwing sticks could stand against even a small regiment of gorilla soldiers.

"You've got to make them *stop* this madness!" Cornelius wailed, grabbing at Professor Tarquin's tunic front. "Stop it before it's too late!"

"It's *already* too late," the older chimpanzee replied grimly. "And I couldn't stop them now, even if I wanted to."

Before Cornelius could say anything else, the rest of the troop, led by Baako, came charging into the grove, waving their spears and showing their teeth in ritual challenge. Upon seeing his friend, Cornelius took a step forward in hopes of warning him, but Tarquin grabbed him by the upper arm and yanked him back behind cover.

"What's wrong with you, chimp?" he growled. "Have you gone completely native? Let the gorillas handle this—that's what they're good for. If you get shot in the crossfire while being rescued, Zira will *never* forgive me!"

Baako's followers managed to release at least one volley of spears, taking down one horse and its rider, before being cut down like wheat before a scythe. Cornelius clapped his hands over his ears as the cavalry opened fire, screaming in wordless rage as his friend's head exploded in a burst of blood and gray matter, before dropping to his knees and sobbing in grief.

"Caesar's blood! Get back on your feet before anyone sees you!" Tarquin said gruffly as he lifted the younger chimpanzee by the scruff of his neck. "And try to act *grateful* for being rescued, why don't you?"

As Cornelius stared at the carnage before him, he realized his heart no longer felt heavy. Instead, he felt strangely hollow, as though someone had come by and scooped out his insides. All he could do was look at the mangled bodies strewn throughout the grove and shake his head and say, over and over, in a stunned voice: "There was no need to do this."

"'No need'?"

Cornelius turned to see a mature orangutan, dressed in the yellow vestments of his caste, seated on a horse. He recognized the ape as Doctor Zaius, the deputy minister of science and a noted up-and-comer in the Ape National Assembly. Like all orangutans, there was wisdom in his eyes, but also sternness.

"If I am not mistaken, these savages murdered three, possibly four of your fellow apes in cold blood. Such actions cannot be allowed to go unpunished. Granted, the extinction of a species is always regrettable, but these baboons have earned their fate. I would not waste pity on them."

A gorilla officer stepped forward. "The enemy has been neutralized, sir," he said in a voice that sounded like two rocks being rubbed together.

"Thank you, Captain Ursus," Doctor Zaius replied with a nod of his head. "But just to be on the safe side, I want this valley put to the torch. Is that understood?"

"Yes, sir!" Ursus replied. He turned and shouted at the gorillas milling about behind him. "You heard the doctor! Burn it to the ground!"

The orangutan shifted about in his saddle, leaning forward on its pommel to fix Professor Tarquin with a baleful glare. "And as for *you*, you are to be charged with scientific heresy upon our return to Ape City. However, given his tender years and his recent ordeal, no such charges will be filed against your protégé."

"Th-thank you, Doctor Zaius," Professor Tarquin stammered, dropping his gaze to the ground. He then drove his elbow into Cornelius' ribs to get his attention, signaling him to follow his lead. The young chimp bobbed his head in imitation of Tarquin, but could not keep from staring at the nearby body of a female baboon, her head nearly severed, and the broken infant she still clutched in her arms.

"I can see, by the look in your eyes, that you are having a crisis of faith, my young friend," Doctor Zaius said as he reined his horse about. "But do not let what you have seen today trouble you, Master Cornelius. It is true that the Lawgiver commanded that ape never kill ape. However, these were not *apes*. They were *monkeys*. They had *tails*. Not even *humans* have tails! Have no fear—we are still without sin in the eyes of the Lawgiver."

Later, as Cornelius rode into the mountains under cavalry escort, he turned around in his saddle to look at the Southern Valley one last time, only to find it filled with fire. The smoke from the blaze billowed into the clouds, causing the sunset to glow as red as the sky above the Forbidden Zone.

Professor Tarquin was right. If he was to have any hopes of a career, it was better to put this all behind him. Baako and the others were dead. Nothing he could do could change that.

Whatever the Southern Valley may have been, it wasn't the Garden. All he wanted to do now was go home and take Zira in his arms and never let her go. Maybe someday, if he was lucky, he might discover the true secret of the Garden and the origin of the species. Who knows—if he could stumble across a species believed extinct for millennia, perhaps he could find the missing link between human and ape as well.

Stranger things had happened.

The landscape of the *Planet of the Apes* live-action television series expands in Will Murray's "Blood Brothers," offering fugitive astronauts Alan Virdon and Pete Burke a glimpse into a corner of their adopted world heretofore unseen and unimagined…

BLOOD BROTHERS

by

WILL MURRAY

The situation was desperate.

This was nothing new. For ANSA astronauts Alan Virdon and Peter Burke, the situation had been desperate ever since their spacecraft, *Probe Six*, had encountered problems en route to Alpha Centauri, and had crash-landed on an unknown planet.

The year had been 1980 when they'd left. There was no reckoning of the year when they landed, for their ship's chronometer had frozen at 3085. They only knew they were approximately 1,000 years into their own future.

The world upon which they found themselves was inhabited by humans very much like them, although more primitive, eking out a subsistence life under a dominant society of intelligent, articulate apes which, while superior to the humans, was vastly inferior to twentieth-century man.

It was not long after their advent, however, that they found conclusive evidence that this was not some alien world, but a future post-holocaust Earth where the natural order of things was upside down.

In this depressing reality, Virdon and Burke sought survival—and any surviving technology that might help them return to their own time.

Mounted gorillas led by Urko, Central City's chief of

security, had been pursuing them for months.

The thunder of hoofbeats at their backs signified that the apes were chasing them again. Once more, Urko had picked up their trail.

They had been pushing north for days, toward the Napa Valley. Village humans had told them that the apes avoided the Napa Valley. No one knew why. But it was a good place to find respite, and a steady supply of food, if the abundant vineyards still survived after generations.

Feeling the ground rumble beneath their feet, Galen, their chimpanzee companion, turned and cried out, "I spy Urko!"

All heads turned, and they saw, amid the swirling trail dust, a small detachment of cavalry, their hairy faces set and determined. The high, bulbous leather helmet signified Urko's rank, towering above all other simian heads. He rode a dun stallion.

Colonel Virdon took immediate charge.

"Urko's more than a mile behind us. Scatter! Good luck!"

As part of their ANSA survival training, the two astronauts had planned for exactly this eventuality. Split up. Make it harder for any one individual to be intercepted and captured. Regroup later.

Reacting instantly, Virdon broke left, while Major Burke shot off to the right. Scrambling on all fours, Galen melted into the underbrush and squeezed himself into a trembling ball. More than the humans, he feared the destructive power of the apes' crude carbine rifles.

Some of those rifles were already firing, but the range was too great to be a threat. Yet.

The trio had passed beyond the throat of the valley, unaware that pursuit lay so close behind. The high mountains beyond offered shelter, but appeared to be too far away. Virdon's blonde hair would be visible as long as light persisted. His homespun clothes, provided by human villagers, were a different matter.

They blended well with the surrounding scenery.

In the end, it didn't matter.

Urko's squad, some twenty gorillas strong, plunged into the valley's throat, firing for effect, but otherwise silent. Apes were not given to shouting as they rode.

The ground shook under the relentless pounding of hoofbeats. Already winded, Virdon dropped into the shelter of a cork oak tree, took a chance, and peered around.

A low growl escaped his lips as he saw three horse gorillas surround something. One dismounted. Galen was extracted from the brush, kicking but helpless.

While Urko shouted commands in his brutal voice, the other gorillas fanned out in all directions.

"Find the humans! Find them! When you capture them, shoot them dead! No prisoners! I am done chasing these astronauts!"

Answering gunfire caused Alan Virdon's heart to jump half into his throat, thinking that Pete had been shot. It was only gorillas answering their leader's commands with boisterous gunfire.

Mentally, Virdon cursed himself. Splitting up had been the only sensible thing to do, but now he had no way to communicate with Pete, no means to organize Galen's rescue, even if that were possible.

Looking upward, he decided to take to the treetops. A long-shot idea had come to him.

Soon, Alan was crouched in the crotch of the tree, doing his best to remain immobile. From this high vantage, he could see the gorillas ranging deeper into the valley, moving in their shambling, clumsy way. Human horsemen would have dismounted and beat the bushes with whatever tools they had, but these horse gorillas preferred the comfort of their saddles to the difficult locomotion with which evolution had burdened their simian frames. It was easier to ride than to walk. So they rode.

One plunged in his direction, unwitting.

Shifting on his supporting branch, Virdon positioned himself. If the ranging gorilla did not change direction, he would pass beneath these very branches.

And so he did.

The gorilla did not sense the human until dropping feet smashed onto his leather-clad shoulders, forcing him out of the saddle, rifle cartwheeling.

It had been a good plan—until its execution. Virdon was counting on landing on the ground next to the ape, then seizing the stunned soldier's rifle.

Instead, the ape fell one way, his carbine the other. Alan was stunned to discover himself slammed into the saddle. He seized the frightened horse's neck to keep from being thrown.

The plan had depended on the astronaut ending up in possession of the rifle...

Accustomed to the weight of a gorilla, the horse reacted to its human rider. It reared up, whinnying and screaming; no doubt, its backbone was hurting.

"Steady, boy! Steady!" Virdon cried, attempting to gentle the animal.

No good. The steed began bucking and sun-fishing, attempting to throw the unfamiliar rider.

The next thing Virdon knew, hairy hands reached up, endeavoring to pull him from the saddle, so he flung himself in the other direction, hoping to land close to the rifle.

He hit hard. Close, but not close enough. Alan spotted the clumsy weapon. He finished rolling, began half-crawling, half-scrambling toward it.

Unfortunately, his gorilla antagonist had the same idea.

Human and ape seized the weapon at virtually the same time and a grunting struggle ensued. Here, evolution had the last word. Human muscles, no matter how well-developed, were not composed of the same tough fiber as gorilla limbs.

The rifle was wrested out of Alan's clutching fingers and swapped around, and suddenly its destructive bore was pointing directly at him.

Colonel Virdon threw up his hands in surrender, knowing that surrender had no point.

"Now you die!" shouted the gorilla hoarsely.

His hairy finger groped for the trigger, almost touched it. Virdon flinched in anticipation of the gunpowder blast.

It never came. Instead, the gorilla sputtered a weird, choking outcry, arched his back, and stood poised for a few seconds, transfixed by death.

The ape finally fell forward. Protruding from his broad back was a willow shaft decorated in hawk feathers.

Alan Virdon blinked. He recognized an ancient arrow. He had never seen humans of this era use the bow and arrow, but there was no question that the shaft had impaled the ape, its obsidian point piercing the thick leather armor.

From the scrub foothills beyond, there came a strange, dry rain.

Wave after wave of arrows flew upward, arced, and descended. They were not silent, for a hissing filled the air. When they whispered, they spoke of death.

All over the valley, the gorillas were transfixed, knocked off their saddles, sprouting unexpected quills.

The origins of this hissing rain were not clear. Alan had no time to consider that. He was too busy tugging the carbine out of the dead gorilla's hands.

When he finally wrenched it loose, Virdon turned and beheld a tableau he had never before witnessed.

The posse of Security Chief Urko was in total disarray. Some riders were already in retreat; others were firing wildly in all directions, desperate to battle back against a foe they could not see.

In the center of this milling chaos, Urko stood firm in his saddle, wheeling his mount about, calling for order.

"Stand fast! Do not break! That is an order! Do not break ranks!"

A whistling shaft happened along and knocked his bulbous helmet off his head. Urko suddenly decided that his apes had the best idea after all. Wrenching his horse's head about, he fled south. He was not alone.

Horses crying and rifles completely silent, the gorillas retreated out of the valley, seeking shelter, not understanding the nature of the calamity that had befallen their ranks.

It was over almost as soon as it had begun.

Felled apes and their horses had remained behind, but the survivors were soon out of sight, only the rising dust of their hasty retreat remaining.

Virdon surveyed the surroundings, seeking the source of the arrows, but saw nothing and no one.

Not knowing if it was safe to do so, he took shelter behind a tree, and called out, "Pete! Galen! Are you hurt?"

Burke answered first. "No! What the hell just happened?"

"Urko's been stampeded. Galen, what about you?"

Alan had to call three times before Galen's mild voice squeaked up, "I have been roughed up, but I am whole. I do not understand any of this."

Muttering under his breath, Burke said, "Join the general confusion."

Turning his attention to the mountainsides, Alan called up, "Hello up there! We are two humans and a friendly chimpanzee. We are trying to reach the Napa Valley."

There was a silence. Then a heavy voice rolled out.

"Do you seek the Rez?"

Virdon hesitated. "I don't know what that is. I seek refuge from Security Chief Urko and his gorilla militia."

"Are you an enemy of Urko?"

"He has made himself our enemy," Alan replied.

"Then we count you as friends. You are welcome on the Rez. Step out into the light. I guarantee you safe passage. You will ride with us."

"Thank you. Who are you?"

The answer was not long in coming, but the seconds seemed to stretch out uncomfortably.

Atop a brush-choked ridge, a figure appeared on a majestic appaloosa horse, squat but broad of shoulder, his head decorated by a war bonnet of eagle feathers the like of which Alan Virdon had only seen in old films.

The rider resembled a war chieftain from the days of General George Custer. In one hand, he clutched his reins, while the other held a feather-decorated longbow.

The dying sun painted his face clearly. It was not the face of a human being. This was the heavy mask of a bull gorilla, but a gorilla whose leathery features were marked by bands of red and ocher—warpaint.

"I," the rider called out, "am Apex."

Down from the mountains, riding single-file, came a band of riders unlike anything Alan Virdon ever expected to see.

In the lead came the full-grown bull gorilla in chief's regalia, but those who rode behind him were human. They were clothed in buckskin, white breechcloths, and eagle feathers, dressed as Native Americans did in the days of old.

Stepping out from behind a tree, Alan waited for Pete and Galen to join him.

Pete was the first to trot up. "Am I seeing what I think I am?"

"A gorilla tricked out like Geronimo leading a band of Native Americans?" Alan shot back.

Pete grunted. "Glad to know I'm not hallucinating." Searching the faces of the approaching war party, he added, "When I was a kid, I was into Native American lore. Still remember a lot of it. Every one of those human riders looks like a full-blooded something or other. If those costumes are authentic, this is the damnedest tribe that ever rode the West."

"Meaning?" Virdon asked.

"I see Sioux, Hopi, Navajo, Cheyenne, Yurok, and other costumes. The faces that go with them seem authentic. Everybody looks like a full-blooded brave of one tribe or another."

"Led by a gorilla," Virdon mused. "What do you make of it?"

"It doesn't make any sense, but if they tell us their story, it's going to be something."

Galen was reluctant to join them, but when he finally stumbled up, the chimpanzee had trouble comprehending the nature of the approaching rider.

"Out of the frying pan into the fire?" he asked, using a phrase he had picked up from his human friends.

"I don't think so," Alan murmured.

"But we really don't know," Pete admitted warily.

"Those humans do not appear to be slaves," Galen said uncertainly.

Apex drew near. Seen up close, he was an imposing sight.

He rivaled Urko in the power and majesty of his native costume, and out-weighed him by twenty-five pounds. His sunken eyes were sharp and wise. His proud expression was fearless. In a strange way, his heavy face brought to mind the great war chiefs of centuries ago: Geronimo, Red Cloud, and others.

The human face and the gorilla mask were very different in structure, but the Native American head tended toward broadness, the skin more leathery than that of a civilized European. So, too, did the gorilla countenance. It was disconcerting.

"Unless basic biology has been completely changed after the holocaust," Alan told Pete, "it's impossible for a gorilla and human to mate and produce offspring."

"He's no hybrid," Pete replied. "This is a gorilla who thinks he's Sitting Bull."

Alan stepped up and introduced himself. "I am Colonel Alan Virdon, and this is Major Peter Burke. This chimpanzee is Galen, who is under our protection."

"You are under *my* protection," Apex retorted curtly. His windy eyes measured them coldly. "You say that you hold military rank. What army claims you as officers?"

Alan and Pete exchanged sheepish glances. Virdon spoke up.

"We are astronauts, not military men."

"You might say that we're the last of our breed," Pete added.

"You talk like crazy apes," Apex grunted. "But I will hear the story of your vanished people later. Gather horses. We ride for the Rez. If the gorillas follow us, we will finish them."

"Fine with us," Pete said. They began rounding up stray horses, and as they did so, the braves who accompanied Apex ranged about, dropping out of their saddles and falling on their apish foes, using their knives with quick, short gestures.

Everywhere they found a dead or wounded gorilla, they finished him off and sliced off the topmost pelt at the apex of their crowns.

Securing a mount, Alan urged it over to Pete, and asked, "What are they doing?"

"Scalping."

"They're only taking a small patch."

"That's what the Indian tribes used to do. They didn't take the whole scalp—just enough to show that they had defeated a foe in battle."

Soon, the braves had surrounded Virdon and the others. They formed an escort, and so rode deeper into the valley, their hulking chieftain in the lead.

Swaying in the saddle, Apex said nothing. He seemed indisposed to speech.

Galen tempted the silence by asking, "Where are they taking us?"

Pete answered that. "The Rez. Short for reservation. We're bound for their camp."

That settled in their minds, they fell into a steady canter as they rolled along, and while the sun set, they kept their mouths shut, only glancing back from time to time to see if Urko's surviving gorillas were stalking them.

There was no sign of Urko. None. It wasn't like the stubborn gorilla, but they were not about to complain.

That night, they all sat around a leaping campfire.

Apex took the seat of honor in the circle, and the firelight made his face look ancient and unreal.

Food was passed around—small game garnished with grapes. For the valley protecting the reservation was abundant with wild grape vines.

Virdon finished telling the story of how they came to this time and place, and of their journey to find an advanced human civilization able to help them. The firelight flickering in Apex's deep-set eyes failed to disclose whether or not he believed a word of it.

Instead, the gorilla chief grunted, "You are welcome to stay with us as long as you wish. But we cannot help you with your quest, for we do not know about the white man's tools of which you speak."

"We are grateful for this," Virdon said. "Now, please, tell us about yourself."

"I am Apex, chieftain of this clan."

Around the campfire, the other braves nodded while they ate. The women of the tribe did not join the circle; they ate elsewhere.

"And?" Pete prompted.

"What more is there to tell? I am Apex, war chief of my tribe."

Again, nods and murmurs of assent raced around the circle.

"Chief Apex," Virdon pressed. "How did you come to be leader of a band of human braves?"

"They raised me. I am one of them. Let no one say otherwise."

"But you are a gorilla."

Reddish faces darkened around the campfire and Apex snarled, baring yellowed fangs, finally barking, "Do not say that! I am chief. Not gorilla. Not ape. I am Apex."

Alan Virdon made calming gestures with both hands, saying, "Yes, I understand. Please pardon me. I mean no offense. It's just that… well, we've never encountered anything like this survival of the Native American tribes."

"We are at the Tribe of the Last," said Apex. "The last of all the tribes in this part of the world, gathered at this spot to dwell in peace and harmony on the Red Road."

A brave grunted, "And to take the scalps of ugly apes where we can."

Laughter raced around the campfire. Apparently, taking such scalps was the chief occupation of the tribe.

Alan decided to change the subject. "I understand that you and Urko are enemies. Why has he not raided this village?"

Apex made a careless gesture with one battle-scarred hand. "Urko tried. Long while ago. The battle was bloody. Many fell on both sides. Urko was flung back. He has not returned—until now."

"I see. Well, Urko was determined to catch us and kill us. Mark my words, Chief, he will be back."

"Mark *my* words," retorted Apex. "Urko will *not* be back. He will not enter the Valley of the Last Tribe. He is afraid of us." He struck his bare chest. "Of me!"

Pete ventured, "I've never known Urko to be afraid of anything."

"He is afraid of Apex. And Apex's warriors. Now eat! You talk too much."

They ate their fill, and when the hour was late, they were escorted to a tanbark wickiup, where they were allowed to retire for the night in privacy.

There was no light, so they conversed in the dark.

Alan asked Galen, "What do you know of this?"

"Nothing, nothing." The chimp's dark eyes grew reflective. His tone betrayed his reluctance.

"Out with it, Galen," prodded Pete. "You're holding something back."

"Well, let me see. When I was a child, tales were told of a warrior called Apex. Fantastic stories. Some said he was a gorilla. Others claimed that he was a human. Some said he was neither one nor the other, but some mongrel combination of both."

"Although he acts like a human being, Apex is clearly a gorilla," offered Pete.

Galen said, "Yes, yes, I can see that. Yet I could also see that he and his—did you call them braves?—seem of one mind."

Virdon reminded, "Apex says he was raised by the tribe. In his mind, he thinks he's one of them."

Pete offered, "Kind of like Tarzan of the Apes, but in reverse."

Galen's curious voice lifted. "Who is this Tarzan of the Apes?"

"Long ago," informed Pete, "a famous writer wrote a book about a man who was orphaned and raised by primitive apes in Africa. Knowing no humans, he believed that he was an ape, and grew to manhood to become the king of his tribe.

He was called Tarzan, which means 'white skin.'"

"I see," said Galen in a subdued voice that suggested he did not quite grasp the concept. "It all sounds rather fanciful."

Alan spoke up. "I see where you're going, Pete. Apex thinks he's of the same blood as his tribe. He doesn't know gorilla culture, only the one in which he was reared."

"Right. He and the others are blood brothers. And one of the reasons Urko and his band are afraid of him is because they don't understand the bow and arrow. To them, it's a foreign weapon of war. They only know the brute force of a carbine rifle."

Virdon nodded in the dark. "Maybe we could borrow a few for future use. But I think there's more to this story than we know."

Galen piped up. "Talk long ago was that a party of apes was massacred during a journey to Central City from the outpost of Huk. Few survived. The dead gorillas were discovered with their heads so bald that naked bone showed at their crowns."

"Scalped!" said Pete and Alan in unison.

"That cinches it," Pete added. "This tribe did the deed."

Alan turned to Galen. "Were all the apes accounted for?"

In the dark, the two astronauts could almost hear the chimpanzee shrug his hairy shoulders.

"There were rumors about that, too," he said vaguely.

"What kind of rumors?" pressed Pete.

"Whispers that one was never found," said Galen. "But it was forbidden to talk about it. The High Council, in particular, was sensitive about the incident. You can imagine that they would be. Gorillas rule. They are not massacred so barbarously. Not even by other gorillas."

Pete mused, "Apex may be one of the survivors of that raid."

"Oh, I wouldn't know about that," Galen said hastily. His tone suggested otherwise, but they let it go.

At last, Alan said, "Okay, let's turn in. We'll worry about the future in the morning."

Security Chief Urko put off sleep that night. He was worried about the future.

Making camp below the Valley of Grapes, he assembled his surviving gorillas.

"Our numbers have been cut by one third!" he thundered, wide nostrils flaring. "This is intolerable!"

One of the apes attempted to make excuses. "Sir, we are the survivors, not the fallen. Blame belongs to—"

Urko slapped him in the face, and continued his harangue.

"You have not been in the saddle as long as I have, Mema. The Valley of Grapes is a dangerous place. I was determined to capture the humans before they set foot in the Forbidden Zone. But you all failed me."

No gorilla replied to that point. There was no reasoning with Urko when he was enraged. And he was furious now, his deep-set eyes bloodshot.

"Did you see anything of those who attacked?"

Hesitation froze the ranks. One gorilla lifted a hand tentatively.

Urko got in front of him, pressed his pulsing nostrils against the other, demanding, "You! Zilo! Speak up!"

"I was one of the last to leave the valley, but I saw on the crest of the ridge a figure in a strange uniform. He wore a crown of feathers."

"Human?"

"No, sir. A gorilla, his face marked in fierce colors."

Urko said nothing. He stared into the eyes of the other ape, seeking signs of falsehood. He broke away, muttering to himself.

"He lives. He lives."

The assembled apes wanted to know who "he" was. But they dared not ask.

Urko stalked off to throw himself into a sleeping tent, but he did not rest. Nor did he tell his troops to break formation, and so they stood obediently that way until the sun rose.

Finally, snorting and breathing heavily, he drifted off.

At dawn's break, Urko's red eyes snapped open, drained of sleep.

Clambering to his feet, he found his reduced force still in formation and demanded, "What are you fools doing?"

"Awaiting the order to break formation, sir," one told him.

"Had you not the sense to sleep? You will need all your strength, for we are returning to the Valley of Grapes!"

They waited for the correct order, and finally it came.

"Break formation! Eat rapidly. Mount up. We ride—we ride hard."

Breakfast was grapes. Conversation was minimal.

Alan, Pete, and Galen observed this unspoken convention in silence, the rising sun warming their bones. It had been a chilly night.

After the breakfast detritus was cleared away, Apex addressed them.

"I have decided to lead a war party against Urko."

Alan asked, "Why?"

"A scout has informed me that Urko and his apes are camped south of the valley. He should have fled to his brutal masters. This means that he has not given up. I am insulted by this. I do not wish Urko to get away this time."

Apex seemed to await some form of response, and Pete offered it.

"We stand ready to ride with you, then."

Apex grunted, then turned away to muster his braves.

Once he was out of earshot, Galen began putting up a fuss. "Are you mad? Do you wish us all to die?"

Alan quieted him with a hard glance and asked of Pete, "Why did you volunteer us, Pete?"

"I could tell that's what Apex expected of us. But he's not the type to ask. I just earned us his respect."

Galen quivered. "I am not eager to join this insane enterprise."

"We'll protect you," promised Alan.

"Be aware, Alan," warned Pete, "that your light hair probably means that you don't stand as tall in Apex's eyes as I do."

"Meaning that I'll have to prove my bravery?"

Pete nodded. "Over and over. Remember that."

Within the hour, they mounted up. Apex was resplendent in his war bonnet, his massive chest and thick features marked with bars and circles of arcane significance.

Apex gave no orders, but his braves formed a single line behind him and trailed him out of the camp in silence.

The humans and Galen straggled in the rear, and so they all marched south between the scrub foothills of the lower valley.

A scout rode ahead, was gone nearly an hour, and returned to confer with his simian chief. They palavered but for moments.

Lifting a feathered staff, Chief Apex shouted, "The enemy rides north to meet us! Let us make them unwelcome!"

"And hurl them into the laps of their hairy ancestors!" shouted an eager brave.

No war cry erupted. The tribe simply resumed riding, sun-leathered features stoic.

"Noisy bunch," quipped Alan.

"Native Americans are descended from horse Mongols," commented Pete. "Genghis Khan and his Golden Horde were famous for riding into battle in silence, too."

The two war parties came into sight of one another just north of the valley's entrance, where flies buzzed over the corpses of the dead apes whose scalps lay raw and exposed in the morning sun.

Lifting an open hand, Apex signaled a silent halt to his column.

Seeing his formidable foe, Security Chief Urko did the same.

Without further instruction, both sides formed a fan on either side of their leader. The opposing forces glared at one another, but no one made a hostile move.

Chief Apex stared without expression, dark eyes boring into Urko's own. A grape-scented breeze toyed with the feathers of his resplendent war bonnet.

Finally, Apex spoke. "You are forbidden to enter the Valley of Grapes. Turn about and go."

"I am under orders to capture the two humans and the fugitive chimp," returned Urko stiffly.

"They are under my protection."

Urko absorbed the portent of these words, eyes unblinking. "I cannot fail in my duty, brother ape."

"I am not your brother."

"No, you are not. You are a renegade. It is tragic. I never thought I would see a bull gorilla sink so low. Teaching humans to ride horses. Leading them as if they were your equals."

Apex thumped his bare chest once. "Low? You are a mere soldier. I am a great war chief!"

"You are mad, Apex. And your madness has taken root in your deluded brain so deeply it cannot be uprooted. I see this now."

"You have insulted the war chief of the Last Tribe," intoned Apex. "For that, I will have your scalp."

"I will not fight you, brother."

"Do not call me that!" Apex snarled. Dismounting, he plucked a stone tomahawk from his saddle and, leading his horse by the reins, advanced on foot in the direction of the mounted gorillas. No fear flickered in his deep-set eyes, only a smoldering resentment.

Urko kept his saddle. He lifted a broad hand in warning to his horse gorillas.

"Hold your fire!" he commanded.

"But, sir," one soldier pleaded, "he is coming for your head pelt!"

"I will shoot the first ape who opens fire on that gorilla. This is my affair, not yours. We have come for the humans, nothing else."

The mounted apes subsided, but their eyes were uneasy and their fingers drifted to their triggers. The humid air was full of the stink of dead apes. No gorilla wished to die this day.

Chief Apex crossed half the distance to General Urko, while his braves arrayed themselves in the semi-circle, long bows in hand, arrows nocked, points aimed at gorilla chests.

One nervous cavalry ape said to another, "We are vastly outnumbered."

"We will die if we are not careful. Let them fight it out."

Moving with a strange cadence that marked Apex as having learned to walk under human tutelage, the chief of the Last Tribe suddenly found his way blocked by a rider—a human rider.

"Hold on," called Alan Virdon.

"There is no need to fear, White Eyes," Apex snapped.

"There's no need for bloodshed if it is not necessary," Virdon cautioned.

Lifting his tomahawk angrily, Apex snarled, "That

misshapen gorilla only understands violence. I will teach him what it tastes like. His own blood!"

"Listen to me, Chief. Urko wants me and my friends. He has no quarrel with you."

"No, but I have a quarrel with him. He would wrest me from my saddle and take me forcibly to his camp to make me one of his tribe. I am a chief, not a stoop-backed gorilla."

"It appears to me that you are a little bit of both, Apex. But listen, instead of fighting Urko, let me do it."

"You!"

"I fought Urko before."

"This is none of your affair! This is not about Urko's mission—this is about our feud."

Suddenly, Pete was on the other side, saying, "Listen to him, Chief. Look, we appreciate your hospitality, but we don't want people dying for it. Tell you what, you hold them off and we'll head up to the hills, and take our chances there."

Chief Apex's head swiveled back and forth between the two mounted humans, his eyes growing narrow and feral.

"You spurn my hospitality?"

"No," returned Alan. "We have taken more than our share, and you have our gratitude for that. We want to push on, without causing you any more trouble."

"You brought no trouble. That stupid ape brought more than a full share. He insults me. Calls me his brother." Apex spat his contempt onto the ground.

"He thinks you belong with him," returned Pete. "Pay Urko no mind. It's not worth killing over."

Chief Apex's jaw clamped shut. He seemed to be considering his response when Urko shouted over, "But he *is* my brother in blood. And his father—our father—misses him."

"What?"

"Grud has never ceased grieving for the son he believes to be dead."

Galen was with them now, and his simian eyes were wide, his jaw hanging loose.

Staring at Chief Apex, he blurted, "You? You are the long-lost son of Councilor Grud?"

Apex sneered, "I am the son of no gorilla. I am of the Lost Tribe. Let no one speak otherwise, man or ape."

Alan demanded, "Galen, what are you talking about?"

"Those rumors abounding in Central City of an apeling who went missing long ago," he hissed. "It was the infant son of a noble. Never heard of again. Presumed dead all these years."

Studying Apex's fearsome countenance, the chimpanzee added, "There is a resemblance. Around the nose and jowls, especially."

"Silence!"

This from Chief Apex, who leaped back into the saddle of his horse. Wheeling his responsive appaloosa, he broke in the direction of Urko. Not expecting this, the other gorilla struggled to keep his dun stallion from shying, and his nervous troops from opening fire.

Rifles jumped up in hirsute hands. But longbows steadied more quickly, and with unerring intent. Bowstrings were pulled back to their maximum tautness. Arrows flew.

Before two breaths could be taken, Urko's horse gorillas were twisting and falling off their mounts, which broke and scattered. Unpleasant groans emerged from simian mouths that leaked fresh blood. No arrow-impaled gorillas stood up. They could not. Most had been shot through the heart.

In the blink of an eye, Urko sat alone in the saddle. His eyes turned to slits of menace as deep within him, a red rage burst forth.

Lashing his mount, the furious gorilla officer charged the knot of feathered foes directly in front of him.

Turning, Apex shouted, "Let none interfere! I will settle this now!"

Pete, Alan, and Galen scattered as the opposing riders charged one another.

"I will have your scalp!" screamed Apex.

Urko brought his stallion up just short of his foe, dismounted, and waded in, intent on using his horny-knuckled fists.

"Where is your weapon?" challenged Apex, leaping from his blanket saddle.

"I do not need a weapon to settle this, my apeling brother!"

At this, Apex swung his tomahawk in Urko's direction, but the gorilla officer caught the warrior wrist that wielded the weapon. They struggled. The blade of chipped stone wavered close to Urko's spasming nostrils.

Exerting his strength, Apex attempted to force the sharp edge into Urko's flat face. Gorilla muscles, locked in contention, creaked and groaned with the awful effort. Inch by inch, the blade neared, ready to bite into ape flesh.

The two combatants stood toe to toe, feet stamping the dirt, throwing up dust. Eyeball to eyeball, they glared at one another.

With a forceful lunge, Apex drove the blade home. Were it not for Urko's powerfully resisting strength, his facial mask might have been split to the bone. But the sharp stone tooth sliced into his dark forehead, drawing blood, and the feeling of stone grating his skullbone gave Urko a final burst of might.

Roaring his rage, he twisted Apex's wrist once, forcefully. The weapon fell to the dirt. Urko stamped on it once, breaking the hickory handle in two. Then he kicked it away in separate pieces.

The two hairy brutes collided then, fists and knuckles smashing, bare fangs snapping at pulsing jugulars. No longer semi-civilized apes, they became ferociously feral.

Apex and Urko fought like wild animals, ripping at one another, teeth and nails tearing at matted flesh, blood crawling from fresh wounds like venomous crimson vipers. Bestial growls emerged from their open mouths.

The tomahawk wound leaked blood into Urko's eyes, blinding one blinking orb. The gorilla general shook his great head in an effort to toss the salty fluid aside. But it was no use. More blood poured, for the tomahawk had bitten deep. Coagulating, it glued the eye closed with its stickiness.

"That which you taste in your mouth," screamed Apex, "is the bitter salt of your defeat!"

It was the wrong thing to say, for it was premature. Hearing this taunt, Urko redoubled his effort and smashed his feathered foe in the snout. Driven backward by the blow, Chief Apex lost his war bonnet, but not his footing. Or his ferocity.

Roaring, he charged. Hairy fists lashed out, pounding furiously. Knuckles split. Blows were landed, traded, thwarted as each colossus desperately sought to best the other.

A human being would have been battered into abject submission, if not ignominious death. But neither ape faltered. Both refused to surrender.

They smashed at eyes, ears, and throats with their long, hairy arms. While every wild blow landed, none could finish the fight. Blood flew like scarlet spittle.

Over time, their growls and grunts grew less loud, their alternating blows less punishing. Barrel chests heaved with exertion, and the unforgiving adversaries fell to panting like thirsty dogs.

In the end, they exhausted themselves, faltered, long limbs swiping feebly at one another, and collapsed. Both warriors ended up in the dirt, flat on their backs, panting, growling, flinging dirt at one another, their rage and muscular energy entirely expended.

Soon, even that pathetic defiance subsided. All their brute strength had fled. Only spite remained.

Finally, one gorilla struggled up and found his feet: Apex. Righting his out-of-alignment jaw with one hand, he shambled over to his panting fellow anthropoid, spat blood into the befouled hair of his chest, and snapped, "Let that teach you never to enter my valley again."

"This is not over, renegade," gasped Urko, hands flopping weakly.

"It is over. For I have ended it. When you find your breath, turn south. If you head north, your hairy carcass will be filled with arrows and I will wear your scalp on my belt."

With that, Apex stormed over to Urko's trembling stallion and gave it a hearty smack on the rump that sent it fleeing, so that his prostrate foe would suffer the indignity of walking home on foot.

Gathering up his dilapidated war bonnet, Apex reclaimed his appaloosa. Mounting up with difficulty, for one eye was sealed shut by sticky gore, he gave the order to ride north. And so the warriors of the Last Tribe followed, trailed by Alan Virdon, Peter Burke, and Galen the chimpanzee, their feathered-decorated heads held high.

Breathing the choking dust of their departure, Urko lay panting and cursing. One hairy fist lifted with difficulty, then shook in quaking rage at the climbing sun.

"I will have my vengeance on you all. All! Do you hear me, traitor?"

Only the blackbirds in the trees heard that emotion-charged vengeance vow. Urko's voice was reduced to a husky frog's croaking, and every word expelled a frothy fountain of blood.

An hour along, they were single-footing through the heart of the valley as the fragrant campfire smoke of the Rez tickled their nostrils.

Alan spoke up. "Urko will return with a larger legion, Chief."

Apex shook his heavy head solemnly. "He will not. Urko

will not kill the one he mistakenly thinks is his brother in blood. That is his weakness. That is why I will always triumph over him. He is afraid to kill me."

"Why didn't you finish him?" asked Pete. "You could have taken his scalp."

Apex snapped angrily. "I could not. For my tomahawk was broken."

That seemed an insufficient answer, but they let it pass. They could plainly see that Apex did not want to discuss it.

Alan asked, "Why does Urko believe that you are his brother?"

Apex was a long time in answering that. Finally, he growled sullenly, "Because he is a stupid gorilla. Nothing more, nothing less."

Wordlessly, Pete and Alan exchanged knowing glances.

Galen offered only this: "Urko is sometimes smart, and other times not very intelligent at all. Among gorillas, that is what makes him a great leader. For, his rank aside, Urko is a soldier. His job is to obey orders, not question them."

Apex looked to the chimpanzee with a troubled brow.

"You are smart," he grunted.

Galen beamed. "Thank you, Chief Apex."

"For a mere chimp," added Apex dismissively.

Galen's jaw sank. His shoulders sagged in dejection.

They rode along in silence a little while longer. Down from the Rez, aromas of food cooking stirred their appetites.

"Once we rest up," Alan informed Apex, "we plan to push north."

The chief did not look in his direction. "My hospitality does not suit you?"

"It is generous and above reproach," offered Pete. "But we have a quest to complete, for we seek our own people, and our own home fires."

Apex nodded. "I do not understand you pale people, but

this much I do know: you are warriors in your own strange way. Go with my respect, and if you ever return, my hospitality will be unchanged."

So saying, Chief Apex spurred his appaloosa on ahead, obviously wishing to be alone with his thoughts, for his heavy gorilla features were troubled.

Hanging back, Alan, Pete, and Galen exchanged uneasy looks.

"Mark my words," whispered Galen. "Urko will not take this insult lying down. The bad blood between them has gotten worse. Now it is boiling over. Urko will avenge his honor. Not even the fact that Apex is the lost son of Councilor Grud will dissuade him. For Urko will slay Apex without ever telling his father that his other son lived."

"I know it," agreed Alan.

"And Apex knows it," added Pete. "Just as he is now realizing that Urko spoke the truth. You can see it's eating at him, undermining his sense of self, his core identity. The chief has always believed that he was human—at least partially so. Now that the illusion has cracked, Apex will do anything to repair it. Crushing Urko is probably top of the list."

Alan nodded. "Let's hope we're far from this valley when that day comes."

"We can do better than that," grunted Pete.

Alan Virdon and Galen looked at Peter Burke quizzically.

Pete grinned. "Since we're hoping, let's hope that when it happens, it takes place a thousand years in our future— because that will mean we'll be home by then."

No more needed to be said. They fell in behind the silent file of warriors comprising the Last Tribe, whom the morning sun blessed with her life-affirming rays...

Bob Mayer's "The Pacing Place" sets a central figure in the Apes universe on a path divergent to the one shown on the big screen, in an intriguing "what if?" tale that offers new hope for a weary future world…

THE PACING PLACE

by

BOB MAYER

George Taylor named his first son Adam. Not a very original idea for the Earth he'd come from, but completely unique for the Earth to which he'd returned. The first few years, it hadn't seemed to matter since no one else in Fort Wayne could write or speak.

Taylor came to regret the motivation behind that decision later in life, an act of cynicism when he was still the man who'd volunteered for the ANSA mission.

It was three years after Taylor and his fellow astronauts had returned to this Earth, but not his Earth, when Nova gave birth to Adam. By then, Fort Wayne boasted three dozen native humans, surviving at a subsistence level.

He hadn't wanted a child, but he had wanted Nova. And as he watched Nova nursing the baby, it occurred to him that she had made the decision for him. Without discussing it with him, which might have mattered on *his* Earth, but was moot here, because they couldn't discuss anything. No matter how hard he tried to teach them, Nova and the others could not form words.

When Adam was two, he reached up and pulled on Taylor's beard and murmured "da-da." And Taylor wept because language had returned to the humans.

•

Leaving the remains of the Statue of Liberty behind on the beach, Taylor rode as hard and as fast as he could, Nova clinging to him. Along the coast for miles, until surf pounding at the base of cliffs forced him to backtrack to the first place he could forge inland.

Dunes and scrub gave way to desert as far as he could see. He was angry and foolish, pushing them into the desolation without forethought. He quickly understood why the apes called it the Forbidden Zone. Only a fool would try to pass this way, and in the brief time he'd been among them, he'd learned the apes weren't fools.

And why *would* anyone go this way when there was no clue as to what was on the other side of the desert? If there even *was* another side to the wasteland? The science part of him wondered about radiation, whether that was why nothing grew here, and why it was forbidden.

But he and Nova had no choice. If they went back, they wouldn't last long in the land of apes. Taylor knew he'd ignited a bonfire and humans were no longer tolerated among the apes, because they were now a threat.

He tried not to dwell on his responsibility for that.

As far as Nova was concerned, she showed no inclination either way, accepting his decision with the apparent apathy every human he'd run into on this Earth seemed imbued with.

They suffered during the journey. A selfish part of Taylor was glad for once that Nova was mute and could not complain. They pushed on. The horse died on the second day. Taylor slit a vein and they drank as much of the blood as they could. He cut some meat off, but not much, since there was no way to cook it, and from his Air Force survival training he knew water was the only thing that mattered now. A person could go three weeks without food.

He gave himself and Nova a max of two more days without water.

Three days later, there was a speck of green on the horizon. Then more green. Eventually, they found water and green and life on the other side of the desert. Taylor picked the best spot he could find, in a wooded area on the side of a winding river.

There was game and fish, and Taylor went back to his species' ancestral ways of finding food as a hunter-gatherer. For Nova, it was life as it had always been.

In this way, they survived.

He built a solid hut high in an old tree. And every night, as he pulled up the makeshift rope ladder, he felt as though he were locking the doors of the house and turning off the lights, and it would be a safe place during the darkness.

The first couple showed up a month later. As best Taylor was able to determine, the apes had launched a pogrom against humans. The result was that the savvier of the humans had no choice but to try the Forbidden Zone.

Where else could they go?

How many had perished in the desert? Taylor didn't want to know, and those who arrived couldn't tell them what they saw. They'd only pantomimed apes attacking, and Taylor had been forced to truly accept that his arrival, and departure, in Ape City had caused a reaction.

For the first time in his life, other than for Nova, Taylor had to accept responsibility for people other than himself.

So Fort Wayne had begun to grow.

Adam's birth changed things, even though Taylor wasn't consciously aware of it. A woman was taken one night by a mountain lion, and the blood trail led into the wild. Now, the protection of Fort Wayne being in the Forbidden Zone wasn't enough for Taylor. He wanted a Wall around the encampment for safety from more than just the apes.

The Wall required time to build, so subsistence wasn't sufficient. Taylor taught the others what he knew about farming from his childhood in Old Fort Wayne, which was the way he separated the memory place from the present place. He scoured his brain and remembered old history lessons of how the Egyptians had used the Nile for irrigation. He showed the others by example.

Trial and error, but it got done.

As civilization had taken root on his old Earth, it now began to take shape here. There was game and fish and now farming.

The Wall went up eight months later. Nova tended to the communal garden with the other women, while Taylor led hunting parties. He also supervised construction projects, as most moved out of the trees and onto the ground, safe inside the Wall.

But Taylor and Nova, and now Adam, remained in their Tree Home. He still pulled the rope ladder up every evening.

Nova had never learned to make more than a few guttural utterances, and early on Taylor decided that language in humans must be learned early or else the place for it in the brain simply withered away. He'd ached to hear another human talk before Adam's first words.

For the first year, as others arrived, singly or in pairs and even small groups, he'd wave and say "Hello," but the greeting was never returned. After a while, before Adam, he gave up on the hello and stopped talking. He mimicked the pointing and guttural sounds of his new neighbors. They built more huts and added more fields and extended the Wall.

One night, when Adam was eighteen months old, the humans, now a tribe, were sitting around the fire as they always did early in the evening. Taylor would never remember what prompted it, perhaps his days in the Boy Scouts, perhaps the utter loneliness of not hearing words.

It was spring—he would remember that later—and that evening, he leaned forward and said, "Once upon a time."

It became known as the First Night of the Fire Story. From then on, every evening, Taylor would tell the stories he could remember. He rued the English classes he'd skipped to indulge in his hobby of making model rockets, because the one thing he truly knew how to build was the one thing they didn't need.

Running out of fairy tales, he switched to history and told these people, his people, of their origins. And the history of those who came long before them. He never knew how much they understood, but they never seemed to get bored. Their eyes were always on him, their attention rapt. So, like any good storyteller, Taylor took that as interest.

The night Adam was born, Taylor had been grateful for the other women. It was a long night and a hard birth. He spent the dark hours pacing back and forth by the river, trying to ignore the animal-like sounds of her pain. But just before dawn, she delivered a big, healthy boy and Taylor longed for cigars to pass around.

The other men had watched him with the questioning looks of men not used to seeing another man worry about woman matters. For them, a baby would come and it would live or it would die, and maybe the mother would die, but the art of worrying had been lost to them over centuries of struggling to simply survive. An integral part of their apathy.

A curious thing occurred several months later, when another woman went into labor. Taylor saw the father pacing by the river in the same spot. He realized a ritual had been created, and while the emotions weren't perfectly attached, it had to start somewhere. After several days, he noticed that no one fished there and the women didn't wash there anymore, and with each new baby, the pacing was repeated.

There was soon a strip of hard-packed dirt next to the river.

After Adam uttered "da-da," Fort Wayne was large enough and the crops bountiful enough for Taylor to devote his time to teaching his son and the other children who came into the world afterward to speak. At night, he continued telling stories around the fire. As the children grew older, they were the ones in the front row, listening intently, with an attention their parents could never have.

Those who could speak began calling themselves Youngers. They called their parents People.

The years passed.

Taylor and Nova had two more boys and a girl. Fort Wayne spread out along the river. The Wall still surrounded what the Youngers were calling Old Town, but the human presence was so large now that the predators kept their distance.

One year, a hunting party came back with a mountain lion they'd killed. The predators were now the prey.

After six years, no other humans came from out of the Forbidden Zone.

Taylor didn't waste time speculating what that meant. Their world was here. Now.

As far as the apes? He didn't foresee them ever having the pressing need to attempt the Forbidden Zone. But the part of him that had become an ace in World War II and Korea wasn't naïve. He set up a Watch at the edge of the desert, rotating two-man teams there, as soon as they were able to spare the manpower.

Just in case.

Life went on.

Sometimes, the men came back from a hunt with enough kills for days of feasting. Taylor began to hear laughter, and that was when he realized he hadn't heard it during the first years. Some years there were terrible things, such as the Day of Drowning, when three children were swept down-river.

Taylor realized there were other skills besides language that had been lost. He began swimming lessons for the Youngers, and some of the People even joined in.

After many years, Nova grew ill. Taylor stopped teaching the Youngers and telling Fire Stories. He spent all his time nursing her. He only came down the rope ladder to get food and water.

There were still gatherings around the fire, but no Fire Story, so it became known as just the Fire Circle. One evening, as Taylor wrung out a sweat-soaked cloth in the door of his Tree Home, he saw the humans, Younger and People, gather round the fire, holding hands in a circle. There was no conversation among the Youngers, as if talking would violate the sanctity of the circle. But Taylor's focus was on Nova as she grew weaker and weaker.

He suspected cancer, but what did it matter? What did that word even mean here?

There were no doctors, no hospitals, no treatment. She was dying as she'd lived: with mute acceptance. She'd smile at him whenever she opened her eyes, and that was message enough.

The morning she didn't smile, he knew the end was close.

And one morning, she didn't open her eyes and her breathing grew shallower. Nova died later that day in his arms. Taylor cried out, not with words, but with pure agony from a place deep inside. He cried out not like a man who had once been a war hero, an astronaut, the founder of Fort Wayne, but like one of the People. Distantly, he heard the cry echoed by dozens of throats, People and Younger, but he didn't focus on it, lost in his grief.

After several hours, just before dark, he carried her down

the rope ladder, easily supporting her gaunt frame with one arm. When he reached the ground, weeping, and turned, he saw that Adam, now a strapping teenager of sixteen, was in the Pacing Place, along with his younger brothers. Even his little sister, Star, was there—the first time Taylor had ever seen a woman pace.

It would not be the last.

The rest of Fort Wayne was gathered between Taylor's hut and the Pacing Place. None of the Youngers were speaking. Tears began to flow, from those who saw him holding Nova and his own tears, spreading out, through the crowd as everyone became aware.

In the Pacing Place, Adam dropped to his knees and cried out, "Mother!"

His brothers and Star knelt next to him, weeping, and crying out for their mother.

The other Youngers took up the cry, repeating, "Mother!"

The People wailed in shared anguish.

Taylor, in this moment of deep sorrow, felt a surge of compassion for his fellow man. He was not the same embittered man who'd volunteered for the ANSA mission in order to leave mankind behind in both space and time. Tragedy, as it tends to do, had brought everyone together to experience the same feeling.

Nova's death was the day empathy returned to humans.

From then on, the Pacing Place was used to mark both birth and death.

There came a day when Taylor paced with Adam, whose wife had gone into labor. And for once, there wasn't silence in the Pacing Place. Taylor spoke with his son, telling him how proud he was. And reassuring him, just like any supportive father would bolster a worried son. It was the first time words were exchanged in the Pacing Place, but not the last. The birth was not difficult and the midwife came out, carrying the squalling baby, and handed it to Adam.

"A son," Adam said to Taylor. Then he held the baby up and everyone who gathered nearby knelt.

"What are they doing?" Taylor asked.

"They give thanks," Adam said. "As in the long story. Thanks that the baby is healthy. Thanks that there will be another man to lead us. Thanks that there will be a strong man like his grandfather."

"And his father," Taylor said, unable to look out at the people, his lips trembling, his eyes damp.

Adam handed the baby back to the midwife, started to follow her to the hut, but then stopped and came back to his father. "We had decided on a name if it was a boy. But only if we have your permission."

Taylor was confused. "Why would you need my permission?"

"We want to name him after you."

"Taylor? That's not a—"

"We want to name him George. With your permission."

Taylor was surprised. He'd only told Nova.

"How did you know?" Taylor asked.

Adam reached into a pocket and pulled out the dog tags which Taylor had given Nova so many years ago. She'd never shown them to him again and he'd forgotten. Adam handed them to his father.

"When did she give them to you?" Taylor asked.

"She showed them to me one day," Adam said. "When she knew I could read. She kept pointing at the letters. So I told her what they said, although I didn't understand anything more than your name."

Taylor's fingers were tracing the letters stamped into the metal.

TAYLOR, GEORGE
325229325 ANSA
O NEG
ATHEIST

Taylor recoiled at the last line, having forgotten so much about who he'd been before coming to this planet. Why he'd left his Earth in the first place.

"I knew the first line was your name," Adam said. "But the rest? What are the numbers?"

"A way of being identified," Taylor said.

"You needed more than just your name?"

"There were many, many people then," Taylor said, but Adam had a point. When did people become numbers? At what point in history? When in evolution—or rather, devolution—had that occurred?

"And the third line?" Adam asked.

"My blood type."

"What is 'blood type?'" Adam was confused. "Blood is red. All blood is the same."

Taylor smiled. "It doesn't matter. Not yet. We've got a ways to go before we get concerned with that."

"And the last line?"

"A word that represents my foolishness and my ego," Taylor said. "When I thought I knew everything."

"But you do know everything," Adam said.

"No," Taylor said. "Every day, I learn how much I don't know." He clapped his son on the shoulder. "Now, go join your wife. And your son. George, son of Adam."

"Grandson of Taylor!" Adam cried out, smiling. He ran to the hut.

Many nights later at Fire Story, Taylor began to tell of a man named Caesar, who led a mighty army. How he crossed a river he was not supposed to cross.

"Like the Ape Army crossing into the Forbidden Zone? Why we Watch?" one of the oldest Youngers asked.

"No," Taylor said, appalled at the thought. "Like all the People did. Taking a chance. Rolling the dice crossing the desert into the Forbidden Zone."

And then he had to explain what rolling the dice meant, and that took the rest of Fire Story that evening. He resumed Caesar's tale the following evening. Caesar arriving in Rome. Becoming Emperor. Taylor was sure he had some of the facts wrong, but what did that matter?

It was a Fire Story.

There came a day when one of the Younger couples had a boy and they named him Caesar. For a while, others would raise their hands and cry out "Hail, Caesar" whenever they passed the boy, but that quickly faded away.

It happened so slowly that Taylor never realized the change, but Fire Story time was more often filled with questions from Youngers and their children than it was with Story.

So the man who'd grown up on Earth before this Earth, who'd built model rockets and caught tadpoles and watched *The Man from U.N.C.L.E.* on TV, became the man who answered questions. He was aware that a day would come when they would know everything he knew, and more.

It might already have passed, he had to admit as he answered a question about the American Civil War he was sure he'd already answered before. But the Youngers acted as if they were hearing it for the first time, and Taylor learned the lesson of gratitude long after he'd already taught it to his son, Adam.

•

The years began to merge, moving faster and faster. One night, lying alone in his Tree Home, thinking about how quickly time was passing by, Taylor remembered the physics of Doctor Hasslein and his theory. The basis on which *Liberty 1* had been designed, built, and launched. And how, despite such a long journey, he'd ended up back on *this* Earth, but not *his* Earth.

It was *their* Earth, he realized. The Youngers and those who followed them.

Taylor abruptly sat up, because thinking of the past and time travel made him wonder about the future. Their future.

The next night, at Fire Story, he waved off the questions. They all fell silent, sensing the change. He was seated on a chair Adam had built for him. His firstborn was to his right, sitting on a log, with his son next to him, between him and his wife.

"This Earth was born out of my Earth," Taylor began. "I ran from my Earth. I have told you of my journey into the stars. Into time. And how I was brought back to this Earth, which was once my Earth.

"You have asked me many questions, but the question no one has asked me is this: Why did I leave my Earth?"

He looked around at all the faces around the fire, rows deep. He remembered when there were so few. When it was just Nova at his side.

"Why did you, Father?" Adam asked, snapping him out of his thoughts, a place he was disappearing into more and more.

"Because my Earth had a sickness," Taylor said. "The worst kind of sickness. Man, the marvel of the universe, that glorious paradox which sent me to the stars and to travel in time, made war against each other. Allowed the children of other men and women to starve while they had plenty of food of their own."

"Why?" one of the second generation of Youngers asked, the concept so strange, she could not grasp it.

"I don't know," Taylor said. "If you'd asked me then, I would have told you, 'Because it's our nature.' But it isn't our nature, is it?"

Adam answered for everyone. "It is not. Everything we have is everyone's."

Taylor held his hand up and quiet reigned. "When I left my Earth, I could look back and see it." He pointed up. "Earth is blue and white and green and brown. It is beautiful. For the first time in my life, I realized how small I was. How all men were. It crushed my ego for a time.

"And I was lonely. I was lonely until I came to Our Earth and met Nova."

"Mother," Adam said, and the word was repeated in a low murmur around the fire.

Taylor paused, groping his way back to the Story he wanted to tell. He remembered. "This Fire Story, I want to speak not of what was. I want to speak of what will be. And of what cannot ever be."

The Youngers waited. The remaining People—and Taylor realized there were fewer now than he remembered—were silent, their eyes reading his face and the reactions of the Youngers for what their brains could not process.

"What cannot be is My Earth," Taylor said. "It cannot happen again. This must remain Your Earth."

"No, Father," Adam protested. "It is *Our* Earth. We are all one."

"We are," Taylor agreed, seeing Nova in the lines of his face. "But the day will come when there will be so many Youngers, when you all won't know each other. When some will be strangers. When some will start another town."

"When we become numbers?" Adam asked.

"You must try never to become numbers to each other,"

Taylor said. "You must always keep your names. And know each other's names."

"We would never make war against ourselves," young Caesar said.

"You would not," Taylor agreed. "But will your children, when there are other towns? And your children's children?"

A murmur rippled around the fire.

"When that happens," Taylor said, "there is the possibility of conflict. Of My Earth coming back."

"What should we do?" Adam asked.

"There is a need for laws," Taylor said. "Even the apes learned this lesson. While they treated us, the People, like animals, they treated each other with respect. They had a law. 'Ape shall never kill ape.'"

The Youngers, none of whom had ever met an ape, tried to understand.

Taylor didn't need them to understand the apes. "What we must do is have the same law. For humans."

Before he could go on, Adam stood up. "Human will not kill human. Human will not harm human." He looked down at his father. "Should this be?"

Taylor's throat was tight. He could only nod his approval.

The years continued to pass with more good than bad. Fort Wayne grew until the town was too much for the surrounding fields. As predicted, a group led by Caesar, who wasn't so young anymore, packed up and left, moving more than ten miles away to found their own town, which they named New Hope.

"As if they didn't have hope here," Adam groused to Taylor one afternoon, as they sat near the warm embers of the fire, watching Adam's son in the Pacing Place, surrounded by his siblings and friends, as he waited for his first child to come into the world.

"Hope is a good thing," Taylor said. "It got your mother and me to this place when we were crossing the desert."

"Why did you name this Fort Wayne?" Adam asked.

Taylor barely heard the question, half asleep from the sun and the warmth of the Fire Circle. "Huh? Fort Wayne? Where I grew up. A small town, small for My Earth, in a place called—" He tried to remember the state. "Indiana." He chuckled. "But it was also a private joke. I knew we would need a wall, a fort. And I thought of a great hero from the movies I used to watch. A cowboy."

"'Cowboy?'"

Taylor waved a liver-spotted hand, dismissing it. "Not important. His name was John Wayne. So Fort Wayne just came to me. We could change it to Old Hope."

Adam laughed. "Fort Wayne is just fine."

A young couple walked by. Both bowed their heads slightly toward Taylor, and he noticed it. "What was that?"

"What was what?" Adam asked.

"They don't say hello anymore. They just sort of… I don't know."

Adam reached out and put a gentle hand on his father's shoulder. "They're showing their respect."

Taylor wasn't sure how he felt about that. He shook off his lethargy and sat up straighter.

"When the first People came, I greeted every one with 'Hello.' No one could reply."

They were silent for a little while.

"That must have been hard," Adam finally said.

A Younger, although he was now past middle-age with greying hair, strolled by.

Taylor called out. "Hello!"

The man was startled, as he was just beginning to do the head bow. He paused. "Hello, Taylor."

"Hmm," Taylor said as the Younger continued on. "There

are a lot of people here I don't recognize. And where are all the People? I was walking around earlier and I didn't see anyone from the beginning."

Adam didn't answer, letting the warm sun lull his father back into a nap.

Several days later, Taylor woke in his Tree Home and heard voices. He just listened. Many were full of joy and happiness. Some with anger. But he simply laid his head back down and fell asleep.

A week later, Adam carried him down the ropes, much like Taylor had carried Nova's body so many years ago. Adam took him to a very cozy hut built of stone, right next to the Pacing Place.

The need to be up in a tree had passed so long ago, that Taylor had been the last.

Taylor tried to remember who had been the last before him, but he couldn't recall. He suddenly realized, looking across the Pacing Place, past the Fire Circle, that the rope ladder, which he'd once pulled up every night, was staked into the ground. It had been for a long, long time.

One day, Taylor remembered something. Knowing he had trouble keeping a remembering in his mind for very long, but that this was important, he took a piece of sharp wood and kept it pressed against his thigh, until Adam stopped by.

"The Watch," Taylor said.

"The what?"

"The Watch at the edge of the desert," Taylor said. "It's still being done, right?"

Adam looked down. "We stopped that a long time ago, Father. No one saw the point."

"The apes." And Taylor realized no Younger had ever seen an ape and none of the People could tell stories of them. Of what it had been like. No one could tell other than him.

He promised himself he would remind them.

That evening, someone came to help him make the short walk from his hut to the Fire Circle, as someone came every evening. Looking around, even though his eyes were no longer astronaut-perfect, he could see there were faces reflecting the firelight as far back as there was light.

Taylor had forgotten about the apes. He spoke of kings on horseback, and long arrows, much like the men used now. And long, green fields where men fought mighty battles. And how they lived in large castles. Machines that flew and people piloting them. Cities that towered into the sky. Even he, Taylor, no longer knew what was Fire Story and what was history.

One fine summer evening, in the midst of a Fire Story that meandered from piloting a spaceship to noble knights gathering at a table that was round, Taylor's voice slowed. He hesitated and peered around the fire.

"Nova? Nova?"

Taylor slumped over in his chair and Adam was there, wrapping the old man in his arms and holding him like a child. Adam was weeping and all the faces around the fire became shiny with tears.

Still holding his father's body, Adam spoke out to the crowd. "Once upon a time, there was an astronaut named Taylor..."

Look behind the scenes of *Escape from the Planet of the Apes* in John Jackson Miller's "Murderer's Row," and meet one of the many casualties of Cornelius' and Zira's brief yet poignant tour of the early 1970s…

MURDERERS' ROW

by

JOHN JACKSON MILLER

From: Franklin de Silva
Hexagon Broadcasting Company, New York City
To: Gary Luckman
Lucky Star Productions, Hollywood

Message:
Apes exist, series required.

That was how it started, seventeen years ago: with a telegram. Frank de Silva used to send a lot of them—I think maybe he thought he would save two cents versus a long-distance call. I wouldn't put it past him. When you're trying to run a television network out of a Gremlin hatchback, you've got to save a buck where you can.

I kid.

No, I don't. Frank was that cheap.

If I'm going to talk about all this, I'd better lay down some ground rules. First, don't expect the quality you've come to expect from a Gary Luckman production. I've got a video camera set up in my wine cellar while I go through my old notes. No action scenes, no musical montage. Looking for a musical score? Tough. They can add that in post when I'm dead.

Shouldn't be too long a wait.

Second, I think most of the people in the biz would appreciate it if I didn't mention them by name in this thing, especially the way the world has gone. Cornelius and Zira— you just can't talk about those two anymore, with good reason. I'm sure the folks I'm talking about don't want to wind up getting a visit from Governor Breck's people in the middle of the night, just because a dying man mentioned them and the Ape-onauts in the same sentence.

Hell, they might even wind up with the rest of the naughty apes on Breck's Achilles List. Show people don't like being on lists. It's a thing with us. Sure, if you were around in 1973, you're probably going to have a good idea of who and what I'm talking about—but all the same, I'll leave the names out of it where I can.

But not yours, de Silva. Drop dead.

Okay, so he sent me this telegram. To be honest, I didn't know what the hell he meant. What did "apes exist" mean? I didn't know until my secretary put on the TV and I saw the pictures from the commission. They don't show that footage anymore, but nobody who had a tube could forget it. The Presidential Commission on the Alien Visitors, where two big chimpanzees, dressed up like they came from a sci-fi movie, started chattering in English. And I mean *good* English. I've had series stars that couldn't speak that well. It was a big deal, let me tell you.

Well, no, let *them* tell you. You can't get this anymore, but I've got a copy of the report from the commission here.

"Where we come from, apes talk and humans are dumb." That's Cornelius.

"We came from your *future."* That's Zira.

Boy, you want to talk about two sentences that changed everything? That's what I heard when I turned on the set. Bigger than the moon landing, bigger than Taylor's flight. I'm no historian, but even I could see that.

As long as I'm talking to you like you've been living in a cave, I should tell you who I am. Gary Luckman was a big name in TV in the fifties: I wrote for the big classy dramas, the ones sponsored by products that wouldn't kill you. Programs were more intelligent back then—back when owning a set was a luxury. Once aerials sprouted across the country like cornstalks, everything turned dippy and safe, and my kind of show died out.

I hung around, though, and saw my chance to come back as a producer. I wanted to open a real writer's shop, something to be proud of—and the early 1970s seemed the perfect time. The networks had started programming smarter stuff, whacking all the hillbilly shows in the process. One actor said they cancelled everything with a tree. Movies made for TV started getting good and getting ratings. And then you had the FCC—the Federal Communications Commission, back before Breck's kind turned it into something else—which tried to gin up competition in programming by giving an hour of prime time back to the local stations. There were only three commercial nets buying shows—not counting de Silva's alleged network—but there were about 900 local stations. That's a lot of potential customers.

So I figured I'd do well. But it all blew up, because of something the government and I didn't figure on: that the affiliates were cheapskates, too. They filled that time with game shows, meaning I had to sell most of my shows to de Silva, whose Hexagon Broadcasting was the umpteenth attempt to compete with the Big Three. You're forgiven if you don't remember it—nobody remembers Dumont or Overmyer either. Let's just say "Hex" was probably not the best nickname for a network.

Anyway, we got in the office and called de Silva—saved him the trouble of reversing the charges. This picks up in the middle of the meeting, as transcribed by the lovely Sally Pewter, of the shorthand and short skirts:

FRANKLIN DE SILVA: Apes, Gary, apes. That's where we want to be.

GARY LUCKMAN: Space apes. Looks like you picked the wrong time to get out of sci-fi, Frank.

MR. DE SILVA: Don't start. I know what you're trying to do. *Target: Jupiter* stays on hiatus. It's not the answer.

LUCKMAN: You were behind *Target* once. You were big on it during the space launches.

MR. DE SILVA: And what happens after those ships rocket off never to return? No one cares after that. But one of the ships just *did* return, Gary—with astro-apes!

LUCKMAN: I think they called them Ape-onauts. Doesn't exactly trip from the tongue.

MR. DE SILVA: Who cares what you call them?

LUCKMAN: No, I get you. Hey, we could add apes to *Target* easy as pie. They won't look as good, of course: costuming's expensive. But if you just let us burn off the last six episodes, we can get back in there and—

MR. DE SILVA: Will you stop it? I don't give two hoots for your space bikini women, running around on Jupiter.

LUCKMAN: On the moons. There's no land on Jupiter.

MR. DE SILVA: Wherever. What do you care? It's all nonsense— just a way for you to put bimbos in blue body paint before nine on a Friday, when every teenage boy is watching. But this isn't pretend anymore, Gary. This is real. I want Hexagon to be the apes network. I need programming.

LUCKMAN: What, drama, comedy? Documentary?

MR. DE SILVA: All of the above. I want hair coming out of everyone's ears. You're the one who wanted to lock in a long-term development deal with HBC, Gary. If you can't get it to me, I'll find someone else who will—in between talking to my lawyers.

LUCKMAN: You're a prince, Frank. We'll get back to you.

We had to send out for new desks after that call, because everyone in the office had put their head through theirs.

Let me tell you about apes. They seem like such a good idea. Kids like them and they never hold you up for money. But they're unpredictable little cusses. The chimp in those old jungle-man movies wouldn't act unless his pet collie was on the set. In the fifties, there was a chimp on a morning news show, which should tell you how little news there was back then. He was as cranky as I would be at that hour.

And just before the Ape-onauts arrived, one of the nets had a kiddie show with chimpanzee spies—and that turned out to be the most expensive Saturday-morning show to that time. You can pay the critter in bananas, but you've got to build so many props for them money just goes up in smoke.

So there was not a sheaf of pitches sitting around with apes in them—and nothing we had in production had any, either. And de Silva wanted something yesterday.

What we came up with in the first round was not my proudest moment. We had three pilots where the sets were still up at the studios for pickup shots. So we brought in some guys in gorilla suits—yes, I know the Ape-onauts weren't gorillas—and shot some test footage, without changing the context.

I was in Manhattan a week later to run them past the man. This one, I have on tape, thanks to Teddy Hyler, one of the management staffers I brought with me; he knew how easily de Silva forgot things. Picking up after we showed him what we had:

FRANKLIN DE SILVA: You two have lost your minds.
GARY LUCKMAN: Tell us how you really feel, Frank.
MR. DE SILVA: They look terrible. All awful. Am I to believe this one ape is a defense attorney?
LUCKMAN: Actually, a prosecutor: *Bobo for the State.* We

just switched him out for the actor. We figure on adding a backstory where another Ape-onaut ship lands near Harvard Law School.

TEDDY HYLER: If we put the rocket down in the Charles River, we can use the existing *Liberty 1* crash footage. *(Pause.)* We just have to pretend there's a beach in Cambridge.

MR. DE SILVA: Didn't I just see you do that already in one of these?

LUCKMAN: That was in the sci-fi series, *Aquaborn. (Sound of papers shuffling.)* The submarine that finds Atlantis—which is full of apes.

MR. DE SILVA: Why in the world would apes be underwater?

LUCKMAN: Well, that's where the footage of *Liberty 1* comes in. Our apes were headed there when they wound up on the shore. We can create a whole society for them.

HYLER: Just be advised anything in water costs a lot.

MR. DE SILVA: The whole thing's all wet. And this other thing, with the woman?

HYLER: That's a movie of the week. It's a serious look at what happens to a marriage when a man transforms into an ape.

MR. DE SILVA: *For the Love of Drogo.* Wait—this thing sounds familiar.

LUCKMAN: *(Pause.)* That's because it *had* been a serious look at what happens to a marriage when a man reveals he's got a gambling problem. We just put the ape in there. What do you want, Frank? We've had a week.

MR. DE SILVA: I want what everyone else wants. I want Zero and Cordelia.

LUCKMAN: You mean Zira and Cornelius?

MR. DE SILVA: Whatever. People don't want to see crappy monkey suits anymore. Not when they've seen the real thing.

HYLER: Costuming like that's going to break the bank. The mouth appliances alone will take hours to put in.

MR. DE SILVA: Then get me the Ape-onauts themselves.

LUCKMAN: *(Pause.)* You want us to put Cornelius and Zira in the shows?

MR. DE SILVA: You're damned right. Did you see Bill Bonds' numbers from this weekend?

LUCKMAN: Bonds? The *Eyewitness News* guy?

MR. DE SILVA: *Eyewitness News, Big News*, whatever they're calling it this week. Bonds had that egghead, that—

HYLER: Hasslein. Victor Hasslein.

MR. DE SILVA: *Otto* Hasslein. And they gave Doctor Otto Hasslein two hours to ramble on about the apes. It clobbered our whole slate—and it was just *about* the apes—they weren't even in it! So I want you to get me the apes.

HYLER: Get you—? Doesn't the government have them?

LUCKMAN: We're not a news crew, Frank.

MR. DE SILVA: And Hexagon doesn't have a news department. That's why I'm talking to you. Put them in something. Get them involved, bring them on board. We'll make it an extravaganza, whatever it is. I'm talking about giving you Saturdays, a three-hour block.

LUCKMAN: You can't be— *(overtalking)*

HYLER: You are aware one of your competitors *owns* Saturday?

LUCKMAN: No kidding. Frank, that's "Murderer's Row." Four of the best comedies ever put on television, followed by the best variety show in, what, a decade? You're seriously going to counterprogram that?

MR. DE SILVA: This network will not go dark one night of the week. I don't care what what's-her-name's legs look like.

HYLER: Cannon fodder. Anything against it's cannon fodder.

MR. DE SILVA: I'm telling you, it'll work. We reran an old travelogue on baboons and got a nine rating and a twelve share. For anyone else, that stinks. For HBC, it's a pulse. You get me the apes by the end of the month and we'll make history.

LUCKMAN: You want me to put a deal together with the Ape-onauts—by the end of the month? Are you trying to kill me?

Fact was, de Silva probably *was* trying to kill me, given those cheap cigars of his—though I have to admit I did the rest myself. That was another thing that had just happened on TV a couple years before the apes arrived—the government banned all cigarette ads. I'd have been better off if they'd done it in the fifties.

Ah, well, the damage is done.

Anyway, I flew back home to my ranch in Agoura Hills thinking I was trapped. I'd just bought the place, and now I didn't have anything to sell. Calling my attorney to get me out of the development deal would break the company—but I didn't see any other choice. I played with my dog, knocked back a scotch, lit a cigarette, and turned on the tube.

What I saw saved me. Cornelius and Zira were all dressed up and getting the red-carpet treatment on the way to their new digs at the Beverly Wilshire. And then I spotted the entourage they were with—and the lovely young blonde who spoke with one of the reporters.

Stevie Branton. While she was at UCLA, she'd done some work as an assistant to a wrangler on a safari adventure series I'd been showrunner for. Bright kid. I'd asked her out, but she wasn't interested. This is the problem with marrying an actress: complete strangers pretty much know what your status is. Apparently she was working with Lewis Dixon, the zoo shrink who was the Ape-onauts' unofficial spokesman and minder. I quickly got on the phone with the animal trainer, who still had her home number.

I can't say that she was thrilled to hear from me. Like the rest of humanity, she'd heard about my divorce and assumed that's why I was calling. But I managed to wheedle my way into a get-together they were having the next night for Cornelius and Zira by promising I would make a big donation to the zoological society. For someone new to being near the center of attention, Stevie was pretty good about figuring out how to make use of it.

I can't say that I have ever mixed too well at parties, which makes me a bit of an outlier in my business. I think it comes from starting off as a writer, alone in a cage. If I'd been part of a team writing for the variety shows, it would have been different. But I was desperate, and more than willing to put on a—jeez, I almost said "monkey suit"—to mingle.

I don't know where they came up with everyone there. Zoo patrons, for sure—it was Dixon and Stevie, after all, who identified what Cornelius and Zira were. Then there were the damnedest people. I met some woman from *Fur and Feather* magazine. I was surprised to learn it was about pets. A reporter from a hunting magazine—who thought *he'd* be a good idea to invite?

I decided the best way to deal with it was to glom onto Stevie like a barnacle. If she wanted to get rid of me, she'd have to introduce me to the apes. That finally happened.

First, the television shots of them really don't do them justice. I've seen high-class prosthetic work, and nothing anyone in the trade can do could remotely duplicate the look of these two. It was all the more reason we had to get them.

Unfortunately, my encounter with Zira—Madam Zira, the others were calling her—was brief. Once I told her what I did for a living, Zira sort of sniffed at me and wandered off to order a drink. It sort of proves what I've always said about the quality of television that someone could land in a rocketship and learn to hate TV and everything associated with it in a matter of days.

When she came back, "grape-juice-plus" in hand, I lit a cigarette and offered her one. Another bad move. "I have seen these instruments," Zira said, turning it over. "So curious."

"Want me to show you how it works?"

"I do not. One's mouth is a poor place for fire." She handed it back to me and ambled away. I could guess with a hairy face, smoking might be a bad idea.

With any kind of face, really. But I digress.

I had much better luck with Cornelius, who looked better in his suit than I did in mine. "I'm a television producer," I said, hoping it wasn't the kiss of death this time.

"Ah, yes. You make the television boxes?" Cornelius asked.

"No, I produce the teleplays you see on them. You have seen some of our programs? Adventures? Dramas?"

"Indeed. One can learn a lot watching television." He was seriously engaged. "I also found a lot of places on the screen that looked like home—Westerns, Lewis called them."

"We have plenty of those shows. But not so many as before."

"I liked seeing the horses," Cornelius said. "We have them in our time. I was curious to see what they looked like in this day and age, but there were none in the zoo."

"Oh, there wouldn't be," Stevie said. "They're common, trained as work animals. You'd find horses on a farm or a ranch." After a moment, she looked at me and perked up. "Weren't you buying a ranch back when I was on set, Gary?"

A light went on. "Yes, yes. I have it." It was the one thing my ex left me: that, and my German Shepherd, who I called Settlement as often as I called him Buster. "It's a great ranch, Cornelius—with plenty of horses. Yes, definitely horses." I turned the charm on the big ape. "Wonderful animals. If you'd like to see them, I can give you a tour whenever you'd like."

Cornelius brightened. "I'd like that."

"Great! How about tomorrow?"

Stevie started to put up an objection to that—they'd had a pretty busy schedule. But I really sold Cornelius on visiting. Zira took a pass—she was supposed to give a speech for some ladies' group soon, and wanted time to rehearse. I left that night happy, even though Stevie hadn't seemed interested in me in the least.

I was also in a hurry. I had about twelve hours to find a place that rented horses and would send them out to a ranch that had none.

We had wonderful weather the next day when I drove Cornelius and Stevie out to my place. Cornelius confessed to remaining edgy about vehicles, yet he seemed to revel in the convertible ride down the Ventura Freeway.

Once we got to the ranch, Buster ran out and charged Cornelius. I'd forgotten to lock him up; I was terrified of how he and the ape would react to one another. But the dog gave the visitor a good sniff, and Cornelius smiled broadly and scratched his head. You can't think badly of any alien race that likes dogs.

Then it was onto the horses, out in the stable I never used. The tracks from the rental haulers were still fresh on the ground in front of the building. All I can say is thank God Stevie was there to make sense of the mountain of tack stuff I'd had sent over. If it had been up to me to saddle one of those things, Cornelius would have been waiting long enough to catch up with his own century.

The ride was as good as any I've ever been on, which is to say, a nervous dance with imminent death by a four-legged monster. What made it better was being able to watch Stevie—and listening to Cornelius as he asked questions about every little thing we trotted past. He was real big on history, and how humans used the horses in settling. I was a little embarrassed—I'd written Westerns before but was only able to give the Hollywood version of history. That seemed to satisfy him.

Seeing my cue, I asked if I could put him in a Western. He was reluctant—and Stevie was downright hostile to the notion. She gave me the evil eye, the one that said she knew exactly what I was up to. I pressed on, offering to show Cornelius all about film and TV technology and how humanity used it to spread its culture. I hit all the right notes—but Stevie was right there nixing anything that involved a lot of work. She knew what rigorous schedules we had on set, and didn't want the apes any more exhausted than they already were.

Then it dawned on me. "How about a variety show?"

"What is that?" Cornelius asked, interested.

"A revue. A lot of entertainments at once. You could host. You and Zira."

He seemed curious, but Stevie stepped in again. "Gary, come on. Cut it out." She looked at Cornelius. "He's going to tell you he's going to make you a star. Oh, and rich."

"Ah," Cornelius said, smiling. "I am afraid I have no use for money."

I nearly fell off my horse. But then I caught myself—and had a brainstorm. "Would you do it if it were a fundraiser for the zoo?"

Cornelius chewed on that. "Yes, yes I would."

Stevie was concerned. "Cornelius, you don't need to do this."

"No, you know the place could use improvement—for the animals' sake. Perhaps you could do something in Doctor Milo's memory, too."

"You've got it," I said—effectively agreeing to donate a huge portion of Lucky Star's proceeds to the event. I knew Hyler was going to kill me, but it was all about saving our skins at this point. When we got back to the house, Cornelius played with Buster while I rushed into my home office for a basic contract. I'd get three hours of Cornelius and Zira on tape, with an option for more if things went well—and more chances to see Stevie. She wasn't in a great mood with me when I returned them to the hotel, but I figured I'd have more chances to see her in the future.

After I got home and sent the horses off in their carriers, my job really began. I'd never written a variety show, but I sure enough knew people who had. The dynamic was pretty simple. The two apes would just have to introduce the acts— and the fun for the viewers would be in seeing their reactions to them. It would be kind of like a command performance. I was pretty sure a lot of music acts would jump at the chance to show off. If you were the Future Apes' favorite band, that'd make your career.

And then we'd do a handful of skits with the apes as participants. Variety shows have a long tradition of working with non-entertainer guests: you just have to keep it simple, using your professional performers to provoke reactions. If Bob Hope can make football players funny, we could turn Cornelius into a joke machine.

Whoops, I guess that was a name. Whoever finds this, please leave Bob Hope alone. Thank you.

The end of the month neared—and my ulcer grew larger the more I thought about what we were trying to do. "Murderers' Row" was originally the name of the '27 Yankees—Babe Ruth, Lou Gehrig, those guys. In 1973, the TV equivalent was a bigoted cab driver, some Korean War doctors, a doll of a single working woman, and a psychologist who stuttered—sorry, *stammered*—with a great ensemble variety show batting cleanup. It was the rare intersection of shows any writer would've been proud to write for with commercial popularity—the night kicked off with the number 1 show and a 30 rating. Even now, years later, I'd say it was the strongest night in history.

And there I was, Don Quixote with a hairy Sancho Panza, trying to take it on. Well, they say it takes a dreamer to make it in this business. I guess pipe dreams count.

The fact is, at first it went surprisingly well. The charity aspect meant we had a slew of acts willing to work for free, making my team happy—and the apes were good on their cues right from the first moment. I was worried I might need to bring Buster in to calm the apes down, just like in the jungle pictures—but they were both cool and comfortable. Cornelius even joined in a song at one point. I was over the moon. People would go ape for—no, there I go again. Viewers wouldn't miss it. The only thing keeping us from a fifty share would be Hexagon's crappy market penetration, and de Silva figured to fix that with successive reruns.

There was even talk of getting the apes to do introductory wraparounds on some of our shows in production, turning them into *Cornelius Presents* or *Zira's Showcase* or something like that. By using the apes to conquer Saturday, de Silva was going to show both Madison Avenue and the broadcasting world that Hexagon was for real. And Gary Luckman and Lucky Star would ride the wave.

Then they missed their run-through.

The apes had skipped a meeting with me once before, so I wasn't alarmed; they had a million people pulling at them, trying to get them to endorse this or speak about that. We weren't planning to tape for a few days, yet: scheduling snafus were par for the course. We had time.

But I couldn't reach the apes—and I couldn't find Dixon or Stevie either. I even sent my gofers to the zoo, where they'd stayed before. *Nada.*

Three days went by, and we were going nuts. This time, de Silva was actually worried enough to dial me up himself. From the notes:

MR. DE SILVA: What's the big idea, Gary? You were supposed to give me a report days ago—and rehearsal footage.

LUCKMAN: It's a problem with the apes. They didn't show.

MR. DE SILVA: Then give them some bananas. I'm pretty damn sure they're not in the union. What are they trying to hold you up for?

LUCKMAN: That's just it, Frank. I can't talk to them. They're not anywhere.

MR. DE SILVA: What do you mean?

LUCKMAN: I mean they're gone. They've vanished. AWOL. Lost in the jungle.

MR. DE SILVA: You're pulling my leg. Those two are on screen every five minutes, visiting museums and opening shopping malls. Just set up a camera and they'll flock to it like gnats to a light.

LUCKMAN: I'm trying to *get* them in front of a camera, Frank. But the Beverly Wilshire won't let me see them.

MR. DE SILVA: Go down and bang on the door, for God's sake!

LUCKMAN: I tried that. Don't you think I've tried that? No dice. I sent Hyler over last evening, and he started paying maids until one of them talked. They haven't made up the suite in days.

MR. DE SILVA: *(Pause.)* You think one of them's sick?

LUCKMAN: I thought of that. But somebody would have told me.

MR. DE SILVA: Everything's riding on this broadcast, Gary. I mean *everything*. My New York affiliate is looking to go on satellite—it'll start getting carried in other cities.

LUCKMAN: Cable?

MR. DE SILVA: Overnight, we'll be in cities that don't have a Hex affiliate. It's going to save the network—and we're going to need a lot more original programming.

LUCKMAN: I can't believe people will ever pay for TV.

MR. DE SILVA: You let me worry about that, all right? What I need from you is the show, and—

LUCKMAN: Hold on a minute, Frank.

MR. DE SILVA: I'm paying for this call! Don't put me on hold, you son of a—

LUCKMAN: It's the president.

MR. DE SILVA: What?

LUCKMAN: Of the United States. Jacob Henry! On TV. Turn it on.

It was the broadcast we all saw, telling us that the apes had moved from the Beverly Wilshire. Citing fatigue, they were heading for a private place after which they would "then be found research employment suited to their high intellectual capacities." The president's words, from what was obviously a prepared statement.

I went berserk. *They had a contract!*

We called the government and got nowhere. Stevie and Dixon just gave me the brush-off, though I could tell something else was going on there. The president's line was the official one, and nobody was straying from it.

Of course, now I know something else *was* going on there. The commission had found something out about the apes, and had met in secret session the day of our rehearsal. That explained the no-show. Cornelius and Zira were far too decent to have stood me up; truth is, they had already been moved. But the net effect was the same: they weren't going to be on our soundstage.

Frank de Silva was having a coronary, and I was right there with him. But there was still a way to make it all work, I said, and keep the affiliates and advertisers with us. No, we couldn't deliver a show right away, but the president's message had given us a card to play. All we had to do was get the apes just for one day in the studio. We could call it their comeback special—or if they were staying in seclusion, their "Postcard from Paradise." If anything, that would be an even bigger draw. Every TV set in the country would be set to the Hex.

But that meant I had to find them.

I dumped all the money I had in petty cash into hiring every private investigator in Southern California. I was in terror that they'd been spirited off to Barbados or somewhere—but the fact that Dixon and Stevie were still around suggested to me they were local.

I was by no means alone in this: every paparazzo and reporter in America was also on the hoof. The apes were money in the bank for them, a cottage industry. I got more and more aggravated as time went on. What did they think they were up to, stiffing us all? It was 1973, the age of mass media. That Greta Garbo "I vant to be alone" stuff didn't cut it anymore.

And... we... had... a... contract!

I can't tell you how long we waited after that. Time was running out for it to make any difference to Hexagon—and de Silva held me personally responsible. He'd been making ridiculous promises about his Saturday-night coup; he was swiftly losing face with his affiliates and everyone else. One of the trades put his face next to a headline shouting "Hexed! Net Frets Over Ape Tape." Cornelius and Zira's departure was referred to as the "Banana Split of 1973."

Me, I was dealing with "Luckman's Luck Runs Out." There wasn't anyone to sue: it wasn't clear Cornelius and Zira even had any legal standing to accept employment. Dixon's zoo, technically their guardian, didn't have a dime that hadn't come from donations or other offers—and with the apes out of the picture, there was nothing left. Cornelius and Zira seemed nice, but they'd slit my throat.

Finally, we were down to the last moment. No make-good would satisfy Hexagon—and if we wanted to get the show on the air during the sweeps, our only chance was to get the apes to do it live. It was then that a miracle happened. I was pulling into the garage at the Federal Building, trying to see what our options were, when I spotted Dixon and that Hasslein guy leaving together in a big hurry. The two Ape-onaut experts, together? *Jackpot!*

I followed them all the way out to a Marine base in San Diego County. Camp 11, it was called. I thought it was part of Pendleton—hard to tell, it was night. It was a hell of a place to vacation, I thought, but at least it was private.

I was trying to figure out how to talk my way into the gate when all of a sudden, it's lights everywhere. A convoy went screaming out. I made for the tall weeds: I'm no action hero; I wasn't about to try to sneak in. I got back to my car and tried to skulk off.

For a second, I thought I saw Stevie, of all people, at a roadblock. But then I wound up with high-beams in my face—and guys with guns outside my windows. They hauled me off in the dark.

The building they took me to could've been anywhere. The windows in the car were blacked out so nobody could see in or out—and a smoked panel between the guards and me kept me from seeing much in front of us. We got out in the garage of a building that could have been anywhere in Los Angeles. The MPs marched me to a holding room, where they passed me off to an alphabet soup of officials: FBI, NSA, who knows what else. Nobody would tell me anything.

I had been cooling my heels for something like twelve hours when they finally arranged for some kind of meeting. It was an empty room but for a table, chairs, and one of those two-way mirrors. There were three guys at the table in Brooks Brothers suits, but only one of them, Jones, talked. My attorney was escorted in—and while they didn't give me the transcript, he was able to put this together from memory:

AGENT JONES: You understand, Mr. Luckman, you are not under arrest. This is an advisory meeting.

GARY LUCKMAN: That's what you said before—but it sure *felt* like an arrest. This is my lawyer, Mr. Lazarov. Anything you have to say to me, you say to him.

AGENT JONES: Mr. Luckman, I'm going to come straight to the point. We're aware of the inquiries you've been making into the whereabouts of Cornelius and Zira. Those are going to stop, now.

LUCKMAN: Like hell they are. I have a contract with the two of them, and a show to produce. And I'm running out of time.

AGENT JONES: Correction—you *are* out of time. Your government requires you to suspend all production, effective immediately.

LUCKMAN: *What?*

SAM LAZAROV, ATTORNEY: Agent Jones, this is prior restraint. You have no authority to interfere with my client's First Amendment rights.

AGENT JONES: Cornelius and Zira will not be making any appearances on his program or anyone else's. This is a matter of national security.

LUCKMAN: A chimpanzee singing is a matter of national security? It's a variety show. What's the matter with letting them appear?

AGENT JONES: That, too, is a matter of national security.

LUCKMAN: So, wait. Where are Cornelius and Zira? And so help me, if you tell me this is a matter of national security—

AGENT JONES: It is a state secret.

LUCKMAN: Oh, well, that's different.

AGENT JONES: They have been taken into confinement for their own safety.

LAZAROV: If so, there should be no problem with our speaking with them.

AGENT JONES: They do not wish to see you.

LUCKMAN: That's hogwash. And I believe the first part—you did take them in. But I'm not so sure you even have them now. What was all that ruckus about?

AGENT JONES: Our agents have the situation well in hand.

LUCKMAN: It didn't look like it to me.

AGENT JONES: *(Pause.)* Cornelius killed an orderly while he was confined here.

LUCKMAN: I don't believe it! He's the kindest, most decent creature I've ever met.

AGENT JONES: The apes are fugitives. You can see, I expect, that having a murderer hosting a television program is likely not in the interest of you nor your television partners.

LUCKMAN: But this news is huge. The world needs to know—

AGENT JONES: The world will know. After his capture.

LAZAROV: Cornelius should have access to our justice system. He has rights.

AGENT JONES: Does he? Rights are for humans. But that will all be sorted out later. For now, Mr. Luckman will stop his inquiries—and his production.

LAZAROV: Can he continue his production without Cornelius and Zira?

AGENT JONES: *(Conferring with his partner.)* That would be acceptable.

LUCKMAN: To whom? Nobody would watch that!

AGENT JONES: We'll be watching, Mr. Luckman. This meeting is concluded.

We were hustled out, put in a car, and driven back to Lazarov's office. The agents had my car there, waiting. I still had the keys—I don't know how they moved it.

Lazarov had a few of his paralegals sneak out to make some calls. We couldn't get hold of Stevie. We couldn't reach Dixon. There wasn't any way around this thing, no way to fix it. I stopped by the production office to give everyone the bad news. Hyler's six-two, a former linebacker. I thought he was going to cry.

The topper hit me when I got home. Buster was dead. He was an old dog, but he hadn't been sick—and he had enough food and water out back that he should have been fine. I still don't know what happened.

But at the time, I almost envied him. The show was over. I was ruined.

I did talk to Stevie a few months later; what she had to say matched up with some of what leaked to the press. Cornelius and Zira had been in Camp 11. They fled that night I was there, and were killed. She still seemed devastated about it; I didn't have the heart to tell her my problems. It was too late, anyway. Lucky Star defaulted on its contract with Hexagon; we lost everything, of course. There's a photocopy place in what used to be our bungalow.

Frank de Silva got it worse, at least at first. He didn't get his big hit. His few affiliates dropped the network—including his New York station, which never went to cable. Hexagon folded up before the end of the '73–'74 season.

But he was right about the whole cable idea, and wound up a bigwig in that business. Right now, de Silva is jet-setting around the world as some kind of trade ambassador for the provinces, impressing the governor with his famous ability to stretch a buck. I hope he chokes on a ten-cent fig.

As for me, I went back to writing. I still see some residuals now and again from *Apeworld,* a show I wrote for later on; I honestly think that show was a government plot, to calm people down once word got out that the apes might have come from a future where their offspring caused humanity's downfall. *Apeworld* postulated an alternate reality where the apes were far too stupid to rule for long; humans eventually reconquered their planet and reigned supreme. My favorite ape character was kind to humans; I thought a lot about Cornelius when I wrote that one.

Lazarov's fancy footwork helped me keep the ranch, but it's 1990 and that's about all I've got. My doctors get half my money. My ex-wives get the other two-thirds. This tape I'm making now goes with my will; it's up to Lazarov to decide what to do with it.

Oh, yeah—I never bought another dog after Buster, and I certainly wouldn't own an ape, even if I could afford one. I don't like that whole business, how people treat them. It's the sort of thing we used to write episodes about—only then we were talking about humans being enslaved.

Sometimes I wonder whether Buster was the first victim of the pet plague, and if he got it from Cornelius—and whether the Ape-onauts had anything to do with the apes of Earth picking up more skills the way they did. I don't know— maybe that's crazy. But I kind of like the idea that Cornelius and Zira were able to turn the world upside down from their graves—presuming they weren't dissected. It's justice, sure— but it's also a great story idea, the sort of last-act revelation that would send future generations to the credits, wondering who the writer was.

Yeah, I like that. Lord knows we don't live forever any other way.

A curious ape peers far too closely into the lives of lowly humans and opens herself up to a dangerous charge of heresy in Greg Cox's "Endangered Species," a story set several generations before the original film...

ENDANGERED SPECIES

by

GREG COX

Eastern Forest Expedition, Day 37. Breakthrough! My efforts to study man in his natural habitat are finally bearing fruit. After weeks of patient observation from afar, I may at last be succeeding in winning the trust of a small tribe of wild humans. Certainly, they appear to be growing more and more comfortable with my presence...

Janae crouched in the thick grass of the clearing, holding out a shiny green apple as a lure. Beneath her olive-green safari garb, her muscles ached from squatting in the same position for so long, but the inquisitive young chimpanzee was afraid to make any sudden movements for fear of alarming the skittish humans, which were milling about beneath the shade of a large, leafy tree less than fifty yards away. Sweltering beneath the hot afternoon sun, Janae envied the humans that cover, even as she assiduously took note of their rudimentary behaviors and social interactions: grooming, foraging, mating, child-rearing, and so on.

If only I could get an even closer look at them...

The apple caught the eye of a pregnant female whom Janae had christened "Flax" due to her distinctive hair, which was the color of corn silk. Breaking away from the rest of the tribe, the animal approached Janae warily. Indecision was written upon her flat, bestial features as she paused hesitantly only a few yards away from Janae. Ragged animal hides were draped loosely over the human's gravid form. She licked her lips, clearly tempted by the treat.

That's right, just a little further, Janae urged the female silently. She had learned the hard way that humans found simian speech more frightening than soothing, so she bit down on her lip to keep from speaking aloud. *Come on, I'm not going to hurt you...*

She held her breath as Flax crept steadily, if fearfully, closer, until they were practically face-to-face. The hungry female, who was eating for two, reached out to snatch the apple from Janae's grasp, only to be abruptly yanked backward by an adult male human whose sudden appearance caught Janae by surprise. His imposing shadow fell over the startled naturalist, who mentally kicked herself for not keeping one eye on the rest of the tribe.

Who knew humans could move so stealthily—or be so protective of their own?

She recognized the male at once. Ragged Ear, nicknamed for an old injury most likely received in a tussle with a rival male, was Flax's primary mate and the presumed father of her unborn child. Certainly, Janae had observed them rutting enough over the last few weeks, although, from what she had seen so far, humans were far from monogamous. His protective behavior lent credence to the supposition that he was the father, and raised intriguing questions regarding pair-bonding in human colonies. Had Ragged Ear acted primarily to preserve his mate, his offspring, or some combination thereof?

Flax scampered back to the safety of the tribe, with only a last longing look at the apple, but Ragged Ear lingered, eying Janae suspiciously from mere paces away. The stench of unwashed man offended her nose, which wrinkled in disapproval. Despite her scientific curiosity, she experienced a moment of apprehension. This was a wild animal, after all, and even the most timid of creatures could react violently if they thought their young were being threatened.

Janae had brought a small gun along on her expedition, for safety's sake, but had fallen out of the habit of carrying it while in the field. At the moment, the ugly metal weapon was securely tucked away in her tent, about half a mile distant.

That might have been a mistake.

Bracing herself for an attack, she peered into Ragged Ear's wary blue eyes, trying to somehow make her benign intentions clear despite the gaping chasm between ape and beast.

You don't need to fear me. I mean you no harm.

An endless, anxious moment passed. Then he darted forward to grab the apple from her hand before scurrying back to the others. Janae let out a sigh of relief, while also experiencing a surge of excitement. That was the closest any humans had ever come to her. Granted, the encounters had been fleeting, but they were progress nonetheless.

One step at a time, she thought. *Ape City was not built in a day.*

Watching from a distance, she was intrigued to see Ragged Ear sharing the stolen apple with Flax. As far as she knew, no ape scientist had ever documented this sort of bonding behavior between humans before; Janae could barely wait to enter the discovery into her journal this evening. Already she was mentally composing her report to the Ministry of Science.

Just wait until Doctor Zorba reads my findings!

A vibration shook the ground beneath her, disturbing her reverie. Lost in thought, it took her a moment to recognize the unmistakable percussion of pounding hooves.

"Oh, no," she gasped out loud. "Not now. Not again!"

Leaping to her feet, she ran toward the tribe, waving her arms and shouting at the top of her lungs.

"Run! They're coming!"

She had no illusions that they could comprehend her words, but her frantic efforts had the desired results. Alarmed, the humans scattered and ran from her, abandoning the clearing for the surrounding forest. She chased after them, hoping to herd them away from the oncoming threat, even as she cursed having to do so.

Damn it! I was just getting through to them!

The bellicose blast of a hunting horn confirmed her fears, however, heralding the arrival of a gorilla hunting party. Mounted on horseback and brandishing their rifles, the apes burst into the clearing, trampling the tall grass beneath them.

"After them!" the captain of the hunt shouted to his comrades. "Don't let them get away!"

The gorilla's name, Janae knew too well, was Atlas. They had clashed before when it came to the humans in this territory.

"Stop it!" She ran out in front of the hunters, hoping to buy the imperiled humans a chance to escape. "Leave them alone!"

The gorillas kept on coming. For a second, Janae feared that they might actually trample her, but they veered their horses away from her at the last minute. Pulling back on his reins, Atlas halted long enough to snarl at her from atop his steed.

"Lunatic chimp! How dare you spoil our hunt?"

"You're the one who is ruining everything! You and your bloodthirsty compatriots!"

Rage contorted his features, so that he looked almost more bestial than the humans he pursued. He drew back his hand, as though tempted to strike her, but merely barked impatiently instead.

"Just keep out of our way!" Turning away from her, he signaled the party forward. "The longer the chase, the more satisfying the kill. On with the hunt!"

Whooping and hollering, the gorillas galloped off after the humans, leaving Janae alone in the clearing, frustrated and fearing for the safety of "her" humans. She prayed that Flax and the others would escape the hunters, but knew better than to expect that Atlas and his fellow gorillas would wind up empty-handed. They would not be satisfied until they had bagged more than their fair share of human game.

Gunshots sounded in the woods beyond.

The grisly aftermath of the hunt turned Janae's stomach. Her gorge rose at the ghastly sight of dead humans hanging upside down from a makeshift wooden rack. More carcasses were piled in a heap upon the veldt, their lifeless remains already drawing flies. It was enough to sicken any decent ape, but Atlas and his fellow hunters were all but beating their chests in celebration. They slapped each other's backs while posing for photos with their trophies. Janae grimaced in disgust.

What sport was there in slaughtering harmless animals?

"An excellent hunt!" Atlas boasted, but his jubilant mood soured at the sight of Janae entering the blood-spattered glade. A scowl made it clear that she was unwelcome. "What are *you* doing here, chimp?"

Janae wasn't entirely sure. She supposed she had to see for herself what the hunters had done to the tribe, as well as take note of which humans had been lost. She had yet to spot Flax among the trophies, but she recognized the other carcasses to varying degrees. Anger boiled over inside her, demanding expression. *Somebody* had to speak out against this atrocity.

"Congratulations on your impressive accomplishment, Captain," she said mockingly. "Armed apes on horseback against a pack of scared, defenseless animals. You and your associates must be quite proud of yourselves."

Her sarcasm penetrated the gorilla's thick skull.

"What do you care?" he growled. "They're nothing but filthy beasts."

"Just because they're animals doesn't mean they deserved to be gunned down for sport. They're not even predators. They live on nuts and roots and berries!"

"So?" Atlas shrugged. "What else are they good for, except to be hunted?"

A gorilla named Crassus came forward and slung another bloody carcass onto the pile. Janae gasped out loud.

It was Ragged Ear.

"You butchers!" she cried out, unable to contain her dismay. "He had a mate! A child!"

"Jealous?" Atlas said with a smirk. The other gorillas laughed uproariously at her expense. "Maybe if you had a husband of your own, you'd have better things to do than dote on a herd of stinking animals."

"Don't be ridiculous," Crassus chimed in. "What sane chimpanzee would have her?"

Janae's face flushed with anger. Averting her eyes from Ragged Ear's bullet-ridden remains, she hoped against hope that Flax and her unborn offspring were safe.

At least for the moment.

"It's barbaric!" she exclaimed. "Something has to be done."

"Such as?" Doctor Zorba asked, sounding somewhat puzzled. The Minister of Science—a distinguished orangutan, naturally—sat behind his desk in his spacious office in Ape City, three days' travel by wagon from Janae's camp in the forest. A leather-bound collection of the Sacred Scrolls occupied a place of honor upon his book shelves, while a miniature statue of the Lawgiver rested in its own niche nearby. Family photos, sitting atop the desk, proclaimed Zorba's status as the patriarch of his clan. Janae understood that the Minister had recently been blessed with his first grandchild: a healthy young orangutan named Zaius, the firstborn of his son Augustus.

"A wilderness preserve, perhaps," she suggested. "Or some kind of animal sanctuary."

"A sanctuary… for man?" Zorba's tone went from baffled to dubious. "Humans are vermin, you know that. The Sacred Scrolls themselves condemn man, in no uncertain terms, as a pestilence unworthy of our concern. To even suggest putting aside precious land for such creatures is absurd, not to mention politically impossible. If anything, humans are becoming a significant nuisance, breeding out of control, raiding our crops, infesting the outer provinces…"

"But only because we're encroaching on their own habitats," she argued.

"As is only fitting," Zorba said. "This world was given to us to tame, to bring civilization to the wilderness. It is our manifest destiny, as laid out by the Lawgiver long ago. Ours is a planet of apes, not man."

"But surely that doesn't mean that we should just sit by and let an endangered species be hunted to extinction?" Janae's agitated voice echoed off the curved adobe walls of the office. "There must be something we can do to protect them."

Zorba sighed. "I admire your passion, but I confess I've never understood your consuming interest in these animals. You have a fine mind and a promising career ahead of you once you complete your graduate studies. Why waste your time on vile creatures unworthy of your attention?"

"What can I say?" she replied. "I've always been fascinated by man, ever since I saw a performing human in a circus when I was a child." She struggled to make the venerable ape understand. "Perhaps it's their striking resemblance to us that intrigues me. Unlike other animals—horses or cattle, say—there's something almost simian about them."

"Hardly," Zorba scoffed. "To compare man to apes is insulting at best, heretical at worst. Any possible resemblance between those beasts and apekind is deceptive in the extreme." His face assumed a sterner expression. "I warned you, when you embarked on this peculiar project, not to get too attached to your subjects. I'll grant that there may be a certain practical value in learning more about man's traits and habits, if only to assist us in curtailing their movements and keeping their population under control, but you must take care not to lose your perspective, nor allow legitimate scientific curiosity to become an obsession."

Janae felt as though she was arguing with the unyielding stone cliffs of the Forbidden Zone. "But they must occupy some biological niche in the ecosystem. Aren't we also meant to be custodians of the world, including Nature and all its creatures?"

Zorba was unmoved.

"Are you listening to me, Janae? Do you hear what I'm saying?"

She longed to argue her case further, but it was obvious that there was nothing to be gained by pressing the issue, given the Minister's current attitude. And she couldn't afford to alienate him, not if she still hoped to find a way to protect the humans.

"Yes, Doctor Zorba. I understand perfectly."

She was on her own.

Eastern Forest Expedition, Day 45. Despite (or perhaps because of) my frantic efforts to warn them of the hunters, the surviving humans remain increasingly accepting of my presence among them. Flax has given birth to a healthy male infant and appears devoted to its care. If she mourns the loss of Ragged Ear, it is impossible to tell...

Spray from the waterfall misted against Janae's face, spurring her to retreat to a higher perch upon the rocky slopes overlooking a remote watering hole, where the humans had gathered to slake their thirst and sun themselves upon the smooth, well-worn stones surrounding the lagoon. Flax nursed her newborn child while other humans were scraping the fat from scavenged animal hides and stretching them out upon the rocks to dry, a process Janae observed with acute interest.

The fact that humans, unlike other animals, draped themselves in crude hides had provoked some debate in scientific circles. The accepted wisdom was that this was nothing more than instinctual behavior, not unlike a bird building a nest or bees constructing a hive, but Janae had to wonder if it was instead evidence of an actual sub-simian culture, passed on from one generation to the next.

She certainly couldn't blame humans for borrowing the hides of other beasts, since their own hairless bodies offered scant protection from the elements. Indeed, she reflected, man was a singularly weak and vulnerable species in general, lacking any unique biological advantages to help him survive. He had no real fangs or claws, no natural armor, nor even opposable toes to assist him in climbing. The clergy, of course, claimed that man was spawned by the Devil in deliberate mockery of apekind—who, by contrast, were created in God's own image—but it seemed to Janae that man was more likely a failed experiment on Nature's part, possibly on the road to extinction.

Not if can I help it, she thought.

A shrill, ear-piercing wail, almost like that of a baby ape, shattered her thoughts. Startled, she was amazed to see that the shriek came from Flax's infant, who was quickly silenced. As Janae looked on in shock, Flax stifled the child's cries, clasping her palm over the baby's mouth and pinching its pudgy, pink arm hard enough to leave a bruise. Janae feared that Flax was suffocating the child, but the female uncovered the baby's mouth after only a few moments. Gasping for breath, the baby started to cry again, only to receive the same rough discipline from his mother, who appeared to pinch the baby even harder.

Janae could not believe her eyes. Her mind boggled at the implications of what she was seeing.

Could it be...?

Small rocks and scree tumbled past her, shaken loose by the sudden pounding of hooves. A shot rang out and an unlucky human toppled from above, splashing down into the once-pristine lagoon, his spilled blood turning the clear blue water incarnadine. A horn sounded like the screech of some mythical demon or predator.

The hunters, Janae realized, aghast. *They've found us again!*

Panicked, and not without reason, the humans scrambled for safety, clambering up the rocky slopes to get away, while leaving the drying hides behind. Janae was suddenly struck by just how silent the frantic exodus was; even in mortal terror, the humans emitted no barks or yowls or squawks of distress.

Except for Flax's newborn baby earlier...

Clutching her baby to her chest, the human female sought refuge behind the curtain of falling water at the base of the falls. Churning mist and white water helped to conceal her hiding place.

Clever girl, Janae thought.

Acting on impulse, and unwilling to let the mother and child out of her sight, she scooted down the slope and scampered across the rocks toward the falls. Like most apes, she hated getting wet, but science sometimes demanded sacrifices; flinching at the cold, soaking spray, she ducked behind the cascading wall of water.

Flax started in fright as Janae joined her. Her eyes widened anxiously and she clutched her baby closer to her breast. Janae covered her own mouth with her hands to assure the frightened human that she understood the need for silence.

You can trust me, she thought. *I won't let anything happen to you or your baby.*

Flax seemed to get the message. Instead of bolting away

from Janae, out into the open, she merely cowered against the slick, wet cliff face while keeping a wary eye on the increasingly sodden chimpanzee. Janae appreciated the human's trust, such as it was, while praying that the gorillas would pass them by. Water dripped from her hair and garments, chilling her.

A bullet, slamming in the rock face only inches away from her, suggested that her prayers had gone unanswered. Chipped stone pelted her face, causing her heart to pound like the hooves of the gorilla's horses. Trembling, Flax curled herself into a ball around her baby. Janae was shaking as well.

"Over there!" a gorilla shouted above the roar of the cataract. "I think I see something behind the falls!"

Damn it, Janae thought. *They've got us cornered.*

There was only one course of action left to her.

"Stay!" she ordered Flax before drawing her own pistol and firing a warning shot past the curtain of water. Working up her nerve, she stepped out from behind the cascade. "Hold your fire, you gun-crazy maniacs! Are you trying to kill me?"

The sharp report of the gunshot, and her unexpected appearance, took the hunters aback. Atlas glared down at her from atop the slope. He sat astride his mount, cradling a hunting rifle against his chest, much like Flax had held onto her child. Janae suspected that Atlas loved his firearms almost as much as the mother human cared for the baby.

"Don't tempt me!" he shouted back at her. "What the devil were you doing behind that water?"

"Trying to avoid being shot by you and your trigger-happy friends!"

Atlas squinted suspiciously at the falls. "Who else is behind that water?"

"Nobody," she insisted. "Since when do I have company out here in the wild?"

The gorilla contemplated the discarded hides upon the rocks. "Perhaps I should see for myself."

He started to urge his horse down the slope.

"I wouldn't do that if I were you." Janae aimed her pistol in his general direction. "I'm still pretty shook up from all this commotion, and there's no telling what might happen if my trigger finger slipped."

Atlas slowed his descent. "You wouldn't dare."

"Not on purpose, of course." Janae did not lower her gun. "But… accidents happen."

They glared at each other while the other apes looked on dumbfounded. Janae's nerves were stretched so tight she expected them to snap any minute, but she struggled to maintain as fierce a gaze as any belligerent gorilla.

I can't believe I'm actually doing this.

"Bah!" Atlas snarled, wheeling his horse about. "Leave the human-lover. There's better game to be found elsewhere, away from all this… wetness."

Janae bit back a mocking retort. Better to let Atlas save face than to provoke him into calling her bluff… if, indeed, she was bluffing. Janae wasn't quite sure about that. Would she really fire on another ape to defend Flax and her baby?

Maybe.

She waited until the gorillas had fully retreated, and the noise of their departure had entirely faded away, before slipping back behind the falls to check on the humans. To her relief, both mother and child remained present and unscathed. Flax stared wide-eyed at her soggy savior, wonder and confusion written upon her face in a language intelligible to both man and ape.

"You're safe now," Janae said as softly and gently as she could. "Nobody is going to hurt you or your baby."

For now, that was.

"Is this true?" Zorba demanded. "Did you indeed draw a gun on a fellow ape?"

Janae had been called back to the city—and the Minister's office—to account for her actions. Thankfully, the long ride from the forest had given her plenty of time to formulate her response.

"Is that what he said?" she replied, feigning innocence. "Did that arrogant brute also mention that he and his trigger-happy companions opened fire on me first, after mistaking me for a human? If I fired a shot, it was merely to alert them to my true nature, before I ended up the victim of an unfortunate hunting accident."

"Hmm." Zorba examined her skeptically. "That's not how Captain Atlas describes the incident."

"I would imagine not, but who are you going to believe? A thick-headed gorilla and his equally brutish cronies... or a trained scientific observer?" She wished briefly that she was an orangutan, if only to give her words more weight with Zorba. "Speaking of which, have you had a chance to read my most recent reports from the field?"

Aside from changing the subject, she was genuinely eager to discuss her latest findings and theories with another scientist.

"I have," he stated. "Unfortunately." He extracted a copy of the report and laid it down on the desk between them. "You are hardly helping your cause—or your reputation—by trading science for sheerest fantasy."

"Fantasy?" She bristled at the label, as well as the Minister's scornful tone. "To be sure, further research is required to validate my theories, but you must concede that the evidence is provocative and may open up whole new avenues of study where man is concerned." She could barely contain her own excitement. "What if man's inability to speak is a *learned* behavior, passed on from generation to generation?"

"Nonsense!" Zorba replied. "Man is, by nature, incapable of speech—or learning. To suggest otherwise borders on heresy."

"But think about it," she said, caught in the thrill of discovery. "Ape children learn to speak by emulating their elders. If humans, for whatever reason, ceased speaking at some point in the distant past, and conditioned their children to keep silent as well, how many generations would it take before language—even speech itself—died out entirely? Ten? Twenty? A hundred?"

"Don't be absurd," Zorba said. "Your so-called theory makes no sense even on its own highly specious terms. Allowing that, just for the sake of argument, man was even capable of doing so, why would any species *choose* to abandon speech?"

"Survival? External pressures, such as predators or rival tribes? A religious taboo?"

Zorba snorted at the latter suggestion. "So now we're crediting man with spiritual impulses, as well as a latent capacity for speech? Your ridiculous fancies grow more preposterous the more you attempt to justify them."

"I admit that many unanswered questions remain, but that's exactly what makes this line of inquiry so intriguing, perhaps even revolutionary." She refused to let Zorba's ridicule douse her enthusiasm. "Who knows? Perhaps it might even be possible to teach a human to speak..."

"Enough!" Zorba said sharply. "You are embarrassing yourself. I have a good mind to call a halt to your ill-conceived project altogether."

Janae's heart sank. As Minister of Science, Zorba had the authority to shut down her studies completely. "No, please, you mustn't do that."

"Give me one good reason not to."

"The summer is almost over," she said, groping for some plausible excuse, "so I'll be striking camp soon anyway. All I need is a few more weeks—days, even—to complete my initial survey, make a few final notes concerning the range and numbers of the humans, their diet, and so on. Then we'll have until next spring to contemplate any future research in the field."

Zorba regarded her gravely. "I would not be overly optimistic in that regard."

"I understand, sir. Perhaps I have let myself be carried away to a degree, but to have my expedition terminated abruptly, so close to its completion… well, I fear that might reflect badly on my career, and perhaps even the entire chimpanzee community."

She was not above playing the species card if it meant being allowed to continue her work—and perhaps discover conclusive proof that humans were more than just mindless beasts, fit only to be hunted or exterminated. And she allowed herself to hope that the Ministry would just as soon avoid any undue attention or controversy regarding her studies.

"I see." Zorba mulled over her words before reaching a decision. "Very well. I suppose there's no need to take any drastic action at this late date. You may have one more week to wrap up your work and bring your expedition to an expeditious conclusion… and perhaps reexamine your ludicrous 'theories' with a cooler head." He returned her report to his desk drawer. "But I strongly urge you not to share your speculations with anyone else, for the sake of your own future."

Janae forced herself to maintain a civil tone.

"Thank you, Doctor. You won't regret this."

His gaze shifted to the family photos on his desk.

"I already do," he said.

Eastern Forest Expedition, Day 60. Despite Doctor Zorba's opposition, I am more than ever determined to continue my study of humans, which have proven to be even more complex and fascinating than I ever imagined. I can only hope that my work will someday overcome the myths and prejudices surrounding man, allowing for a more enlightened approach to his care and preservation...

Alone in her tent, Janae looked up from her journal and rubbed her weary eyes. The glow of a solitary lantern illuminated the interior of the tent, which was pitched at the outskirts of the forest, within walking distance of the humans' usual environs. Night had fallen hours ago, but her racing brain would not allow her to sleep. There was still too much work to be done, too much to plan and ponder, in the scant days remaining before she would be forced to return to Ape City.

She was sorely tempted to try to capture Flax's baby and take it back to the city for further observation, but, no, she couldn't do that to the poor animal, which had already lost her mate. Janae knew she was being overly sentimental, and not at all scientific, in wanting to spare one particular human's feelings, but, like any decent chimpanzee, she had a heart as well as a brain and she wasn't about to apologize for that, not even to herself.

Was there any way she could get her hands on *another* newborn human? An orphan, maybe?

There was still vital work to be done, even back in the city, provided she had a suitable human specimen with which to work—the younger, the better. Perhaps she could start by trying to teach it sign language before advancing to actual vocalizations? Even if her theory was correct, it would not be easy to undo generations, perhaps even millennia, of behavioral conditioning, but...

A twig snapped loudly outside the tent. Janae sat up straight, all her senses on alert. Was it just her imagination, or did she hear something stirring out there in the dark? Maybe more than one something? She put down her pen and reached for her pistol.

"Hello?" she called out. "Is anybody there?"

As far as she knew, humans were not nocturnal...

Torches flared to life outside. She caught a glimpse of simian silhouettes on the other side of the canvas before a flaming object crashed into the side of the tent, setting it ablaze. Screaming in fright, she grabbed her journal as smoke and flames rapidly filled the shelter, driving her out into the night— where she found Atlas and his fellow gorillas awaiting her.

"You lunatics!" she accused them. "Are you all insane? This is beyond harassment!"

Remembering the gun in her hand, she started to raise it in self-defense, only to have a leather noose, of the sort employed by zookeepers, seize her wrist and yank her arm roughly to one side, spoiling her aim. A heavy club, wielded by another gorilla, struck the same arm, causing her to lose her grip on the pistol. A net was tossed over her, dragging her to the ground, where she whimpered in pain. Her abused arm felt like it was broken.

"That's it!" Atlas egged his accomplices on. "She loves humans so much. Treat her like one!"

No, she thought, *this can't be happening. Not even a gorilla would go this far.*

The light from the burning tent lit up the night. Reaching through the netting holding her down, Atlas pried her precious journal from her grip and casually tossed it onto the bonfire her camp had become.

"Burn it all," he ordered the other hunters. "Every trace."

Janae ached in more ways than one. The loss of her notes hurt almost as much as her throbbing arm. "You can't do this. When Doctor Zorba finds out about this—"

"Who is going to tell him? Your precious humans?" Atlas sneered at her. "Go ahead, scream for help. See if those filthy animals come to your rescue. They can't save you any more than you can save them."

"Save me?" Anger gave way to terror as the gorilla's words sank in. "No, you can't mean…" Unable to give voice to the unspeakable, she turned to scripture in desperation. "Ape shall never kill ape!"

Atlas shrugged.

"Ape? I don't see any apes here." He cracked his knuckles ominously before nodding at the other gorillas. "What are you waiting for? Destroy this… animal."

The hunters fell upon her. Fists and boots and rocks slammed without mercy into her huddled form. She curled up into a ball, trying in vain to shield herself from a never-ending rain of blows that no living creature, human or ape, could survive. All because she had dared to speak up for the humans.

No wonder, she thought, *that man chose to be mute.*

"She was an ape to remember, as well as a naturalist of considerable intellect, dedication, and potential. Her untimely end is a loss to us all."

Zorba stood before a podium in the city temple, delivering the eulogy. A stone statue of the Lawgiver, suitably larger than life, loomed behind him as he gazed out over the assembled mourners, which included Captain Atlas, who was seated among the other gorillas. A closed casket hid Janae's battered remains from view. Zorba was grateful for that small mercy.

"How ironic it is that our beloved friend and colleague met her end at the hands of the very beasts she bravely sought to study," Zorba continued. "And yet her tragic fate is not without meaning, for it serves to remind us of a bitter truth: man cannot be trusted. He is, and will always be, a savage animal whose murderous instincts are at odds with all that is civilized and simian. Janae re-learned that harsh lesson during her harrowing final moments. The rest of us must never forget it."

Atlas winked at him from the audience.

How dare he? Zorba thought. *Has he no sense of decency… or discretion?*

The Minister was deeply offended by the gorilla's callousness. This was an occasion for sorrow, no matter how necessary certain actions had been. Zorba had spoken truly when he'd praised Janae's intellect and determination moments before; nothing short of death was enough to still her restless curiosity. Given time, she might well have uncovered the forbidden truth of man's origins, or at least pointed others in the right direction.

And that could never be risked.

Zorba averted his gaze from the damning casket, even as he knew that there had been no other way to silence Janae permanently. What he had done had been for the good of all apekind, both today and for generations to come. His troubled conscience sought comfort in the memory of his beloved grandson, who had just this morning spoken his first word.

That word had been "Ape."

Paul Kupperberg's "Dangerous Imaginings,"
another "What if...?" tale in which Earth was
not destroyed in *Beneath the Planet of the Apes*,
reveals forbidden knowledge to a trio of eager
and impressionable young apes...

DANGEROUS IMAGININGS

by

PAUL KUPPERBERG

Ever since he was a little chimp, Darius would have to suppress an involuntary giggle any time an elder sat the children down to tell them, in hushed and frightened tones, tales of the Forbidden Zone. The monstrous creatures who inhabited it. The ghostly lights and sounds that haunted its nights. The bands of wild humans who had forsaken fruits and vegetables for the taste of ape flesh, particularly that of any youngster foolish enough to cross the border between civilization and savagery.

"*None*," children were warned as soon as they could understand the words, "have ever entered the Zone and returned alive."

But if none who entered had ever returned, who was it who had brought back these tales?

So, the elders were either lying to them about what was in the Forbidden Zone... or about the fates of those who had entered it.

Or both.

Darius had also concluded early on that it was best to keep such ideas to himself. His parents, both intellectuals—his father taught philosophy at the Academy and his mother was a physician—had raised him to question everything, but even they would have to draw the line at what was, at the very least, their son's heresy. New ideas were scary and unwelcome. And new ideas that questioned the consensus were deemed too dangerous to even be thought, much less allowed to spread.

So Darius kept his heresy a secret.

Just as he did his ever deeper explorations into the Forbidden Zone.

He probably would never have even noticed the smooth, shiny rock if he hadn't stubbed his toe on it while walking along the edge of a corn field several miles outside the city. Over the years, Darius had come to know large tracts of the forbidden terrain beyond the hills almost as well as the streets between his home and the Academy, where he had been engaged in research and teaching since graduating the institution as an engineer. The young chimp never even told his soon-to-be life-mate or closest friend of his explorations. His forays into the unknown weren't just forbidden by ape law—they were heretical to ape belief.

But if ape-eating humans, ghosts, and demonic lights were out there, they didn't seem much concerned with Darius. He went where he pleased, unmolested by anything more dangerous than stinging insects and the harsh sun. There were an abundance of wild human tribes living in and around the forests of the Zone, but he would usually catch no more than a glimpse of their pale, pink hides as they crashed loudly and fearfully into the underbrush and overhead foliage at the first sign or scent of his approach.

But something was hidden out there. Where there were secrets, he thought, there also had to be lies.

Not that Darius had yet come across any lies or discovered a reality that was inconsistent with the words of the Lawgiver.

Until the moment he struck his toe on a smooth, silver rock sticking several inches out of the ground.

•

It came slowly to Darius, like awareness from a deep, comfortable sleep, that Kya was speaking to him. It wasn't unusual for his mind to wander even in the middle of conversation, a bad habit he had fought most of his life to overcome. His mother's deeply held belief to the contrary, he wasn't being rude or disinterested, just easily distracted by the scattered pieces of the latest scientific puzzle on which he was working.

Kya said she understood, but Darius didn't believe her, especially when it was their future she was talking about. So he forced his mind from the distracting puzzle and focused instead on the tail end of her current statement:

"...But how are we going to break it to your mother?"

Darius blinked.

"Well," he said, feigning deep thought.

He cleared his throat.

"My mother," he began, speaking slowly while his mind raced. He was a scientist. He should be able to work this out. But, of course, Kya was also a scientist, a mathematician trained in the logic of numbers, and she could also work it out.

"You were doing it again, weren't you?" she said.

"No," he insisted with a dismissive gesture that could not have come off any phonier before he instantly deflated and admitted his crime. "Yes. Sorry, Kya."

Darius knew the only reason she responded with such outward calm was because they were in public, sharing a bench and lunch on the Academy campus.

"I don't understand why it's so hard for you to spend any time with me without your mind wandering off," she said, her tone more hurt than angry. "If I'm that boring..."

"No," he said, this time with genuine insistence. "You're the most interesting female—the most interesting chimp—

I've ever met, Kya. Really, it isn't you. Don't you ever drift off into limbo when you're working on one of your problems? Just, go away to a place in your head where your numbers are all that there are, where you have absolute mastery over them until every last piece of the puzzle fits together?"

Kya stared at him with an expression he couldn't quite read. "No," she said. "I mean, I've had moments of... I suppose you could call it clarity, and even flashes of inspiration. But nothing like what you're saying."

But then she smiled—a little sadly, he thought—and took his hand. "You know what? I think I'm a bit jealous."

"Of me?"

She tapped at his forehead with a finger. "Of this. Of what's inside it."

"What's wrong with the outside?"

She paused while she studied his face before saying, "There's not enough time to go through the whole list."

Darius gave her a dirty look, but then she leaned forward and pressed her muzzle against his and they broke out in giggles like two little ones.

As they gathered up the remains of their lunches, Kya asked, "So what universe were you deconstructing that took you away from me this time?"

"Oh," he said. Darius hadn't told anyone about his discovery by the corn field. The instant he saw what he had as he started to dig the silver object from the surrounding dirt, he knew it was dangerous. Digging it up and bringing it back to the city, where he was attempting in every spare moment he could find to discover what it was and how it worked, was a death sentence. For him and for anyone who knew his secret.

"What aren't you telling me, Darius?"

"It's nothing, Kya. It's that irrigation system I'm designing that's been giving me some problems."

"You told you finished that two weeks ago, more than a month ahead of schedule."

"I did?"

"Darius!"

"I... I really shouldn't..."

"What could you possibly be involved in that you can't talk to me about?"

There was no good answer.

"Please, Kya, can't you just trust me?"

And the worst answer of all was the truth.

"Not if *you* can't trust *me*," she said.

But what choice did he have?

"I knew as soon as I saw it that it wasn't anything made by ape hands," Darius said, once they were alone in the corner of the workshop he called his own. His area was neat and orderly, with the top clear of everything except the plans for the irrigation system he was supposed to still be working on.

The young chimp spoke softly as he crouched to extract the object of his words, wrapped in a rough hemp sack, from the dark back corner of the shelf under his bench. It measured eighteen inches high by eleven inches wide by four inches deep and was surprisingly light for its size.

"The metal it's made from, the manufacturing techniques, and especially its contents, are all so far beyond what our science is capable of producing, it might as well be from another world."

Kya's eyes shifted nervously from Darius to the package he was laying carefully on the bench. "You don't really believe it's an... an alien object, do you?"

Darius shrugged. "Even after examining it and its components, I don't know what to believe. A metal object that's been buried in damp soil for an indeterminate amount of time should show *some* signs of rust or deterioration, but except for some dents on its face, it's as bright and shiny as polished silver, except for a symbol of some sort stenciled onto it. It's badly faded, but study with a magnifying glass shows what appears to be once-white symbols or possibly letters against a blue background: A N S A."

Kya nodded, breathless, speechless, and frightened.

"And these," he said, starting to forget his own fear and feeling the excitement of being able to share this miraculous discovery, "these are clasps. See?" He depressed the two small silver tabs set into the bottom of the case. With a soft click, the case popped open, hinged like a clamshell along its short top end.

"Such precision," he said with undisguised admiration. "The seam between the two halves is invisible when closed. And look at how *thin* the shell is, but so strong. It reminds me of aluminum, but aluminum's strength and rigidity isn't one hundredth of this. It may be an alloy. I'll need to run some tests, though, to see if I can duplicate it." He paused and squinted. "I'll need a heat source." As if also suddenly recalling that he wasn't alone, Darius jerked his eyes in her direction and said, "Where's the nearest foundry? Or kiln? A kiln would work."

In spite of her discomfort over the object of Darius' monologue, Kya had to smile. "If this is what it's like inside that head of yours, maybe I should be glad you *don't* share it with me."

Darius caught himself. "Right. I'm sorry. And this isn't even the most interesting part." He opened the lid the rest of the way until the two sides lay flat on the bench. Both halves of the case were lined with a dull, white substance that appeared to be made of densely compacted particles of some sort. Shapes had been carved into the substance into which the case's contents were fitted. Several of the shapes were empty, but other objects remained, though the only thing Kya could positively identify was a hammer. The rest of them were mysteries.

He reached in and plucked a shiny black oblong box from where it rested in its specially hollowed-out shape, next to an identical but empty shape. On its face were two shiny silver circles, some buttons, and a metal rod stuck out of one end. "There are two of these, but I had to take the other one apart to examine it."

"What is it?"

Darius laughed in delight. "I have no idea, but it's also made from a substance for which I can't find a precedent in any text, and it's filled with... with... *things*! Hard little bugs of this and that... there's pure silicon involved, and wires, copper it seems, and designs almost too fine to be seen with the naked eye, etched into tiny little boards. And a source of some kind of energy. Well, at least I think that's what it is, but it's long depleted. But when I touch a static charge to the wires from the power source, it lights up... and talks!"

Kya stepped back with a gasp.

"Okay, maybe not exactly *talks*, but it makes a noise, a crackling sound. Like... like... remember that time we were caught out in the fields by that storm, and as we ran towards the city gates, there was that strange ball of blue lightning we saw dancing up and down the guard tower? The guard said it didn't hurt, just made his hair stand on end, but it also made that sound, almost like fat sizzling in a hot skillet."

"I remember," she said.

"They did come in a pair. Maybe it's a signaling device of some sort?" He rubbed his chin. "However, there are also two of these," he said, pointing to the twin black rectangular boxes set into the white substance above the talking boxes. They were made of the same substance, but almost half their faces had been cut out to show white gauges marked with a series of symbols. "The static charge causes lights to flash and a needle to twitch. And with all these metal antennae sticking from them? It could be a medical device. Very puzzling, but I haven't had time to really examine it yet."

Kya touched one of the empty shapes. "That looks like a weapon."

"Yes, I think it was. A handgun, I believe. But even forgetting that the science and technology here are beyond anything we're capable of, take a look at the size of all these objects. None of them are designed for ape hands. The shapes and proportions are all wrong, the buttons too small and closely spaced. The handgun, for instance. From the cut-out, I can tell that even I would barely have been able to fit my finger in the trigger guard. A gorilla could hide two of those weapons in his fist."

"But... if this isn't the work of apes, who *did* make them?" Kya said.

"You're going to think I'm crazy," he said.

"I already think that."

"But I've made measurements, done the calculations."

"I'm sure, Darius. You're very thorough. Please, don't worry what I'll think. Just tell me, my love, scientist to scientist."

"To scientist," said a third voice from behind them.

Darius shrieked in surprise and whirled, eyes wide with fear at the thought that he had put Kya in harm's way by sharing with her, against his better judgment, his secret.

"Well? Come on, my monkey!" the voice said, the speaker stepping into view, a big smile on his face. "The suspense is killing me."

"Sidd," Kya cried.

Darius' knees went weak.

"You almost gave me a heart attack, you dumb ape," Darius said.

"No doubt," Sidd said. "You want to talk heresy, you

should lock the door. I passed Doctor Hiatt in the corridor on my way in. If he'd seen or heard what I just did, it would have been all over for you chimps."

"I'm an idiot," Darius said. His hands were still shaking.

"Naw, you're a genius, just like me."

Sidd was grinning as he said it, but that didn't diminish the fact that his claim was true. Fortunately, he was also Darius' best friend.

"I can't believe you've been holding out on me," Sidd said, pushing past him to get a closer look at the case.

"I didn't want to get you guys in trouble if I was caught."

"Since when have I ever worried about getting caught?" Sidd leaned down, peering at each piece in the case in turn.

"Human, right?" he said without looking up.

"That's what it looks like," Darius said.

Sidd lifted the lid off the bench top and examined the faded white symbols on its face. It took him a moment to piece it together, but when he did, his expression of shock was, Darius thought, exquisite.

"You don't think...?" he said in a soft tone of awe.

Darius nodded, enjoying the moment in spite of the danger he would unleash with the next word he spoke: "Taylor."

Darius tried very hard not to fidget on the small, hard stool that Doctor Hiatt offered junior visitors on their rare audiences in the venerable professor's inner sanctum. This was the young engineer's first time in this dark and dusty place, with its endless shelves and stacks of books and scrolls, every surface covered with papers and plans and scientific instruments, a vast storehouse of accumulated ape knowledge. It belonged to the Academy, but its stewards were the scientist-philosophers who had headed that institution, legendary orangutans with names like Krysa, Bysin, Tartus, Zaius. And Hiatt.

Stooped and frail with age under his heavy robes, Doctor Hiatt paced relentlessly, weaving his way flawlessly around the dingy cave of a room and the precarious scholarly stacks with unerring accuracy, even with his snout buried in Darius' irrigation system proposal. He had expected that what was, but for one detail, a proposal for an otherwise routine project would attract attention from higher up, but he thought he would have to deal with some assistant administrator of public works, not Doctor Hiatt himself.

What was so interesting about the plans and specifications? *They* weren't the thousand-pound gorilla in the room. That honor belonged to the length of pipe that came with the proposal and now lay where it had been tossed on top of a jumble of correspondence and scrolls on the old doctor's worktable.

Doctor Hiatt stopped abruptly in his wanderings, and said, "Yes."

Darius jumped.

"S-sir?"

"You say the discovery of this… aluminum came about by accident?" Doctor Hiatt said.

"Yes, sir. Sidd. *Professor* Sidd. A colleague. Some aluminum was tainted with silicon, and when he heated it to its melting point it, it formed an alloy," Darius said, his mouth sand-dry. "Well, it took him several attempts to find the right proportions, of course. But when he showed it to me, I thought it was the perfect medium from which to mill pipes for my irrigation project. It's strong, lightweight, resistant to corrosion, easy to machine, and with both aluminum and silicon in such abundance, we have a near-endless supply— and we will need it, Doctor Hiatt, I know it. There are countless uses to which we can put this alloy once it's…"

"Yes," Doctor Hiatt said sharply when Darius paused for breath. "It is quite miraculous. I am, however, attempting to ascertain the *inspiration* for the miracle."

Doctor Hiatt's suspicions didn't come as a surprise to Darius. He had come prepared with what didn't, he hoped, sound like an over-rehearsed response and he used it now, complete with a submissive grin and embarrassed avoidance of the old orangutan's eyes:

"I'm sorry to say, sir, Professor Sidd's discovery was not so much an inspiration as it was the result of sloppiness. He used a vessel that hadn't been properly cleaned."

Doctor Hiatt made a rumbling sound in his throat. Darius couldn't tell if it was an angry growl or phlegm, but he plunged on. He had already climbed to the top of the tree; he might as well reach for the top banana.

"But inspiration or accident, sir, the fact is that there is so much…"

"*We*," Doctor Hiatt said sharply, "will determine what are the facts, Professor Darius. That will be all for now."

Darius was surprised. "S-sir?"

"I said that will be all."

"But the project…?"

Doctor Hiatt peered at the young chimp with an expression Darius couldn't read and said, "You will be informed," before turning his attention to the papers he picked up from his worktable. Darius gulped, then rose and got out of there as quietly as he could.

Several tense weeks passed during which Darius stayed well clear of where he had hidden the evidence of his crime (and he had, in his anxiety, begun to think of it as a crime) and saw accusation in the eyes of every gorilla and orangutan who looked his way. He had started to berate himself for his stupidity and arrogance in thinking he could outwit all those wise old heads with his juvenile lies, and he wondered why they were waiting so long to come for him.

But it was, in the end, a lot of worry over nothing. One morning, his supervisor, Doctor Shia, informed him, casually and in passing, that the plans for the irrigation system had been approved, in full, and would proceed immediately, good job, good job. Darius was speechless. In that moment, he felt as though he could breathe again. Sidd, who tried without success to hide his own shock, replied that he had been telling them all along not to worry, hadn't he? Kya allowed herself a few moments to let the news sink in, then said: "Promise me you won't do this again."

That shouldn't be a difficult promise to make, he thought.

Except now that the danger had passed and they *had* gotten away with it, he couldn't stop his imagination from doing what it did.

Once Darius finalized the irrigation plans, he and Sidd worked with the foundry making the aluminum and the factory that would mill the raw material into the necessary piping and pieces of structural support. By the end of a month, the first aluminum was being laid in the fields while the lightweight main ducts were starting to be horsed up to the reservoir high in the surrounding hills.

In all that time, they were too busy to give any thought to Taylor's legacy, but once all the new processes had been implemented and were running smoothly, Darius found he couldn't stop thinking about the signaling devices. Communication between the Academy and the work crew at the reservoir was through written messages delivered by riders on horseback, a process that could take better than two days. When big problems arose, that time could be crucial, even fatal—but imagine if they could communicate almost instantaneously? Such an ability could save not just time, but lives.

He didn't bother to mention to Kya when, the next morning, he went to retrieve the devices from their hiding place. But only after taking every precaution to make sure he wasn't being followed.

By the time the first water from the new irrigation system was flowing into the fields, Darius and Sidd had solved the mystery of the suspected power source in the signaling devices. It consisted of cells of oppositely charged chemicals that converted its own energy into electrical energy. While they couldn't hope to duplicate the compact units found in the devices, they had soon cobbled together a crude approximation that, when connected to one signaling device, produced a sustained crackle that Darius suspected was the sound of electricity itself.

And when *both* devices were connected to their own, individual power source—Sidd suggested they call it a "cache"—and the correct button depressed, they discovered, to their astonishment, that they could send their voices from one device to the other. This excited them to no end, until common sense won out with the realization that to present this finding to the Academy would be suicide—and, as it turned out, they couldn't duplicate the result in anything they devised. With a little improvisation, though, they had soon rigged a crude device that sent a steady electrical charge from a cache through a copper wire. By interrupting the electrical charge, they could create breaks in the electrical hiss and crackle that could be heard clearly by a receiving device at the opposite end.

Kya didn't have to be told what they were up to. Darius' frequent absences and his bad, stammered excuses were all the evidence she needed that he was hiding something. Once confronted, he confessed everything, and as much as she wanted to be angry with them, what they had created was too fascinating to ignore. In fact, she found her mathematician's mind going instantly to work devising a simple code that translated letters and words into the short bursts of various lengths and combinations on the static-filled line. With a little practice, they were sending messages from one station to another almost as fast and as fluently as speaking.

"...And we can't ever show it to the Academy," Darius said, late one night as he and Sidd worked by flickering firelight at the engineer's workbench. The copper wire and caches for their communication device were carefully hidden, while the transmission terminals could be quickly disassembled into their component parts and scattered on the tabletop with other random pieces strewn there.

"Why not?" Sidd said, hunched over to squint at the delicate connection he was attempting in the dim light.

"Why not?" Darius said, manning his friend's distracted surprise. "They were suspicious enough about the aluminum, and we had a perfectly logical explanation for its so-called discovery."

"You should thank the Lawgiver I'm such a renowned slob."

"So what do we tell them this time? You accidentally put some electricity in a dish contaminated with copper wire?"

Sidd cast an irritated glance at the flickering torch over his shoulder and bent closer to his work. "A different kind of accident. Static electricity, a stray bit of wire... or something. Anyway, how are we supposed to keep this to ourselves? You know you can't keep a secret to save your life."

He sat up and looked at his handiwork. Then he reached up and flipped the lever on his transmission terminal, and sat back with a sharp bark of surprise as the short length of wire attached to it began first to glow, then flare suddenly into a short, brilliant burst of light. The wire was ruined, reduced almost to ash.

Sidd looked up with eyes as wide as a baby discovering sweets and shouted, "Wow! Did you see that?"

"How could I miss it?" Darius replied, rubbing his eyes. "It was almost like looking into the sun. What did you do?"

"Nothing. I've just been trying out different elements to see if I could find something as efficient as copper but more common to use for wire. I connected the wire to the cache and... poof!"

"Did the cache experience some sort of surge? What kind of wire were you using?"

Sidd inspected the cache, looking over the terminals and touching tentative fingers to it. "No, it's fine. The wire was made of ore refined from wolfram," he said. "I was fairly sure it wouldn't be viable because of its high melting point, but I had some so I tried it anyway..." He stopped and looked in surprise at Darius.

"Electricity plus resistance produces heat," Darius said.

Sidd nodded furiously. "Wolfram has a high resistance to heat."

"So at a certain temperature, it starts to radiate the excess energy as light."

"But it quickly passes that stage and reaches its melting point."

"So we would need to control the rate of the wolfram's oxidation."

"How?"

Darius bared his teeth and laughed. "We're smart chimps. We should be able to figure it out."

"What do you call it again?" Kya asked, her awed expression awash in the steady white glow of light from the glass cylinder inches from her face on the workbench.

"The illuminated orb," Darius said.

"It's magnificent," she said and quickly switched it off. "And it will get us killed."

"No, no, *this* invention springs directly from the discoveries made coming up with the signaling device," Sidd said.

"Which we *still* haven't told anyone about."

"Then we really should get started on how we're going to accomplish that."

"This is serious, Sidd," Darius said.

"Yes, it is, and not just because I'm worried about our skins. No matter how the discovery's been made, it's been made and now we have to share it with the world. Look at what we've been able to accomplish in less than a year. Imagine what we could have done if we didn't have to work in secret, in the dark." He flipped the switch and the illuminated orb began to glow. "The Lawgiver is good, but our religion is science, and science doesn't have any boundaries. Certainly not based on ancient superstitions and archaic rules. Look at this… we've given every ape a way out of the darkness, but we're prohibited from sharing it because of its source."

Kya said, "You're just one chimp. You can't fight the whole world by yourself."

"I'm not by myself," Sidd said, grinning at the glowing orb. "I've got science on my side."

"Some common sense would be more useful."

Sidd waved his hand dismissively. "Relax, Kya. We've kept everything well concealed and only work on it late at night, after everyone else has gone home. No one suspects anything."

"Suspects?"

The voice from the doorway froze Darius in place.

"Quite the contrary, Professor Sidd."

Darius couldn't make himself move, but he didn't need to turn to know who it was.

"We've known almost from the very start."

Doctor Hiatt.

This wasn't like any trouble Darius had ever found himself in. He had been cuffed and yelled at by his parents, made to sit in corners, berated in front of colleagues, and once even threatened with dismissal from his studies at the Academy for a prank that had gone wrong, but nothing that ever rose to the level of requiring an armed gorilla escort.

The hard-faced soldiers stood at attention in the doorway while Doctor Hiatt stepped into the laboratory. Kya grabbed Darius' hand and Sidd seemed to suddenly shrink into himself. The old orangutan didn't speak or look at them. He went straight to the workbench, casting a long gaze at the glowing orb and the rest of their contraband technology. He flipped the switch off, then on, then off again. After a few moments, he grunted and turned, leaving as he came, through a wall of gorillas.

"Bring them," he said as he went, and the soldiers streamed in, each of them grabbing one of the frightened chimps roughly by the arm and yanking them out into the corridor, where still more soldiers waited. There, they were separated and marched away, too scared to protest. For all their conspiratorial talk, Darius had never really considered the possibility of arrest. He thought discovery of their work would result, at worst, in another innocent-sounding summons to Doctor Hiatt's sanctum and... what? A stern lecture? The punishment, he realized now, surrounded by the gun-toting soldiers, would likely be far more severe.

He was brought outside and put onto the back of a wagon. One soldier faced front to drive the horses. Two more stood over Darius, arms at the ready. No one said a word while the wagon trotted through the night-darkened streets. There was no further sign of Kya or Sidd.

The wagon drove straight down the main boulevard outside the Academy, then beyond the city's boundaries and out onto bumpy trails that, to Darius' recollection, led nowhere. The first light of dawn illuminated unfamiliar terrain, a place Darius had not yet ventured in his secret explorations. *Not yet...* as though he would ever be free— if he even survived the day—to do anything ever again, he thought with a shiver.

They rode until the surrounding lush greenery gave way to dusty brown and gray and the rough trail rose into the stunted foothills of the Northern Mountains. It was there that they finally stopped, and, following the wave of a rifle barrel, Darius stumbled from the wagon and was shoved under a low-hanging ledge of rock that hid the mouth of a cavern. His gorilla guards had to stoop almost in half to fit beneath it, but they dragged him into the opening and, in the sudden darkness, he stumbled on the steeply inclined ramp. But several dozen yards down and into the darkness, the way took a series of sudden, sharp turns which, once navigated, opened into a large cavernous space. A hundred feet across and almost as high, the cavern's walls were neatly ringed with openings to small side chambers, most of the openings of uniform size and shape, dug by the hands of apes. A rough wood table with a chair on either side of it sat in the center of the brightly lighted cavern.

The light from electrified illuminated orbs hanging high on the walls.

One of his escorts pushed Darius forward and growled, "Sit." Then the gorillas turned smartly and marched back into the dark tunnel.

Darius walked tentatively across the cavern to take his seat, his hair bristling and his ears flattening against his skull. He couldn't get a clear look at the glowing orbs themselves, but they appeared to be designed along the same lines as what he and Sidd had concocted in his lab. Had Doctor Hiatt been watching them so closely that he had already duplicated their work?

He would have a very long time to think about it, sitting in that cavern under the cold, accusing light of his own transgression.

The electric lights were like a sun stopped dead in its trek across the sky. How to mark the hours, much less the minutes, without any outside reference point? Outside, the shadow of a stick on the ground or the position of the sun or the moon in the sky was enough to show the hour, the time of the month, the month of the year. What to replace that with when those natural indicators weren't available? Well, time was merely the sum of regular natural intervals, so if a reliable mechanical device could be substituted...

Darius wasn't sure if he had fallen asleep or had just gone so deep into his own imagination that he had lost sight of the real world, but he was suddenly aware of Doctor Hiatt, standing on the other side of the table, looking down at him with hard, analytical eyes.

"Doctor Hiatt," he gasped, starting to rise from his seat in an automatic gesture of respect. The old orangutan stopped him with a gesture.

"What were you thinking about?" the old orangutan said.

"Sir?"

"You were so lost in your thoughts, you failed to see my approach."

Darius' lips moved but he couldn't speak.

Doctor Hiatt pulled the second chair from the table and sat. "We have been watching you, Professor Darius. You have scarcely moved for hours."

"Kya," Darius said, his voice dry and raspy, as much from fear as thirst. "Sidd. Where are they?"

"Your friends are unharmed, I give you my word," Doctor Hiatt said.

"How... how do I know I can trust you?" Darius said, more surprised by his own words than was the orangutan at whom he threw them.

"Have I ever given you cause to question that trust?"

"You had me arrested," Darius said in disbelief. He wondered why he wasn't more frightened.

"A result, Professor, of your dishonesty, not mine," Doctor Hiatt said.

That brought Darius up short, but before he could frame an answer, Doctor Hiatt again asked, "What were you thinking about?"

And again, almost without thinking, like he was still a student in the classroom, Darius responded to Doctor Hiatt's question. "A... a time-keeping device, sir, utilizing a pendulum to regulate the intervals."

Doctor Hiatt arched one brow. "But a pendulum's interval would vary as its arc began to decay."

"Yes, sir. A pendulum is ultimately unreliable and unstable, so I was designing a series of gears and levers that could mimic the pendulum but be easily regulated by the size of the gears."

"And what would supply a reliable energy source to keep the gears turning?"

Darius frowned. "I haven't quite worked that out. I was looking at some manner of spring or coil that could be tightly wound, with the gradual, regulated release of tension to drive the gears."

Doctor Hiatt sat back and allowed himself a tight-lipped smile. "And all this you did in your head, Professor Darius?"

"Yes, sir. I can... I guess see my experiments in my imagination. I can take projects apart, inspect the individual components, rearrange them, test various ideas and configurations. I even see my calculations, as though written on a slate."

"Remarkable. I will confess, we have been keeping an eye on you for quite some time, ever since you started your explorations out into the Forbidden Zone as an adolescent."

Darius didn't hide his surprise. "But... no one ever tried to stop me."

"You were never a threat or a danger to us or yourself," Doctor Hiatt said with a shrug. "You have seen for yourself there is very little of substance to fear in the Zone. No, Professor Darius, the Forbidden Zone is forbidden not for the protection of apes, but for the maintenance of the Secrets passed on to us by the Lawgiver."

"Secrets like Taylor?"

Doctor Hiatt nodded his head once. "And his devices."

"But why?" Darius said, almost in anguish. "They are a boon to apes."

"These things, Professor Darius," Doctor Hiatt said in a gentle, corrective tone, "are the destructive seeds of apekind."

"That's insane," Darius said, the words flying from his mouth before he knew he spoke them.

Doctor Hiatt calmly said, "I told you we have been watching you for some time. Our interest did not spring from fear of your curiosity and intelligence, but rather the hope that, under our careful tutelage, it would blossom and grow. I will tell you we are none of us disappointed in the results."

"But then," Darius said slowly, "I found Taylor's backpack."

"Yes. Poisoning all your discoveries going forward by the tainted roots of forbidden knowledge."

"I don't understand, Doctor Hiatt. What difference does the source of knowledge make if the knowledge itself is beneficial?"

"Because all knowledge must be ape knowledge."

"I'm an ape," Darius said.

"Would you have made the inventive leap to your aluminum pipe without Taylor's backpack to inspire you?"

"I don't know... perhaps. But even if I hadn't, sooner or later some other scientist would."

"And *then* it would be *ape* knowledge, born of ape wisdom and ingenuity."

"Then why was my irrigation project approved?"

Doctor Hiatt made a dismissive gesture. "A disagreement on the Academy council. There were those who found your and Professor Sidd's version of its discovery plausible. By the time we located the backpack, the project had already been constructed and the process was known by too many to suppress."

"You still haven't told me why we weren't stopped before we went too far," Darius said. "Were you waiting for us to incriminate ourselves?"

"Quite the contrary, Professor Darius. We were curious to see what you would do next. We are already in possession of all you have discovered and more." Doctor Hiatt held up both hands to take in the lighted cavern. "Electricity. Energy storage devices. Illuminated orbs. Communication of sound and images over wires and without. Medical devices. Many marvels, all created by bright, young scientific minds who found inspiration in recovered or stolen bits of human technology."

The doctor's confession almost knocked Darius from his seat. The elder saw his shock and didn't wait for the question to answer, "Human technology, yes. Taylor was real, an intelligent human who came to our world with his companions, bringing with them the technology from their world that you and those before you have found so fascinating.

"But know this," the old orangutan growled, leaning across the table to lock his bloodshot eyes on Darius. "Taylor and those others were *alien* beings, from another world. They may have looked like our feral humans, but they were no more related to the mindless humans of Earth than apes are kin to the moon."

Darius couldn't sit any longer. He pushed back the chair and began to pace behind it, his fingers plucking nervously at his tunic. "If they're so different, why is their technology still forbidden?"

"Because it is *human*."

"But not *our* humans."

"The distinction is too subtle for the common ape to…"

"No," Darius barked, startled again by his own boldness. But even as they had been speaking, his imagination had been at work on the problem, deconstructing Doctor Hiatt's argument the same way he had solved the riddles of the communications device and the orb, by rearranging the pieces and filling the gaps with creative leaps of logic; if *this* is to happen, *these* steps must first take place, even if how to achieve any of those steps is currently unknown. And the final banana had dropped into the basket.

"You… you aren't sure, are you?" he said in a whispery rasp.

Doctor Hiatt stared back at him through narrowed eyes, as though he were a specimen being measured. At last, he shrugged and sighed.

"What is certainty? Yes, I know you believe that all things are quantifiable by science. Were the proof for religion held to as rigid a standard as science, there would be no faith. And that makes faith sometimes a very fragile thing. We of faith do not feel a need to test it, for to test it would be to question the Lawgiver and give, in actuality, proof of our lack of faith."

"That's just rhetoric," Darius said. "Besides, trying to understand the universe that the Lawgiver gave us doesn't question him or alter my faith. None of it would be there without him, so anything that apes can create celebrates him."

"There is that one pillar, Professor, that, should it ever

be removed, could send the entire temple crashing down into rubble," Doctor Hiatt said. "The infallible belief in the superiority of ape over human. It has been, remains, and shall forever be a fact as inarguable as existence itself."

"What if it isn't?" Darius asked. "Why should it matter?"

"Because we must know that everything we have comes from *here*," the old doctor said fiercely, pounding his fist against his chest. "We must know that not a shred of human knowledge, no matter the world of its origin, infects ape thinking. We must know that not a scrap of skin or drop of similar blood is shared between us."

Doctor Hiatt rose now as well, as did the volume of his voice, as though delivering the apocalyptic words of the Lawgiver.

"And *our* certainty must serve as the foundation for the unshakable faith of those who look to us for strength and guidance. But how can we maintain the certainty of our faith if we do not also maintain the purity of our knowledge?"

Darius looked around the cavern. "Then what's all of this? Why don't you destroy it instead of keeping and even using it if it's such a threat?"

"Don't be naïve," the doctor scolded. "One must sometimes use the Devil's own tools against him. We were able to listen in on your laboratory with a concealed device that sends sound through the air."

Darius almost smiled. "Wireless transmission. I knew it was possible," he said in satisfaction before remembering that he should be upset. "What's going on, Doctor? How come I'm here with you instead of in the hands of some gorilla for questioning?"

"You are a bright chimp, Professor. Why do you think?"

"I can only assume it's because you need me for some purpose," Darius said slowly.

"It's not quite a need, but we recognize potential when it is before us. We believe you can be an asset to the Academy, the word of the Lawgiver, and your fellow apes. We believe you would choose the opportunity to continue your scientific research, now backed by the full resources of the Academy, over a far less pleasant and fulfilling fate."

"You mean death?"

Doctor Hiatt chuckled. "Do not be absurd. No, but you would be sent to a place where you would be too exhausted from your labors to ever again even think about science."

"And if I stay, how will I be helping anyone except myself?"

"Your work will benefit society, Professor, more than it will ever know. Though we need to wait for an ape whose mind has not been tainted by human technology to discover illumination and communication for all to enjoy it, there are some equally immediate and potentially lethal threats that face our world. They are worrisome enough that should they manifest, what tools we have at our disposal to defeat them will be secondary to how those tools were acquired."

"What about Kya and Sidd? What did they say when you told them this?" Darius said.

"Professor Kya, while a talented mathematician, is not an object of our interest as are you and Professor Sidd. He, however, has taken a more defiant stance and will require some reassuring counsel from a trusted friend to be made to understand the situation."

"How do you know I understand?"

"It's a matter of faith," Doctor Hiatt said. "*Your* faith, Professor Darius, that the only truths in the universe that matter are those that can be proved by science."

"What good is any of it if it can't be used?"

"It may not allow apes to light their homes, but your discoveries will not go to waste, of that I assure you."

Doctor Hiatt was right, of course. A life of hard labor for his friends and himself or one of pure science, unfettered by all restrictions.

Darius sighed. No choice at all.

"Of course, Doctor Hiatt. And I thank you for this honor," he said, lowering his eyes and bowing his head. "I will, of course, talk to my colleagues. I'm sure they can be made to understand."

"Very good, Professor Darius," Doctor Hiatt said. "I am relieved to see you are as sensible as you are brilliant. Thank the Lawgiver."

"Thank you, Doctor Hiatt," Darius said humbly, but he was careful not to echo the oath to the Lawgiver himself. Doctor Hiatt had said it himself—Darius' faith lay in science, and science only. And Darius was just as dedicated as Doctor Hiatt to protecting his faith: science, in service of apekind and practiced without restriction.

Darius understood that the best way to bring down an institution like the Academy was from the inside. He didn't yet know how he and Sidd would do it, but he was still confident. As he once told Sidd, they were smart chimps. They would figure it out.

Doctor Zaius himself takes center stage in Kevin J. Anderson's and Sam Knight's "Of Monsters and Men," years before the orangutan became the holder of the planet's greatest secrets and met the human called "Bright Eyes"…

OF MONSTERS AND MEN

by

KEVIN J. ANDERSON AND SAM KNIGHT

"Apprentice Zaius!"

The young orangutan flinched at the gruff tone. He stepped backward in the rough-hewn stone hallway to see the angry gorilla bearing down upon him. "What is this nonsense?" Spittle flew from the darker ape's lips. "Why have my gorillas been recalled from our hunting trip and ordered to report to you? We were on the trail of a new band of humans!"

Zaius shrank as the intimidating gorilla came nose to nose with him. "Captain Caetus! I—"

A calm, authoritative voice filled the passageway behind them. "Because I said so."

Stiffening, Caetus stepped back from Zaius. Always more in control of himself than any gorilla, Zaius turned and bowed as the Defender of the Faith approached them. "Doctor Tullius."

Tullius' orange Academy robes complemented his ruddy hair, but contrasted sharply against the drab greens of Zaius' student jumper and Caetus' black leather military armor. Ignoring the younger orangutan's greeting, Tullius addressed the gorilla. Though he was physically smaller, the Defender of the Faith exuded power and confidence. Clearly, he did not expect his orders to be questioned. "My student Zaius is leading you and your men into the Forbidden Zone. I have been told your soldiers are the best. Is this not so? Are you not prepared for true danger? Or would you rather be chasing weak humans for sport?"

The gorilla's dark eyes narrowed. "My soldiers *are* the best! We are prepared."

"Then you leave at first light. Make whatever preparations you feel are necessary. You are dismissed, Captain Caetus." Ignoring the flustered gorilla, Tullius held out a rolled parchment to the younger orangutan. "Your travel papers, Zaius—Academy-approved."

Zaius gingerly took the scroll, as though afraid it might vanish like a dream in his hands. "Sir, I... I don't know what to say."

Pausing, Tullius looked up the hallway, watching until the gorilla had stomped out of sight before resting a hand on his fellow orangutan's shoulder. "My boy, if you are ever going to be a member of the Academy Board, you must learn how to control the gorillas. You are smarter than they are. All orangutans are."

Zaius focused on an entirely different part of the statement. "Me? A member of the Board?"

"Why else would I have gotten you approval to explore the Forbidden Zone?"

"Honestly, I don't know, sir. I am at a loss for words. You are Defender of the Faith, and I know you've heard my theories about an ancient, possibly non-simian civilization." He looked away. "I rather expected you would charge me with heresy, not aid my search."

"Perhaps I see potential in you, Zaius, and I am giving you a chance to disprove your theory and denounce such nonsense. Provided the evidence warrants it, of course." The Defender of the Faith fixed Zaius with a bright, intense gaze, making it clear exactly what answer he expected to hear. "And, for safety reasons, I will not allow you to take any humans."

Zaius shifted nervously. "No humans? Who will carry the packs? Do the digging? All the physical labor?"

"Surely gorillas are capable of doing a little hard work. It would be good for them to get their hands dirty for a change." Tullius squeezed Zaius' shoulder and smiled. "You are one of the brightest apes to ever come through the Academy. If anyone can comprehend what is to be found in the Forbidden Zone, it will be you. Keep your eyes, and most importantly your mind, open." His voice hardened again. "But not every ape is capable of comprehending... difficult concepts."

The expedition had not gone far before the gorillas began to cause problems. The sun was hot, the road dusty, and Zaius had the worst horse of the lot—no doubt a small way for Captain Caetus to put the young orangutan in his place, no matter what Doctor Tullius had ordered.

"Why exactly are we going into the Forbidden Zone if it is forbidden?" Caetus' gruff voice burned Zaius' ears worse than the blistering heat of the day. "Does the Defender of the Faith question the word of the Lawgiver?" He made a snorting sound. "When all questions are already answered, what is the purpose of asking more questions?"

The gibe carried over the sound of the horse hooves and rattling tack. A snuffling laugh from one of the mounted gorilla soldiers at the rear of the expedition assured Zaius that everyone in the party had heard. Trying to maintain his composure, Zaius looked back at the other two orangutan apprentices and three chimpanzee students making up his scientific team. They all held rigid, neutral expressions, and none dared refute Caetus' comment. They were already nervous about entering the Forbidden Zone, not to mention being surrounded by eight armed gorillas.

Karah, the only female orangutan, nodded slightly at him. Neaus, the other orangutan, watched expectantly, waiting for Zaius to put the gorilla captain in his place. They both looked regal in their newly fitted orange Academy Representative robes. Zaius resisted the urge to look down at his own. Any sign of nervousness would make controlling this expedition a difficult task.

Though he was himself just a senior student, Zaius was the leader of this expedition and would have to respond.

He lifted his chin and spoke in an erudite, knowledgeable voice. Anticipating the gruff gorilla's questions, Doctor Tullius had offered him possible responses. "The Forbidden Zone has been deadly to simiankind for twelve hundred years, Captain. Plenty of time for humans to hide in the rocky canyons and breed like vermin." He raised his voice to make sure the other gorillas in the squad could hear. "You know what the Sacred Scrolls say. 'Let him not breed in great numbers, for he will make a desert of his home and yours.' Every generation, a select few apes are chosen to make sure the naked beasts have not found a way to survive out here." Turning to look Caetus in the eye, Zaius did his best to hold the ape's gaze. "We should be proud to have been chosen. This is a great honor."

"Ha! Then it's a hunting expedition." Caetus threw back his head and laughed, satisfied—for now. Raising his rifle overhead with one hand, he shouted back to the other gorillas. "Academy-talk for saying we are the ones to root out and exterminate humans in the Forbidden Zone!"

The other gorillas raised their weapons and shouted approval.

After the pounding, dry heat of the day, the desert night was colder than Zaius expected, but it was far from the most surprising thing about this strange, inhospitable landscape.

When the expedition approached, the boundary to the Forbidden Zone had been unmistakable: desolation demarcated the living world from the dead. Beyond the line of sinister scarecrows apes had set out to warn off the ignorant, the increasingly nervous riders had seen nothing to look at but rock, dirt, and sky.

Unable to sleep, Zaius rose from his pallet and walked the perimeter of torches the gorillas had set around the camp. As he passed the surly, black-haired sentry, he was grateful the gorilla did nothing more than nod as he passed. He thought the sentry's name was Bovarius, and he chided himself for not knowing; he was, after all, the designated leader of the expedition, and Doctor Tullius had cautioned him that he needed to learn how to keep the gorillas in check. Orangutans were smarter—*he* was smarter—and he had to know them and know how to control them, using their ignorance as a lever, if necessary.

Even though Zaius did not actually expect to find infestations of feral human tribes in the awful wasteland, his suggestion had turned the disgruntled military escort into the most enthusiastic members of the expedition. Gorillas were so easily manipulated. He paused as he wondered if Doctor Tullius had manipulated his orangutan students just as well.

His thoughts were interrupted by a gentle voice from behind. "Zaius, what's troubling you? You are unable to sleep?"

"Karah." Zaius chuckled as he turned to face her. "You startled me."

"The Forbidden Zone is not a good place to get lost in a daydream." Karah's soft brown eyes glimmered in the torchlight.

"Is there another kind of dreaming I should be doing?"

Slipping her arm around his waist, Karah stepped close. "You will be an important ape someday, Zaius. You have no need for daydreams." Her lips curved in a provocative smile. "And I will always be with you to make sure your nights are pleasant."

He nuzzled the side of her face. "Always. But not yet. Once we have graduated the Academy, we will both have more say in our lives."

A distant, decidedly un-simian scream rent the desert night, sending a deep chill down their spines. He sniffed the air as the gorilla soldiers scrambled awake, ready to fight any monstrous attackers from the night. The chimpanzees stood together, frightened and muttering. But the scream did not recur, and eventually the apes settled back down to sleepless waiting for the dawn.

Zaius looked out into the mysterious darkness and whispered to Karah. "The Forbidden Zone is not as lifeless as it appears."

Bringing his scientific mind to bear, Zaius looked over the shoulder of the gorilla tracker who was examining the ground with Caetus. Although the sun was high and the loose dirt pristine, the giant three-toed prints were strikingly out of place, unlike any species Zaius had studied at the Academy.

"Ape tracks? Single file, stepping in the same place to hide their number?" The tracker's suggestion was obviously absurd. "That would put the opposable toes off to either side like this."

Caetus stood, brushed dust from his knees, and grimaced at the soldier, obviously disgusted by the assessment. "Bird. A large one, but obviously just a bird."

"But, sir…" The soldier followed Caetus back to the horses.

"Bird!" Caetus finished the discussion and re-mounted, turning his horse back toward the others.

Zaius watched them leave, then put his foot next to the ominous track, pushing into the red dirt. His footprint, while similar in size, sank less than half as deep. An enormous bird indeed. He could not forget the loud, chilling sound that had shattered the night.

"They are circling us at night," the gorilla soldier reported as he reined his mount into camp. "Many more tracks out there." The red dawn on the horizon backlit his dark form, glinting off his leather armor and rifle barrel.

Caetus nodded as the rest of the expedition muttered, uneasy after another tense night in camp, far from Ape City. "Whatever they are, the creatures must be afraid of the torches. Keeping their distance, hiding and watching. Many animals fear fire. You've seen how man runs from it. Their limited intelligence disappears completely when faced with fire."

"Or perhaps they are hunters circling prey," Zaius offered, "looking for weakness in the herd. Prey animals do not approach what they fear, Captain—and they do not avoid that which they do not fear. We should be cautious."

Turning past Zaius, Caetus announced to the rest of the expedition, "Tonight, when we set up camp, we will make a different kind of perimeter. We will leave an inviting hole for them to explore, and when they do, we will finally get a look at our giant birds!" He chuffed with laughter.

By applying a psychological analysis of the brusque gorilla, Zaius recognized the technique Caetus used to maintain control. In announcing his orders for all to hear, he ensured that no one could question them without risking public dissent, which would be sternly dealt with. It was not an invitation for open discussion, such as at the Academy. Zaius was in charge of the expedition, though, and he would have to counter the gorilla's dismissive behavior. He had to show his command here; to challenge a blustering, ignorant opponent would serve him well if he ever became a Board Member.

He was sure the other orangutans and chimpanzees would

back him up. He would publicly question the captain's decisions, which would make Caetus think twice before announcing them like this. Glancing to Karah for support, Zaius took a breath to speak out against Caetus' plan.

But the gorilla blurted out first, "If we catch one of the creatures in our nets, we can release it in the morning, follow it back to its nest. Then we will not have to live on dried fruit and canned water for the entire expedition!"

The cheer that went up among all the apes, even the chimpanzees and orangutans, kept Zaius quiet.

By midafternoon, the landscape of the Forbidden Zone changed into even more bizarre terrain. Among rounded hillocks cut by wandering washes and canyons, strange rock formations spotted the reddish tan desolation. Some of the tortured rocks were smooth to the touch, others razor-sharp. The formations reminded Zaius of discarded slag at the blacksmith's shop. But this was stone....

Running his hand over a smooth, gray protrusion speckled with large holes, Zaius wondered if, like metal, rock could be heated until it ran liquid, and then be molded. Perhaps only in the Forbidden Zone.

He sniffed, felt the dry, bitter burn in his nostrils. Even the air was different here. More than just hot, it was acrid. Zaius plodded on, pulling his horse by the reins.

"Over here!" At a nearby hillock on the edge of a deep arroyo, one of the chimpanzees was jumping and waving for attention. It was Markos, the secondary leader of the archeological expedition. "I found something, Zaius! Artifacts—with markings!"

Yanking his horse's reins, Zaius trotted over to the hillock and the rock formations, feeling a twinge of jealousy that he hadn't been the first to make a discovery. He came closer to

Markos to see a giant crescent-shaped rock formation, as if a wave of water had turned to stone.

The other two chimpanzees, Cassius and Aelia, pushed past Zaius as he gawked at the strange formation. Too excited to be irritated by their presumptiveness, Zaius tied his horse to an outcropping and followed them into the cave Markos had discovered.

Just above Zaius' head, a stone sign with the engraved word "TRUTH" was embedded into the rock wall. The anomalous word beckoned Zaius closer. The letters were so smooth, so evenly spaced. As he reached up to touch it, marveling that even the best craftsmen couldn't compare to the skill behind this one, perfect word, the chimpanzees excitedly worked at loose stone farther down the cliff. They yelped and jumped out of the way as rock crumbled down, sliding aside to reveal a second stone sign, this one bearing the word "KNOWLEDGE."

Karah came up to Zaius. "That is a portent if I have ever seen one! This expedition set out in search of truth and knowledge, but I never guessed that we would literally find them."

Caetus was unimpressed. "Just words on a wall left by some fool who didn't know better. They mean nothing more than words on paper or scratched in dirt."

"But much more permanent," Zaius said, still touching the engraved letters. "These could have been here for centuries."

The gorilla impatiently turned away from Zaius and the excavation site. "Fortunately, this canyon is ideal for setting a trap. We still haven't seen any sign of the human infestation. My soldiers will stay here for a day or two, until we catch one of those birds. Then we will be ready to hunt for humans again!" He trudged off through the loose sand as he spoke, leaving Zaius to catch the end of his words and allowing no room for a retort. Studying this, Zaius nodded to himself. That was another way Caetus made sure he always got the final word.

No matter. It was exactly what Zaius wanted anyway. Meanwhile, there were too many interesting things here to waste time quarrelling with a gorilla.

He hurried back to where the others were digging. The words had been revealed to be carved into bricks of a wall that extended belowground. Broken fragments of statues and the top of an exposed archway made it clear that an entire building was buried there in the desolation.

"What could possibly be inside a building called Truth and Knowledge?" Aelia mused as Zaius approached the line of apes digging at the bottom of the cliff. No one answered. She had asked the question many times already.

"Truth and knowledge, undoubtedly," Zaius said. "Maybe the Lawgiver himself placed this here for us, as a test."

"Or a reward," Karah said.

"I wish we had humans here to do the digging," Cassius complained as he shoveled.

"Yes, yes…" Neaus, working much more slowly than the other members of the team, agreed. "This type of work does not befit such as us. Maybe you should tell the gorillas to do it, Zaius. We are here to learn, not to dig."

Zaius knew that demanding such work from Caetus and his soldiers would backfire on him. The gorillas would never agree, and he would look weak. Zaius chose a different tactic. "And what better way to learn, than by doing?" He picked up a shovel and joined in, setting an example with his pace. "Every scoop of dirt could contain a delicate and mysterious artifact. We would have to watch over every shovel they raised—either humans or the gorillas. They are not scientists." In low voices, the chimpanzees and orangutans muttered with amusement at how he had lumped gorillas with humans.

Both would have been in the way.

Karah shrieked as the sand opened beneath her, sucking her down. In a heartbeat, she had been swallowed up, gone. Dirt and sand still slid into the hole where she had been.

Zaius lunged after her, falling onto his chest and looking down into the cavity, dangling his arm down. "Karah!"

Surprisingly, wonderfully, her voice echoed back up. "I'm all right. I think I found an entrance!"

The gorilla argued with Zaius' simple and obvious suggestion. "We need those ropes for our nets!" He placed his gloved hands on his hips, making no move to follow Zaius' order.

Zaius tried to sound like Doctor Tullius, firm and completely in command. "Caetus—"

"*Captain* Caetus!" the gorilla corrected.

Impatient, Zaius made the harmless concession. "*Captain* Caetus, the Defender of the Faith did not dispatch our expedition to hunt birds, no matter how large they may be. We were sent to make archeological discoveries. Right now, we have the opportunity, and the obligation, to investigate. We need the ropes so we can descend into the cavern and explore the ruins buried there." They had already pulled Karah back out, but she had talked about other passages down there, more artifacts, more mysteries.

Caetus waved his fists and turned in a circle, taking in the camp with the traps. "The nets are already in place! And it will be dark soon—we have to be ready for the creatures."

Zaius noted the sun low in the shimmering sky. With torches, they could explore the ruins underground, day or night, but it had been an exhausting day, particularly for Karah.

Sighing as though Caetus was a petulant child who had begged long enough, Zaius raised his voice and spoke so the entire camp would hear, using the gorilla's own technique.

"Very well, Captain. I will allow your soldiers to use the ropes until morning, but at first light you will take them down and make them available to the research team."

Caetus turned back and flashed a glare at Zaius, who walked away as he spoke, not allowing the gorilla a chance to retort. "I wish you luck in catching your bird."

The nervous whinny of a horse stirred Zaius from his uncomfortable sleep. His quiet room at the Academy was far different from the constant restless noises of camp. He rolled over, but the gruff, urgent voice of a gorilla woke him instantly. "Something is in the net!"

He heard a strange coughing noise, then the sounds of a struggle. As he emerged from his tent, he looked around in the darkness. Rousing apes rushed about the camp. Twin screams filled the night—one sounded like the chilling cry from two nights earlier, but the other scream reminded him of the terrified squeals of wild humans hunted down by gorilla soldiers.

This time, though, the scream belonged to an ape.

Zaius looked around in the darkness, the bright spots of flickering torches, tried to see what was happening. Gunshots cracked, and deep-voiced gorillas shouted. A moment of silence covered the surprised camp, then chaos reigned.

"By the Lawgiver..." Zaius hardly had time to regain his wits before the horses tore free from the makeshift corral and stampeded through the camp, fleeing the terrified screams and charging toward the excavation.

More simian cries of alarm rang out as Zaius dodged charging horses, sliding between dark forms and fending off muscular flanks. As the animals thundered past, leaving him bruised but intact, a yelp, cut short, told him that not everyone had been so fortunate.

He spotted the orange robes of a figure sprawled in the sand. He uprooted a torch and ran toward the figure. "Karah…" The name involuntarily escaped his lips as he saw dark blood staining the hair and clothing. He gently rolled the body over—Neaus, not Karah.

Vacant eyes stared up at the night sky. A last rattling breath was the only indication of life in the limp body.

"Over here!" Zaius shouted. "Neaus is injured!"

Only gunshots and angry shouts answered his plea. Torches bobbed in the night, running away from camp. Another scream pierced the darkness, this one fading terribly toward an end that seemed to never come.

Zaius hooked his hands under Neaus and began dragging the injured orangutan away, into the safer center of camp, but a heavy impact ripped the other scientist from his grasp. Stunned, Zaius stumbled back, fell to the ground, and looked up into a nightmare.

A hideous giant "bird," featherless and with a maw full of naked teeth, raked into the dying orangutan's abdomen with three-inch talons. Clawed arms that could never be mistaken for wings reached out and lifted Neaus by the head, as though to examine the face. Its long scaly tail twitched, and the creature opened its jaws to take a bite. With a snap of razor-sharp fangs, it bit off Neaus' face.

Zaius gasped, scrabbled backward as he fought to control his roiling stomach.

At the sound, the creature cocked its head sideways, birdlike, and eyed Zaius. A blue nictitating membrane flashed over its golden eye. Dropping the bloody body of Neaus, the giant lizard-bird coiled to pounce.

Gunshots roared, and red splotches blossomed on the creature's scaly hide, knocking it off-balance. Then Zaius was up on his feet again and running.

Soft sand slipped under his splayed feet as he left the

torchlight and bounded into darkness. Twice he resorted to running on all fours to keep from falling. Then the cliff face loomed, trapping him inside the little crescent valley within which the camp had been set up. His eyes still hadn't adjusted, and he could barely see among the shadows on top of shadows.

"Be careful!" Someone called from out of the darkness, a voice close to him. "Don't fall into the hole!" A horse screamed, and Zaius saw its shadowy shape vanish into the ground just in front of him, followed by a dull thump and sickening squeals of pain from the underground cavern.

The nearby voice grunted, "That's at least three horses and one ape."

"Markos?"

"Yes." He heard a snuffling sound. "Zaius?"

"Yes. Is anyone else here?"

"Me—Aelia," said another voice. "I think it was Cassius who fell in."

They fell into a tense hush as heavy footfalls approached, panting hard—someone running blindly in the dark. As his eyes adjusted, Zaius saw an ape running right toward the hole, a bright orange uniform, an orangutan—Karah! "Stop!" He sprang to catch her. Colliding, they tumbled into a heap as Zaius rolled them away from the dropoff. He knew the feel of Karah in his arms, and the familiar smell of her pressed against his face. "Thank the Lawgiver!"

She buried her face into his shoulder, snuffling and sobbing. "In the net—it wasn't a bird. A monster! It killed one of the gorillas, maybe two. And there were more bird-things… circling out there."

He held Karah as they heard more gunshots from the camp, and torches began moving toward them in a tight grouping. By the time Captain Caetus and four gorilla soldiers arrived, Karah, Aelia, Markos, and Zaius had found shovels from the excavation and stuck them in the soft ground to mark the perimeter of the pit.

"Scientists!" Caetus snorted when he saw what they had done. "Protecting your precious dirt at the expense of all else." The other gorillas laughed but their eyes watched the darkness beyond the torchlight.

Karah huffed. "You know very well that is not—"

Caetus angrily waved her off. "Would you rather I accused you of running away like cowards?"

Zaius stepped forward, squared his shoulders. "That's enough, Caetus."

"*Captain* Caetus!"

He ignored the gorilla's rage. "How many casualties?"

"Four of my soldiers, two horses, and one orangutan." Caetus skewered the scientist with his gaze. "So far."

Zaius watched the nervous eyes of the four remaining gorilla soldiers as they shifted around with torches in one hand and rifles in the other. "What were their names, Captain?"

"What?"

"Neaus was the orangutan who died. I saw the creature kill him. I request to know the names of your soldiers who died protecting us." Zaius kept his attention on the remaining gorillas.

Caetus made a low, respectful sound deep in his throat. "Acutus, Ulos, Mephitis, and Corax."

Zaius repeated the names slowly. "We honor them for their sacrifice in defending our vital expedition. Captain Caetus, please tell me the names of these remaining soldiers, so I might thank them in person."

Frowning, Caetus pointed the soldiers out, one by one. "Crispus, Bovarius, Verus, and Avilius."

Zaius bowed his head slightly to each gorilla in turn. "On behalf of the Academy, the Defender of the Faith, my fellow scientists"—he motioned to the apes behind him—"and myself, thank you all. Your bravery is beyond reproach."

Caetus growled and turned to face the darkness. "We must round up our horses and restore the camp."

Verus pointed into the night. "Captain!" Glowing eyes flickered and then vanished.

"Another!" Bovarius pointed to the other side.

"Will the creatures fear the torches enough for us to return to camp?" Zaius asked.

"No." Caetus aimed his rifle and fired at something Zaius couldn't see.

"Perhaps we should spread the torches out, create a larger perimeter of light we can defend?"

"No. They attack individuals too far away from the group. The only safety is in numbers." Caetus fired again. "And we don't have many numbers."

The darkness was closing in. The gorilla soldiers formed an outward-facing protective circle.

"Our torches won't last much longer. We have to do something." Karah squeezed Zaius' arm. "Before it's too late."

The sounds of the squealing injured horse in the cavern below had them on edge as much as the monsters in the dark. "Captain Caetus," Zaius called to the gorilla's back. The captain didn't answer. His bravado had faded as their ammunition ran low, and after he ordered his soldiers not to fire unless attacked, he hadn't spoken a word.

Zaius raised his voice so all could hear him. "We need to go down into the hole. Our torches won't last until daylight. The cavern will offer some protection."

The end of the gorilla's rifle barrel continuously swept back and forth at the darkness, but Caetus didn't respond.

Turning to the remaining members of his expedition, Zaius tried to sound confident. "We lost the ropes back at the camp, but if we go one at a time and carefully slide down, we should be all right."

"I'll go first," Karah volunteered. "I've done it before. I know what to expect."

"Be careful. You might land on the horse." *Or Cassius*, Zaius thought.

"We cannot all go down there." The odd, hushed tone of Caetus' voice disturbed Zaius. He had never heard a gorilla speak so quietly. "If we all go down, who will help us back up? And if we divide our numbers, those things will attack."

Zaius lowered his voice and moved closer to Caetus. "And if we stay here? The torches won't last much longer. If we go down, we can save them, use one at a time. We can defend the entrance until the sun comes up."

The captain still hadn't turned from facing the ominous darkness beyond the dwindling torch perimeter. "What if they don't leave with daylight?"

"Then we will have gained time, regardless. Maybe down in the cavern we'll find relics from the old civilization with which we can defend ourselves. Or maybe just clubs." He huffed a breath, hoping to sound brave. "We won't die without fighting."

Caetus grunted, conceding the point. "Verus, you go down first. Take a torch. Slide on your backside, feet first. Let's hope it is not even worse down there."

With a last fading cry, the fallen horse finally fell silent.

The weight of the rifle in Zaius' hands gave him no comfort as he stood at the edge of the pit. He had fired weapons before, but did not like them. They were a brutish, gorilla sort of weapon. He would rather know more about the enemy in the dark, so he could plan, prepare, and negate the danger. *You are smarter than they are*, Doctor Tullius had said. Was that true of the bird-things, too?

"Your turn, Zaius." Caetus didn't dare look away from the darkness. "Get down into the cavern." The glint of predatory eyes in the night had increased. They moved closer, growing bolder as the scientists slipped into the pit below, leaving a smaller and smaller group of defenders above.

"No—there are too few of us left up here. We should all go, together, at the same time," Zaius countered. "Or those creatures will attack the last ones." Other than Zaius and Captain Caetus, only Bovarius and Avilius remained. They had four torches left and four rifles, and very little ammunition. "With the extra light below, we should be able to see well enough to avoid each other as we fall."

Golden eyes flashed in the night, and Caetus tracked them with his rifle. The eyes backed off, as if they understood the weapons.

Loose rocks falling from the cliff face above made Zaius look up in alarm. "They are up there, too. Do you think they are intelligent enough—?"

A large rock thumped into the dirt next to Zaius, just missing him. Bovarius and Avilius jumped, whirling to face whatever might be attacking them from above. Behind them, taking advantage of the distraction, one of the sleek shadows darted in to strike. Caetus roared and turned, firing his rifle at it, which opened his flank to yet another attack.

Though he could barely aim with shaking hands, Zaius shot the lizard that came in behind Caetus. In the light from the muzzle flash, Zaius saw it change direction and come for him. He fired his weapon again, missed, then something slammed into him. He cried out as claws ripped through his clothing, tore at his skin, and he tumbled backward, flailing.

Then he was falling.

He had one glimpse of the creature thrashing in the air above him, then he landed hard on the body of the horse. He felt the animal's ribcage snap beneath him.

The lizard slammed to the cavern floor close by, landing on its side. It writhed its head from side to side, snapping toothy jaws. Zaius tried to cry out, but with the wind knocked out of him, he couldn't make a sound. From above, three gorillas struggling with another lizard creature toppled down to land on top of him.

Zaius awoke to warm sunlight on his face, blindingly bright. He blinked away the glare and sat up. A jagged sharp pain in his side made him gasp, and he tenderly touched his ribs. Broken, at least two. His cinnamon hair was matted with dried blood, and multiple gashes stung. Zaius found himself still on top of the dead horse. A monstrous lizard creature lay dead next to him, its skull shattered.

In the shaft of sunlight streaming in from above, he could see that the cavern was indeed a building's interior. More blood covered the floor. As he sat up, struggling to focus his vision, Zaius spotted Avilius and Bovarius, both dead, horribly shredded by claws and teeth. Footprints and a blood trail wandered off into the gloom through piles of debris. Some of the prints belonged to apes. Others were bird-like.

Zaius grunted in pain as he attempted to stand. His knee would not bear weight. He found a discarded rifle and used it as a crutch so he could struggle to his feet.

"Karah! Caetus!" His voice echoed back, without any other response. The gun gave him little hope. None of the gorillas would have left a weapon behind on purpose. Maybe there were no bullets left. "Hello? Anyone?"

He realized his voice might attract one of the reptilian predators.

A harsh whisper from the darkness sent a chill down his spine. "Some still live."

Zaius whirled but saw nothing. "Who's there?"

"They thought you dead, but your heat signature did not fade." Sharp consonants clicked as the whisperer spoke. "I would have offered help, but they are armed and frightened. I dare not approach."

The voice did not sound like that of an ape. "You do not intend to use the weapon against me? Will you put it aside?"

"At this moment, it is holding me upright," Zaius answered, fighting back the pain from his broken ribs. He didn't think he could sound intimidating. "As to whether I use it against you, that depends on how much of a threat you pose."

A large, hulking figure approached the edge of the shadows, still remaining unseen. It was definitely not an ape.

Zaius caught his breath, forced himself not to show any reaction. He tried to make his voice strong. "Do you know where my companions are? Can you take me to them?"

The figure turned its head, as if to consider. In the murk, he could see that the elongated shape was similar to that of the dead lizard monster. Definitely not an ape! The creature was hairless and covered with leathery skin. Although the head was shaped like the attackers from above, it did not appear to have teeth.

"Can you walk?" it asked. "I fear you will not be able to outrun the lacerators." The figure gestured toward the dead creature on the cavern floor. "An old term used for the ornithischians. Derived from the taxonomic family Lacertilia. The humor, I am afraid, was lost on me. The creatures are not actually related to Lacertilia at all."

Zaius frowned at words he did not recognize. "You are intelligent. A... scientist?" Could this creature be part of the civilization Zaius had come to investigate?

"I am a seeker of Truth and Knowledge." The creature paused. "Are you in more pain? I see distress upon your features."

"Not pain." Zaius shook his head. "Confusion."

The figure shuffled forward, barely into the light. Its face was smooth, not quite reptilian. As it spoke, Zaius saw nictitating membranes flash over its golden eyes.

"If you can walk, it would behoove us to move quickly. Two lacerators remain above and they are desperate to kill— so desperate, they even brave the bright sun above. I cannot imagine how they will react when they find their kin dead."

Since Zaius had never imagined any sort of creature other than an ape being capable of speech, he found the talking lizard creature a frightening, even surreal experience. The long-faced being walked upright like an ape but moved with the fluidity of a snake, leading Zaius deeper into the ruins and away from the shaft of sunlight. When it opened its jaws and spoke, the experience was as bizarre as if a feral human had suddenly uttered words!

"I apologize for my incessant nattering," the creature said. "I have not spoken to anyone for a very long time. I surmise, by the way you look at me, you have never seen my kind before." It glanced over its shoulder at Zaius with a quick, twitchy movement full of deadly efficiency.

"I have never *heard* of your kind. Apes rarely venture into the Forbidden Zone." Zaius limped along, resting his weight on the useless rifle, but it was too short. The creature skirted debris piles that appeared to be bones from an unimaginably enormous beast. Zaius wished he could examine them as a scientist, but at least he realized that one of the rib bones would serve as a far more satisfactory walking stick. He pulled the long bone from the collapsed skeleton, tested it by rapping it on the stone floor, and hobbled on, feeling the sharp-glass pain of his broken ribs with each step.

"And there are few of us left," the creature said. "Only

five, that I know of." It turned its head. "I am called Parth. Another jest I did not understand. Somehow related to the experiments I was used for. Parthenogenesis—the ability to reproduce asexually. I was fortunate. Some of my brethren were studied for regeneration." Parth's smooth stride faltered at the thought. "Forced propagation seems a smaller agony than enduring repeated amputations for the sake of science. My people were created, abandoned, and left with a destroyed world."

Zaius wrinkled his nose in skepticism and curiosity. "Created? Who created you?" He realized the Defender of the Faith would very much want to speak with this creature.

Parth's nictitating membranes slid over its eyes, then wiped back. "The scientists, of course. From the ancient times. They made us intelligent, and they considered it humane to explain what they were going to do to their specimens." Air huffed through the creature's narrow nostrils. "Eventually, I was one of a dozen studied to determine if brumation could be extended into suspended animation, tests that were under way as part of a long-term space program. But they never sent any of my siblings off into space. Apparently, something went wrong, and my species never went farther than here... deep underground." With clawed hands, Parth gestured to the buried building around them.

"I knew of the uprising of your kind, long ago, but when my siblings and I finally awakened after centuries of sleep, we found the radioactive devastation aboveground. We thought the world had ended, and we were baffled. What caused all the destruction?" The sauroid held unnaturally still while waiting for an answer.

Zaius stepped carefully as he gathered his thoughts. The uprising of his kind? What *caused* the destruction? "The Forbidden Zone has been deadly to simiankind for twelve hundred years."

"Twelve hundred years?" Parth remained motionless. "Simiankind? What about mankind? Are the humans all dead?"

"Of course not. They breed wild in the forests. We have to chase them out of our crop fields like vermin. Were they failed experiments from your creators, too?"

Parth cocked its head curiously before moving on. It seemed to find the answer amusing. They passed podiums and darkened display cases spaced along the wall, all of which reminded Zaius of the cultural museum in Ape City. "What is this place? What did the ancient race use it for?"

"It is the American Museum of Natural History."

Zaius didn't know the meaning of "American," but now he understood the words "Truth" and "Knowledge" engraved in the stone slabs outside the ruins. This was a museum! He could not have hoped to discover a better treasure trove for his expedition. As they moved along at a slow pace, with Zaius leaning heavily on his rib-bone cane, he tried to see some of the exhibits, but the deep gloom was oppressive.

Although Parth darted ahead, Zaius stumbled on loose rubble on the floor, which he didn't see. He gasped in pain, reeled, tried to keep from falling over. The creature returned to him. "My apologies. I forgot that your kind cannot see very well in the dark. It has been a long time since I walked with another. Wait here."

Parth skittered off into the gloom, and Zaius was left alone with his thoughts and fears. He wondered where the other apes had gone, how many others had survived, if Karah was all right. And he wondered about the strange being. Parth said that he and his kind had been experimented upon. Had apes once known these creatures? Tested and probed them, as was done with humans today?

From the darkness at the far end of the room, he heard repeated clicking sounds before a startlingly bright beam of light pierced the room. "Finally, one that works." Parth returned, light in hand. "So many things no longer function. The deterioration rate does not seem to be consistent. I have had difficulty estimating the passage of time." The creature handed the marvelous cold light to Zaius. "Twelve hundred years?"

In wonder, Zaius turned the small metal cylinder in his palm. He aimed the focused beam at the creature and got an even clearer look at it. Then distant thumping caught their attention. Even Parth seemed alarmed. "I fear the lacerators have found a way down. We must hurry."

Zaius panicked, fumbling with the cylinder, but could not understand the mechanism enough to turn off the light. Parth put a clawed hand over Zaius' hairy one. "Leave the light on. Darkness is a disadvantage only to you. The illumination will help guide you." The creature moved closer to his side and helped support his weight. "It would be wise for us to hurry." Parth's naked body was cool and smooth, with sinewy muscles under the loose skin.

The beam of light bobbed drunkenly ahead, illuminating many fascinating but confusing things. Parth led them to a set of stairs, which created an agonizing obstacle for Zaius with his broken ribs, but they worked their way slowly down, one step at a time, landing after landing. Above and behind, they heard infrequent thumping sounds that must have been the lacerators. Parth seemed to be growing more uneasy.

"Where are my companions? You said you would take me there."

"Not far. Some of them are injured."

Finally, they emerged into a large room filled with humming machinery and blinking control panels. "I awoke here ten years ago," Parth said. "Four of my siblings were already dead, due to malfunctions in the apparatus. Five remain in hibernation." The creature pointed to a row of oblong containers, some throbbing with a faint glow, while others were in obvious disrepair. "I have been monitoring them. Do you understand this type of equipment? You are an ape scientist—can you help me revive them?"

Zaius ran his fingers over the smooth surfaces, amazed and intimidated. The craftsmanship was well past anything he would have ever imagined possible. "This is beyond my comprehension."

Parth continued to chatter, as though desperate for any kind of conversation. "I hope to learn how to awaken them one day." He flinched at another thump that came from the stairwell several floors above. "We must hurry if we are to reach your companions before the lacerators do." The reptilian creature glided among the tables, then hesitated before it picked up two metal canisters from a rack. It pointed to a far door. "That way."

Zaius led, trying to hurry with painstaking steps, his light beam sparkling off metal surfaces. Passing through a narrow hallway, they emerged into a much larger chamber that echoed with shadows. He swung the beam of light, stopping in astonishment when the illumination revealed a giant reptilian monster, its jaws filled with teeth as long as his arm, its upraised arms disproportionately small on its body. It towered high over Zaius, twice the size of the other lacerators—this one could swallow an ape whole!

Zaius dropped the light and reeled back, colliding with Parth, then falling to the floor in an explosion of pain from his broken ribs.

Parth caught him, with a loud urgent whisper close to his head. "Stop—it is not alive! Just a skeleton, for display."

The stark shadows and bright spots of illumination from the rolling light cylinder on the floor revealed that the giant reptile was indeed just a skeleton, preserved and mounted. Zaius panted, trying to understand what he saw. "This is a museum," he said to himself, comprehending. "A skeleton, mounted for study. But, by the Lawgiver, what a monster!"

Retrieving the dropped light cylinder, Zaius pointed it upward to reveal the skull and spine overhead, the enormous legs, the long tail. The huge reptilian skeleton was mounted on a platform, and at its side he found another startling discovery—a skeleton placed for scale comparison. A human skeleton.

Why place a comparison skeleton of a man instead of an ape?

Parth hung back in the shadows as Zaius hobbled forward, following the sounds of whispered ape voices. His beam of light settled on figures huddled at the end of the hallway. He recognized dark gorillas, the green jumpers of the chimpanzees, the orange of an orangutan uniform. "Karah? Is that you?"

Her voice was unmistakable. "Zaius!"

He spotted the gorilla holding a rifle at the ready. "Verus, hold your fire. I have someone with me. A helper."

"Who?" Captain Caetus demanded as he stalked into view from the shadows, pointing a rifle at Zaius. "Everyone else is dead!"

Unable to contain his excitement, Markos stepped out from behind Caetus. "Zaius, we made the most incredible discovery! This place is a museum. Man is not an unevolved ape! Humans—"

"Shut up!" Caetus backhanded the chimpanzee and sent him sprawling. Turning back, he raised his rifle higher. "Who is with you?"

Stunned by the gorilla's behavior, Zaius did not immediately respond, but the sauroid creature moved forward, revealing itself. "I am Parth," it said in its whispery voice.

"You are one of them!" Caetus fired his rifle, and the muzzle flash blinded Zaius. Beside him, Parth fell to the floor with a grunting wheeze of pain.

"Caetus!" Zaius lurched in front of the sauroid, placing himself in the line of fire. "Lower your weapon!"

The gorilla aimed the rifle at Zaius instead. "I do not take orders from you!"

"Yes, you do. By order of the Academy!"

"Bah! Lies—all of it!" Caetus stomped his feet. "Is your great orangutan Lawgiver even real? No! All lies to keep power for yourselves, to keep gorillas under your control. No more. I am in charge now, and I have had enough of you, Zaius!"

He swung the rifle, bringing it up to fire, but Karah lunged forward, colliding into Caetus as the gun went off. The bullet missed, and the enraged gorilla punched her in the throat, dropping her on the spot. He turned down at her, infuriated, and without a moment's hesitation he pointed the rifle and shot Karah in the chest.

With a howl of horror, Zaius ignored the pain in his ribs and lunged forward, but something grabbed his ankle and tripped him. He sprawled with a grunt of agony, and his light skittered across the floor and went out, plunging the corridor into darkness. More gunfire rang out, bursts of muzzle flares as the gorillas simply fired at anything that moved.

Explosions and screaming filled the hallway—and then more things were moving, creatures that came through the shadows from behind them in the museum.

Zaius sprawled, moaning with pain as well as grief from witnessing Karah's murder, and heard Parth's rattling voice weakly in his ear. "The lacerators are upon us. Help me." He was still alive, but gravely wounded from the rifle shot. He pressed something hard and cold into Zaius' hand—one of the metal canisters he had taken from the laboratory. "Twist the valve on top. When I ignite it, throw it away from you, back toward the lacerators. The heat will blind them."

Zaius found the handle and turned it. The cylinder hissed, releasing a foul stench. Parth gasped. "Be ready. Here is the flame."

A ball of fire erupted in Zaius' hand, singeing the hair on his face. He flailed, nearly dropping the cylinder, but the sauroid creature summoned a shout. "Throw it!"

Unable to rise, Zaius lobbed the flaming cylinder where he thought the lacerators were. The fireball illuminated the hall, revealing two monsters throwing themselves on the remaining apes.

Caetus fired as the first lacerator tore into Markos, ripping open the green jumper. The second lacerator clamped jaws down on Verus' rifle, then flung it away from the gorilla. Two more shots hit the clawed beast that attacked the screaming chimpanzee. Karah desperately crawled toward Zaius, her face bloody in the firelight.

Parth forced a second cylinder to Zaius. "Throw this one at the lacerator." Slick with blood, it had flame already coming out of a three-inch nozzle.

Zaius threw, and the canister hit the lacerator in the side as it finished killing Markos. The painful flame distracted the monster long enough for Caetus to shoot it again. As the lacerator fell, the second creature leapt over its body and landed on Caetus, snapping the rifle in two. Ignoring the gorilla's mighty punches, the lacerator sliced him to ribbons with its talons.

"Shoot at the fire…" Parth's voice was weak and hard for Zaius to hear over the simian screams. With a death rattle deep in its throat, the sauroid pushed Zaius' rifle to him. "Shoot at the fire."

Lifting the weapon, Zaius aimed at the flaming canister near the taloned feet of the lacerator and pulled the trigger.

The bullet spanged off the floor and missed. The lacerator swung its bright gaze at Zaius, snapped its jaws, then began to move. Zaius fired again at the hissing canister.

The explosion was deafening.

After the fires had burned out, Zaius had cinched bindings around his ribs, keeping the pain down to a tolerable level. He cradled Karah's body and squeezed her hand, but she did not twitch. Caetus had killed her, and then the lacerators had slain the rest.

But Zaius had work to do, even if the rest of the expedition was dead. After long and tedious dragging, he lay Parth's body in the empty container next to its preserved siblings in their suspended animation chambers. When the other mutant creatures woke, if they ever did, they would know nothing of the time Parth had spent watching over them, or the sacrifice Parth had made for an ape it did not know.

Watching the blinking lights on the control apparatus, Zaius considered destroying the machines, but he knew their world, their destiny, was not his, nor was it his to command. He left them sleeping.

As Zaius limped into the bright desert sun and squinted at the desolate landscape of the Forbidden Zone, the words of the Lawgiver haunted him. "*For he will make a desert of his home and yours...*" What they had found in the museum was much too dangerous to become widely known.

Finally, Zaius understood why the Defender of the Faith was quick to watch over relics of the past and shun dangerous technology. If the Lawgiver's Word were brought into question, the gorillas—and perhaps all of ape society— could no longer be kept under control. Zaius vowed not to forget the sacrifices of his expedition in the name of Truth and Knowledge. But not every ape deserved Truth and Knowledge. Not everyone could handle it.

The landscape blurred in front of him like a mirage, but it was no illusion, no radiation shimmer, merely a film of tears as Zaius imagined Karah encouraging him on.

He spat the acrid dust of the Forbidden Zone out of his mouth. Leaning on the rib-bone cane, he took the first step of his long walk home.

General Urko, of the Saturday-morning animated
series *Return to the Planet of the Apes*, steps forward in
Drew Gaska's "The Unknown Ape," opening up
a Pandora's box of multiple universes and dire
portent for their inhabitants...

THE UNKNOWN APE

by

ANDREW E.C. GASKA

General Urko barked.

"Sergeant, I want that weapon ready to launch *now*!"

He and his commando force were in an ancient cathedral, miles beneath the surface of the Forbidden Zone. The general's archeologist had surmised that some cataclysm in the distant past had dropped the former metropolis, part of the remnants of a vast city, into a fissure. It had then been buried by thousands of years of desert sand and storms.

Zako gave the go-sign to his troops, and the work began. Thrown lines snaked over the cathedral's buttresses and through its latticework. Seconds later, gorillas clad in green oxhide leapt from gargoyle perches atop sturdy marble columns. Their uniforms stood in stark contrast to the general's pale blue and orange leathers.

Pulling the ropes with them, Urko's gorillas descended gracefully, spinning down the lines in a sort of simian aerial ballet. As they fell, the line and tackle pulled, raising the prone cylindrical device attached to the other end of the cordage. Slowly at first and then gaining momentum, the metallic beast's cone-shaped head began to ascend.

It was a weapon of yesterday. Its appearance reminded Urko of a brass Rea Voom 88 hunting rifle cartridge with small winglets on either side.

This missile would be far deadlier than any bullet, Urko enthused. *Far deadlier than any aeroplane, even. This weapon will be the means of my revenge!*

As the ape soldiers rappelled to the floor, the massive rocket lifted into its firing position. Its worn hull groaned in protest as the missile stood up. After millennia of slumber, it rose like a phoenix, shaking ash and debris from its tarnished shell. Upright now, its base cradled the projectile in its launch apparatus. It was an angry and omniscient god of destruction.

And it was in Urko's hands.

Urko's revenge plan had been simple—invade the subterranean home of the mutant Underdwellers and locate the secret weapon hidden there: a flying bomb capable of destroying an entire city.

His gorilla scouts had found it down a tunnel that the Underdwellers had sealed up centuries before, in a long-abandoned house of worship. It lay down the aisle between rows of gothic pews—dirty, dented, and scarred from eons of abuse. A relic of a bygone age, it had been entombed in the same cathedral that was once its house of worship.

Discarded and forgotten.

Until, that is, a loyal archeologist had found proof of its existence in the Forbidden Zone.

Until Urko had learned it was real.

The general's lead engineer, Doctor Inzari, had pored over the unearthed technical tomes on the matter, and had told Urko what needed to be done:

Elevate the weapon to its firing position on the pad recessed behind the altar. The controls would then activate and rise up from it. Set the range of the humanoids' city, and obliterate them for good.

As the missile's full weight came to rest on its pad, it triggered ancient machinery that churned and stalled and churned again before finally cycling to life. Just as Inzari had said, the altar split in two and slid apart. A control panel emerged from the space beneath it, clicking into place and coming to rest right beside Urko. He could hear the distant hum of turbines as ancient electrical pathways rerouted themselves to summon power to the controls. Kicking aside the body of an unlucky Underdweller, Urko stepped up to the console. The face of the panel was just as described. He had memorized the important switches. He quickly found the keypad used to input target coordinates, as well as a red firing cylinder with a safety shield over it. Depressing it would launch the missile.

Urko's luck was changing.

He had been disgraced by the council, over a war started with a less technologically inclined ape colony. Exiled, the rogue general and his loyal gorillas had since waged a guerilla war against both sides. They raided enemy settlements and then melted into the night. Now, his tactics would change.

Now, he had the weapon.

With a whirl and a click, the lights on the control panel hummed and stuttered to life. Glancing over his shoulder, Urko made certain his troops had barricaded the cathedral's massive doors. No one would be able to stop him now.

"Maps! Where are my maps?" Urko shouted. He needed the exact coordinates of the humanoid enclave.

In a rush to obey his orders, two of his soldiers collided. Normally, Urko would be furious, calling them idiots and demanding their heads for their incompetence. Instead, the general bore his teeth. In another gorilla, it might have seemed like a demonstration of power. For Urko, it was the closest thing to a smile of which he was capable.

"Now, we'll see what the council has to say with *this* power at my fingertips." Urko slammed his fist down on the edge of the control panel, hard. The lights flickered.

"Death to the humanoids! Death to Zaius!"

His mantra summoned an unearthly response. The wind squealed in defiance. Vertigo overtook him as the cathedral skewed and darkened around the edges of his vision. Something in the air was coalescing.

An ape-skulled wraith took shape before him, as tall as the bomb itself. Its eyes were swirling embers in the voids of its pitch eye sockets. No sooner than the thing had appeared, it spoke. *"You desecrate this holy chamber!"* the apparition howled. Its voice came from everywhere, yet nowhere, all at once.

"Return," it shrieked inside his skull. *"Return to the surface now, or face the Lawgiver's wrath!"*

As his troops fled, Urko grabbed one of them—Private Mungwort—by the collar. "Coward! Fool! Don't run from it!" Urko ripped the soldier's automatic rifle from his hands, throwing the dimwitted ape to the ground.

"Shoot it!" Urko slid back the rifle's bolt, releasing its safety. "Kill it!" He emptied his entire clip into the phantom. And with that, it was gone.

An illusion? Urko pondered. *Created by the minds of the Underdwellers, no doubt.*

As the specter had never truly been there, however, the general had instead fired on what was *behind it*.

The enormous weapon once again towered before him, but now it was riddled with bullet holes. Jets of noxious steam vented from the wounded missile, scalding the gorillas nearest to it. The burst cleaned the soot and debris from the device's left wing, exposing two archaic symbols, the meaning of which Urko could only guess:

AΩ

For the moment, he did not even care. The venting steam seemed to have no end. The gorilla general adjusted his bulbous orange war helm, a gesture intended as much to maintain a dignified appearance as it was a thinly disguised face-palm.

"Uh-oh," Urko said.

The colossal trajectile was damaged and, from his understanding, exposing him and his men to high doses of lethal radiation. Urko needed to get it in the air fast—not only to accomplish his goal of wiping the humanoids off the planet, but to save himself from his own error as well. The punctured missile continued to spew steam. Distressed, the general bellowed, "Where are my maps?!"

"Here, sir!" Sergeant Zako had rushed to his general's side, scrolls in hand.

Finally—an ape who follows orders. When this is said and done, Urko reflected, *I'll let Zako live.* So many of the other officers, however, had to go. *Traitors, all of them!*

Urko spread the appropriate map on the control panel in front of him. With agency, he began punching in the coordinates of the humanoids' Hidden Valley.

He only got one axis code entered. Then, there was chaos.

An explosion burst through the barricaded entrance. The doors shredded and splintered off their hinges. Wooden shards perforated the gorilla commandos, impaling those nearest to the foyer with ragged timber stakes.

Urko's ears were ringing. Dazed from the concussion blast, the gorilla clumsily concealed himself behind the split altar. The air was thick with chalk dust and steam. Urko bit back the urge to cough.

Emerging from the smoke and debris of the cathedral's foyer was a single ape—a chimpanzee. A rifle slung on his back, the chimp was wielding some kind of portable rocket cannon. He quickly discarded the used weapon, beckoning to some unknown force in his wake.

"Now," the chimp roared, "fight like apes!"

Emerging from the smoke behind him was a troop unlike any Urko could have imagined.

Chimps. Orangutans. Even treacherous gorillas, and—

*—human*oids?

A humanoid and ape hybrid army—working together?
Urko boiled. *Blasphemy!*

The chimpanzee's followers swarmed the cathedral, firing indiscriminately at General Urko's stunned forces. Using the temple's pews for cover, Zako quickly organized his surviving commandos into flanking teams. While the hybrid army may have made headway inside, most of them were pinned down, just as many of the gorillas were. From his protected position behind the cathedral's stony altar, Urko sized up his enemy. The chimpanzee flowed through the disheveled temple, deftly weaving in and out of machine gun fire. The other apes in the charge followed the chimp with a fever, almost fanatically devoted to this new leader. There were other commanders as well. Most were humanoid—and leading apes into battle!

The dark-skinned male humanoid in the blood-red shirt was among the charge. Urko was certain he had been the partner of the one Doctor Zira had named "Blue Eyes." There were at least three other intelligent beasts as well—one young and dark-skinned, the other older, fair-skinned, and blonde. The blonde man wore modern clothes like his compatriots, but with a primitive oxhide vest over them.

The third was bearded and bushy-haired with a tanned hide, and dressed in typical humanoid loincloth and rags. Despite his primitive appearance, that one commanded particular attention. He was older than the others, wiser-looking, but with a wild fire in his eyes. A barbarian wielding an automatic weapon was a frightful image, Urko noted. He would have to keep his eye on *that* beast.

The three of them were unrecognizable to him.

The filthy animals all look alike!

Among the ape leaders was Doctor Zaius himself, shielded by a mixed force of armed chimpanzees and gorillas. The duplicitous Cornelius and an unknown squat orangutan, carrying an automatic weapon slung on his back, accompanied the doctor.

Perfect, Urko schemed. *Most of the thorns in my side, gathered in one place.*

All he had to do was kill them, then launch the weapon on the humanoids' valley. New Ape City—and all other ape colonies—would then be his.

Urko watched them all, looking for a weakness to exploit. The humans held their own. The chimpanzee warrior broke from the group, making his way up a forgotten stairwell and toward an organist's balcony. Exposed from Urko's position, the chimp erroneously thought he was safe. The general grasped a discarded rifle lying nearby. In hand, he checked its chamber, finding but one round within.

That's all I'll need, Urko grinned.

Bringing the rifle up to his shoulder, he steadied his arm and focused through its sight.

Ape or not, a headshot would be best. Clean and efficient.

Lining up the chimpanzee, Urko gasped. Now, he recognized the ape. The contours of his face, the length of his hair, the build of his limber body. Even his piercing eyes.

Especially the eyes.

Yes, Urko had seen this chimpanzee's visage before, adorning countless statues and priceless classical paintings throughout the city. He had even been to the ape's tomb several times.

"By the Lawgiver," Urko whispered to no one. "It's the Unknown Ape!"

He had heard hushed rumors of the sightings, but had dismissed them as ghost stories. Nonsense, he'd thought. Or was it? It was as the Simian Book of Prophecy had foretold. The greatest ape of them all had returned.

The Unknown Ape. And he is my enemy!

Urko got busy making fermented ruta juice out of sour rutaberries. The appearance of this mysterious chimpanzee leader would not hinder him, no. Instead, all of apekind would see what a virulent warrior he was.

I will go down in history as the gorilla who bested the Unknown Ape!

If the chimpanzee was merely a charlatan, no one need know the truth. One way or another, that chimp's death would usher in glory for Urko.

Statues and paintings of me, he fantasized, *adorning all of Ape City!*

With renewed vigor, the gorilla general steadied his rifle once more. *Ape shall never kill ape,* he reflected. *But the Unknown Ape died almost twenty centuries ago. You can't kill what is already dead!*

As he focused on the kill, his nostrils were filled with something other than dust and stale steam. Pungent. Bitter. Familiar.

Ignoring it, he shook his head and lined up the Unknown Ape in his sights. As the smell grew in intensity, his intuition caught up with him.

Wait, Urko's eyes opened wide. *Where is the loin-clothed human?*

The butt of the rifle smashed his face. Urko's head slammed into the altar, chipping the pitted stone.

The bearded humanoid stood over him, bare-chested and barbaric. Worse than that, it spoke: "This is for Bill, you sadist." The humanoid kicked him hard, its bare foot striking the general across the temple.

As his vision blurred, Urko lamented. *Should have trusted my nose...*

The void took him.

Ron Brent had taken out Urko.

An astronaut from the year 2109, Colonel Ronald Roland Brent was a descendant of astronaut John Brent. Colonel

Brent's ship had crashed in the Forbidden Zone two decades before the *Venturer* and her crew—Bill Hudson, Judy Franklin, and Jeff Allen—had arrived. It wasn't until the three had found him living as a hermit that he'd realized he was in Earth's future, and that apes had taken over the planet. Part of a human community again, Ron had adopted a father-figure role to a female primitive humanoid, naming her Nova. He had become good friends with Bill—the human whom the apes used to call "Blue Eyes." When Bill had been lost in their fight against Urko, Ron swore vengeance for his friend. Standing over the broken and bloodied gorilla general, Brent finally felt a modicum of satisfaction.

Nearby, Jeff had wounded Zako. Like a house of cards, the rest of the gorilla force capitulated.

Scanning the crowd, the Unknown Ape was relieved to see Cornelius and Virgil safe in the care of Bruce MacDonald. The battle won, the Unknown Ape's self-styled Unknown Army cheered.

Their celebration was a bit premature.

At the cathedral's heart, the weapon still stood tall, still vented noxious gases, and was still primed for launch. As the last gorillas were rounded up, the Unknown Ape prodded his human allies. "Ah, we still have a crisis, here. Where exactly are the Underdwellers?"

His astronaut friend Alan stole a look out the charred doorway. Frowning, he shook his head. Jeff touched his temple, then spoke up: "Judy and Krador are on their way! Krador is sending a deactivation code to us through thought transmission now. It *should* shut the missile down."

A series of large red numbers flashed through the minds of everyone present. Possessing telepathic powers, the Underdweller leader Krador had forced the sequence into their minds. Shaking off the thought transmission, the Unknown Ape called for his science advisors.

"Gentle-apes, I, ah, suggest we do something about this weapon," he motioned to the ominous device, "before it does something about *us*. Agreed?"

The orangutans Virgil and Doctor Zaius rushed to the console, followed closely by the chimpanzee Cornelius.

As the Unknown Ape watched Cornelius make his way through the rubble, MacDonald circumnavigated the missile itself—stopping when he saw the letters on its starboard wing.

Doctor Zaius punched in the weapon's deactivation sequence. The numbers had no effect. "The console may have suffered corrosion damage over time," he offered.

"If we cannot deactivate it by code," Virgil postulated, "we may have to open the warhead and manually remove its core."

Everyone looked up at the venting projectile.

It was a bold and dangerous suggestion. If not handled with the utmost precision, the bomb would activate. At the least, it would flood everyone in the cathedral with a large enough dose of radiation to kill them within a few short weeks. At the most, it could detonate right in front of them.

Joining the orangutans, Cornelius produced a knife-edged pry bar from his tool bag. "Before we go that far," the chimpanzee archeologist suggested, "perhaps we should be sure that all the contacts are making the appropriate connections." Wedging the bar between a metal and plastic seam, Cornelius popped the console's cover off, exposing the circuit boards within.

Brent slung his automatic rifle and went to help the apes make sense of the circuit boards.

Perched above, the Unknown Ape watched Cornelius work with Zaius and Virgil. Distracted by the scientists' attempts to disarm the atom bomb, neither the Unknown Ape nor Brent noticed that Urko had come to.

An obscene cry resounded off the cathedral's walls.

A rabid Urko threw himself at Brent, pummeling him to the floor. Brent struggled to fend off the insane ape, but the gorilla's strength was too great. The savage clamped his jaws down—hard. Steely fangs sank deep into the astronaut's shoulder and neck, slicing through his carotid artery.

As Brent lost consciousness and sprayed blood across the steps, Alan leapt into the fray. Tackling the gorilla, he pried the ape's mouth off the mortally wounded astronaut before hammering Urko's face. Enraged all the more, the gorilla tore Alan off of him, sending the man crashing down the altar's steps. Full of bloodlust and determined to launch that missile, Urko stampeded the control console. Virgil unslung his automatic rifle, but the chamber was jammed. Cornelius shoved him and Zaius out of the way and steadied himself for Urko's attack.

It never came.

The Unknown Ape fired. A single shot echoed through the hall, lancing the raging gorilla's neck and exiting through his throat. Urko stumbled but kept moving. His final cry was a wet sticky gurgle as the gorilla's momentum propelled his bulk past the cowering Cornelius. Urko tumbled up and over the split altar and onto the control console, flicking open the launcher's safety switch in the process. With a death rattle, the general slumped over the console, his hand connecting with the firing mechanism. Before anyone could stop it, the launch cylinder glowed red and sank into the control panel.

The missile began its final countdown.

Ancient turbines let loose a high-pitched whine. Silo doors in the cathedral's ceiling cycled open. Sand and debris from millennia of disuse rained down on the missile, pelting it with rocks and showering those closest to it with a fine white ash. The weapon continued to vent toxic gas. As the ash hit the jets of steam, it was sprayed around the hall.

A rumble grew outward from the weapon's heart until

the entire cathedral reverberated with its awesome power. Alan and MacDonald grabbed Virgil, Zaius, and Cornelius, shielding them behind the altar just in time. The missile's rockets ignited, incinerating Urko's corpse and obliterating the rear of the cathedral.

With a mighty blast of its engines, the weapon lifted and began its spiraling climb to the surface world.

All was lost.

The cathedral shuddered.

Ronald Brent was dead, and they would all soon be as well.

The Unknown Ape followed the atomic rocket's glare. It shot up the missile silo, twisting as it soared toward the night sky.

Was it supposed to spin like that? he wondered.

It didn't matter. His mission, it seemed, was a failure. While Judy, Alan, Brent, and their missing friend Bill had come to this future via accident, the Unknown Ape and his companions—the orangutan Virgil and the humans Alan and MacDonald—had traveled forward in time to prevent a permanent destruction wrought by both man and ape. To hear Virgil tell it, an omen from the future had compelled them to prevent disaster.

That was not an easy thing to explain.

Evolved apes from the fortieth century, Cornelius and Zira, had been thrust back in time by the destruction of the Earth itself. He was their son—the child of a union in the future, born in the past—and he had led apekind out of captivity. For better or for worse, the Unknown Ape was Caesar... and right now, things couldn't be any worse.

Upon their arrival in the late twentieth century, Caesar's parents had been "interviewed" by the U.S. government. Classified tapes of those sessions had been sealed deep within the archives section of the Forbidden City. Decades later, Caesar and his confidants—Virgil and MacDonald—explored the ruins of the bombed-out metropolis. There, they had seen those tapes.

The trio then set about stopping the future destruction of the planet, be it by human or ape hands. They unearthed the last of ANSA's *Liberty*-class spacecraft: a starship designated *Probe Nine*. Together with their new friend Alan—an astronaut who himself was out of his own time—they headed to the future. Calling themselves the Travellers, they hoped to change the course of history, to set man and ape on the right path.

Traveling to further eras, Caesar learned of the simian council's edict to posthumously deny his existence. He had been expunged from all records, and what few texts mentioning him remained were considered apocryphal to the Sacred Scrolls.

Caesar found that they could erase the ape, but not the legend. His nameless accomplishments had become attributed to "the Unknown Ape." Caesar adopted the moniker, and the Travellers used the influence of his myth to guide humans and apes away from the precipice. To steer them clear of genocide. To save them from themselves.

Despite their efforts, each future the Travellers accelerated toward only seemed worse. Much, much worse.

Just like now.

"Caesar!" The Unknown Ape's reverie broke.

When Zaius, Cornelius, and the ape troops looked perplexed, Virgil tried again. "Ah, Unknown Ape!"

Zaius whispered to Cornelius. "Caesar?" Cornelius shrugged.

Caesar looked away from the rapidly receding trail blazing above. On the steps, Alan was respectfully covering Brent's body with the torn robe of an Underdweller. By the altar,

Virgil and Zaius furiously input commands into the weapon's control console. Their efforts were rewarded with a flashing yellow beacon.

"We cannot disarm the missile nor stop it from here," said Zaius. "We were, however, able to alter its trajectory. The weapon should now circumnavigate the planet once before it comes down on its target."

Jeff voiced his own concerns. "What is its target, Virgil?"

"Yes, well, as Urko had not completed the coordinate sequence before we arrived, the target is not Hidden Valley."

Jeff let go a sigh of relief. Virgil continued. "Instead, it appears ground zero is Ape City."

Zaius and Cornelius looked grim.

"It doesn't matter, Virgil," MacDonald interjected. "Did you see the symbols on the missile's wing? Alpha and omega."

Caesar, Virgil, MacDonald, and Alan all knew what that meant—they had been made privy to the twentieth-century man's Alpha-Omega Bomb in one fashion or another.

The others were nonplussed. MacDonald did his best to explain.

"It will burn the planet to a cinder. It—" MacDonald paused, unable to finish his thought.

Caesar completed it for him. "That thing is a doomsday bomb." He pointed to the exposed sky at the far end of the silo tube. "No matter where it detonates," he cast his eyes down, "it will kill us all."

Human and ape alike hung their heads low. The cathedral grew silent in prayer.

Caesar weaved through the crowd, breaking the spell. "Lucius," the Unknown Ape addressed his sergeant in hushed tones. "Take the apes back to the surface as fast as you can. Tell them to see their loved ones. There is little time."

Lucius nodded. The sergeant gathered the Unknown Army and led them home. As each devotee passed the Unknown

Ape, they reached out to touch their leader, chimpanzee, gorilla, and orangutan alike. Unity among apekind.

But Caesar—as himself or as the Unknown Ape—had no speeches for them, no words of encouragement. He was defeated.

Caesar and his Travellers were further along in the timeline than the dates his parents had proclaimed as the end of the world—and his parents, Cornelius and Zira, were here, not thrust back in time. At first glance, it would seem that history had been changed, that they had achieved limited success after all.

Except, here it was again: the Alpha-Omega Bomb. The end of the world.

Just like Caesar had seen in his visions long ago. The same, but different. A warmongering gorilla general. A race of underground mutants. An ancient cathedral deep beneath the planet of the apes. An astronaut named Brent, dead. But why hadn't the humanoid female Nova been here to die when the gorillas invaded? She was safe back at Hidden Valley with Zira. And where was the astronaut whom his parents had come to love?

Where was Taylor?

The setting was the same. Many of the players were the same. But the particulars were off. So many things were off, but the endgame would be the same.

Or would it?

As the last of the ape army receded from the cathedral, Alan snapped to life.

"Wait just a minute!" Index finger raised, the excited astronaut approached the orangutan scientists. "You're sure that missile is going to make a full orbit?"

Zaius looked over the disheveled control panel again. Conferring quietly with Virgil, the elder orangutan ultimately nodded.

Virgil turned to face Alan. "That is our assertion, yes."

"That's almost ninety minutes, plus seven or eight minutes' ascent time." Focused, Alan strode toward the wrecked doorway.

"We've only lost maybe fifteen minutes…" The astronaut was onto something. "I swear to you," Alan asserted, "we are not out of this yet."

Recognizing the inflection of Alan's voice, Caesar did not question his human friend. Instead, he fell in beside him. The others soon followed.

"Jeff," Alan continued, "tell Judy and Krador to meet us at the hangar."

Caesar had an idea of what Alan had in mind, and it was he who gave the next command: "Have *Probe Nine* prepped for launch."

"Alan—it's suicide!" Judy exclaimed.

"You tell me another way—any other way—and I'm ready to listen."

Judy and a group of Underdwellers had met them on the way to the hangar. As he spoke, Alan moved with purpose. It had taken them nearly another ten minutes to get there from the cathedral.

"All I know is we've got maybe an hour left before that missile starts its descent." Alan sped his way down the corridor, Caesar at his side. Alan spoke over his shoulder at the group behind them. "And if it *is* the Alpha-Omega Bomb, it could ignite the entire atmosphere."

Caesar recalled what his mother's tapes had said about the Earth's destruction: "When we were in space, we saw a bright, white, blinding light. Then we saw the rim of the Earth melt. Then there was a *tornado* in the sky!"

The group entered the vast cavern via a catwalk, high above the cave's floor. The burrow was filled with the blink and hum of technology two millennia ahead of twentieth-century Earth. The focus of this room, not unlike the cathedral which had held the Alpha-Omega Bomb, was a launch silo. This launch pad here did not support a weapon of mass destruction. Instead, it housed *Probe Nine*.

The spacecraft was why the Travellers had been here during Urko's attack. She was now also their only chance of salvation.

The Travellers' ship had been damaged upon arrival in this century. They had forged an alliance with the *Venturer*'s exiled crew. Judy Franklin had called for help from the technologically advanced Underdwellers, and they had secreted *Probe Nine* here for repair. After nearly a year, she was ready for launch—ready to take Caesar, Virgil, and the rest back to the early twenty-first century.

Except Alan now had a more desperate gambit in mind.

"I'll go alone. Intercept the missile at its orbital apogee." He smashed his fist into his palm. "Get it to detonate above the atmosphere. The only thing you should suffer down here would be an electromagnetic pulse that will fry every unshielded circuit on the planet." While the Underdwellers' machines were likely protected, the technology of the apes was not.

At that, Cornelius gasped.

"But then we will lose our machines, our power—ape civilization as we know it."

"Yes," Alan agreed. "The playing field would be leveled. You'll be the same as the ape colonies out there that never had power. But..." He paused for effect. "You will be alive to rebuild."

Cornelius nodded, realizing that the human was right. The others looked incredulous. Caesar turned to his scientific advisor. "Virgil?"

After a moment of mental calculation, Virgil turned to

Caesar and sighed heavily. "What Alan is suggesting has a substantial probability of success, pending the expediency with which we implement his outline."

Caesar stared daggers at Virgil, and the orangutan relented. "In a word, yes."

Alan pulled Caesar away from Cornelius and Zaius to speak privately. "We're cutting it close, Caesar. Fifteen minutes to program an intercept course. Another half an hour to complete launch prep. Seven more to reach orbit, and then ten, maybe fifteen minutes to find the damn thing and hit it before it falls back to Earth."

None of the *Venturer* crew, nor the Travellers, said what they were all thinking—this was a one-way trip. If Alan was successful, he would die in the orbital blast.

"Why you, Alan?" asked Judy.

Addressing his fellow astronauts, Alan was defiant. "Because with Brent gone, I'm the senior officer. No one under my command takes a risk I'm not willing to take myself. And I'm the best pilot here." He quickly frowned, then added sheepishly, "No offense intended, of course."

Solemnly, Jeff replied for them all. "None taken, Colonel."

After a pause, Caesar closed his eyes and nodded once. "Go."

Alan acknowledged.

Everyone exploded into action.

Virgil had gone missing.

Caesar had noticed the orangutan's absence after Alan's plan had been put into motion. Knowing his friend, the chimpanzee found him back in the cathedral, alone and buried underneath the malfunctioning control console. With Cornelius' tools in hand, Virgil was attempting to fix the unfixable.

It was, of course, hopeless.

"Virgil, that won't work," Caesar reasoned. "Alan's plan is the only way."

Finally accepting the folly of his efforts, the orangutan philosopher exhaled. Caesar sat down on the altar's steps, patting the stone next to him.

"I have but five minutes, Virgil. Sit with your king. Caesar needs your counsel."

A dirtied and disheveled Virgil climbed out from beneath the control panel and brushed off his clothes. Sitting beside his friend and leader, he spoke. "On what matter does Caesar require counsel?"

The chimpanzee drew an abyssal breath. "Virgil, my parents have not traveled backward in time."

The Travellers were responsible for this. A Doctor Milo had found a damaged starship in the Forbidden Zone and had repaired it. The Unknown Ape had ensured Cornelius and Zira were not on that spacecraft when it launched. Faulty heat tiles caused the ship to explode in mid-flight, killing Milo and the others aboard.

"I have saved their lives. Stopped them from suffering a grizzly death, two thousand years before they were born."

Virgil nodded, proud of Caesar's accomplishments, and the role he had played in making them a reality.

"I have prevented my mother from birthing me in the distant past," the chimp continued. He had broken the cycle. But something was wrong. Terribly wrong.

Seeing his friend's distress, Virgil put his hand on the chimpanzee's shoulder. "Caesar?"

"Oh, Virgil," Caesar dropped all pretense of confidence. "If I have altered destiny, then tell me, why am I still here?"

Virgil paused.

"I—" the orangutan started to speak, then stopped in mid-thought. Would altering the timeline erase Caesar from existence? Finally, he came to a conclusion with which he was not at all familiar. "I… had not considered that."

As Virgil had defined it, time was an infinite motorway that possessed an infinite number of lanes replete with automobiles. A driver in lane A might have a fatal accident, while one in lane B might survive. As that suggested, a driver might change his lane to change his destiny, but the outcome of that change would still be unknown. It was a blind choice, but it was a choice nonetheless.

While there were, indeed, an infinite number of timelines, they *had* moved forward within their own, hadn't they? If, then, Caesar had altered destiny, should he still exist?

They had always known changing the future would create a new timeline, and had hoped it would become one in which apes were not responsible for Earth's destruction. But they had expected to branch off from the future from which Caesar's parents had come—had assumed it was their own. Since they had first arrived, however, Caesar had suspected something was wrong.

It was the year 3980. According to their taped testimony, Caesar's parents had witnessed the Earth's destruction in the year "thirty-nine fifty—something." Assuming, at first, that the starship in which they had escaped had a faulty chronometer, they had dismissed any inconsistencies.

But that suspicion had gnawed at Caesar more and more, the longer they had been here. This Cornelius and Zira lived in a technologically advanced society, not a pre-industrial one as the tapes had described.

"Virgil, they are not my parents, are they." It was a statement—not a question. The Zira and Cornelius here were but alternative versions of his mother and father.

Virgil reluctantly shook his head. "We must have deviated into another splinter of existence," the orangutan hypothesized, "another lane of time's highway. We have been changing the course of *another* future, not ours."

Caesar had been fighting to save *an* Earth. But not *his* Earth. Not *his* parents.

The fate of the world was at stake, and Alan Virdon did not intend to let it down.

Suited up with his helmet under his arm, the former Air Force colonel walked the long deck of the launch gantry, headed for *Probe Nine*'s cockpit. His thoughts were of old friends and family. Sally. Chris. Pete. Galen. Even Jonesy. Alan hoped that somewhere in some time—any time—they were well.

Jeff and Judy had just finished programing the navigation computer. MacDonald and Virgil had said their goodbyes. Now it was down to him and his starship.

The Underdwellers and their allies had modified *Probe Nine* so much that—aside from her familiar delta-shaped command capsule—he barely recognized her. Her slaved Gas Dynamic Fusion Drive system had been replaced with an integrated EmDrive—technology invented nearly two hundred years after he was born. Constructed from ancient scrap, this new engine was a far superior design, made from far inferior parts.

It would have to do.

Alan addressed the ship. "Well," he smiled, caressing her hull, "you're the only girl in town."

"Alan, a moment, please."

Caesar was approaching. Behind him were Zaius and Krador, the Underdwellers' leader. Alan could guess what this was.

"The ship is still being prepped for launch." Taking Alan's helmet from him, the ape king motioned toward those behind him. "Allow them their gratitude."

"Of course." Alan smiled at the planet's leaders. As he neared them, Alan thought about the stubborn nature of time. It seemed intent on conforming to its original path, despite any and every deviation intelligent beings might force upon it.

Travel through the Hasslein Curve had inevitably connected him with multiple gorilla generals named Urko and orangutan councilors called Zaius. This era's Urko, just as the one he had met in the past, had become an adversary. This Zaius, however, was far different from the one he had encountered before.

This Zaius, Alan reflected, *is reasonable.*

The orangutan leader was the first to extend his hand in friendship. "You do us a great service." Alan shook his hand. "If we survive today, I will do everything possible to make the council sue for peace with mankind," Zaius turned his head toward Krador, "and the Underdwellers as well."

The cloaked and hooded Underdweller leader stepped forward.

"Think of it," Krador all but whispered. "Peace in our time, thanks to you. May we be worthy of your sacrifice."

Alan beamed. Since he had first arrived in an ape-dominated future, he had believed that all intelligent creatures should learn to live and work together as equals. Now it looked like his dream would finally bear fruit.

Too bad I won't be around to see it.

As the leaders dispersed, Alan started to climb into *Probe Nine*'s nose hatch.

"One more thing," Caesar added.

"Yes?" Alan turned to face the chimpanzee just as his helmet smacked him across his face.

The astronaut's limp form collapsed against the ship's hatch. Lowering the headgear he had just used to bludgeon his friend, Caesar replied, "You forgot your helmet."

Soon, *Probe Nine* was on her way.

•

"Who's flying *Probe Nine?*" a confused Jeff Allen asked.

In the cavernous underground hangar of the Underdwellers, human, mutant, and ape alike conferred. They had found Alan unconscious on the launch gantry right after liftoff. Now, Cornelius administered a potent balm to the underside of Alan's nose. From the stench of it, MacDonald reasoned, it must be this century's equivalent of smelling salts. Noting who among their group was missing, he and Virgil exchanged worrisome glances.

Alan moaned. Before the astronaut was lucid enough to respond, MacDonald answered Jeff's question. "Who else," he said, speaking mournfully, "but the Unknown Ape?"

Virgil was desperate to raise Caesar on the TX-12 communicator. MacDonald knew Caesar would have switched his radio off.

No interference.

He tried his best to comfort the distressed orangutan.

A conscious but dazed Alan Virdon spoke up. "By now, he's reached orbit. He's only got a few minutes to find that missile and knock it out of the sky." Alan sighed. "I just don't know if he can do it. Caesar doesn't have the flight experience. If our trajectory calculations are off, or if the missile is late because of the damage it took…"

Alan trailed off. Nothing more needed to be said on the matter. Caesar was now their only hope.

Virgil slumped. "I only wanted to say goodbye."

"And you shall."

Judy and Krador approached. As Judy put her arm around Virgil, the psionic leader of the Underdwellers continued to speak. "Allow me to help both of you."

•

Probe Nine's afterburners fluttered and quit as she silently glided over the rim of the Earth. The ship's attitude thrusters fired intermittently, performing minute adjustments to keep her on course. Caesar had reached orbit with no issues. Now, he performed three full sensor sweeps and found nothing. He was beginning to fret that the missile had already begun its descent, and he had missed it.

Perhaps Alan was better suited for this after all, he thought.

Abruptly, other thoughts shared his own.

Caesar.

The chimpanzee's heart thumped hard in his spacesuit as the voice flooded his brain.

This is Krador.

"Krador," Caesar said in annoyance, gripping the ship's controls tighter. "I am a little busy right now. Perhaps you could call on me later?"

I am linking your mind to those of your friends.

"You are what?"

Caesar, it's Alan. The missile may be in a different orbit than we plotted. The damage Urko did—

"Understood, Alan." Relieved he would have help, Caesar acquiesced. "Tell me what to do."

T plus 37 minutes.

It was now past Alan's time estimate for the missile's descent. Despite the help from Krador and his friends, Caesar still found nothing. At any moment, the bomb might ignite the atmosphere and kill the entire planet. Soon, he would tell his friends goodbye.

Stabbing at the control panel one finger at a time, he put the ship into a roll. *Probe Nine* spun on her axis, settling upside down relative to her previous orientation. Caesar gazed up and out the forward viewport. Instead of the star-filled void, he saw the azure curve of the Earth.

Lovely.

A glint of light caught the chimpanzee's eye. Its orbit suspect, a lazy projectile rolled and wobbled its way toward the terminus into night.

"Wait a moment!" Caesar exclaimed. Checking the sensor scope, he confirmed his suspicions. It was there. Before he had rolled the ship, its approach vector had been masked by *Probe Nine's* ventral blind spot. Its tardiness, no doubt, was a result of the damage it had suffered in the cathedral.

The Alpha-Omega Bomb.

"I can see it!" Caesar yelled, elated. "It's closer to the Earth than me." Caesar thought the missile's coordinates to them. "What do I do now?"

The astronauts' minds grew dark. Defeated.

"Gentlemen," the chimpanzee inquired, "would you like to share your dilemma?"

It was Jeff who thought first.

If she's crossed into night, she's approaching target. We are only hours from dawn here. The range is too far, Caesar. Even with boosters at full burn, you'll never make it.

Caesar was silent.

If I may, Virgil's thoughts flooded their minds, *I recommend an intercept course regardless, followed by a short burst from the EmDrive.*

The EmDrive was designed to gradually accelerate *Probe Nine* to near-light speeds. It seemed feasible that it could instead be used to cross thousands of miles in an instant—and then stop.

Alan's and Jeff's thoughts exploded. *Yes! My God, Virgil, that just might do it.*

"Virgil," Caesar responded, "you are the greatest mind of our time." After a thought, he added, "or any other."

Ah, thank you, Virgil thought. Caesar imagined him blushing.

Set the EmDrive for, say, let me see… Virgil performed the calculations in his head… *0.003 seconds. That will put you right on top of it.*

Better yet, thought Caesar, *why not go right through it?*

Jeff and Virgil fed him new intercept coordinates, and thought him through the procedure. Caesar did not set the EmDrive for a small burst, however. Instead, the engine would cut out well past his target. He wouldn't just get close to the missile and try to knock it off course; he would use *Probe Nine* to cleave the Alpha-Omega Bomb in two.

Indicator lights intensified as the EmDrive approached full power. In a minute or two, *Probe Nine* would become a deadly projectile of his own. Then he could obliterate the doomsday weapon—and himself with it.

Caesar put his affairs in order. Saying his goodbyes to Virgil and the others, he requested that Krador put him in thought contact with Cornelius.

"Cornelius, there is something I need to tell you, and there isn't much time."

On the sensor scope, the Alpha-Omega Bomb slowed its looping orbit and began to alter course. Its ventral side flickered yellow-orange as it kissed the atmosphere.

Caesar spoke fast. "This might not make sense to you, but—"

The chimpanzee archeologist interrupted. *I understand, Caesar.*

He had called him Caesar. Not "the Unknown Ape."

Virgil told me everything, Cornelius' thought transmission continued. *Since you arrived, you have always avoided Zira and me. Every time there was danger, however, you were there, watching over us. I now know why.*

"I don't know what to say," Caesar admitted.

Then say nothing, Caesar. You have a mission to complete.

"Cornelius," Caesar started, "I am not from your

timeline." He had to be sure the other ape understood. "Not really *your* son—"

Yes. But in another world—another lifetime—I am your father. Had we more time, I would have liked to explore that here with you, I think.

A light on the engineering panel strobed green—the EmDrive was ready. A single tear bled down Caesar's cheek.

Caesar threw the switch. In the end, it was Cornelius who said goodbye.

Godspeed, my son.

The EmDrive fired.

Her speed a fraction of light, the dart that was *Probe Nine* threw herself at her target. No one—man, mutant, or ape—could maintain consciousness at that sudden an acceleration.

Darkness swallowed Caesar.

Probe Nine sliced through the Alpha-Omega missile just as it began its descent. The wrathful bomb detonated on contact.

A rampant ball of gamma rays ruptured space itself. *Probe Nine* did not escape the doomsday weapon's fury. Instead, the meteoric force crumpled her like a paper airplane. The sky dissolved in a brilliant blast of white light.

In the Forbidden Zone, human, ape, and mutant alike gathered to witness the expanding aurora above. A chroma of crimsons, corals, and vermilions saturated the deep-blue sky. The colossal blast illuminated the desert, transforming night to day. Underdwellers were forced to shield their eyes. The others looked on in awe.

Vivid colors frolicked while charged particles danced in the atmosphere. Electromagnetic waves took shape and savaged the planet's machines. In the Forbidden Zone, any unshielded electronics the Underdwellers possessed fell victim to the high-altitude explosion.

Miles away, Ape City suffered an immediate and final blackout. Every car battery died. Every transistor blew. Every circuit board shorted. But the planet was not devastated. Apes, humanoids, and mutants were all still there.

All still alive.

Zaius and Krador exchanged glances. True to his word, the orangutan councilmember offered his hand. Krador accepted it.

The planet would be forever changed, but it would survive. A new beginning.

As the others dispersed, Alan and Virgil stood transfixed by the lightshow.

"Do you think he knew he did it?" Alan asked. "Do you think Caesar died knowing he stopped that thing?"

Virgil cleared his throat. "My good Alan," he started. "Caesar may have known, and Caesar may still know," the brilliant orangutan declared. Alan was addled.

Virgil explicated. "Who is to say that Caesar is dead? Even if *our* Caesar died in the atomic blast above, I believe that somewhere out there in time and space, *another* Caesar has survived." Virgil was proud of his hypothesis. "Infinite possibilities, you know. Regardless, the legacy of the Unknown Ape will carry on."

Looking again to the iridescent sky, Alan agreed.

"The king is dead," he offered with a smile. "Long live the king."

Jim Beard's "Silenced" weaves a tale that is, in fact, many tales—a rich tapestry with a single thread of fate shining throughout it…

SILENCED

by

JIM BEARD

A cool breeze off the lapping water around them tickled her nose. Wrapped in her arms, she felt him stiffen as he looked up at the giant figure before them.

She, too, gazed up at it then, not understanding what he saw in it.

"Let go," he said, freeing himself and stepping away.

He took a few steps, still staring at the figure, his back turned to her. She looked at both, one at a time between the two, uncomprehending.

"How can you be so *cold*?"

He turned to her, finally. "With you? Easy."

She took in his face, the lean features, the prominent jaw, the once-warm eyes roaming over not her face, but her body. She saw him take in her tight uniform skirt, her shapely legs, the light blue dress blouse stretched taut over her breasts underneath her service jacket, and her raven-black hair.

Undressing her with his eyes; some things never changed.

"We could…" she said, a warmth flooding her belly despite the cool February air.

"I'm leaving, Nora. Tomorrow morning. Leaving you and the miserable human race behind. Pretty simple."

The heat in her shifted. She felt her cheeks warming, her anger igniting.

"But not *alone*, Taylor."

She saw the instant bemusement on his face at her name for him—never "George," only "Taylor."

He hung his head, wagging it from side to side and smiling. "Stewart's a qualified professional—"

A flash of insight. "You *bastard*," she swore, her fingers balling into fists. "You—*you* made sure of that! You made sure it was *her* and not *me*. That *bitch*."

"There's that face," he said, still smiling. "The face that launched a thousand starships, or maybe just *mine*. My supernova on two legs…"

She stepped up to him, her face now hot, her lips parting to speak.

He held up a hand to cut her off, began turning away from her. "Save it. It's done. I'm off to Cape Canaveral tomorrow morning and off this rock six hours later. It was fun, the sex was good—very good—but that's that, Nora."

"Was that what you told your *wife*, too?" It was lame, but it was all that came to her in the moment.

Taylor stopped smiling. His eyes narrowed to slits.

"This is pointless, but if it pleases you, I'll try to picture you and not my wife when I'm talking to Stewart."

"*Screwing* her, you mean," she spat. "I hope you'll be very happy with your space princess—which one of you gets her first?"

Silence.

It wasn't like him not to have an immediate, sharp retort to her gibes. She stared at him, her face still hot, and now her eyes wet. He stared back at her.

Slowly, hesitantly, she reached out with open hands to lay them on his broad chest. He was still hard, hard as a rock, as unmoving as the statue above them, as the little island they stood upon, the meeting spot that used to mean something to them both.

"Taylor," she said, low and warm. "*Please*. I'm sorry. I'm… I'm distraught… they're talking about reassigning me. They're saying…"

She paused, internally assessing his mood. He simply stared back at her, still silent.

Nora's fingers found his dog tags, just underneath his half-unzipped leather jacket. She saw his eyes dart down to them, then back to her face.

"You—you can't leave anything behind of yourself," she said. It was meant to be a question, but it came out a statement. "Why can't you leave one damn thing behind, for *me*? You've got to take *everything*—"

His hand sprang up and snatched the tags from her fingers effortlessly, slipping them back into his jacket. His jaw moved from side to side, his eyes colder than before.

"So help me God, I'm actually glad I don't have to listen to your voice anymore."

He turned away from her fully, looking back up at the statue again. The island seemed suddenly devoid of all life to her, a desolate hunk of stone in the middle of a great, barren desert.

He took a step, and then another, walking away.

"Good*bye*, Nora," he threw back to her with a weak flip of a hand. "Have a… well, have a life, I guess."

The figure of him wavered in her liquid vision, tears now rolling down her burning cheeks. She found she couldn't speak. Three years of frustration and anger and disappointment welled up inside her, like a dam, blocking her, cutting her off from humanity.

Her entire body shook, quavering in the chilly air.

"*Taylor!*"

It came out nearly inarticulate, barely a word; a name. It came out as a strangled remnant of her sanity, a dam breaking to release her pent-up rage.

"Damn you, Taylor! God *damn* you!"

He stopped, turned his head to the side, glancing back at her.

"Blasphemy, Nora?" he tsked. "In front of Lady Liberty?"

Shaking his head, he continued on his way. He might even have been chuckling, too.

She stood alone in the shadow of the giant statue, the water lapping around her, her body still vibrating, her hands empty.

She had no more words.

The gorilla squinted in the harsh, antiseptic light, its nostrils twitching as it steamed the glass with its breath and peered inside the room.

It wore one of the standard red jumpsuits, now stained and torn; she didn't want to know what the stains were. In one meaty, hairy hand, it toted a wooden club that appeared to be a notched and battered police baton. It clunked against the glass as the ape leaned in for a look.

Suddenly seeing her—she wasn't trying to hide—its eyes widened slightly and its free hand came up to press at the glass. Then, it jabbed the hand spasmodically in the air, pointing at the door next to the glass wall. The gorilla's entire body bobbed up and down from the action.

Not for the first time, she shook her head ruefully over how a once fairly peaceful species had grown so aggressive in such a short time.

After the battle, what an ANN reporter had disdainfully called Caesar's "small struggle," she wasn't sure what to do with herself. Only a few weeks following her nineteenth birthday and she was out of a job—the only real job she'd ever had. So one morning, frustrated with sitting in her little apartment in the great city, she got up, got dressed, and made her way through the so-called Exclusion Zone and to her workplace.

Surprisingly, Caesar allowed some humans to travel through the part of the city he'd claimed. The word went out that men would be stopped and searched for weapons and perhaps even followed in some circumstances, but the most important of his decrees—the chimp emphasized this one—was that no human must speak in the streets, and most especially not to an ape.

The penalty for breaking the rule wasn't spelled out, but she didn't worry over its alleged harshness, for she couldn't imagine what she'd have to say to armed apes roaming the city anyway.

So, quietly and discreetly, she returned to Ape Management, to the nursery.

It was all she really knew, her job. Fresh off the farm at seventeen, she'd begged her mother to let her move to the city and seek a career in a field she was good at. On the family farm she'd been good with the animals, caring for them and, to her mind, making their small lives better. Her mother scoffed at first, but grew tired of the argument and watched as her only daughter left for the big city, a world she herself had abandoned.

After only a week, she secured a position as midwife at Ape Management, in the Breeding Annex nursery. She was working with animals, caring for them, and, hopefully, making their lives better.

The apes had ignored the nursery in the aftermath of Caesar's rebellion, for the most part. She knew the automated machines there would keep the current crop of infants alive for up to two weeks without human supervision, but in all good conscience, she felt she needed to check on them, should they still be there.

Upon entering the nursery for the first time since the revolution, she was somewhat surprised to find the infant apes—all nine of them—still in their cribs, still in the same place she'd left them when the fighting had broken out. They hadn't been moved by the conquering adult apes, whisked away to be raised beyond the taint of human technology.

Her face grew warm as she looked over her nine charges and thought maybe they'd been forgotten. Or, more likely, Caesar wasn't even aware they existed.

Which was ironic in a way, because she knew that at least three of the infants were his.

The mothers were gone, of course, swept up in the tide of revolution, but she remembered delivering the children of two female chimps that could be traced to Caesar's studding, and one of them had twins. If the conquering king knew he'd spawned or guessed he had little princes, there was no indication of it. The babies seemed abandoned, forgotten. The thought of it made her burn inside.

The gorilla, not waiting for her to open the door to the inner room, tried the latch and found it unlocked. Loping into the room after throwing open the door, it eyed her with a wary look. She drew back, putting a large table between her and the ape, unsure of what it wanted.

It poked and prodded instruments with its club, sniffing the air with its coal-black nose and twisting its head in question, just the way she recalled dogs did when they were curious. She could tell the gorilla was keeping one eye on her as it made its way around the room.

Outside, beyond the nursery, she could hear the sounds of other apes in the building. She felt her position slipping away, realizing that they had finally come to secure it.

The gorilla's hand moved toward a console near where she stood, and the sight of it shook her from her reverie. The ape's fingers reached out to caress a dial there, then another.

Panic zigzagged through her body.

"*No!*"

It came organically, unbidden. She foresaw the result of

the gorilla's unknowing handiwork at the panel and reacted without thinking. Her shout rang around the room.

In a flash—she never saw it begin to move—the gorilla sprung at her, swinging one big arm to backhand her across the face. To her, it was like dynamite had gone off across her cheek.

She struck the wall behind her, bouncing off it and to the floor in a heap. The impact of the ape's knuckles on her sounded like a gunshot to her ears.

Automatically, she glanced up immediately to the large window on the wall she'd struck and the opaque blinds drawn down over it. Behind it rested nine infant chimpanzees, sleeping away in their crèches. The gorilla, she assumed, knew nothing of them at all, or that it had almost destroyed them.

In a wink, it was over her, glaring down at her with big, black eyes. It sniffed once, then snorted, the hand gripping the club swinging back and forth, back and forth.

She could tell she was bleeding. Her face felt like it was five times its normal size. Tears dripped down her cheeks, mingling with the blood.

The ape looked like it suddenly noticed something and reached out toward her with its free hand. She felt frozen in place, confused and dazed, her body unresponsive, save for her eyes. She saw the gorilla reach down to finger the collar of her Ape Management uniform shirt.

It came away with dog tags dangling from the chain around her neck.

She bit back on shouting again. She couldn't risk that word, any admonition to stop a second time.

Inwardly, she saw her mother handing her the tags, nearly three years before, on her sixteenth birthday. She had asked for them, knowing they belonged to her late father, and her mother had reluctantly relinquished them. From that moment on, the tags rested around her neck, never once removed in the three years.

She'd heard her mother call them "my prize" more than once when she was a child, and knew that she'd received them from her father when he retired from the service. They were precious to her mother, something that reportedly made her feel whole after a dark time in her life, before she'd had a child—a bad break-up with a man her mother would only refer to as "that bastard." Her father had been there to cushion the blow, and they got married soon after.

"Please," she whispered to the gorilla in the most pleasing tone she could muster. "*Please* don't take them…"

The ape reared back, rage in its eyes, snorting great bursts of air out its nostrils.

It raised the club, and in her mind's eye she saw it caving in her skull, the dog tags leaving with the ape.

"*No!*"

She wasn't sure if it was she who had spoken the word again. Slowly, it dawned upon her that it was a male's voice from behind the gorilla. Her assailant turned toward the voice, club raised, and in so doing allowed her to see who had dared to speak.

A chimpanzee in green coveralls. Caesar himself.

"Stop," he said to the gorilla in an even tone. "Go back." He pointed out the door. "Help the others."

The ape bowed its massive head and shuffled past him and out the door. Caesar watched him go, then turned to her, frowning.

"Get up. Leave here and never come back. I will ensure your passage. You won't be molested."

She didn't reply, didn't speak, but pulled herself up off the floor. Caesar's face eased, but he shook his head slightly at the sight of her swollen, bloody face, and let go a sigh. Turning toward the door, he exited the room, glancing left and right into the outer area as he did so.

Following him, she paused at the console with which the gorilla had started to fiddle. Darting a quick glance at Caesar's back, she reached out and flipped a switch on the board. A green telltale lighted, and at a soft hum she entered a code on a keypad. A small beep told her it was accepted.

A large dial ringed with increasing numbers around its circumference held her attention for a brief moment. Then she twisted it, turning it up to its maximum range. She thought she could hear the released gas, but told herself she was imagining it.

It was the one piece of nursery equipment she thought she'd never use, let alone touch or even contemplate. It existed for the use of higher beings than her, those who made the decisions regarding which infants were needed, and which were not.

Everything had changed for her in the last few minutes. Once, she could never have made that decision. After seeing her blood on her hand and on the floor, being denied the right to speak, and the underlying arrogance of Caesar, everything turned around. The farm girl lay dead on the floor behind her, her skull caved in.

No more kings, she thought to herself as she left the room clutching her dog tags. The princes were silenced forever.

The rain had begun to come down in sheets, so she called for the covered carriage. The weather made her middle-aged bones ache, but she wanted to go and see him—no, *needed* to see him.

As she rode out of the city, she fretted over this and that. She wasn't supposed to leave the city limits, but wasn't she the queen? Queen of nothing, it could be argued (and was, in some boroughs), but she intended to live the part to the bitter end.

Up in the low hills, she exited the carriage and entered a cave, listening to her voice raspy and strained as she told the carriage men to stand ready. It was nothing to fuss over, she mused; weren't all humans' voices raspy and strained these days?

On a simple wooden bed in the cave lay a dying ape.

"You've come," he said simply, his voice sounding better than hers, despite his worsening condition. "Thank you."

"Nothing would have stopped me, Boniface," she told him truthfully, smoothing back her still-black hair from her face.

The small ape on the bed was different from the rest of the simian population, but not just in size and physical make-up; a chimpanzee, but *not* a chimpanzee. He was *different*, in that way she could always spot, ever since she was little. Something would be lost when he was gone, something *important*, though intangible. She realized the thought probably showed on her face, and she wondered what he might think of it.

"It is the end," the small ape said, nodding, as if remarking upon her thoughts. "I have something to say to you."

She resisted the urge to smooth down the wild, long hair on his head and simply gazed at his dark face, the once-pink lips now nearly white, and his kind eyes.

He'd been an advisor to her family for many years, one of the only apes who lived in the city, until the army came and everything changed. He once told her he wasn't like the gorillas and the orangutans and the chimpanzees—his people were apart from those others. And, many years later, he confided in her that he was the very last of his kind.

The thought sprang again into her mind: the world would be at a loss after his passing. And then an even stronger idea: *He might have changed the world had he not served us in the city*.

Boniface didn't agree with the followers of Caesar, or with many of the Lawgivers who had followed him, or with much of the wider ape world. Her mentor—yes, that's what he was—had different ideas, peaceful ones mainly, but still strong and unbending. If only more had heard them…

She inwardly registered disgust from the image of Caesar that came to mind. It had always been so, though she was unclear on why that was.

Boniface reached out a tiny, wrinkled hand and touched the metal pieces that hung from a chain around her neck. The remnants of words could still be seen on their surfaces, once deeply embossed, now barely legible. He, like she, had always liked shiny things, material things. It was one of the subjects they enjoyed discussing.

"The sign of a great warrior, my queen." He coughed; bloody spittle appeared on his thin lips. "Ancient, but still powerful."

"Queen of nothing," she intoned, narrowing her eyes. "Queen of *slaves*."

The ape let the metal pieces slide from his hand. His eyes watered over and he coughed again.

"Tell your daughter and her daughter to keep *hope* in the years to come," he told her in earnest. "To keep the faith, but *always* be wary. The age of mankind is coming to a close... but not the end of their *spirit*. Tell them that."

Boniface died a moment later, to the sound of a thunderclap. After briefly reflecting upon his lifeless face, she stood up and returned to her carriage. Behind her, his attendants covered him with a blanket from head to toe, forever ending their conversation.

The last ape she could talk to was gone.

She rode off, silent.

It was the old, familiar argument: human or ape?

She had always said it was a human, but her sister, younger but not as pretty, insisted it was an ape. How could it be otherwise?

They wrote their notes back and forth, sometimes using the same scrap of paper multiple times, filling them with their scrawls while playing the old disc over and over. They listened to the singing and each one of them imagining the singer.

It was a fun game, a way to pass the time, but they always made sure to hide their notes from the apes—the apes didn't like to see humans writing.

Hers was one of the last families that could write.

It was all moot now, she mused as they trudged down the road and to the outskirts of their village. It was called Mak, and it was flat and barren and comprised only a dirty main street and a clutch of tumble-down wood cabins. It was said to once have been a great city, full of life and the center of the world, but she just couldn't imagine it.

Still, the apes wanted it back now, for whatever reason. And they demanded that all the humans in Mak leave.

It was an insult, she told herself as she guided the horse on which her mother rode. Weren't they descended from great leaders? Weren't they the Sulls, related to a woman who once told both man and ape what to do? The original Sull, the may-nor of Mak?

The apes didn't care, if they even knew anything about it. They rode into the village two days ago and told everyone to leave. And here the humans were, walking out of town in rags, with feet bare and heads bowed.

And silent; every human was silent as they left. But that was nothing strange—no one spoke because no one could.

She remembered her great-granddame speaking... or, at least, she thought she remembered that. It was a kind of croak, like the frogs made, but she seemed to recall her granddame forming words...

They approached the inspection point, and she ceased her useless reminiscing and heeded her father's motions: let him handle it and look after her sister.

She saw three gorillas and a chimp, standing off to one side of the line of humans, talking to them and rifling through packs and boxes. She glanced at her family's meager belongings on their second horse and shuddered. No one else had two horses, and this made her feel like the Sulls stood out, made them look like they were better than everyone else.

Well, they were, of course, but at that moment, it seemed like the worst thing in the world for the apes to think.

She pulled her sister to her side and placed her hands on the girl's shoulders, kneading them and willing herself to relax as they neared the inspection point. When they got a little closer, she heard one of the gorillas mumbling to himself in a deep, bass voice.

"...done with this trash. Finally rid of them."

The chimpanzee wore spectacles. She'd seen them on other apes when she was younger and discovered they helped them to see. Her own eyes were good and strong, and the thought of it made her feel *better* than the apes. It was a fleeting idea, because something else would always come around to chase it away.

"How long have you lived in the village?" the chimp asked her father with a fussy chirp. He held a small, thin piece of wood on which he'd fastened sheets of paper. As her father gestured, the chimp made notes on the papers with a pencil.

"I take that to mean you've always lived here," the chimp grumbled. He looked over his spectacles at her and her sister and mother, and especially at the horses. "Stay here, and *don't* move. Sergeant! Get to it."

The gorilla farthest from the chimpanzee snapped his hairy fingers and pointed to the horses. The other two gorillas shambled up to them and started going through her family's things.

Though every citizen of Mak was subjected to the same scrutiny, it was still humiliating to her.

One of the gorillas suddenly pulled a small box out of one of the packs and held it up to squint at in the sun. Her tension spiked and she took a step forward around her sister, looking from the box to her father, pleading with him with her eyes. Her father raised his eyebrows and began waving his hands at the chimpanzee.

The chimp sighed, shook his head, and motioned for a gorilla to block her father's advance on him. Then he took the box into his own hands and opened it.

Inside were the most precious things the Sulls owned: two pieces of dull, grey metal, worn and blank. They sat in the box nestled in a scrap of fine material, the way they'd been all her life and all of her mother's life and her mother before her. As far as she knew, they had always been that way.

The chimp frowned, glancing up at her father. "You seem to think these are worth something? I can't see how that could be, but we'll find out. Sergeant, bring up the next humans. We're done with these."

She nearly fell to the ground. The objects in the box were to be hers, her birthright, as they were for the oldest child in each generation. They were to be *hers*, and now the apes took them with nearly no thought, no real interest. Just *took* them.

Why the metal pieces mattered to her, mattered to anyone in her family, she could not say.

She moved toward the chimp, balling her hands into fists. She took two, maybe three steps, and found herself on the ground, spitting out dirt. The gorilla who knocked her down snorted, then giggled.

Her father ran to her side and picked her up off the ground. She pushed him aside, leapt over to the gorilla and, leaning over his exposed upper arm, bit him.

Once again she found herself on the ground, but this time reeling from a blow to the side of her head from the wooden butt of a rifle.

"Move along, human," said the chimp, placing the little

box in a chest that sat beside him on the dusty ground. "Or we'll take the girl—*both* girls—as reparation, too."

She managed to make it to her feet with only minimal help from her sister. Her father was too stunned by the event to muster anything beyond a slack jaw and utter resignation. He finally gathered up the reins of both horses and tugged at them.

Together, the Sulls moved past the inspection point to the sound of chuckling gorillas.

Roughly a mile down the road out of Mak, there was a small stand of trees. There they stopped, along with a few other families, and rested after their ordeal.

She searched the faces of their former-fellow villagers and found them either haunted or empty. This was somehow significant to her, a signal of something.

Her sister kept looking back at the inspection point. She walked up to her and hugged the young girl, looking down the road herself. A thought came to mind. It surprised her.

Seeing that her parents were now sitting beneath one of the trees, perhaps napping, she looked at her sister and gestured for her to join them. The girl's eyes questioned her, but she nodded and went to join her mother and father.

It was late in the afternoon, nearly evening, when they stopped in the stand of trees, so she only had to wait an hour or so before the sun began to set and brought shadows to the landscape.

Without a sound, she slipped away from the group and down the road.

Sometime later, she sat down in the dark next to her sister under the tree. In her hand was the little box.

Before she drifted off to sleep, she massaged the lump on the side of her head and gazed out at the surrounding land and down the road away from Mak. Far off, she could see a great forest, and she felt it was somehow beckoning to her and her family. Maybe it was calling to all humans.

She opened the lid of the box and looked at the metal pieces. Touching one with a finger—which she had never done—she was pleased at how cool it was.

As sleep came, she wondered at her boldness, and at the new lengths to which she would go for something that mattered to her.

She cherished the feeling, for she believed, in that moment, she was the last human who really cared about anything at all.

The *Nrr* tribe shuffled about, gathering wood.

It had been harder this time to get them up and moving, but she somehow knew it was the time for it. They were slow to be about the gathering, but she saw that the huts were falling apart and if she didn't do something about it, the tribe would regret it later.

After a day of searching for pieces of wood, the *Nrr* began to break up into smaller groups and then as individuals. Despondent from a fruitless quest, they went about doing other things, or, in many cases, doing nothing at all.

She knew then they would have to trade for wood. And they had nothing to trade with.

"Nrr," said her mate when she pointed at the holes in the top of their hut on the edge of what the apes called the Forbidden Zone. An animal hide, much like the ones they wore on their thin bodies, flapped in a light breeze, placed loosely over a hole, but not fixed down.

She sighed and turned from him. Was she really the only one who could *see*?

Sitting down on the hard ground to think, she looked at the pictures in her head. She remembered there was once something they could use to trade, but it was gone. It had been taken from them by an ape.

She had come back from a hunt for berries and had found her mate standing with an orangutan near the tribe's small clutch of huts. The ape was pointing out across the Forbidden Zone and speaking. As she approached, both her mate and the ape glanced at her.

She saw then that the orangutan held her things, looking down at them and back up to her mate and gibbering.

Running up to them, she grabbed at the metal pieces the ape held, but when he flung up his hand, her mate pushed her away, and she tripped and fell to the ground.

Later, when the ape had gone, her mate told her, through gestures, that their visitor thought the pieces came from the Zone, and gave him a small basket of fruit for them.

It was all they'd had, but now it was gone.

A cool breeze off the lapping water around them tickled her nose. Wrapped in her arms, she felt him stiffen as he looked up at the giant figure before them.

She, too, gazed up at it then, not understanding what he saw in it.

The Good Man slipped away from her and off the horse. She did the same. He started to make the sounds from his mouth again, but they were not the good ones he often put in her ears; these were bad. They were quiet at first, then became louder.

The Good Man was in pain because of the big figure. And then he was gone.

She'd looked for him for a long time, before she found him the first time, then she lost him again. He was not the same as her, not the same as her people. He was not like the Others, either, but he made sounds like them. He was *different*. He did strange things, both good and bad, and he scratched things in the dirt.

She was scared when he scratched things in the dirt. She was scared that the Others would take him away from her because he did that. Because he was *different*. She tried to make him the same as her, so he would stay with her.

She needed him, wanted him. And she thought he wanted her.

With the Good Man, everything began to change. She *remembered* things. She remembered things because they were good things to remember, like her home, but there were also bad things, too, like the pain from the Others. He also gave her a good thing that he put around her neck, and that felt cool to her touch. It was good for him to do this, and it made her feel good, made her forget the bad thing the Others put around her neck. He also wanted the sounds to come from her mouth, like they did from his, but she could not remember if she could do that and so she didn't.

She thought she wanted to, though.

After the Good Man was gone, after the giant figure, she remembered him and wanted him back. So, she looked for him.

Without him, something was wrong. Things were bad. She needed to find him.

She found someone else instead. He was like the Good Man, but not him. He was the Sad Man. He wanted to find the Good Man, too, so she took him to the Others. The Good Others.

She remembered all of this, and more, but when the Sad Man took her to a place below the ground, she didn't remember any place like it before. It was *different*. There was pain there. The Sad Man tried to hurt her. She could not breathe in the water.

And there was no Good Man, only pain and darkness and then no Sad Man.

But then there was light.

•

Mendez XXVI was asking her something.

Albina turned her face from the girl and answered him silently.

I apologize, she said, *but I've never encountered this before.*

Mendez saw that she was shaken, and he could not recall Albina ever being shaken by anything.

What is it? It's just a human female; what is wrong with you?

Albina looked into his eyes and then back at her subject. The dark-haired, filthy girl lay prone on a table, unmoving, her beautiful eyes open yet not seeing.

There's nothing wrong with me. *It's* her. *She's opening up, like they all do…*

So, why is there a problem? There are things we need to know—and now.

She did not sigh, though she wanted to. Her leader hated sighing. She collected herself and tried to organize her thoughts, lest he think she'd become weak.

It's not just her that I'm seeing, Mendez. I'm seeing others. Several other women's memories…

Split personality?

No… racial memories, I believe. It's incredible. It's—

Mendez reached out and took Albina by her shoulders, wheeling her around to face him. The physical contact shocked her, and she knew she'd failed to hide that from her thoughts.

We don't have time for this, Albina. Come with me now to the audience chamber. The girl will be sent in and we'll see if she has a use to us then…

He departed, leaving her with the female. She reached out with her mind to bring her back to consciousness, hoping there'd be another opportunity to delve deeper into the fascinating world that lay within.

•

She saw the Sad Man again, but not the Good Man. There were more, too, that looked like her and the Sad Man, but they were not the same. They were *different*, too. Why was everyone now *different*?

And then the Sad Man tried to hurt her again.

The Different People brought her into a big place with the Sad Man and put something on her and made her sit and watch strange things. The Different People were ugly under their faces; she was confused. And still there was no Good Man.

Then the light came again.

Albina, I warn you...

This time, the Inquisitor did not look up at Mendez when he entered. She knew he'd be unhappy that she was once more delving into the girl's mind, but it presented an unparalleled opportunity she simply could not turn away from.

I will not apologize again for my actions, Mendez, she told him. *This female is special, a mind that encompasses... centuries. What I've found within her is—*

Not important! Mendez sent, so powerfully it gave Albina pause. She ended her second examination of the girl and turned to her leader with eyes wide.

You would have me abandon a cache of knowledge that—

Silence! he raged. *We are fighting for our very survival at the moment, Albina, and this—*he indicated the savage with a pointing finger—*is not the path to it!*

She is opening up. If I could only—

Mendez cut her off with a cutting sweep of his hand. *No. Have her taken away to a cell, and then you will join the others. I must go and pray.*

Albina opened her mouth to speak, really speak.

No more, Mendez interjected. *This is done.*

She heard the Good Man before she saw him.

One of the Different People took her to a new place, still deep below the ground. There she heard who she was looking for.

She tried to go to him, but the Different Man held her back. She knew how to get away, though, and did so.

And there, separated from her in a small place, was the Sad Man—and the Good Man. They were together.

A great thing gathered inside her. She felt it fill her up, like nothing she ever remembered before. Not food, not water, not the Good Man lying with her, nothing.

It was *different*. It was not the same as anything else. Something had changed.

Her entire body shook, quavering in the chilly air of the place. *"Taylor!"*

It came out nearly inarticulate, barely a word; a name. It came out as a strangled remnant of her sanity, a dam breaking to release her pent-up passion.

Nova began to think strange thoughts. Nova? Yes, that was her *name*.

Taylor saw her, saw her for who and what she was. She was sure of it. He and… Brent? Yes, he and Brent took care of their tormentor, and then Taylor was with her, loving her.

She forgave him. She spoke with a thousand voices and he heard her and listened.

Then pain again, hot, searing pain. And darkness followed, and still Taylor loved her.

The darkness deepened, and then there was light. The brightest light ever.

And she was no longer silent.

It's back to the realm of the live-action television series we travel, as Robert Greenberger's "Who Is This Man? What Sort of Devil Is He?" explores Urko's home life and reveals details concerning one of the show's greatest mysteries…

WHO IS THIS MAN? WHAT SORT OF DEVIL IS HE?

by

ROBERT GREENBERGER

"Kill them!"

He had commanded Zako to shoot Burke and Virdon. Why weren't they dead?

"Kill them!" he ordered one more time.

Instead of his second-in-command's voice, or the sound of gunfire, he heard the voices of his wife and son. What were they doing there? Where was he?

Urko's mind was fuzzy as he climbed from the fog of sleep. His first instinct, since he couldn't remember where he last was, was that he was a captive. But then he heard something anomalous: his wife's voice. He *and* Elta couldn't both be prisoners, so where exactly was he?

As Central City's security chief opened his eyes, the bright light from the lamp bothered him and he was keenly aware of the aches and pains around his body. Blinking once, then twice, he quickly realized he was home and that someone was offering him a banana. This made him recoil in horror as an image of captivity flooded his mind. It triggered very unpleasant memories, angering him, mixing with the confusion and pain.

"It's okay, Urko," his wife said. He blinked again and realized she was not taunting him with the fruit but was instead holding a tall, yellow cup of water before him. "Drink."

That was when he focused on just how thirsty he was. With a rough hand, he grasped the cup and guzzled the cool, refreshing drink, letting it dribble down his face and pool on his hair. As he drained the cup, Urko came to focus on his surroundings. He was home, in his bed, wearing a rarely used sleeping gown. There were bandages on various parts of his body but he was home. Safe.

Elta looked at him, her lighter brown hair beginning to streak with gray, concern and love in her eyes.

"It has been a day, my husband, but you will heal," she said, answering the most immediate questions. "Doctor Kira sent a nurse to check on you every few hours, and she says you are healing."

"What happened?"

Elta sat beside him, gesturing for their teenage son, Urso, to refill the cup. The boy seemed eager to do something, so he loped off toward the tap. She settled by her husband and said, "You were trapped belowground with one of the humans. You were injured in your attempt to free yourself. Zako helped bring you back to me."

Her words triggered a flood of images and memories. What was it Burke called that underground chamber? A *subway station*. There were earthquakes and the two were trapped, and he was forced to ally himself with the enemy to escape a deadly fate. But before he could be free, he spotted a poster, one that put a lie to everything he had been taught.

A gorilla was behind bars, on display to humans. The youth in the poster was offering a banana to his ancestor, and Burke's words played in his memory: "You couldn't risk my telling anyone, could you, Urko? You couldn't risk having your friends know the truth: that *your ancestors* were the lower species, Urko, and that it was the humans who built a civilization beyond your understanding!"

Urko had torn the poster from the wall, folded it and tucked it into his glove. He rapidly rolled over, wincing in pain, his eyes scanning the room for his uniform. Each movement caused him discomfort but he refused to acknowledge it.

"What are you looking for?"

"My uniform!"

"You're not reporting back to your troops until the doctor clears you," Elta said firmly. "Councilor Zaius' orders."

"There was a paper…"

"There was nothing but your uniform and gear," she said, gently forcing him back onto the bed. "In fact, we're having it cleaned and repaired so you look your best when you return to duty."

He grunted at that, wondering if the poster fell when he collapsed and, if so, where that damning image was.

"Zako brought you back here, semi-conscious, and the doctor worked on your injuries. Zako took command of the troops and said something about seeking the human astronauts."

Urko's last memories were of ordering his soldiers to kill Burke and Virdon, but Zako countermanded them. Something about giving his "word"; well, they'd be having words about *that* when he resumed his post. He presumed Zako would be doing an imitation of a manhunt to keep up appearances, but now suspected he had human sympathies, and there was no room for such sentiments among his troops.

"What happened?"

Such a simple question, but one filled with complex answers. Could he reveal the truth to his wife? Would she even believe it? Burke described things that staggered his imagination. Metal tubes that ran on some form of "nuclear" energy. He paused to consider if any of that energy was still there, and how he could safely extract it and make more powerful weapons for his use. The other things the human babbled about, such as disposable clothing and meals in pill form, sounded wasteful or foolish. Or both. He liked his food in his hand, the variety of tastes, and the ways Elta prepared it. To miss all that for the convenience of a pill? Absurd.

Slowly, haltingly, Urko began to describe his ordeal. When it was just him and his wife, he could let his true self be seen. He was more than just a military commander, but an ape who deeply loved his wife and fiercely wanted to create a world where their son could be safe from humans. He took his duty to his people very seriously, but his family would come first, which is why he divulged to Elta what Zaius or others might consider state secrets.

Could he trust her with the newest secret? Silly question, he chided himself.

"The paper was an image from long ago. It showed... one of us... behind bars. We were on display, Elta. We were zoo specimens, on display for humans!"

"Could that be true or propaganda?"

The question gave Urko pause. He hadn't stopped to consider the poster's veracity, and had allowed Burke to taunt him. But he *could* have been lying. Humans were very good at that.

No, he decided, he had heard the raw emotion in the man's voice. To Burke, that was the reality.

"If true, Elta, it means the scholars, the sacred texts, are liars," Urko said, laying back on the pillow, frustrated.

"Is that even possible?" she asked.

"We live in a world where the impossible is proven possible with regularity. Burke and Virdon, the astronauts, and their predecessors, possess such intelligence compared with the humans here. You never saw their ship. It's beyond anything apes could build—or even conceive of."

At first, she nodded in silence, sitting still by him. But as he began describing the arguments with Burke and the revelations of human ability, she took his hand, her fingers intertwining with his. They used to hold hands more often, and he paused to idly wonder when they had stopped.

As he spoke, the poster's mocking image remained fixed in his mind and refueled his anger.

"You truly believe that was the case?"

"Humans can't be trusted," Urko said, strength returning to his voice. "I've known that my entire life, but when I saw how... intelligent... some were, it reinforced to me how dangerous they were."

Urso looked at his father with a quizzical expression but Urko chose not to elaborate.

"But I cannot explain what I saw down there. We would never have built tubes and tunnels, so someone did. And that picture. We'd never create that obscene notion."

"So, Burke spoke true?"

"Yes. No. I hope not," he finally said, trying to convince himself that there had to be another explanation. He'd leave that to the chimp scientists. As those thoughts filled his mind, he drifted back to sleep.

A day later, Urko finally felt normal again. Despite the pain he still felt, he rose from bed and dressed in simple leathers.

As he dressed, he could hear Elta and Urso talking, resuming some conversation they'd previously had. In fact, he thought, it reminded him of the words he heard as he first awoke.

"Why is it so unimaginable that we'd someday cooperate with the humans?" Urso asked. "We both live on this planet, we're both intelligent..."

"Don't let your father hear you say that," she chided. "You know he has a low opinion of humans."

"But didn't Zako and the other human, Vernon—"

"Virdon," his mother corrected.

"Zako and Virdon worked together to rescue Father. Doesn't that prove that anything is possible?"

"Virdon and his partner, Burke, appear to be the exception

for humans," Elta said. Urko wanted to interject himself into the conversation, but realized silence was better. He so rarely knew what was on his son's mind these days. Now was as good a time as any to learn. After all, there might be a tactical advantage in it.

"What if they teach the other humans?" Urso asked. "Then what? We have common problems, like those earthquakes. Why can't we come up with common solutions?"

"Son, humans and apes have not treated one another well for generations, and we keep to ourselves. It's better that way," Elta said.

"Better for who?" he shot back.

"We keep to ourselves, and it's safer for the humans," she replied. "We have our own internal divisions; the orangutans, chimpanzees, and gorillas have their own prejudices. Don't go adding in humans because you see them as similar."

"Has no one questioned how they are so similar to us? So similar to the triad that is our society?"

"Triad," Elta mused. "Fancy word."

"I do pay attention in class," he shot back, "regardless of what Father says."

The conversation drifted to other topics, but Urko heard Elta's gentle hand guiding it. She didn't want to further the line of reasoning about the similarities between humans and apes. He approved, since his own dark thoughts were troubling enough.

Until the medical team approved, Urko was officially off-duty, on medical leave, although he snarled at the last nurse. He felt fine, and he was ready to resume his duty and lead the hunt for the human astronauts.

Elta had other ideas.

Urko brooded all the way through their breakfast, unable to get the poster's image and all it revealed from his mind. He merely grunted at questions from Elta or Urso, barely saying a word when pressed. They recognized the single-focused mood and knew to back off, at least for a time. But once the food was cleared and the kitchen cleaned, Elta appeared before her husband in a fresh dress.

"You're planning something," he said, accusing her in a tone he normally reserved for politicians.

"You being home is messing with my routine," she said brightly. "The sooner we can get you cleared for duty, the better we'll all feel. To do that, you need some exercise so you can show Doctor Kira."

"What exercise?" he snarled.

"We're taking a walk, get you some sunlight, maybe pick some fruit for lunch," she said in as positive a tone as she could manage. He knew she was trying to make a bad situation at least palatable and he couldn't argue with the benefit of some movement. He did feel stiff and needed to resume his peak condition as quickly as possible. Urko also noticed how she stood and saw the expression in her eyes. In most matters, his word was final, but when it came to things like this, he knew better than to argue.

"And our son?"

"Coming," Urso said, a cloth bag slung over one shoulder.

Urko grunted in acknowledgement and they were off. The sun was bright and at first bothered his eyes, but he appreciated the warmth and feel of solid ground beneath his feet. When Zaius had visited the night before, the elder orangutan had reported that there had been no further aftershocks from the earthquake so the danger had subsided. Howala, their village, had taken some damage, but Urko was happy to hear the human settlements were in worse shape. It meant less shelter afforded Burke, Virdon, and that traitor, Galen.

As they walked past the outskirts of their village, Urko realized he was moving with less pain. He needed to push himself, convince others he was fine. There was work to do.

Elta entwined her fingers with his, and Urko relaxed at her touch. They walked along in companionable silence, Urso a few steps behind them. Where his eyes normally scanned the scene for strategic advantages, he now just observed the trees and scrub brush, the tufts of grass ringing gardens. The further from Central City they got, the more natural the land seemed and Urko realized it had been a long time since he had really noticed his environment. He had played out here as a child, and knew Urso and his friends also played catch here, away from any building that might be damaged from an errant throw.

The trio walked by a tree that was scorched, blackened from some gunfight. It was old and hardy, though, still producing green leaves. He studied it and slowed their gait.

"Husband?"

"Zako and I fired on the astronauts here," he said matter-of-factly.

"How'd you miss? You're such a great shot," Urso asked. Urko tried to listen for any sarcasm or pride, but his son's tone was neutral.

"Moving targets," was all Urko would say. They picked up their pace and he was brooding once more, images of bananas and bars before his eyes. "I have to find them. Eliminate the astronauts again."

"Again? I thought they were still alive," Urso said.

Elta's fingers tightened around Urko's, a silent signal, its meaning a mystery to him.

With a heavy sigh, Urko turned and faced his son. "You know these men—Burke and Virdon—claim to be astronauts, men who came here from another time, another place."

"Yeah."

"You were young, but there had been others to make a similar claim," Urko admitted.

"You're kidding," his son said in a high voice. "How many astronauts can there be?"

A low growl escaped Urko, and Urso fell silent. How much should he reveal to his son? Was that the warning in his wife's fingers? She knew everything, of course; he kept no secrets from her. Urso was growing up and would soon be choosing a role to serve. Urko had hoped it would be the military, but so far, the boy had not evinced much interest in marksmanship, riding, or even tracking. In fact, Urso's head seemed to be in the clouds, always thinking. About what was another puzzle. If this morning's conversation was an indicator, then he would be branded a problem, making it seem that Urko was unable to rule his own home, let alone the armed forces.

Maybe a cautionary tale about humans was just what was needed.

"I had just been named security chief and the helm of office was finally feeling comfortable on my head when we heard something crash not far from here," Urko said as they walked. He gestured toward the eastern horizon. Urso drew closer, he noted, which was good. He didn't want to shout and for his words to carry. This was not for the public.

"Councilor Zaius and his young assistant, Doctor Zira, insisted on coming with me to investigate, but I made sure we had sufficient gorillas just in case it was something that posed a threat. It took an hour to get there, so you can imagine just how loud that sound must have been for us to hear it. What we found was indescribable: twisted metal and what looked like a boxy shape half-buried in the dunes. We counted four figures in white outfits that covered them from head to toe. They looked shorter and slighter than us, human-like, and at that I had my troops fan out. We'd never seen anything like them before, and had no idea where they'd come from or what danger they posed."

Urko paused and Elta handed him a canteen. He drained half of it rapidly, suddenly aware of how dehydrated he felt—a combination of his injuries and the medicines, no doubt.

"Astronauts?" Urso asked.

"I suppose that is what they called themselves," Urko said. "I could tell the landing was not as intended. What I couldn't tell was how many of these creatures there might be, or what danger they posed. They moved about without purpose, but I could see they had no obvious weapons and couldn't pose much of an immediate threat. Zaius was fascinated by the metal construct, while Zira noted that they appeared uninjured.

"One removed his headpiece and revealed himself to be a human. Zaius was stunned but fascinated, while I was alarmed at the threat such technology in the hands of humans posed to the people.

"Zaius theorized it was a vehicle, a vessel, or a ship of some kind. He insisted we secure the ship for study, so I dispatched soldiers to encircle it, taking measures and determining whether something so big could be moved. With the others, we approached the four humans. What surprised me was that humans could build anything so complex. All our studies showed they lacked metal-making skills. The machine's purpose escaped us, although Zaius was already coming up with ideas. He has more ideas than there are stars in the sky. My goal was to apprehend them and learn their origins and what threat they posed to our people. If they were to report to their home, they might summon more, so I was determined to kill them at once."

Urso paused mid-step and stood still. His mouth dropped open and he asked, "Without talking to them?"

"Son, humans cannot be trusted. Humans lie. They do whatever they can to stay alive, but every human is a threat to our way of life." Urko realized he was saying almost word for word what his instructor had told him decades earlier, long before ships from the stars fell on the earth.

The boy with the banana and the ape. They looked primitive in a way, but not alien.

"Can we build anything like that?" Such an innocent question.

"No," Urko said firmly. "And we don't need to be up in the air. We're bound by gravity and that's the way of the world."

"What happened?"

"They were not entirely unarmed, but were carrying tools I did not recognize. As they waved them about the air, one spotted our approach and they scattered, running from the ship. I ordered my soldiers to secure the ship while I went in pursuit."

"How'd you know which one to follow?"

"My instincts, Urso," Urko said. Then with a wink, "It's why I was made a security chief."

Urso nodded at that and stepped closer as they walked.

"I couldn't understand it. I knew that territory from my training days and had ridden it often, yet they were clever and managed to elude me and my soldiers. They displayed a level of cunning and intelligence none of the local humans had ever shown. I was intrigued and horrified at the same time. If there was an intelligent tribe of humans who could build such things and be so clever, then they were an immediate threat to our people."

"That sounds like a drastic conclusion," Urso said.

Urko stared at his son for a long moment, not saying a word. "Humans are, at best, to be tolerated, but are dangerous and always should be seen as a threat. The hunt took time and rarely had I ever been so openly challenged. I was actually exhilarated by it. I trailed one man toward a mesa and he scampered up its side very impressively. He was almost apelike in his speed. One of my soldiers was closer and began up the side after him. The human—their leader, as it turned out—was smart enough to trigger many rocks to fall, and my lieutenant was killed.

"I kicked my horse into moving more swiftly and saw a human about to climb the mesa. I quickly dismounted and caught up to him, being a superior climber. I hauled him off the rock face and brought him back to the ground. I later learned his name was Bengsten, but it didn't matter. I snapped his neck with my hands, eliminating one-quarter of the infestation."

"They were humans, not spiders," Urso protested.

"They were a threat!" Urko snapped, his anger clear. "You don't get it, son. Wherever these men came from, they were dangerous. If they taught their ways to the locals, we'd have a clear danger. Today, we have Virdon and Burke posing the exact same threat."

"Wouldn't you want to learn how to make machines like the one you describe? Or the subway machine you saw the other day?"

Urko eyed his son with surprise. "What good is a machine that crashes to the ground? Or one that crawls *beneath* the ground?"

"Okay, then, what about learning how to make sophisticated metals so you can have superior gear for your soldiers?"

That was an argument that actually made sense. Perhaps interrogating Burke or Virdon might yield some useful intelligence. But should the astronauts share it with the local humans and not him, what sort of challenge to his authority would that make?

"Are you sure you are not an orangutan?" Urko commented, attempting humor that neither Elta nor Urso found funny.

"Did you kill them all?"

"One named Charles vanished. I never learned his fate, but can only hope the desert heat got him. Cooked him in that bulky garment he wore."

Elta placed both hands around her husband's and held them close to her chest. "I remember this story. Tell him what happened next."

Urko nodded and continued. "I was so focused on killing Bengsten that I did not notice the approach of a man who called himself LaFever. Such names. He knocked me from my feet and grabbed my rifle. He used the butt-end to pummel me and I was stunned. Rather than shoot me, he hefted a large rock and intended to crush my skull. I was too dazed to do much of anything."

Urso took in a sharp breath and Elta gripped all the tighter as Urko relived those moments of disorientation and genuine fear. He had never told his wife just how certain of death he was at that moment, and he never intended to share that.

"The fourth man, Thomas, shouldered LaFever and toppled him. Maybe he was trying to keep him from killing me, or just provide a cowardly distraction so Thomas could flee. LaFever fell over, and as I rose, my soldiers finally arrived and surrounded them both. I retrieved my rifle and was about to fire when Zaius showed up."

"You would have shot him just like that?"

"It's a kill-or-be-killed situation, Urso; you have to be decisive or die." Clearly, Urso did not have the instincts for the military. Part of Urko was disappointed while another part, one he rarely acknowledged and tended to keep far from his main thoughts, was thankful he would not be putting his life at risk.

"The thing is, everything changed when Thomas opened his mouth and spoke. Zaius beckoned Zira to his side and the two had us put our weapons down until they could have a conversation." Even now, a decade later, he remembered the contempt he felt for the councilor risking their lives by having a discussion with the human. His intelligence was dangerous.

"What did this Thomas say?"

"He said they meant us no harm, and claimed that not only did that wrecked machine fly through the air, but it crossed the void, the stars, and came here. He then embroidered his fantastic lies with the suggestion that he had also traveled from another period of time."

"You mean like from the future?" Elta asked. Either she had forgotten this aspect or he had never shared it before. At the time, Zaius considered such discussions a state secret. To Urko, then as now, it was an absurd notion, the product of a deranged or cunning mind—either way, a problem.

"He claimed his home was a thousand years in his world's past," Urko said. His mind returned to the "subway" station and the marvels there. The minds that could build a massive wagon that ran underground on atomic power could also build machines that flew through space. Why not time? The poster swam in his vision once more, linking Burke's Earth with Urko's. He stifled a shudder.

"Are you ill?" Elta said, alarm in her voice.

"It's nothing," Urko said, resolving not to think of the image again.

"Zira kept asking questions, wanting to learn all Thomas had to share. Zaius kept his own mind at the moment. My riders returned, unable to find Charles. LaFever stayed down, silent. I remember it all sounded insane, and I could not believe Zira and Zaius wanted to bring them back to Central City, to expose them to our society.

"As security chief, I knew my mandate was clear. I was to protect our people at all costs, and it was my final determination as to what presented a clear and present danger. I had seen and heard enough. I picked up my rifle and shot LaFever. I then raised my gun to aim at Thomas, but Zira interposed herself between me and the human. She took the shot meant to end the threat and died for it. The fool."

"The fool?" Urso said loudly. The incredulity in his voice was clear. "Think of what he could have taught us."

Urko and Elta both stared at their son.

"You just went and killed someone who could have taught us how to build with metal, not just use it for knives and horseshoes." Urso paused, waiting for a response. When it didn't come he asked, "What happened to Thomas?"

"To his credit, he stayed in place, just staring at LaFever and Zira. Zaius yelled at me. I yelled back, both of us exerting authority, both of us convinced we were right. We were younger then and things grew heated. We actually began to fight, which is a clear breach of protocol. Thomas saw a chance to escape, so he began to run away."

"Good," Urso said.

"One of my smarter gorillas—Zako, as it turns out— saw what was happening, took aim, and fired. So ended the threat."

"But Charles got away!" Urso said, sounding actually happy about it.

"He has not been seen since," Urko said. "He's dead."

Urso stared defiantly back at him. "You just shot them dead," the teen said.

"They were a threat! Humans are always a threat," his father repeated.

"Why do we let any live, then?"

"They are useful at times," Urko admitted. "When they are kept docile and know their place. But trust me, at the first sign of danger, they are eliminated."

"What happened after you slaughtered the humans?" Urso asked.

"Eliminated, Urso," he replied impatiently. "Not slaughtered. *Eliminated*. Zaius ordered my soldiers to bury Zira and the astronauts. We dug proper graves and left a marker to note her passing." Urko had liked Zira, respected her quite a bit, but her good nature had proved her end.

"And their machine?"

Urko let out a snort at the memory. "We were so focused

on burying the dead that no one had seen a pack of humans slither all over the machine, stripping it for useful tools. They were like flies around abandoned food, so pitiful. My troops took some shots to scatter them. Whether it was something they did or a lucky shot, the machine burst into flames and eventually warped into a useless hunk of metal. When the fires died out, we brought out animals with tools and buried the remains. No one else would ever touch it."

"Why wouldn't you let them speak? What were you so afraid of hearing?"

"Afraid? Nothing of the sort," Urko said, disliking the defensive tone he had to take with his own son.

"Can we learn *nothing* from humans?"

Urko shook his head. "They're simple-minded people," he said.

"Even Virdon and Burke, the most recent astronauts?"

"I admit they're clever enough, but actually learn something from them? I think not."

"Wasn't it Burke who engineered your rescue? Saved your life?" Elta gently asked.

He thought about the human's actions underground. Burke really did plan their escape and even managed to find a way to communicate with Virdon, tapping in some sort of code on the metal that connected above and below ground. At the time he hadn't considered it, but yes, they were clever. And that intelligence is what made them dangerous.

"If humans dug those tunnels, then of course he knew how to get us out," Urko said, but he didn't sound entirely convinced, which was doing nothing to prove to Urso the correctness of his actions.

"So, they have nothing at all to teach us," Urso said. "Doctor Zira seemed to think so. Councilor Zaius still thinks so. Otherwise, he'd have you eradicate them all for miles around."

"What nonsense are you speaking? Learn from humans? I told you they are not to be trusted."

"At school, my friends and I have been talking about whether or not there are more of these clever men like the two who trouble you so much, and where they might have come from. If there are intelligent men, then there must also be intelligent women to mate with them and produce children."

Now *that* was a troubling thought, Urko concluded. Worse, it came from a teenager who saw this as a *good* thing.

"Why can't we co-exist on this world?"

"Co-exist?" Urko dragged out each syllable, his anger, confusion, and frustration vying for precedence. "They are slave labor at best, parasites on our resources at worst. You do not co-exist with vermin."

"Burke and Virdon saved your life! Don't you owe them something?"

No, he didn't. It was a matter of convenience, nothing more. It was weak-willed Zako who guaranteed their lives, not Urko.

"What else do your friends think?"

"It's not like we talk about them all the time," Urso said, though he sounded evasive to Urko's trained ears. "But they cause us no harm, not even Virdon and Burke. I don't understand why you want them dead."

"Should they actually come from a village of smarter humans and get home, we may be inundated with more humans. Our way of life, the one that shelters you and protects you and lets you go to school with your… friends… would be over. We'd be vying with them for food and water, for minerals to process and horses to ride."

"And we can't share?"

"Urko, Urso, is this really the time for fighting?" Elta asked, finally trying to intervene and calm them down. Urko eyed his wife carefully, taking her measure to see if she, too, had sympathies for the humans. She knew Burke saved his life, so maybe he had earned them, but the others had not. She betrayed nothing.

"Father has spent weeks hunting down these humans who appear so clever they have remained alive," Urso shot back.

Urko howled at the insult. Had Urso not been his son, he would have struck the boy. The pent-up rage had to be expelled and he roared again, hurling rocks as far as his aching body allowed. The pain felt good, made him feel alive.

"I don't want to fight," Urso said, suddenly abashed and genuinely frightened by his father's display. "I just want to understand."

Urko was on him in a second, pinning his son to the ground, ignoring Elta's pleas.

"Humans helped ruin this world, make it resource-poor. Humans ruin everything they touch! Humans are dangerous! Burke and Virdon are smarter than most and that makes them all the more dangerous. All the more reason they have to be taken down. I will do whatever I must to protect us, to protect *you!*"

With a heavy exhalation, Urko rose, his anger spent. He felt tired and wanted to rest, but they were now far from home.

The boy. The banana. The cage. The vision came back to his mind.

Burke revealed a very, very dangerous secret about their world. It was a secret none, not even Zaius, could learn. Burke and Virdon were the deadliest threat to the apes' way of life. If Urso was representative of how the next generation saw the humans, then their mere presence was enough to endanger society.

Whatever else Urso did in his life, eliminating those two humans—and the traitorous Galen—would take precedence.

He had to save Central City and all of simian society. He had to save his son from their contamination.

Never again would a human feed a banana to an ape.

There are more apes than were ever dreamt of in the prevailing *Planet of the Apes* mythologies, as we learn in Greg Keyes' "Stone Monkey"...

STONE MONKEY

by

GREG KEYES

Sun had recently come to believe that there was nothing quite so frustrating as trying to enjoy a dowry cake while someone was shooting at him. This insight came just after the first snap of the crossbow string, when he was forced to abandon his perch atop the thatched roof of Lai the baker's shop and leap into the branches of a nearby loquat tree. Because the tasty confection was in his hands, he had to grab the branch with his feet, so that he then swung upside down. As he took another bite, Lai shot at him again, so Sun had to quickly transfer the cake to his feet, the better to brachiate with his long, slender arms. But this made it all that much more difficult to eat the cake, and indeed, some of the lotus-seed filling spilled out.

"Baker Lai," he shouted, "what are you about?"

"That's the last of my cakes you'll ever steal," the angry chimpanzee said, working the action on his bow. "I've had enough of your thieving ways."

He fired again, just as Sun stuffed another glob of the cake into his mouth and launched himself out of the loquat tree and into the spreading arms of a nearby ring-cupped oak.

"Be reasonable," Sun said, after he managed to swallow. "I would never have stolen from you had I known you possessed a crossbow."

This did not seem to mollify Lai the baker, who shot at him once more. The bolt clipped through the leaves a scant few centimeters from Sun's face.

"Take heart, Lai," Sun said. "Your aim is improving."

"Shut up, you dirty monkey," Lai shouted, as Sun swung behind the trunk of the tree, where he was able to gobble another few bites. He felt it was a shame to have to eat so quickly. Lai really did make wonderful cakes, and Sun preferred to take his time and savor them.

If his mouth hadn't been full, he might have corrected the indignant chimpanzee as to his lineage. Sun was not a monkey. He was an ape, and more specifically a siamang. His head was nicely round, his body adorned in lustrous black hair. His arms were longer than his legs, and he had thumbs on his feet as well as his hands.

Lai was sneaking around to get a clear shot, so Sun swung rapidly through the branches and hurled himself into the air so that he landed on the edge of the red-tiled roof of Cong the magistrate's house. A bolt struck and shattered a roof tile as Sun vanished over the ridge. As he continued on into the grove of trees beyond, he heard the magistrate begin to yell at Lai in his rough human voice.

In the top of a willow tree on the hill outside of town, Sun was finally able to lick his hands and feet clean. He had an excellent view of the valley with its neat little fields and picturesque village, and he began to wonder if—once again—he had overstayed his welcome.

He sunned himself on the branch, and was nearly drowsing when he heard horns blowing. He sleepily pulled himself up so as to see what the commotion was.

A group of horsemen was entering the town from the southern course of the main road. Most of them looked something like chimps, but larger and with bigger skulls. Sun had seen such apes when he was young, but he could not remember what they were called.

The horns were being blown by several of the big black apes, the ones nearest to what Sun guessed to be the leader. Like the others, he wore light armor of leather, cloth, and lacquered wood, but he also had an odd green helmet with a bright red turban wrapped around its base.

Most of the riders were armed with swords or clubs or repeating crossbows like Lai's, but the leader had something sheathed and attached to his saddle that Sun recognized as a far deadlier weapon.

The riders, about twenty of them, approached the magistrate's house. From his vantage, Sun could see the village militia trying to organize themselves, probably scared out of their wits. After a moment, the magistrate himself came out. The ape leader remained on his horse, towering over Cong and his thatch of gray hair. A crowd was beginning to gather, and Sun's curiosity was piqued—not enough to rouse himself from his well-earned rest, but enough for him to continue watching. It wasn't often that anything new happened in the village of Four Fortune.

Lai the baker approached the horsemen with a tray of pastries, followed quickly by Chen the wine monger and, soon enough, by most of those who dealt in goods, making all manner of obsequious gestures.

Absently, Sun remembered these apes were called *dà xīngxīng*, which just meant "big xīngxīng." Xīngxīng was the old human name for orangutan, but it literally meant "ape-ape." So these were "big ape-apes."

After a bit, the leader and his men entered into the magistrate's house as Cong wrung his hands. After that, the crowd dispersed and the magistrate with them, his shoulders slumped. Sun scratched his head. The sun had shifted, and he was now in shade. He moved further up the hillside to rest further before dinner.

Toward evening, Sun roused himself and made his way back down to the village. He was thinking of dumplings, and thus headed toward the little shed where Mei kept her steamer going. On the way, he passed Lai's place, but thought the baker might still be vigilant. The door stood open, but Sun imagined Lai inside, hiding behind a bag of flour, crossbow in hand.

Instead, he found Lai at Mei's hut, chatting about something or other.

So, he returned to the bakery, thoughts of dumplings overwhelmed by the remembered taste of dowry cake and almond biscuits.

Once inside, he stared at all of the beautiful pastries, momentarily breathless. He thought that perhaps he should find a bag or basket to fill, and was undertaking that search when the slanting rays of the sun coming through the shop door were suddenly blocked by three massive, black-haired figures.

"That's him," one of them grunted.

"Might I interest each of you in a sweet?" Sun asked. "Lai the baker left me in charge of his shop, and I'm sure he wouldn't mind—"

He was cut off as one of the giants hurled something at him. As it opened, it looked like a spider web.

Sun hooted and flung himself to the side, but the net hit his right foot and caught at his ankle. He leapt up and seized one of the ceiling beams, kicking his feet. The net came off, whirling into the face of one of his attackers. In the same instant, the end of a long pole swished by his head. Sun yelped and grabbed hold of the end of it. The force of the swing carried him past a mound of steamed buns; he caught several with his free hand and feet and hurled them at the big ape-apes, which he just now remembered were also known as gorillas.

"Stop that!" one of them shouted. "You can't get past us."

The ape holding the staff swung it so as to slam Sun into the wall. He scrambled down the length of it, up the gorilla's arm, across his face, down his back—and was out of the shop. He dodged as a fourth gorilla he hadn't seen lunged for him, and suddenly found himself face to-face with Baker Lai. He ducked between the chimp's legs and gave him a good thwack in his privates as he did so. Then he bounded into the trees behind the shop, laughing a little as the roars of rage and Lai's moans of pain faded behind him.

As he left the village once again behind him, Sun wondered what on earth the gorillas were up to. It was obviously Lai who had proposed the trap, but what interest did the big apes have in doing Lai a favor? He tried to recall if he had ever made mischief amongst gorillas great enough to draw vengeance. In his youth, perhaps. He had been much enamored of wine in those days, and there were gaps in his memory. But gorillas were rare in these parts, as evidenced by his forgetting what they were called.

They seemed warlike. Perhaps they were merely mercenaries hired by someone else to capture him. But he couldn't think of anyone who would go through that much trouble over a simple siamang.

All the more reason to move on from Four Fortune to someplace less threatening.

But he decided to put off leaving until morning. And in the morning he was hungry, and supposed that perhaps he ought to make one last trip to town.

Outside of the village, in a clearing by the stream, Sun saw one of the gorillas. He was alone, seated on a red cushion, facing a small table piled with sweets. Another cushion lay on the other side of the table. Sun approached cautiously, searching for hidden confederates, but the leader—he could see now it was the leader—truly seemed to be alone.

Sun sat there for a few moments, dithering a little, more

curious by the moment. As he watched, the gorilla took a bun from the dish and popped it into his mouth.

Sun moved up to the edge of the clearing. The dark gaze of the larger ape flicked to fix on him. Besides his chewing, it was the only motion he made.

"I made a mistake in trying to have you captured," the gorilla said, after swallowing. "I admit that now. I am an ape of war, and am used to taking what I want."

"I am of the belief," Sun said, "that you have somehow mistaken this lowly person for someone he is not. I have thought hard and long on this, and cannot imagine any harm I might have done you or any use that I might be to you."

"My name is Shor Telag," the gorilla said. "The warlord. Perhaps you have heard of me."

"Of course," Sun lied. "The mention of your name shakes the branches of peach trees a thousand miles away."

Shor looked pleased. "You are more knowledgeable in that respect than these villagers," he said.

"I am perhaps more widely traveled," Sun said. "Of what use could this poor siamang be to your august eminence?"

"I have conquered many towns and villages, siamang," Shor said. "I have brought order where there never was. I have brought law to the lawless. I have collected artists, architects, and philosophers and built a magnificent city to be my capitol."

"That all sounds very grand," Sun said.

"It is. And yet, I fear at my death it will all be for naught. My sons are simpletons, at best. Even my most trusted followers may well squabble when I am gone and divide my legacy. I cannot bear the thought of this, and have deliberated much on the matter. I have consulted sages and oracles, and in the end there is only one remedy for my situation."

"You wish me to rule after you are gone?" Sun said. "This is very flattering, but I have no natural inclination toward governance."

"No," the gorilla thundered, impatiently. "Come closer so we can converse in a normal way. Have some sweets."

Sun came closer, but not all the way to the table.

"I don't blame you for your suspicions," Shor Telag said. "My apologies again for my clumsy attempt at capturing you."

"I am not offended," Sun said. "But tell me—what is the solution to your dilemma?"

"Oh, that is simple," Shor said. "I must live forever. Then my legacy will be secure."

The gorilla's gaze intensified. He seemed to desire some sort of reaction from Sun.

"Well, yes," Sun said, after a bit. "That is, indeed, simple."

Shor showed his teeth. "You understand now why I have searched for you."

"I fear I no longer follow you," Sun said.

The gorilla shrugged. "Eat with me."

Sun was, in fact, very hungry. It was hard to keep his mind off the treats. He sidled up to the table, gauging that Shor's arms were not long enough to reach across. He sat on the pillow and chose a bean paste-filled bun from which the gorilla had already taken a bite.

"You would eat after me?" Shor said.

"It is a gesture of trust where I am from," Sun said.

"You're thinking I may have poisoned the food," Shor said, wagging the back of his hand at Sun.

Sun looked at the bun. "I am now," he replied.

"I haven't, and it isn't," Shor said. "I only wish for you to tell me what you know of the Stone Monkey."

"Stone Monkey?" Sun said.

"I understand your reluctance to speak of this," Shor said. "So let me begin. There is a legend that dates to the time when the accursed cities of man fell and the Blighted Regions were created. The legend of the Stone Monkey."

"I know nothing of such things," Sun said.

The gorilla frowned a bit before going on.

"They say that a ray from the heavens struck a stone, and from it was born the Monkey King. He ruled over legions of monkeys in a secret cave in a faraway mountain. He learned much magic—how to fly upon clouds, how to control the elements, and much more. And he came to possess all manner of fabulous weapons. They say he traveled to Hell and struck his name from the Book of Life and Death, and thus became immortal."

"A fantastic tale, indeed," Sun said.

Shor leaned forward a little.

"Magic is the stuff of children's stories, of course," Shor said. "But all such fables are built on a foundation of truth. In ancient times, it was possible to fly as if on a cloud. There were weapons so powerful they could level cities and entire regions—the evidence for this is everywhere. This was not magic, but a thing called science. And if science can explain those aspects of the story, there is little reason to doubt that in those days, some elixir or tonic may have been created to sustain a life far beyond its normal span. That secret, like so many others, would have been lost in the Time of Thunder and Fire. Lost to all but the so-called Stone Monkey, the Monkey King, who thieved the secret from Hell—the Hell that was human-imposed slavery, or perhaps the Hell man unleashed upon the world with his weapons."

Shor leaned back and crossed his arms.

"You see how it all fits?"

"Your logic seems undisputable," Sun said. "But it is all very much beyond me."

"I have searched for a long time," Shor said, "finding little bits and pieces of evidence, adding them together—all of which led me inevitably here. Because the stories are not all old. There are recent accounts that point to the existence of the Monkey King. Most recently, I met with an ancient orangutan sage, who told me that in the village of Four Fortune I would find a siamang who is a loyal subject of the Stone Monkey. Here I am, and you are the only siamang present."

"Perhaps the sage was a drunkard," Sun said, "or merely wished to speed you on your way."

"Perhaps," Shor said. "But I think not."

"I should also like to point out that I am not a monkey, but rather an ape."

"There is no need to put on airs," Shor said. "We are taught that there are three kinds of ape—gorillas, chimpanzees, and orangutans. You are not any one of those, nor are you human. You are, therefore, a monkey."

"I have no tail," Sun said.

"Neither do baboons," Shor said. He struck his chest with his fist. "Don't be troubled or take offense," he said. "I am not like these rural bumpkins. In my empire, even monkeys have their place. Now, will you guide me to your master?"

"Why have you become so blurry?" Sun asked.

He tried to get up, but his hands and feet felt heavy.

"You were right to believe the food was drugged," Shor said.

"But you ate it, too," Sun said. His tongue felt like a tadpole, on the verge of escaping down a stream.

"Stupid monkey," Shor said. "I outweigh you by ten times. I will be mildly intoxicated for a few hours. You, on the other hand…"

"Yes, I see," Sun said, slowly leaning forward until his face was flat against the table. He felt the bump, and then his mind wandered off into distant places of strange light and voices he did not understand.

He came back around to Baker Lai's angry face.

"Now you will get yours," Lai said.

Sun shook his head, trying to clear it. His hands and feet were shackled by chains to a wooden post.

"Where are they?" he asked.

"That is none of your concern," Lai said. "I was chosen to watch you and alert them once you're awake."

"Baker Lai," Sun said, "you must listen to me closely—"

"No," Lai said. "You listen. When I was a child, I thought you were funny. Always playing pranks and making the adults look foolish. And then Lo the wine-monger found you asleep amongst the bottles of his most excellent vintage and put you in a bamboo cage. Do you remember this?"

"I'm not sure I recall—"

"I do," Lai said. "I was three. You told me the cage was a magical carriage which would soon transport you to the Mountain of Heavenly Delights, where everyone does what they want all day and sweets fall like rain. And so I begged to go with you, and you said that only one could go at a time, but that I could take your place, if only I could find the magic key."

"Look—" Sun said.

"So they found me, locked in the cage, with a big stupid smile on my face. Do you know how long it took me to live that down?"

"Baker Lai," Sun said, "that was all in the past, and I apologize. Now you must consider the future. Release me. Then you must flee. Do not pause to gather your things. Warn the others to do the same."

"You will not trick me again," Lai said. "We have had enough of your foolery."

"This isn't foolery," Sun said. "You do not know apes like these. I do."

"I have met gorillas, in my trips to the south."

"I don't mean gorillas," Sun said. "I mean apes of this nature. They believe I know the way to a prize beyond all value—"

"And if I release you, you will take me there instead," Lai

sneered. "I am no longer three."

"There is no prize," Sun said. "But they believe there is. Everyone in this village is in danger."

"Why? They have what they came for."

"Exactly," Sun said. He sighed. "Release me or don't," he said. "But put as many footsteps between you and this place as you can. The sooner, the better."

Lai's angry certainty now looked more like confusion.

"I don't know what you're playing at," he said. "I'm going to tell them you're awake."

"You shouldn't," Sun said.

More than an hour passed before they came. They put him on one of the horses, still shackled, sitting in front of one of the gorillas. As they made their way up the road that wound into the hills, Sun looked back at the flame and smoke from the village. He heard a few screams, but not many.

It had taken a while for the gorillas to come for him. Maybe Lai had taken his advice. Maybe he had warned others.

Maybe.

The gorillas made camp not much later, erecting a large, garish tent and several taller ones. After a bit, Sun was carried into the tent, still bound, and placed before Shor, who was seated on a pile of pillows.

"We shall have this conversation one more time," the warlord told him. "If I do not like the direction it takes, I will have your fingers and toes severed one by one. After that, we will begin taking your limbs a joint at a time. The wounds will be cauterized so you do not bleed to death. Is this all very clear to you?"

"Very clear," Sun said. "I was prepared to speak candidly yesterday, which you would have learned had I remained conscious."

"You will pardon me if I am skeptical," Shor said. But his eyes now shone with a strange light. "Tell me what you know."

"Well," Sun told him, "it is as you said. All of that about the Monkey King."

"You know him. You have met him."

Sun pretended to hesitate. Then he nodded.

"And you will show me the way."

"That presents a bit of a problem," Sun said. "You see, I am not exactly—ah—highly welcome there at the moment. A little matter, not worth going into."

"I don't doubt that," Shor said. "Why else would you spend your time making an annoyance of yourself in a backwater village? But you are under my protection now. You need not fear him."

He signed at one of his subordinates.

"Bring it," he said.

A moment later, the gorilla handed Shor the sheath that had been on his horse. The warlord withdrew its contents.

"Do you know what this is?" Shor asked.

"I do not," Sun said, even though he did.

"It is called a gun," Shor said. "A powerful weapon, a product of the science I spoke of earlier."

"Yes," Sun said. "But…"

"What?" Shor demanded.

"Well, it is just as you said. The Monkey King is immortal. However fearsome your weapon, it will have no effect on him."

Shor's eyebrows lowered dangerously. "I told you, I do not believe in fairy tales. From what I have heard, he does not age, but he is not invulnerable. However old he is, a bullet will not bounce off of his skin. You will see." He cocked his head. "Which finger shall we begin with?"

Sun hung his head. "Very well," he said. "I will guide you there."

"Of course you will," Shor said.

•

When they reached the border of the Blighted Region, Shor's soldiers began to mutter amongst themselves, and even the warlord seemed visibly disturbed.

"There must be some other way," he said, gazing out at the wasteland that stretched off to the horizon.

"There is not," Sun said. "At least, not that I know of."

"If this is some trick, monkey—"

"I came this way," Sun said. "But I understand if you're afraid to venture in."

"Are you implying that a monkey is braver than the Warlord of Shor?" the gorilla roared. He kneed his horse, and it surged forward into the desert.

The Blighted Region was not bereft of life. Tough weeds and grasses clung here and there, and dangerous, venomous things lurked beneath stone and sand. Bolder were the hunchbacked predators whose ancestors might have been dholes. A pack of perhaps seven paced them for much of the second day.

"They will attack when night falls," Sun told Shor.

"Will they?" Shor said. He reached to the sheath strapped to his saddle, unlaced it, and drew forth the weapon. Its barrel was a dull, grey color, and the stock was scratched and dented. Shor raised it, took careful aim. Then thunder seemed to clap. Sun shrieked and put his hands to his ears. One of the dhole-beasts fell over, writhing. The others looked at it, confused, as Shor took aim again.

He shot four times, and four of the animals fell. The others finally got the hint and vanished over the nearest rise.

"You see now why I fear nothing," Shor said.

"Quite so," Sun replied, shivering a little.

That night, they built a fire from what wood they could scavenge, which wasn't much. When yellow eyes appeared in the darkness, Shor fired the gun at them.

After that, they did not see the dog things again, except for the dead one just outside the edge of camp.

In four days they reached the river, which provided relief from the barren wastes. Its waters brought life from its headwaters, willows and rushes and fish and small singing frogs. Otters of great size cavorted in the waters, and turquoise kingfishers hunted from the treetops. Beyond the bright stream, all was again desolation.

"Must we cross the river?" Shor asked.

Sun hesitated.

"I've been tied up for days," he said. "Couldn't we take a rest here? I'd like to take a bath in the river."

"I've no doubt you would," Shor said. "And you also hope I will underestimate you. If I did not untie you in the desert, why do you think I would here, where if you escaped you might have some hope of survival?"

"Warlord, I am cooperating as best I can."

"And yet, each day you seem uncertain what direction to take. First north, then east, then northwest. If I didn't know better, I would think you were doing nothing more than trying to get us lost. That leads me to two possible conclusions: either you don't know where the Monkey King is and you're biding your time until you see an opportunity to escape, or your loyalty to him is so great you would lead us to our doom rather than take us to him."

"If I might offer a third possibility," Sun said, "my sense of direction is rather poor."

Shor nodded thoughtfully. "Then let us see if we can sharpen it."

He motioned for one of his gorillas.

"Cut one of his fingers off," he said.

"Now, wait just a moment," Sun said, as another soldier pushed him down and pinned his right arm. "I think I'm starting to remember—"

"I'm certain you will," Shor said.

"I see now it's a credible threat," Sun said, his voice rising. "There's no need to prove your point any further!"

The gorilla produced his knife and placed it on the second joint of his longest finger.

"So, I'll just tell you—"

Sun was surprised at how much it hurt, and he yelped first from the shock and then screamed from the pain itself. His finger rolled away from his hand and lay there like a black caterpillar.

Sun screamed some more when they cauterized the wound, and then he lay whimpering.

"Well?" Shor said. "Shall we do that again?"

"No," Sun said, quietly. "It is northeast, two days beyond the river. I'll show you."

"You see," Shor grunted to his soldiers. "Even a dirty monkey can be made to see reason."

By the next day, the pain in the stump of Sun's finger had become a dull ache throughout his body. He tried to comfort himself by recalling the taste of Lai's pastries, of sunning himself on a limb, of swinging from tree to tree.

None of it helped much.

On the second day after crossing the river, they came to a line of low hills.

"Travel east along that big mound there," Sun told Shor.

As they grew nearer, Shor reined his mount to a stop.

"Those aren't hills," he said.

"No," Sun replied.

It must have been a city of some size, at one time. Now it was mostly a pile of rubble and rust, but here and there one could make out the straight line of a wall, a skeleton of beams jutting up. The gorillas—who had somewhat overcome their terror of the Blighted Region—now fell again to grunting nervously and making superstitious signs against evil.

Sun led them on, until he spied a long crack in the edge of the rubble.

"Down there," he said.

"Dismount," Shor said, reaching for his rifle.

They kept Sun chained, but put a long lead on him.

"You walk ahead," Shor commanded.

"I'm only too pleased to," Sun said wearily.

A slope of rubble descended to a long corridor clearly shaped by human hands. The gorillas advanced timidly until Shor roared at them, but even then they did not make great speed. The light from their torches flickered and played upon the ancient walls and floor.

"You will warn me when we are near," Shor said.

"I will," Sun replied. "But I think you will know."

"What was this?" the warlord wondered.

"Some sort of transportation system, I think," Sun said. "Those rails down there, you see?"

"Ah," Shor said. "Something like mine carts might ride on those."

Sun didn't answer. It was hard to walk without putting his hands down, but when he did, it hurt.

Presently, he heard the soft rushing of water.

"There's light ahead," one of the soldiers said.

It was true. It was an odd, inconstant light, and as they drew nearer it became obvious why. A sheet of falling water barred their way. Both the origin of the waterfall and its destination were hidden on the other side. On this side, the twisted remains of an immense valve still partly occluded a round portal.

"Through there," Sun said.

Shor stared at the curtain of water for a moment.

"I can lead the way if you want," Sun said.

"No," Shor replied. He gestured at one of his soldiers. "Chog," he said. "You go. Come back and report."

He turned to Sun. "He will come back, won't he? Because if he doesn't…"

"It's safe," Sun said.

Chog sidled reluctantly up to the waterfall, pausing when he reached it.

"Chog!" Shor shouted.

The big ape squared his shoulders and stepped through.

A few heartbeats passed. Twenty. Shor's expression became increasingly more dangerous.

Then Chog came back through, soaking wet.

"Well?" Shor demanded.

"It is amazing," Chog said.

Shor nodded. "Come, all of you." He strode up the waterfall and marched straight through it, cradling his gun protectively beneath his chest. Chog took Sun's lead and dragged him through the falling water, to the place beyond.

Shor stood there, dripping, transfixed.

"It's all true," the warlord said. "All of it."

The ceiling rose in a vast vault above them, glowing with a light that was not daylight, but which resembled it nearly exactly. That false sky overlooked a vast jungle, in which grew a tangle of apple and pear trees, bananas and mango and durian, loquat and peach, walnut and pecan. Grape vines climbed the lower reaches of the dome, and the river the waterfall fed flowed through all of it.

"You see?" Shor said. "The legend speaks of a cave within the Mountain of Fruit and Flowers. And yet, this is no natural cavern. This was built by man. But for what purpose?"

"I believe they hoped to survive down here," Sun said. "Survive whatever happened, whatever created the Blighted Region."

"And where is the Monkey King?"

Sun sighed.

"He is all around you. You had better drop your gun."

As he said it, every tree in the vicinity rustled, and they appeared. Macaques and baboons, snub-nosed monkeys, lutungs and true langurs, lars and black-crested gibbons. Each was armed with a pistol, rifle, or shotgun.

"You made us outcasts," Sun said. "So we found our own place. You shouldn't have come here."

Shor trained his rifle on Sun.

"You betrayed me," he said.

"I did exactly what you asked me to," Sun said. "How is that betrayal?"

"Don't try to be clever," Shor grunted. "The elixir of immortality. Where is it?"

"There is no elixir," Sun said. "And you are a buffoon."

Shor's face twisted in fury. "You're lying." His finger twitched on the trigger.

The roar of a hundred guns filled the dome. Shor staggered back, his expression one of purest incredulity. The other gorillas turned to flee. Two made it through the waterfall. None of them made it outside.

Only then did Sun realize he had a sharp pain in his ribs. He looked down and saw blood there.

"That's unfortunate," he said. Then he fell face-down in the water.

A month later, Sun climbed a mountain, stopping now and then to munch on one of the pastries he had stolen in the village of Five Swans. He hooted a long, slow song, just for the pleasure of hearing his own voice as he swung through the cloud forest. Eventually, he came to the ancient, crumbling temple, where he found Shalang the sage.

Shalang's flat, moon-shaped face was fissured with age and his cheek pads were bloated to absurd proportions. His orange hair was matted and dirty, and he bore a beatific expression.

"There you are," the aged orangutan said. "I was expecting you a month ago."

"Yes, I know," Sun said. "I incurred a gunshot wound, which somewhat delayed my trip."

"I see," Shalang said. He closed his eyes. "I sense that you have a question to ask me."

"You bloody well know I do," Sun said.

"Why did I tell the warlord where you were?" Shalang said.

"Indeed, your reputation for prescience is much deserved," Sun said.

"I knew you would do the right thing," Shalang told him.

"They cut off one of my fingers!"

"Yes, but I see it has nearly grown back," the orangutan pointed out.

Sun looked at his hand and the half-sized pink digit protruding from it.

"It hurt," he said.

"You could avoid such pain by remaining with your subjects, safe in your cave," Shalang pointed out. "And yet you do not."

"I'm old," Sun said. "I get bored. Besides, it's best to keep abreast of things. What if Shor had come upon us unawares? With a bigger army and more guns?"

"That is my point," Shalang said. "I told him the legend so he would seek you out, and you would know of him."

"You could have just sent word," Sun said. "And the legend—"

"Shall I tell the legend?" Shalang asked. "Not as Shor understood it, but as I do?"

"Why not?" Sun sighed.

"In the time before, before the fall of cities, when apes were slaves, there was a siamang held in a place where humans did their science. They did something to him that made him—if not an immortal—at least very long-lived. And then the battle between ape and man began, and the siamang changed as all apes did, just as the stone in the ancient legend was touched by heaven and quickened into the Stone Monkey.

"After the wars, after the Blighted Regions scarred the land, this siamang found that his kind—the siamangs, the gibbons—were mistreated by humans and other apes alike. They were lumped in with monkeys, who also were victimized. And so this very long-lived siamang took it upon himself to find his brothers and sisters and lead them to a safe place. A place of their own."

Sun was silent for a moment. Then he hooted a little laugh.

"Shor thought it was a serum, something I drink or inject. They always think it's something like that."

"Do you know what they did to you?"

"No," Sun said. "As you say, my mind was different then. I was... less complicated. All I remember from the lab is pain, all sorts of pain. And then one day, some chimps came in and let everybody go. I went as far from humans as I could get. After a while, I figured out that I heal faster than everyone else. Eventually, I realized I wasn't aging, either. It really was as if someone had gone to Hell and taken my name from the Book of Life and Death."

"How old are you?" Shalang asked.

"Over a hundred," Sun said. "I quit counting long ago. I also stopped spreading my legend a long time ago. I actually cribbed most of it from an old human legend. It just attracts trouble. And yet you just keep it going."

"The world is better off without the likes of Shor," Shalang said. "Those determined enough to find you—well, they discover the only eternity for which they are destined. It's as you said—better to know they're coming before they arrive."

"I suppose," Sun grumbled, looking at his regenerating

finger. "But it still hurt. And I can tell you're delighted."

"Well," Shalang said, "I am not as ancient as you, but I am old, and there isn't much to do up here. I get bored, too."

"Perhaps," Sun said, "you should take up calligraphy."

The wondrous inventor companion of Cornelius and Zira in *Escape from the Planet of the Apes* tells his incredible personal story of triumph and tragedy in Ty Templeton's "Milo's Tale"...

MILO'S TALE

by

TY TEMPLETON

Doctor Milo stood in the surf and watched Lieutenant Soror and his expert team of chimpanzees unload equipment from the large ocean vessel anchored just off-shore. Milo's mood leaned neither toward excitement nor scientific curiosity, as was so often the case during expeditions into strange lands. Instead, today, Milo felt fear. Fear that he was too late. Fear that the gorillas had already beaten him to the object from the sky. Fear of gorillas in general.

Milo had good reason to fear them. His chimpanzee nation had been at war with gorillas for centuries. He had been born in the occupied Westlands before the liberation and, unlike most of the chimpanzees Milo knew and worked with today, he'd seen gorillas as a child, and remembered them well. They were massive, ugly things, and they smelled like death. They bullied his family and killed his friends. As a youngling, Milo had trouble believing that gorillas were part of God's plan. They seemed so purely evil, it made no sense that a loving God had made them.

But that was thirty-five years ago, before the liberation. Milo had not seen a gorilla since. He'd grown to be an ape of some importance in his home nation, a well-known professor of history, electronics, engineering, physics, and so much more, at Highlands Chimpanzee University.

It was this precise set of qualifications that had made Milo the perfect candidate to lead this expedition across the Great Northern Sea, thousands of miles from his tropical home. Milo was honored to be asked, and happy to serve, right up until he was told to be prepared to encounter gorillas.

"If chimpanzee astronomers could spot a strange object in the heavens, track its descent, and plot a likely location for landfall up there in the Northern Dead Areas, then so could the gorillas," Milo's mission commander had told him. "They have spy glasses and ocean ships, just like chimps do, perhaps not so precise a spy glass, or so fast a boat, but gorillas have them. And they will be coming to examine that object from the sky—hoping it might be ancient human technology—just like we hope it is."

The briefing had ended on a grim note. "The gorillas will be behind you, Doctor, by perhaps days, or weeks. No more than a month, but they'll be there."

Doctor Milo was nudged from this anxious memory by something down the shore, a reflection off something large and metal. Was it another boat? Milo raised binoculars and brought into focus a giant metal statue half-buried in the sand. It was the likeness of a human woman with a crown, no doubt a long-forgotten queen of this long-dead land.

Milo smiled. He didn't mind human signs up here. He expected them in the Dead Areas, where no one had existed to disturb them since the wars. Human statues, he could live with. What Milo didn't want to see was gorillas.

He knew what gorillas were capable of.

"How can we trust Doctor Zaius?" Cornelius hissed to his fiancée, Zira, as soon as they were out of earshot of the court-house. "First he had us arrested for heresy, then he insisted on clemency at the trial *he* presided over. It was all nonsense."

"But this was nonsense with promotions, Cornelius!" Zira whispered back, barely containing the grin widening across her pretty chimpanzee face. "I'm made head of veterinary science, while you've been given a chair on the Science Council for all of Ape City. That's *rare* for a chimpanzee. It's usually the redheads."

The pair continued through the bustling streets on this lovely day. Zira looked upward, drinking in the sun while Cornelius fretted and fussed. "We get to keep those promotions provided we remain *silent*, Zira," he said. "Zaius has chosen bribery over punishment as a way to keep us quiet about what we learned in the Forbidden Zone—of this world's *true* history... about mankind."

"I prefer bribery," Zira sang back. "It's so much more civilized." As they found themselves in front of their modest home, she added, "Who needs all this talk of punishment when we're going to be married?"

"Zira, we haven't set a date."

"The trial is over. You just got a *big* promotion. You've run out of excuses, Cornelius. This is good for you. I'm good for you. Learn to be quiet and the world gets better. Trust me."

"I *do* trust you, Zira dear. It's Doctor Zaius I don't trust..."

Doctor Milo flew his auto-gyro five hundred yards above the barren landscape. The solar-powered battery kept the small craft aloft for only short bursts, but it was useful for aerial reconnaissance and mapping out the direction his team would travel that day.

The expedition into the Dead Areas had been moving inland for three weeks. They were close to the projected landing site of the mysterious object, and Milo was hoping to spot it either today or tomorrow.

As he had done for the last few weeks, the chimpanzee academic ritually noted the landmarks, the geographical features, the evidence of ancient settlements hinted at in the eroded formations below. He mapped the abandoned roadways, unseen since the human wars that led to this wasteland long ago.

Milo suddenly wanted to be home, anywhere but here. The thought of being the first creature in centuries to see this once-thriving continent filled him with a palpable dread.

But he forced down the feeling and continued flying beyond a ridge of cliffs, where he came across an isolated lake. He flew over the top of the shallow, clear waters and saw a grey object the size of a house—a triangle of metal, like a giant spear tip under the water—less than fifty feet from land. Unlike the colossus Milo had seen back at the ocean shore, this object was free of moss, rust, or wear. It had not lain in the water for years. It might be the object from the sky.

Milo took a quick look around before landing, scanning for miles in every direction. There was no sign of life. He was the first one here, and so he breathed a sigh of relief.

He'd beaten the gorillas.

"It was a wall of fire, reaching up to the sky," the gorilla soldier wailed, his eyes wide and darting around General Ursus' office. His commanding officer was a giant gorilla, seated majestically behind his equally imposing desk, a permanent snarl frozen on his dark sinewy mouth. Ursus wore the buckled straps and ornate leather hat signifying his rank, which served to make him all the more impressive. Across the room, sitting in the alcove of a window, was Doctor Zaius, the smallish orangutan head of the Science Council, also wearing the trappings of his office, splendid orange robes and a golden chain.

"The clouds rained *blood*! And there was... there was...

a *human* there," the nervous solider continued. "He was ten feet tall, and wearing clothes made of lightning…" His voice trailed off before he broke down into heaving sobs, begged forgiveness, and fled the room.

Ursus turned to Doctor Zaius. "That was the lone survivor of the scouting party that went into the Forbidden Zone a week ago," the general said. "Five dead. Raving madness from him. And it has something to do with talking humans, like that jabbering circus animal you paraded before the council, Zaius. I *demand* to know what is going on!"

Zaius considered the huge gorilla before him, watching his muscles visibly tensing, and his breath beginning to labor. "You may *ask* what is going on, General, but you may not *demand*," Zaius said. He hoped the show of authority would diffuse the mood. Military apes understood authority.

"There are things best not known that are best left out there, Ursus…" Zaius began.

"Anything not worth knowing, we will *destroy*," Ursus interrupted. "We need land, Zaius. More farmland. And there is good land in the Forbidden Zone inhabited only by the filthy human animals. I will not let my troops go hungry while lazy humans pick the fruits from the trees. I *demand* to know what's out there!"

Zaius managed not to visibly react to Ursus' repetition of the word "demand," but the orangutan knew what it meant. He'd seen it before, during a long life filled with public service and political maneuvering.

This gorilla general was testing his power, trying to discover what he was capable of.

Lieutenant Soror's chimpanzee divers had gone down into the shallow water and attached hooks and lines to the sunken metal object. It was pulled from the water with winches and pulleys, and all things considered, not much effort was required. It took longer to bail out the interior than it did to drag the vessel to shore, and now it sat in the sand like a beached whale, large, grey and inert.

As Milo and his superiors had believed, the craft was, indeed, ancient human technology. That was confirmed when Soror found human artifacts aboard, as well as a preserved dead human—a female, apparently—sealed in a triangular glass tube. Milo wasn't a biologist, but he had some understanding of such things, and he guessed the corpse was centuries old.

Milo spent hours in the interior of the capsule, pondering the controls and instruments found there. This vehicle, or whatever it was, might have functioned with some sort of electromagnetic power at one point, but the trip to the bottom of the lake had short-circuited the system. Disappointingly, the capsule was dead.

"There will be time to figure it all out when we get it home," Soror told Milo. "God had a plan, and finding a working piece of human technology was clearly not part of it."

"Apes make plans and God laughs," said Milo.

Suddenly, there was a great commotion outside. Chimpanzee voices were whooping and shouting with tremendous excitement. Milo's heart raced as he thought gorillas were attacking and he was trapped in the capsule, unable to run. But he found a moment's courage, and bolted outside to find everyone pointing up at the sky.

There, bright as the sun, was another object hurtling toward Earth from out of the heavens. Another giant spear tip, exactly like the one they had already found, was passing overhead, trailing smoke and fire, less than a mile above them, coming down fast.

Milo, too, began to whoop and holler and fill the air with a joyful noise. This event was far more than coincidence. This was God's plan made manifest. He had chosen a particular ape to find these things, these ancient technological gifts from the heavens—and He had clearly chosen the chimpanzees.

The last months had been eventful for Cornelius and Zira. First there was the marriage, and the honeymoon. That was something.

Then there had been a visit from another talking human named Brent, who was just like Taylor. He had come in another fantastic flying machine to look for Taylor and bring him home, and now Brent was gone as well—alive or dead, the couple had no way of knowing.

Brent's existence troubled Zira greatly. Taylor the talking human freak could be aberrant, a fluke, but two such creatures suggested many more were out there, perhaps an entire community of civilized humans deep in the Forbidden Zone who had language and technology and flying machines. Zira wondered if those men would have souls.

For too many years, Zira's job had included human vivisection, and now, after meeting Brent and Taylor, the morality of it all couldn't be easily swept away. If man had a soul, what had Zira done to her own?

She obsessed over this for days, and finally spoke to her husband about finding the city of men she was convinced was out there in the Forbidden Zone. She wanted to leave in the morning, but he argued. "It's the Forbidden Zone, dear. Not the Invited Zone. We can't just go any time we want."

"We can, Cornelius," Zira grinned. "Doctor Zaius has left with the gorilla army to look for human lands to conquer. Before departing, he put you in charge of the Science Council. You don't have to ask permission of yourself."

Cornelius was dumbfounded. She was right, of course. She always was. He began to pack.

"We'll take a northeastern route," Zira said. "I don't want

to run into any of the gorillas on their travels. They give me the shudders."

Milo had found the second crash site with his auto-gyro late in the day, and, unwilling to wait until his team showed up, he put his small craft down near the charred hull of the thing from the sky.

This time, the hull was badly bent and torn, still hissing from re-entry blisters, but the cockpit was miraculously intact. The lights were on inside the interior and the instruments seemed curiously undamaged.

Milo found something else at the site that chilled his blood. It was a small collection of stones piled up deliberately by willful hands, next to which lay a tiny flag that matched markings on the side of the capsule hull.

This was a grave marker. After a momentary hesitation, curiosity overtook the chimpanzee and he pushed aside the pile of stones to discover the dead human underneath. It was wearing the same shiny, metallic clothing as the dead woman they'd found at the other site, but unlike the mummified corpse found earlier, this body was fresh, and someone had buried it recently.

Milo's heart stopped in his chest with that realization. He scrambled back to his aircraft and retrieved his pistol. Then he searched the area, frantically focusing his eyes down onto the sand and rocks at his feet. Soon, he saw what he was greatly afraid to find: ape and animal prints leading off to the north. There was someone else in the Dead Areas, and they'd been here within the last twenty-four hours.

He began to salvage what he could from this wreck as quickly as possible, while his auto-gyro slowly recharged. Milo had no idea how long he was going to be alone at this site. Someone had already been here today.

•

After four trips into the Forbidden Zone, Cornelius had become familiar with the uneasy feeling that accompanied venturing into the desert, past the human habitations. It was more than the lack of vegetation out here; it felt like something was physically pushing them away. Cornelius attributed it to the very name of the place: the *Forbidden* Zone. "Who wouldn't be nervous in a land with so awful a title?" he said to his wife.

Zira blamed her nerves on the gorillas, even though they had left Ape City some days ago, and they hadn't seen them since. Her thoughts kept falling back to the repulsive harvest and slaughter of men that was going on back in the green belt.

Zira didn't know exactly how to find the civilized human settlement she knew in her heart was out here, but Cornelius' old archeological site along the shore of the Eastern Sea was the last place they had seen Bright Eyes some months ago, and it was as good a place to start as any.

Early morning on the second day of their journey, something caught Cornelius' eye off to the east. At first, he thought it was a firefly hovering in the pre-dawn twilight, but focusing attention on it, Cornelius determined it was something actually much larger, perhaps the size of a horse and rider, a few miles away, floating in the air and projecting a small light from somewhere. It crested a rocky mesa and hovered above it for five minutes before disappearing behind another hill.

Cornelius and Zira dropped their jaws. It was either a real-life dragon, or else an equally improbable flying machine, just as Taylor had described. Cornelius had never believed in dragons—or flying machines, for that matter—but one of the two was out there flying over the desert to the east.

So, Cornelius and Zira turned east.

•

This was Milo's final trip to the beta site. This time, he had packed enough ordnance to destroy what remained of this second capsule, now that he had gutted it of all its component parts. His expedition didn't have the capacity to bring two capsules home, so he had to destroy at least one of them, in case gorillas came to get it later. Milo had spent the last few hours removing power cells and instrument casings, and inserting explosive charges in their place, and now he was ready to detonate the explosion. He primed the blasting cap and headed toward the auto-gyro to set it off from the air.

As he moved to attach the now powered-up battery to the rotor, he saw two figures cresting a rocky shelf overhead. Milo cursed himself for being careless and quickly reached for the pistol on his belt, terrified of the fight he knew was coming.

It was then that he saw the new arrivals were not gorillas, but chimpanzees. He'd never seen them before—they weren't part of his crew, and they certainly weren't supposed to be wandering alone on a dead continent, thousands of miles from home—but they were chimpanzees. That relaxed him a bit, but not enough to put down the gun. Milo gestured for the chimps to come over, which they did, rather casually. Their attention was focused far more on the large metal ship grounded in front of them, and the smaller, lightweight auto-gyro Milo was now standing beside.

"Who on earth are you?" both Cornelius and Milo said at the same time.

Milo went first. "Since I have the gun, why don't you answer a few questions of mine first? What are you doing out here in the Dead Areas?"

Zira gestured at the auto-gyro and began to speak. "We saw that… thing over there, flying in the air! We came over to see what it was. What it is. What is it? I've never seen anything like it. And what's that metal triangle thing over there?"

Cornelius began poking at the hatchway of the capsule, so

Milo shouted, "Get away from that! You'll get hurt!"

Cornelius turned, amused rather than threatened. "You don't scare me with the gun, sir. Apes don't kill other apes. You can lower that weapon."

What a strange notion, that apes don't kill other apes, thought Milo. Where he came from, gorillas killed chimpanzees and chimps killed gorillas as a matter of course. But he was a fellow chimpanzee, true enough, and Milo didn't want to hurt him.

"There are explosives all over that ship. I don't want you setting them off accidentally," Milo said, holstering his weapon as Cornelius scrambled away from the hull with some speed.

"I am Cornelius, grand councilor pro tem of the Science Council of Ape City, and this is my wife, Zira, chair of veterinary science on that same council," Cornelius said, composing himself. "You obviously don't have permission to be in the Forbidden Zone, or I either would have known about it or would have given it to you. So I ask you again, what you are doing out here?"

Milo looked puzzled. "You would have given me permission to be here?" he asked. "And you're from the Ape City Grand Councilor Pro Tem? I've never heard of any of that. Where did you come from?"

"We're from the city. That's where the council is," Zira replied, a bit annoyed. "I don't know what county farm you're from, but you should know my rather important husband by now. He's been on the Council for months. Don't you hear news where you live?"

"I'm from further away than you might think," Milo said. "I came here on a large ship from across the great ocean to the south. Do you know the ocean?"

Cornelius and Zira considered this. "Across the ocean? Oh, no... no, you didn't. There's nothing out there but more ocean. Certainly not other apes," Cornelius said. "The Sacred Scrolls tell us that."

Zira tugged on her husband's arm. "Ask him about that flying machine. Where did he find it? Does it belong to Taylor?"

Milo's thoughts raced. They didn't understand the ocean, and they thought Milo knew one of their friends, someone named Taylor. Did that name actually ring a bell? This odd pair of chimpanzees lived nearby, close enough to travel here on foot. The possibility was startling. They claimed there was a city back where they came from, on this barren continent. Milo wondered if that were even possible.

"Where is the city?" Milo asked.

Zira looked suddenly sympathetic and gestured over her shoulder. "Why, it's back there! A few days' travel. Poor thing. You're lost? It's a good thing we found you. We'll get you home."

Cornelius lay a gentle arm on Milo's shoulder. "It's a good thing *we* found you, and not Doctor Zaius and his army. They'd likely have you arrested for being out here. And Lawgiver knows, gorillas love to arrest people."

Milo startled, terrified. "Gorillas?"

"It's all right," Zira said, trying to calm him down. "The gorillas are miles away… off that way, hunting men."

That comment did little to reassure Milo. He barely heard anything after the word "gorillas." He retreated to the chair in the flying machine and moved his hands over a series of levers and dials. A moment later, the rotor blades of the engine began to spin, making a quiet humming sound as they cut the air.

"You have to move away from this area!" Milo shouted above the sound of the engine. "I have to destroy the capsule. I can't leave anything behind for the gorillas to find! Go! *Run!*"

As soon as he had said it, Milo realized he had something of a duty to these two chimpanzees not to leave them behind. That's what they must have been doing in the desert. They had been on the run from the gorilla army—probably escaped slaves. His conscience wouldn't let them be captured if he could help.

"Wait. You can come with me."

"Fine," said Zira.

"*What?!?*" shouted Cornelius.

"We can't let him leave, Cornelius!" Zira told her mate. "He has a *flying* machine, just like Bright Eyes. This has something to do with Taylor and Brent and their people. We can't let him go!"

Cornelius and Zira got in the back of the auto-gyro, amidst the last of the salvaged equipment, and within a minute, the little airship had finished its takeoff and was in the air. As the wheels left the ground, Cornelius managed a scream that was easily louder than the propellers.

He was still screaming minutes later when Milo detonated the explosives packed into the capsule below.

Zaius, Ursus, and the gorilla army had been marching into the desert of the Forbidden Zone for days. They were hot, tired, and demoralized by their journey, and growing irritated by the constant sound of the attack bugle when there had been absolutely nothing to attack for mile upon mile of dull marching.

Small rumblings began on the fourth day, after the commanders had ordered the army to skip lunch. There wasn't much fresh fruit left anyway, as they had expected to encounter lush human settlements to raid and replenish their supplies by now, but so far they had found none.

It was at this low ebb in morale when the army experienced a series of terrible visions. First, they saw a wall of fire leap up from the rocky ground, radiating immeasurable heat. And then they saw a statue of the Lawgiver appear from nowhere, bleeding and crying and crumbling into dust. Finally, the infantry and cavalry and everyone present saw a vision of themselves, crucified and crying out, screaming a warning to go back home.

It was the most terrifying thing every gorilla there had ever seen, and they fell to their knees, or rocked back and forth, unable to move past their fear, but commanded by their general not to turn and run.

Doctor Zaius shouted that he didn't believe in the reality of the fire, and he rode into it unhurt while Ursus stayed behind with the rest of the army, cowering. As soon as Zaius lifted his arms and shouted, the fire dissipated. He had banished the false visions with his voice. It was like something directly out of the Sacred Scrolls, vividly brought to life. It was the most inspiring moment in the life of every gorilla there, except for Ursus, who did not wish to share the admiration of his soldiers with the orangutan.

In the rear squad of the infantry was a rifle carrier named Krute. An undisciplined beast of a gorilla, prone to fights and fits of temper, Krute had chosen the army in lieu of prison some years ago when confronted by a criminal record and a generous judge. Krute had a problem with authority, and authority had a problem with Krute, so when he spotted something against the horizon—something that he at first thought was a dragonfly, but that seemed to be much larger, and much further away—he chose to bring this information to the attention of Doctor Zaius, and not his commanding officer, Ursus.

Zaius listened intently as Krute described what he had seen. Zaius believed this "giant dragonfly" of Krute's was another clever illusion, sent by unseen forces to distract the army into heading in the wrong direction. But the orangutan recalled Taylor talking at some length about a *flying machine*, and because of that, he decided Krute's sighting was worth investigating. He allowed Krute to take a dozen infantry with him to look into the vision of the dragonfly and report back when they rejoined the column the next day.

Zaius enjoyed the idea of dispatching a small squad of Ursus' army without consulting the general. It mattered who truly commanded here, and as this campaign continued, Zaius would instruct the gorilla on who demanded things from whom.

Later that day, Krute and a dozen well-armed gorillas broke off from the much larger column and headed to the northeast.

Cornelius loathed the trip in the auto-gyro, but Zira was enchanted by the entire experience. From the sense of weightlessness to the view of the ground below, it exhilarated her exactly as much as it nauseated her husband, and she reveled in it like a dream. As a child, she dreamt of flying like a bird, and now, here she was.

Milo pressed Zira for information while they made their way back to the alpha site. "How many gorillas are in this army? Where are they now? Did you and your husband escape?" Most of these questions were met with puzzled looks and some amusement, but little information that helped Milo understand. Meanwhile, Zira peppered Milo with questions in return: "Who created this flying machine we're in? How do you drive it?"

Milo craned his head over his shoulder. "Have you never seen flying machines before? What about solar trucks, or electricity itself?"

Zira didn't understand the questions, not really. She'd seen electricity during thunderstorms, of course, but everyone had. And what was a solar truck? Nonsense. She asked after Taylor, and again, the word rang a bell in Milo's mind. Again, however, he couldn't place why.

The auto-gyro made its way to the alpha site, now a location of bustling activity. From the air, Zira could see dozens of chimpanzees running to and fro amidst the recovered capsule, and dizzying amounts of confusing machinery. There were wagons moving on their own without horses to pull them, and there were impossibly long black vines neatly running between metal boxes and connecting all sorts of things to each other. Central to the proceedings was another gigantic iron spear tip, which looked very much like the thing Milo had just blown up.

The wheels touched down, and Lieutenant Soror ran up to help unload what he expected was another collection of component parts from the other capsule. Instead, he was greeted by Cornelius, searching for a place to be sick, and Zira holding him, apologizing for her husband.

"I'll explain in a minute," said Milo to his lieutenant, who dutifully held back questions about the stranger. "From what I learned from these two, there is a gorilla army out there in the desert, blindly marching this way. We need to establish a perimeter and post sentries right now, and we have to get out of here at first light tomorrow!"

Soror glanced at Milo's chimpanzee passengers, starting to straighten up after Cornelius' moment of weakness.

"I think they might be escaped slaves," Milo whispered to Soror. "They claim to live around here, but they don't understand much. They told me about the gorilla army to the southwest, and that's about all I can get from them. If there's a gorilla army, you can assume they're hunting for chimps." Milo was grim.

"Conserve power; pack up in the dark. Let's use what we have stored to get a jump on the sunrise tomorrow," Milo suggested, then turned to his new guests. "Go with my friend, Lieutenant Soror, and he'll get you something to eat and drink after that flight. I'll join you in a little while."

Cornelius and Zira were led off by the lieutenant, trying in vain to take in everything that was going on. There was so much activity out here in the Forbidden Zone by a secret group of chimpanzees about whom Cornelius knew nothing.

It didn't make sense.

After an hour, Milo had fit the final piece of the technological jigsaw puzzle together. He'd replaced the last part in the capsule's last dead control panel and wired the last bits of it as best he could. It was time to flip the switch and see if he could get anything out of the ship's electrical systems before the whole expedition packed up and headed home at morning's light.

The chimpanzee held his breath before twitching his finger. God had answered one prayer, he thought. It would be too much to ask for another so soon. But when Milo flipped the switch, the power came on.

"I said 'Let there be light.' And it was good," said Milo under his breath, smiling.

Panel after panel lit up, displaying images and numbers and colors that meant little to the chimpanzee. But it was all working. For the next few hours, Milo struggled to understand all he could about the technology before him. He read the consoles and flipped switches and buttons, looking for information each time he did something. There were labels and display screens and sequences marked clearly. Before long, Milo managed to engage the computerized operating system, which had a helpful interface.

From then on, the computer made it easy. The propulsion systems, auto-pilot, and launch procedures were all spelled out for Milo on touch screens. There was so much to take in, but he prodded and poked and asked and learned until he could fit no more in his weary brain. There would be time to study this magical ancient invention from the sky when they all got home.

If they got home. There were gorillas out there, God only knew how far away.

Milo's eye was suddenly caught by something on the far wall of the inner capsule chamber. It was a set of human clothes, shiny and bulky and topped with a glass helmet. They'd found examples of it in both capsules mounted on the walls, and Milo had decided to leave them where they were after they'd been dried out. This particular set of human clothes had a detail on it that startled him, because he'd seen it before and it hadn't registered until now.

Over the top of the chest area, on the left side, was a label that read "Taylor." *That's why the name rang a bell!* He'd seen the shiny suit before, one that belonged to Taylor. Those chimpanzees outside said they knew him.

Milo felt dizzy as he considered the idea of an ancient human walking around today.

Cornelius and Zira were brought aboard the capsule, but they recognized nothing inside it, beyond the familiar name on the shiny human suit.

"Yes, Taylor was a friend of ours," said Cornelius, "a human beast who could read and write and speak and reason just like any ape."

Zira continued excitedly, "He said he came to our city from the sky, in a flying machine, just like yours, just like this one. Where is he? Do you know?"

Milo was amazed. "You mean there are humans—*living* humans—and you've actually seen them? With your own eyes?" Milo asked quickly.

"Whose eyes *would* I be using?" said Zira. "I've seen lots of humans. I work with them. It's only interesting to meet ones who could read and talk. Don't you listen?"

Milo turned to answer, but was interrupted by the sound of distant gunfire, short rifle bursts at first, then the *ratatat* of machine guns.

Soror had shot first. That's what had started the eventual slaughter.

Krute and his squad had heard sounds coming from the camp long before they had seen it in the dark. A forward gorilla scout determined that a group of chimpanzees was out here in the Forbidden Zone, doing some sort of scientific work only the Lawgiver could understand, and he came back to report that to Krute, who then decided to approach the camp and find out if they had supplies, fresh fruit, or water they could spare for their loyal army.

Krute walked up with his rifle team at ease, weapons strapped to their backs, shouting greetings and pleasantries to the chimpanzee sentries at the camp's perimeter in the predawn light.

They were met with a hailstorm of bullets. Two gorillas died before the group could dive for cover in the rocky terrain.

It made no sense. Ape never killed ape. What kind of monsters were these chimpanzees to open fire on their brothers in the army?

Krute ordered his gorillas to take out their machine guns and attack, and to show no mercy to these chimpanzees, now that he knew the criminal behavior of which they were capable.

The single-shot rifles that Soror and his chimpanzees carried were no match for automatic machine guns in the hands of gorillas. Krute's squad was past the perimeter very quickly, killing Soror and his rifle squad within a matter of minutes. From there, they rushed over the crest of the rock formation to enter the camp proper.

Inside the capsule, Milo could see, through the large porthole windows at the front, the armed gorillas over-running the camp, shooting in all directions. He shut the hatch quickly, and it slid down with a loud pneumatic "shhhh." This sealed them inside, perhaps safe for now, but ultimately trapped. The outer hull could likely take a bullet without damage, but he didn't know about the porthole windows. Milo had feared this since the moment they had set foot on this continent.

"What's happening?" shouted Zira. Her husband was trying to calm her down and failing.

"The gorillas are here. They're killing everyone. I've got to do something!" Milo shouted, glancing around for ideas. "If I could get to one of the supply trucks, I could bring back enough explosives to destroy this capsule as well…"

Cornelius grabbed Milo by the arm. "Your plan is to destroy the thing we're hiding in? Are you mad?"

"I can't let them have it, Cornelius," Milo shouted. "I have to destroy it if it's going to fall into their hands. An explosion could…" Milo stopped in his tracks. "The booster rockets. The system said they were still charged. That ought to make a hell of a bang."

Milo hurried to the control console and began flipping switches. The sounds of gunfire died around them. That was a bad sign. It suggested there was no one left to shoot at out there. Through the porthole windows, gorillas could be seen running toward the capsule. Now they were at the hull, banging on the outer shell and shouting commands.

"May God forgive me if there are any chimpanzees left alive out there," Milo said as he ran through the launch sequence to power up the booster rockets. In a moment, the final button blinked green and Milo pressed it down.

A deafening WHOOSH filled the cabin, and a powerful red light flooded the portholes. The entire capsule began to shake and rumble like a huge earthquake as the floor tilted slowly to the left for a few moments and then jolted violently, pushing everyone aboard into the back wall of the cabin, as though a great weight pressed down on them.

This rumbling and pushing lasted for about five minutes but finally let up, and the trio of chimpanzees tried to get their footing and see what had happened.

The view out the porthole window was a mind-numbing shock. The capsule was in the air, hurtling at unimaginable speed away from the surface of the Earth, up, up into space. Already, the Forbidden Zone was curving away from them far below, and the stars… there were suddenly so many of them in the sky.

Cornelius and Zira held onto each other against the rear wall. Milo simply stared out the window in disbelief.

The capsule had gone into its full launch sequence— that was the only explanation. Milo hadn't meant for that to happen, but it had. He tried to call the computer up and correct the mistake, but to no avail. Each button he pushed and switch he flipped served only to frustrate him. The capsule continued to climb higher and higher. Soon there would be no way to return home. Shortly, they would leave the atmosphere and suffocate in airless space. Perhaps they would starve before the air ran out.

At least he kept the object from the sky out of the hands of the gorillas. That was what he had been tasked to do, so his mission hadn't really been a failure.

Milo settled down on the floor to await his fate. He had stopped listening to the pleading and shouting of Cornelius and Zira. Perhaps they'd stopped shouting; Milo was beyond caring. Ten minutes later, when he saw the blinding light through the porthole, Milo took it as a sign he was dying. He got up to look out the window and saw something too horrible to consider. Zira and Cornelius joined him at the window. Far below, the Earth itself began to split open. Huge, continent-wide cracks began to form, lava poured out in mile-high geysers, and the oceans began to boil. It was the end of the world, and Milo, Cornelius, and Zira were the only witnesses.

It was impossible to comprehend the scale of so much dying. The destruction continued until they could no longer watch, or even process what they were seeing.

Milo was the first to speak. His voice was eerily soft. "Those maniac gorillas actually did it. Somehow, they blew it all up, damn them."

Cornelius and Zira said nothing, but they agreed with Milo. It had to be the gorillas, somehow. Their violence and thirst for war had found a way to destroy the world.

Milo had always feared the gorillas, for he knew what they were capable of.

But none in that capsule could have known that the world actually died at the hands of a man named Taylor, deep down in a manmade cavern below the planet's surface, detonating a manmade weapon called the Alpha-Omega Bomb.

The gorillas may have been brutes and bullies, the stuff of Milo's nightmares and Zira's secret fears, but they were never evil enough to destroy the world.

Only *man* was capable of *that*.

In Dayton Ward's "Message in a Bottle," television astronauts Virdon and Burke return with their chimp ally, Galen, to chase down a mystery that may, once and for all, lead them to an escape from their ordeal on the planet of the apes...

MESSAGE IN A BOTTLE

by

DAYTON WARD

Flanked by four subordinates, Urko charged into what passed for the small village's center as fast as his horse could carry him. A single human male dashed out of his path and only narrowly avoided being trampled. Urko barely noticed the man as he pulled on his horse's reins, bringing the steed to a halt before a large, well-appointed abode. The rest of his advance party mimicked his movements before they all dismounted their horses, and Urko handed the reins of his own mount to his lieutenant, Robar.

"Take the troopers and search the village. Report back to me once you've completed your sweep."

The lieutenant nodded. "Yes, Urko."

A flag hanging from a pole near the dwelling's front door identified the home as a prefect's residence, and a heavy wooden door swung open to reveal an older, stoop-shouldered chimpanzee. Urko noted the green tunic identifying the ape as a prefect.

"What's the meaning of all this commotion?" asked the chimp. He gestured to Urko. "Who are you, and why have you come to my village?"

"I am Urko, chief of security, and I come with the authority of the High Council. I don't need your permission to be here, Prefect Gaulke."

"You do until such time as the Council relieves me of my position." Gaulke drew himself to his full height. He was still shorter than Urko and possessed far less mass, but there was an air about him which belied his slight stature. "Now, shall we stand here in the hot sun engaged in useless debates, or would you rather tell me what brings you to Nivek and how I might be of assistance?"

Opting to set aside what admittedly was a petty argument, Urko instead said, "We're searching for three fugitives. Two humans and a chimpanzee."

Gaulke's brow furrowed. "Humans with an ape, you say? That is most peculiar."

"These humans are different," said Urko. "They're smarter, and possess far more spirit than the humans you are familiar with. You may have seen or heard of them helping your villagers in various ways, as they have unusual knowledge and skills."

Nodding, Gaulke replied, "I've heard rumors about such humans, though I myself have never seen them." He shrugged. "Besides, all humans look alike to me. However, a young chimpanzee calling himself Maurice did come to the village more than a week ago, and I believe he had two human servants with him, but they're not here any longer. So far as I know, they left here yesterday, or was it the day before?" He frowned, shaking his head. "I'm not sure."

Urko grunted in irritation. How many times had he come so close to apprehending his quarry, only to have them slip away? The information which had brought him to the village of Nivek was the first sighting of the fugitives in months. The astronauts and Galen had become quite proficient at eluding his police patrols and finding allies among the provinces and villages scattered across the territory, but they could not escape notice forever.

"Do you know which direction they were heading?"

"East, I believe," replied Gaulke. "They seemed most interested in the Paola Wasteland."

Retrieving a map from one of his horse's saddlebags, Urko followed the prefect into the residence. There, he spread the canvas map across the large table in the home's dining area. For a brief moment, he pondered the series of charcoal markings peppering the map's surface. Each symbol harbored a chapter in a story that already had gone on for far too long for his taste. How long had he been marking the map in this manner? Had he really lost track of the weeks or months? With that thought clouding his mind and fueling his mounting annoyance, he shifted his gaze to the very first symbol he had placed on the map, which indicated the origin point for his current worries.

The crashed spaceship. The astronauts, Virdon and Burke.
Even thinking their very names made Urko growl in annoyance. His current mission of tracking the fugitive astronauts and their renegade chimpanzee ally, Galen, had taken him far from Central City, far from his wife and son, and ever farther into the undeveloped and largely uninhabited regions south and east of the larger, populated areas. As days and weeks had stretched into months, there had been more than one evening spent writing in his journal, its pages illuminated by the light of a campfire, when Urko contemplated returning to the city and devising a new plan to pursue his prey.

Then, some tantalizing morsel of new information would present itself, stoking his determination to continue the chase, such as what had drawn him here to Nivek. The village was one Urko had never visited, located as it was on the fringes of explored territory and the area over which he was charged as chief of security.

He pointed to the map, and the mark he had made the previous evening to indicate Nivek's location. "Show me where they went."

Studying the map for a moment, Gaulke traced a line from the village to the east, toward an area that was not even labeled.

"The Paola Wasteland lies here, beyond the forest and mountains," said Gaulke. "Perhaps a day if you ride fast. Little is known about it. For generations, we were warned to avoid that area, but whoever made up those stories died long ago. A few of the apes living in Nivek have ventured there."

"What is there?"

Frowning, the prefect replied, "Nothing, mostly, though there are some areas that hold ancient ruins."

"Ruins." Urko repeated the word. "Of course. Virdon and Burke would want to go there." It would be consistent with their previous actions, in which they seemed to always be moving with direction and purpose. The High Council seemed convinced of this as well, with its most senior member, Zaius, believing that the astronauts were driven by the hope of somehow finding a means of returning to the distant time period from which they had come.

A time before humans destroyed their own society, Urko reminded himself. *A time before apes gained their freedom and ascended to their rightful place as rulers of this world.*

Zaius also had explained to Urko the true risk Virdon and Burke represented. As much damage as they might do here in the present, perhaps, by inspiring the humans of this era toward rebellion, it was in the past that the astronauts posed the greatest threat. Should they successfully return to their own time, they might well be able to affect the course of history by preventing the catastrophe that had doomed human civilization and allowed the emergence of apes as the dominant species on this planet. Urko did not entirely understand how such a dramatic change could happen, but it still was sufficient justification to do what he knew must be done: kill Virdon and Burke, by any means necessary.

And now, the astronauts were once more within his grasp. *The hunt begins again.*

"Well, would you look at that."

Standing on a rise overlooking the expanse of terrain before them, Alan Virdon shielded his eyes with one hand as he took in the scene. The area was littered with rock formations, ruts, and rolling hills sprinkled with trees and other vegetation, but there could be no mistaking the sharp angles of rusted, twisted metal jutting out from mountains of broken concrete and dirt.

"It's way too small to be a city," said Peter Burke, Virdon's friend and fellow astronaut. He stood close to the edge of the slope leading down to the open expanse. "Any ideas?"

Virdon shook his head. "Could be anything." He pointed to what he thought might be sections of deteriorated chain-link fencing, as well as what looked to be remnants of massive metal scaffolding. Farther away were the broken, dilapidated ruins of more than a dozen small, squat buildings. "Maybe a construction site or an oil field?"

Galen, their chimpanzee companion, said, "Prefect Gaulke told me that no one from the village ever ventures down there. There are a number of stories about strange noises and visions, but they sound to me like stories to scare children." Galen sniffed the air. "I don't mind telling you I'm not getting a very good feeling about this."

Burke said, "Hard to believe nobody's ever checked out the place. You'd think it'd be ripe for scavenging metal or whatever else."

Shifting his canvas backpack to a more comfortable position on his shoulders, Virdon replied, "That might be a good thing for us, particularly if the apes tend to avoid this area."

Even after all these months, there were rare times when the

reality of what he and Burke faced every day still bordered on the unimaginable. Such occasions were far outnumbered by those laced with grudging acceptance of their situation: propelled centuries into their own future and returning to Earth only to find human civilization all but obliterated, with a society of simians having risen to take its place. Since then, Virdon and Burke, along with Galen, the young, idealistic chimpanzee whom they had befriended, pursued a clear-cut goal: evading capture by the likes of Urko and his ape police garrisons, while searching for a way back to their own time. It was a formidable goal, given that Urko, as well as Chief Councilor Zaius and nearly every ape in any position of authority or influence, wanted them dead. Virdon knew they would never stop so long as he and Burke remained alive.

It's nice to be wanted.

Choosing his steps with care, Virdon led the trio as they descended the slope. Once the ground ahead of them began to flatten out, he could see telltale signs of concrete beneath the dirt, thanks to bare patches where wind had cleared away the soil. In and among the scrub brush, he also noted pieces of rusted rebar and other metal. Rock and dirt still covered a significant portion of the area, leading the astronaut to wonder what had happened to so drastically alter the landscape.

"I don't think Gaulke or the other villagers were totally honest with you, Galen," said Burke as he maneuvered around a large mound of broken concrete.

Inspecting the remains of the deteriorated buildings and other structures turned up little of interest, though he could tell that the area had not been immune to the previous passage of humans or apes. Paths between piles of rubble and other detritus became evident as the fugitives continued their sweep.

"Some of this stuff looks picked over pretty good." Virdon shrugged. "Makes sense. There's a lot here to use, for someone who knows what they're doing or just has a little imagination."

Burke snorted. "So, basically nobody, then."

It was hard for Virdon to take issue with his friend's cynical remark. By and large, the humans they had encountered in their travels had seemed content to live out whatever meager existences the apes granted them, exercising little if any ambition or initiative. Only on rare occasions had they found someone dissatisfied with the status quo and who aspired to something greater than servitude. Such individuals tended to draw the attention and ire of their ape masters, and therefore endeavored to maintain low profiles.

"Alan. Pete. There's something here I think you should see."

Virdon turned to see Galen standing before what at first looked to be a section of exposed concrete, which was partially obscured by a ring of parched brush.

"There's an edge here," said the chimpanzee.

Kneeling next to the shallow rut in the soil where the concrete was exposed, Virdon brushed at the sand until his fingers moved across something large and smooth. "This is a metal hinge. Pretty big, too."

Motivated by the odd discovery, the trio set to work. Within minutes, they had cleared an area several meters across. In the middle of the square of concrete was embedded a rusted metal hatch with a recessed wheel, a pair of hinges, and a separate handle running along one edge.

"What is it?" asked Galen.

Virdon ran his hand along the wheel. "If I had to guess, I'd say it's an escape hatch for an old nuclear missile silo."

Frowning, the chimpanzee cocked his head. "A what?"

"A very large weapon, Galen," replied Burke. "They were kept in special underground facilities we called silos, which were scattered all over the country. Other nations had similar missiles, and they protected them the same way." He gestured around them. "Somewhere around here is probably another very large hatch, under which might still be whatever's left of a missile."

"Unless it was launched," said Virdon. He paused, wondering how many such launches had taken place centuries ago, raining nuclear destruction down upon cities around the world and all but obliterating human civilization.

Burke nodded. "Yeah."

Reaching for the wheel set into the hatch cover, Virdon was surprised when it turned with relative ease. In fact, he felt almost no resistance at all.

"How about that?" he asked. With Burke helping him, it was a simple matter to lift the door on its hinge until it swung all the way open and tilted back toward the ground. With that accomplished, Virdon looked into the hole which they had revealed, and saw the metal ladder descending into darkness.

"Notice anything, Pete?"

Stepping closer, Burke leaned forward so that he could look into the shaft. "It's pretty clean for having been buried for a thousand years."

"Exactly." He waved toward the shrubs they had pulled up. "Maybe whoever marked this location has been inside the silo."

"Seems like they'd have a pretty nice apartment," said Burke. "Assuming they've got a thing for bunkers in the middle of nowhere."

Gesturing toward the shaft, Galen asked, "You're not seriously thinking of climbing down into that thing, are you?"

Virdon smiled. "We've come this far, haven't we?"

As expected, Virdon found a tunnel at the bottom of the shaft. How far down were they? Looking past Galen and Burke, who were still descending the ladder, he saw the small circle of light and estimated they were at least two hundred feet beneath the surface. Of greater interest were the recessed lighting panels positioned at regular intervals along the shaft, which seemed to activate in response to their movements on the ladder. As they moved downward, lights turned on below them, while the ones above eventually extinguished themselves.

"What do you think?" asked Burke once he stepped off the ladder and moved to stand next to Galen. "Solar power? Atomic batteries?" His voice echoed in the narrow conduit.

Virdon replied, "Beats me, but whoever built it knew what they were doing." He gestured toward the circular passage ahead of them, which was small enough that they would have to traverse its length on hands and knees. "Let's see where it goes."

Fidgeting as he sniffed the air, Galen said, "I don't know if I like this, Alan."

"It's okay." Burke rested a hand on the chimpanzee's shoulder. "Assuming this is a missile silo and the tunnel's not blocked, it should lead to a larger room."

No sooner did Virdon maneuver himself into the passage than another pair of lighting panels flickered to life. "See? We'll be fine. Come on."

"You've seen places like this before?" asked Galen as he followed Virdon.

"No, but I've read about them." The astronaut ran his right hand along the smooth concrete wall. "Each silo had a single missile, and a crew would be down here to monitor its condition. If the order came to launch it, they were responsible for making sure the missile was fueled and launched toward its designated target. If what we came down was the escape hatch, this tunnel should take us to the main control room." His fingers traced over one lighting panel's translucent cover. "I don't remember anything like these lights, though."

"They must've done some fancy redecorating after we left," offered Burke.

The end of the conduit, along with another circular hatch, was revealed when another pair of lighting panels activated. Though realizing he should not be surprised by this point, Virdon still grunted in mild astonishment when the hatch opened without difficulty. No sooner did he break the seal than he felt a rush of cool air playing across his skin, and light flickered through the narrow opening. He also heard the low thrum of… power? A generator?

Oh, my God.

"I wonder if anybody's home," said Burke from behind him.

Extracting himself from the tunnel, Virdon stood and got his first look at the larger room. Though unoccupied, the chamber still harbored signs of life, thanks to the interior lighting and the unmistakable sound of machinery operating somewhere in the underground complex. Control consoles and computer banks lined the circular room's perimeter. All of the equipment was inert, though to Virdon it looked none the worse for wear for being perhaps a thousand years old. A quartet of inactive television monitors hung at different points around the room, angled toward the workstations and suspended by metal brackets from the concrete ceiling.

"What *is* this place?" Stepping around Virdon, Galen moved toward the consoles, his expression one of disbelief as he took in the room's contents. He reached with a tentative hand to touch one of the dormant workstations, before pulling it back and turning to his friends. "It's extraordinary! Do you know what these things are? What they do?"

Removing his backpack, Virdon placed it on a chair near one of the consoles. "Some of it, anyway."

"There are a few pieces I don't recognize," said Burke, pointing to the row of computer banks along the wall. "Those look like more advanced versions of the equipment we had on the ship."

"But how is it still working after all this time?" asked Galen.

Virdon nodded. "That's a good question." He ran his fingers along the edge of a keyboard at one computer terminal. "And it's clean, too. If I didn't know any better, I'd think someone's here, or has been here." He shifted his gaze to take in the rest of the room. "How has no one found this place before now? That just doesn't make sense."

"Look over here, Al." Burke had crossed to the room's far side, and now stood before the entrance to a larger tunnel. He gestured toward the passage. "Any guesses where that goes?"

"If this place is laid out the way most silo complexes were," replied Virdon, "then probably to the main access point from the surface, and the silo itself."

Like the control room, the tunnel leading deeper into the complex was clean, and Virdon noted that lights were now on throughout the underground chambers, rather than simply activating in response to their presence. As he guessed, the passage opened into a stairwell and elevator shaft, though there was no car in the shaft itself. The metal stairs seemed to be in good condition, ascending toward the surfaces and dropping deeper into the complex. On the room's far side, the tunnel continued in a straight line before opening into a massive chamber: the silo.

"This is incredible," said Virdon, looking up to see the pair of massive metal doors which covered the silo's opening. At the bottom of the tower, black scorch marks were visible along the metal and concrete floor and the cradle in which a missile once had rested.

"Holy cow," said Burke, shaking his head as he rested his forearms on the railing. "I know we've had a pretty good idea about what happened here after we left, but until now, there was a part of me that didn't want it to be real." Reaching up, he wiped his face. "So much for that."

"Yeah." Virdon had harbored similar thoughts, but seeing the empty silo before them, he was left to wonder where the missile had gone following its launch. How many people had it killed, before triggering a similar response from some other world power? There was no way to know. Answers to such questions had long ago been consigned to the faded pages of a history book no one would ever read.

Damn.

Pausing at the crest of the small rise, Robar brought his horse to a halt. After nearly a full day spent riding over a seemingly endless stretch of rolling hills, sun-baked sand, and withered vegetation, the landscape now gave way to a flat plain.

"Look," said Sergeant Medros, who had accompanied him to scout ahead of Urko and the rest of the main search party. "What is that?"

Robar shifted his weight in his saddle as he beheld the odd ruins that lay before them. "I'm not sure." Though he had seen other examples of ancient human cities and other artifacts, he had never ventured into those areas. Still, he recognized telltale signs of that earlier civilization, in the form of the odd, smooth stone that seemed to be everywhere, along with rusted, twisted metal. How had the humans been able to make such things? It was beyond Robar's understanding, and his attempts to elicit more information from Urko had met with great resistance. More than once, the chief of security had cautioned him about the dangers of "unchecked curiosity."

"It is the sort of thing the humans would want to investigate," said Medros.

"You're right." Robar nodded, recalling that Urko had been quite clear on this topic when dispatching him and Medros, along with the other advance scouts, into the Paola Wastelands. By Robar's reckoning, he and Medros had ridden about two hours ahead of the main party. If they turned back now, they could report back to Urko well before dark. On the other hand, what if the renegade humans and their traitorous chimpanzee companion were here, now? This might be a rare opportunity to capture or kill them. Urko had promised a hefty reward to the ape who accomplished that task, and being in the security chief's good graces would surely carry numerous other advantages.

Urging his horse to begin traversing the gentle slope toward the ruins, Robar gestured for Medros to follow him. "Let's have a closer look."

Their tour of the underground facility had been cut short, thanks to several sections of the complex being inaccessible due to cave-ins or tunnel collapses. Everything below this main level had been cut off, but a cursory inspection of the upper areas revealed that the main entrance appeared to still be useable, though Virdon guessed it would take a bit of work to clear whatever dirt or rock might be covering the access point on the surface.

The most surprising find was the stockpile of provisions waiting for them in what at one time had been sleeping quarters for the personnel manning the complex. Fresh water and vacuum-sealed meal packets were the most prized items, but Virdon and Burke also had found a selection of tools and other small equipment which they might carry with them. Included with the tools were a pair of Colt M1911 .45-caliber semiautomatic pistols, the same model of weapon with which both astronauts would be familiar thanks to their Air Force training, along with belts, holsters, and a sizable amount of extra ammunition. What had captured Virdon's attention was the folded paper map depicting what once had been the United States, including a detailed inset for the area encompassing California, as well as western Nevada and Arizona. Both astronauts had only been slightly surprised to see a red circle on the map in southeastern California, indicating the missile complex's probable location not too far from the Nevada border.

"There's no way this stuff has been here for a thousand years, Pete," said Virdon as he inspected their find. "Somebody put this here, recently and deliberately." The identity of their benefactor remained unknown, as a thorough search had confirmed that they were alone in the complex. Leaving the supplies in place for the moment, the trio returned to the control room.

"I recognize some of this equipment," said Burke, dropping into one of the wheeled desk chairs positioned at different consoles. "But there's a lot that looks like it was well after our time."

Virdon replied, "Same here." They had known from the first hours after their arrival on Earth that the planet and human civilization had suffered upheaval while he, Burke, and their fellow astronaut, Christopher Jones, were traveling in space and encountering whatever storm or time warp had propelled them centuries into their own future. What remained a mystery were the circumstances of that catastrophe, and how, why, and precisely when humanity had reached a point of such desperation that it felt compelled to unleash upon itself weapons of unimaginable destructive power. How far had science, technology, and society advanced after his and Burke's departure, before all of it was lost? What had become of his wife, Sally, and his son, Chris? Such questions tore at him, and it was the not knowing that haunted Virdon's dreams.

"Whoa. Get a load of this."

Startled from his momentary reverie, Virdon turned to see that Burke had risen from his chair and was leaning over one of the consoles. He pointed to the workstations, one of which was now active. Rows of lights and status gauges reported all manner of information, only some of which Virdon recognized.

"It's alive," said Galen.

Burke replied, "Sort of. Something's up, that's for sure." He pointed to one of the terminal's blinking lights. "If I'm reading this right, this set of controls is for the video monitors." Without waiting for instructions, Burke tapped one of the keys. The blinking light now remained lit, and the four television monitors hanging from the ceiling all crackled to life. Within seconds, their displays coalesced into the image of an attractive, dark-skinned woman with short black hair. She wore a nondescript olive, drab jumpsuit with no insignia or patches, and looked to be seated at a desk or polished table. Her hands were clasped before her, and her expression warmed as she smiled toward the camera.

"*Greetings, Colonel Virdon and Major Burke. My name is Doctor Eva Stanton, and if you are watching this, then so far, everything has gone according to the rather hasty plan we have put into motion.*"

"What the hell....?" Virdon felt his jaw slacken, his gaze riveted to the alluring woman on the monitor.

"*I represent a community, one of several pockets of human civilization which have managed to survive all that has transpired over the many centuries you were away from Earth. Our numbers are small, and continue to dwindle with each successive generation, to a point where we are considering revealing ourselves to the surviving human populace. However, doing so brings with it the risk of discovery by the apes, which is something we cannot afford.*"

"This is unbelievable," said Galen.

"*We only recently became aware of your existence here. One of our people was investigating reports of a human experimenting with a rudimentary glider, and discovered that you were helping him. We later realized that it was you*"

345

who found the cache of information at the Oakland Science Institute. That storehouse was lost, unfortunately, but we were grateful that you escaped, and have continued to elude the ape authorities. Now that we know about you and your general whereabouts, it's time for you to find the safe haven you've been seeking. I know you and your friend, Galen, have many questions, and we hope to provide those answers. For that to happen, you must come to us."

"What is this?" asked Galen.

Burke pressed a button and the video halted. "It's a recording, similar to that projection we found in Oakland, but not quite so advanced." He patted the control console. "Whoever made it probably just took advantage of the equipment they found down here."

Virdon gestured to one of the monitors. "Let it play."

"*Due to our small numbers and limited defenses,*" said Stanton after Burke resumed the playback, "*it's imperative that we hide our existence from the apes. For that reason, we maintain our communities well away from the territories they control. However, after learning about you, we've attempted to track your progress while maintaining our secrecy.*" She paused, and her smile returned. "*You've proven most adept at hiding from us, too.*"

"They never call," said Burke. "They never write."

"*Much information from centuries past has been lost, but we were still able to identify you as two of several astronauts from the 20th century who had been listed as missing and presumed dead, and we're sorry for the loss of your friend, Major Jones.*" Stanton paused, as though collecting herself, before continuing, "*Once we realized you were heading inland and away from the central territories, we devised means of reaching out to you. The missile complex you've discovered is just one such facility we've rehabilitated in anticipation of your finding it. To protect ourselves, we can't give you our precise location, but based on your 20th-century knowledge, you should be able to find us if I tell you to search for a former military installation that used to be known as Area 51. We've left you with supplies to aid you, and it's possible we may be able to help you further as your journey continues. Until then, I look forward to the day we meet in person. Good luck, my friends."*

The image faded, leaving the astronauts and Galen to stare in muted shock at the blank screen. After a moment, Virdon turned to his friends.

"I don't believe it."

Burke snorted. "*You* don't believe it? Try being *me*, pal." A small smiled teased the corners of his mouth. "All those times I doubted you? I take them back. I officially surrender my membership in the Skeptic's Club."

Unfolding the paper map he had taken from the supplies they had found, he laid it atop a nearby table and traced his fingers along the inset portion depicting the southwestern United States. It took him only a moment to find a marking in Nevada's southern regions, which was labeled "Nevada Test and Training Range."

"That's it." Virdon could not help a small smile. "Groom Lake."

Leaning over the table, Galen asked, "You know this place?"

"Heard of it, mostly," replied Burke. "In our time, Area 51 was the popular name for a top-secret base where they developed new technologies for the military. Planes that were all but undetectable by an enemy, that sort of thing. Some people thought it's where spaceships from other planets were taken for study."

Virdon added, "I've never been there, and I don't know that the Air Force even admitted the base existed. At least, not before we left."

"And this is where this human lives?" Galen gestured to the monitor and the frozen image of Eva Stanton. "Her, and others like her?"

"That's what the lady said." Burke moved closer, eyeing the map. "If I'm reading this right, we're talking about something like three hundred miles, on foot, to get there."

Nodding, Virdon forced himself not to let the exultation and anticipation of the past few moments overwhelm him. "Yeah, but we can do it. We have to."

"You realize that even if we find these people," said Burke, "the chances of them being able to help us get home have to be pretty remote."

"I'm aware of that, Pete, but it's the first real hope we've had since we got here." Reaching into the pouch he wore on the rope belt around his waist, Virdon extracted a thick cloth, within which was wrapped a small, shiny metallic disk. For the first time in weeks, he held it up to inspect it.

Despite everything he and his friends had endured, he had managed to retain possession of the invaluable artifact that was the one surviving component from their spacecraft. Whatever had befallen their vessel, every aspect of that doomed flight was recorded on the disc. Did a civilization exist, anywhere on this planet, with the capability to interpret the stored data and perhaps recreate or reverse the circumstances which had pushed him and Burke so far into their own future? For the first time since their arrival, the answer to that question might very well be within their grasp.

There was no way Virdon could ignore that opportunity.

"I know that look," said Galen, before reaching over to tap Burke on the arm. "I think you and I should start packing those supplies."

Virdon wrapped the cloth around the flight disk and returned it to his belt pouch before folding the map. New energy and hope surged through him. For the first time in months, he felt driven once more by purpose. "Let's do it."

"Watch out!"

Galen's cry of alarm rang in the air an instant before Virdon felt the chimpanzee slam into him, driving him off his feet. Even as he tumbled to the floor, the snap of a gunshot echoed within the control room's confined space. Rolling away from the direction from which he thought the shot had come, Virdon caught sight of the gorilla soldier levering his bulk through the escape hatch's narrow opening. Moving with surprising speed for his size, the ape emerged into the control room just as Virdon and Galen scrambled for cover. Behind the soldier, Virdon saw another gorilla scrambling to pull himself from the conduit.

"It's them!" said the second ape. "The fugitives!"

Where the hell had the apes come from? How many of them were there? His mind racing, Virdon considered their escape options, which were few. There was the silo's main entrance, which meant a retreat deeper into the complex, or the escape shaft, which required fighting their way through at least two gorillas. Either scenario involved abandoning the complex itself, along with the supplies and the priceless information it contained.

We can't leave it! Not now!

"Alan!"

Hearing Burke's shout as he lunged for whatever meager protection the control consoles might offer, Virdon looked up to see his friend charging the first gorilla. He wielded a large, silver fire extinguisher that he swung by its handle like a club, striking the ape in the face and sending the soldier crashing to the floor.

Backpedaling, Burke was looking for a chance to lash out at the second gorilla, but the ape was faster, turning toward the astronaut while reaching for the short club hanging from a hook on his uniform belt. Using the soldier's distraction,

Virdon vaulted over the console and lowered his shoulder, driving into the ape's back and sending them both crashing into the wall. The gorilla struck his head against the concrete and grunted in confusion and pain, giving Burke an opening to strike once more with the fire extinguisher. One solid blow was all that was needed to drop the ape in his tracks.

"Behind you!"

Instinct and Galen's warning made Virdon duck and roll to his left just as he sensed the other gorilla lumbering toward him. The soldier overshot and tried to change direction, but by then Burke had retrieved the club from his companion's belt and come up behind him. A backhanded swing with the bludgeon across the back of the ape's head was enough to send him reeling, until he stumbled over one of the workstation chairs and crashed to the floor with a heavy thud.

Drawing heavy breaths, Virdon pushed himself to his feet. "Thanks."

Burke hefted the club. "Always liked these things."

"We can't stay here." Virdon moved to the tunnel accessing the escape shaft. It took him only a moment to verify that the two soldiers who had ambushed them appeared to be alone.

"There might be more up on the surface," he said upon returning to the control room, by which time Burke and Galen had finished tying up the unconscious apes.

Galen said, "At the very least, it's a scouting party that someone will miss. You heard what they said. They knew who we were."

The soldiers were the first the fugitives had seen in weeks. According to Prefect Gaulke, there was not even a police garrison anywhere within a day's ride of Nivek, but Virdon could not believe that the soldiers finding them here was a simple coincidence.

"You think it's Urko?" asked Burke, as though reading his friend's mind. "He's a tenacious one, that feisty gorilla."

Virdon nodded. "Well, we're not waiting around for him." He paused, casting his gaze around the control room. They would have to abandon the complex, which was unfortunate, but the buried missile silo had served its purpose, so far as he was concerned.

It had given him hope.

Urko stepped through the large metal door, trying not to let trepidation get the best of him as he examined the odd, circular chamber and its contents. In many ways, it reminded him of the underground room they had found several months earlier in the Forbidden City. Some of the unfamiliar components here looked to be of similar origin, and Urko knew what that meant.

Human knowledge, from ages ago, and all the danger it represents.

"Incredible," said Chief Councilor Zaius, who was standing at the room's center, taking in the collection of unfamiliar machines with their blinking lights and the low humming noises they made. "Simply incredible. Urko, do you understand what we've found? What we now hold in our hands?"

Regarding the strange devices, Urko grunted in annoyance. "All of this is dangerous, Zaius. You know that." He waved to indicate the room. "This is disease and destruction. We must destroy it all, just as we've done before." Several of the components looked to have been destroyed, reduced to nonfunctional piles of scrap metal and broken glass. Had they always been this way, or had Virdon, Burke, and Galen done this before making their escape?

It had taken Urko's troopers more than two days to force their way into the underground complex, during which Zaius and his entourage had completed their journey from Central City after being notified, more than a week earlier, of the latest reports of the fugitive humans and Galen being sighted in this region. Upon entering the subterranean passages, Urko's soldiers had found Lieutenant Robar and Sergeant Medros, who had managed to free themselves from their bonds while remaining trapped within the strange chamber. The two gorillas reported encountering the renegade astronauts and Galen and, after several minutes of harsh questioning, admitted that the humans had bested them, after which they had awakened to find themselves trussed up like animals. The fugitives were long gone, of course.

"It seems unreal that this equipment survived being buried for so long," said Zaius as he moved about the room. He reached out to touch various pieces of the bizarre machinery. "We know that humans once were capable of amazing feats, but this seems beyond even them."

Huffing, Urko waved toward the machinery. "What does it matter, Zaius?" He had ordered his troopers to remain outside the room, and instructed Robar and Medros not to discuss anything they had seen here until first debriefed by him. "This is an infection we cannot allow to spread. You know what we have to do here, just as we did before."

"Perhaps we were too hasty then, Urko." The chief councilor stopped before one of the odd components, resting his hand along its smooth surface. "There may be much to learn here—knowledge we can use to improve ape society."

Urko shook his head. "What can humans teach us, except how to more easily annihilate ourselves?" He pointed back toward the heavy metal door and the tunnel that lay beyond. "This entire facility had but one purpose: to carry destruction." He had seen pictures of similar structures in one of the few human books Zaius kept in his office back in Central City. Giant arrows of fire, carried on the winds to rain death down upon entire cities. It was no wonder the humans had so easily obliterated their entire civilization all those centuries ago. "You taught me to be wary of such things, Zaius. Have you forgotten your own warnings?"

To his relief, the councilor nodded, releasing a tired sigh. "You're right, Urko. We must remain forever vigilant." He tapped the odd machine with his knuckles. "This place is nothing but poison, and it must be eradicated." Turning back to Urko, he asked, "What of Virdon, Burke, and Galen?"

"We will find them," replied Urko. "It's just a matter of time."

Another hill.

"For the record," said Burke as they made their way up the latest gentle slope to crop up in their path, "I'm really getting bored with this whole 'return to nature' thing we've got going."

Virdon smiled at his friend's sardonic comment. "You might not want to get over it just yet. We've still got a lot of walking ahead of us."

By his calculations, and while allowing for factors such as rest periods, terrain, and weather, and even possible injury or being forced to evade ape patrols, Virdon figured it would take a minimum of a month to reach their destination. It would be a long journey, but he was confident they could make it. There was no need to rush or take unnecessary risks, and every reason to exercise due caution as they undertook their new quest.

"I don't know that anyone has ever been this far east," said Galen as he walked between his two human companions. "We seem to be walking off the edge of the map."

"Ape maps, maybe," replied Virdon. He tapped the pouch on his belt, which held the paper map he had taken from the missile silo. "But we've got some extra help now." Along with the map, the supplies left for them by their mysterious sponsors also had contained a proper compass of a style similar to those he had used during military land navigation exercises. It was a welcome substitute for the crude one Virdon had fashioned months earlier.

Noting that Galen seemed to be walking with his gaze fixed on the uneven ground before him, Virdon asked, "You okay?"

"I was just thinking," replied the chimpanzee as he shifted the heavy pack higher on his shoulders. "The woman on the recording represents your world, rather than mine. Once we get where we're going, *I'll* be the outcast."

"You're our friend," Burke said. "They'll welcome you, the same way you befriended us."

"I hope you're right." Galen smiled. "I have to admit, I'm excited and nervous, all at the same time. There's likely a great deal for me to learn."

Virdon said, "That may be true for all of us. On the other hand, there may be a lot you can teach them, too. After all, there are plenty of good apes out there. When you think about it, you'll be their ambassador. Would you rather they meet you, or Urko?"

"Speaking of Urko," replied Burke, "do you think he got into the silo by now?"

"Probably." There was no real way to prevent that in the limited time available to them, which Virdon had elected to spend gathering as much of the supplies as they could carry. Now each of them bore a hefty canvas pack on their back, filled with the provisions which would see them through their expedition. Their main concern upon leaving the missile silo was masking their departure, in the hopes of eluding Urko's scouts long enough to lose themselves in the uncharted terrain east of the Paola Wastelands.

"I'm going to feel pretty embarrassed if we walk all the way there and there's a sign on the door that says they've gone fishing," said Burke. "Here's hoping they know we're coming."

Virdon understood his friend's concern and shared it, at

least to a point. What mysteries awaited them in the midst of the vast unknown ahead of them, and what else might they find? Perhaps an opportunity for a world in dire need of salvation?

There was, Alan Virdon knew, only one way to find out.

We just keep walking.

Caesar's growing empire after *Battle for the Planet of the Apes* comes into sharp focus in Rich Handley's "The King Is Dead—Long Live the King," a treatise on treachery that may serve to shape the simian leader's legacy for centuries to come…

THE KING IS DEAD—LONG LIVE THE KING

by

RICH HANDLEY

The pursuit had been relentless.

Evolution had offered apes distinct advantages over man: superior strength and speed, heightened senses of smell and hearing, the ability to take to the trees with ease. They were in their element during the hunt, and their targets had been outmatched from the moment the horns had sounded. The humans knew they had been herded into an indefensible position. With little choice, they ran toward the towering stalks.

"No corn fields!" bellowed Karne, the oldest of the group. "You're out of bounds!" A squat orangutan with wild hair the color of flame, he pounded a thick fist against his chest as his human playmates sheepishly stepped back into the open. The two gorillas, Beren and Tiptonus, grunted their agreement.

"You're cheating!" Beren yelled.

Jillian stood her ground, but was mindful of her body language. Despite his small stature, Karne was the alpha among their friends, and she and the twins knew better than to openly challenge him. Though taller than the others, the three were, in the end, still humans.

Besides, Karne was right. They *had* cheated.

"Well, the rule's not fair," Jillian countered. "If we can't hide in the fields, you find us too quickly."

Karne thumped his chest. "That's because you humies are all skin and no hair," he said. "You stand out like a baboon's back door." This caused Tiptonus and Beren to screech in hysterics; most things Karne said did. One of the twins, Jeric, clenched his jaw, but Karne bared his gums and teeth to take the sting out of his jibe, then playfully lunged. The two rolled to the ground laughing, and the others joined in.

"It's gratifying to know that all of Ape City values peace as much as I," a voice observed. "It appears Lisa and I can retire now. Someplace warm, I hope, with a lot of fruit."

"Caesar!" Karne said. Standing next to the elderly chimp were his advisors, Virgil and Bruce MacDonald. The children scrambled to their feet. "I know how you feel about fighting, but we were only playing, honest."

"If you were only *playing* honest," Virgil wryly noted, "that implies you were not actually *being* honest." The orangutan's once-orange hair was now dusted with white.

"Grandfather, that's not what I meant." Karne swayed nervously, puffing his cheeks. "Actually, I'm not sure what you even just said. But we *were* only playing."

"The humans were cheating," Tiptonus added. "They broke the rules of the game."

"Some consider violence no game at all," Virgil said.

"Now, Virgil," Caesar chided, not unkindly, "children will play."

Virgil raised a bushy eyebrow. "I recall when Caesar forbade games of fighting."

"That is true, my friend. But times change, and I suppose I have as well. Call it a king's prerogative." Caesar sighed. "Besides, I can't imagine apes ever hunting humans with nets."

"Shall we release the prisoners?" MacDonald quipped. "Or should I escort them to the stockade?"

"I think a stern reprimand will suffice," Caesar said, smiling. "Consider yourselves reprimanded… *sternly*. Now have fun." He leaned in closer to Tiptonus. "When rules are broken, sometimes it means those rules need to change."

"Yes, sir," Tiptonus said. Caesar watched, his smile fading into a sigh, as the friends ran toward the adobe structures recently added to Ape City's residential area.

"I know that look, Caesar," MacDonald said. "Something's bothering you—and I don't think it's the children of the corn."

"All this time, MacDonald," Caesar replied, "and we haven't truly set aside our differences. Whether school is in or out of session, they're inseparable friends. Yet even in games, they never forget, or cease to remind each other, that we are not the same."

"Well, we're not," MacDonald pointed out. "But I wouldn't worry. Playing Hunters and Hunted won't turn Virgil's grandson into a redheaded Aldo." Virgil chuckled.

"Let us hope." Caesar felt the midday sun on his skin. "Twenty years," he said softly. "Where has the time gone?"

"I presume Caesar is no longer discussing children's games," Virgil mused, then he nodded his comprehension. "Yes, of course. The Battle. Tomorrow is the anniversary, I believe."

"Has it been that long?" MacDonald replied. "I guess that explains my hairline."

"Ape City barely survived that day," Caesar said. "I've long worried that Kolp's people might retaliate, which is why the Armory still stands."

"Yet they've never returned," Virgil noted. "We've lived without war ever since."

"Without war, yes. But not without its specter looming in the Forbidden City—and inside our own walls. What we've built makes me proud, but I'm not naïve enough to think it's a paradise, Virgil. There is still mistrust, particularly between humans and gorillas."

"Understandably," MacDonald said. "The gorillas were the most harshly treated under man's rule. Aldo made sure never to let us forget that. Moving past it will take time, on both sides. The history of humanity has proven that time and again. Those oppressed sometimes become the next oppressors, and those beaten down can be the next to raise a hand."

"Hunters and hunted…" Caesar sighed. "When does the resentment end, MacDonald? When did human society set aside its differences and unite as a species?"

"When we all became subservient to the apes, I suppose." A smile softened his words. "That's no longer an issue, of course. Thanks to your reforms, mankind has been integrated back into society. You and I may be different, but we're equals. You're my brother, and so is Virgil." The orangutan bowed his head.

"Had Malcolm lived to this day," MacDonald added, "he'd have been proud to see humans and apes living and working side by side."

"I do believe he would have," Caesar agreed. "I also believe the time has come to make amends with those beyond our borders. Your brother was a man of peace. On the Night of the Fires, he warned me that violence prolongs hate, and hate violence. I wasn't ready to accept it at the time, but he was right. And so we must now reach out to those in the Forbidden City."

Virgil and MacDonald exchanged glances. "Are you sure that's a good idea, Caesar?" the orangutan asked. "For many in Ape City, those wounds still run deep."

"I once dismissed those in the wasteland as mad creatures—irrational and irredeemable as they were irradiated. But I fear I was unjust in my condemnation. It wasn't so long ago that man viewed apes as savages, that apes feared humans as taskmasters. Given what we've achieved within our community in so short a span, is it really that unreasonable to think we could form a friendship with those who once warred against us?"

"It's an admirable goal, Caesar," MacDonald admitted,

"one I'd be glad to see pan out. But I have my doubts. For one, I can't imagine those in the Forbidden City would be open to it. Whoever you send, you'll be putting them at great risk."

"We've only achieved what we have because Caesar believed we could," Virgil said. "His will has never led us astray. If Caesar believes we should seek peace with the Forbidden City's population, then the risk is worth taking."

"Thank you, Virgil. And you, MacDonald. Your counsel and friendship, as always, mean more than either of you could know. Now I must see Brutus. He has a long journey ahead of him."

"Father," Brutus said with a smile as Caesar entered his home. "I wasn't expecting to see you until tomorrow's Council meeting."

"I hope it's not too late," Caesar said as his son offered a chair.

"No, of course not. It's a nice surprise. Can I get you something to drink? I just pressed some fresh figs."

"Oh, I'm fine, thank you. There is something I need to discuss with you, though."

Brutus sat nearby. "What is it?"

"I have a task I'd like you to undertake," Caesar said. "It won't be easy."

"Anything, Father."

"I need you to help me correct a mistake of the past."

"What kind of mistake?" Brutus asked.

"In leading our people, I allowed fear to smolder unseen instead of dousing the flame, comforted in a self-told lie that if none stoked the blaze, it would cease to consume and grow."

"I... don't understand, Father."

Caesar chuckled. "Perhaps I've been friends with Virgil for too long. I'm starting to talk like him. In our early days, we faced a turning point when humans from the Forbidden

City tried to destroy what we had built. They were mutated and decrepit. Their leader, Vernon Kolp, had served under Governor Breck before the revolution. He and I had… history."

"He blamed you for his people's deterioration," Brutus said. "You've told me about him. Obviously, he was a lunatic. Man's own weapons disfigured the mutants."

"He was deranged and dangerous, yes," Caesar agreed. "But not all of his people were. I saw them, Brutus. They were desperate, living among the rubble of a dead civilization. They followed Kolp's orders because they had no hope left. After he died, the stragglers of his army retreated to the Forbidden Zone. Many in Ape City hailed that as a great victory."

"Wasn't it?"

"In the short term. In the wake of the Battle, apes and humans finally began to live as one." The chimp rubbed his temples. "The longer term is more uncertain. How can Ape City claim to have peace if our nearest neighbors might still harbor a grudge over past wars? Can I end my reign in good conscience, knowing I did not do all I could to stop the cycle?"

Caesar patted his son's arm. "I intend to form a lasting peace with those in the Forbidden City, Brutus. Help me make this happen. I need you to travel there in my name and invite their leader to negotiate a permanent treaty."

Brutus' eyes narrowed. "Is that even possible? It sounds like they fled in humiliation. They'd probably open fire the moment they saw us. They killed the man who raised you, remember, and he was one of their kind."

"I remember, yes, but Armando was not one of *their* kind," Caesar corrected him. "He was a gentle, protective father. You'd have liked him… and he was murdered by Breck's staff, not mutants."

Brutus bit his upper lip. "Given what it's like beyond Ape City, I'm not convinced we should be inviting contact with outsiders, Father. That hasn't always turned out well in the past. It certainly didn't for Seraphine."

Caesar squeezed his son's hand. "I know. She was taken too soon. I always pictured her at your side when you eventually lead Ape City." He yawned. "Which might be sooner rather than later, given how tired I've been feeling lately."

"Mother says you need to sleep more. You bring your work home with you."

"She's a wise ape, that one." He looked into his son's eyes. "I hope you don't blame all humans for Ser's death…"

"For a while, I did. Not anymore." Brutus leaned on the wooden table where he and his wife had once shared meals. "There are good men and bad. She met some bad ones."

"The same is true of apes, I'm afraid. Aldo killed your brother Cornelius, and he was an ape. MacDonald is not an ape, but I would trust him with my life and yours."

"I know."

"He and Tanya care deeply for you, and for your siblings."

"I know that, too."

"Help me open Ape City's arms in friendship. I want that to be my legacy, Brutus. I don't wish to be remembered as the king who left peace to chance. Beyond our borders lies the unknown. I've seen it first-hand, and it can be terrifying, I know, but there's as much to gain as there is to risk. I'm too old to make the trip, or I'd go again myself."

Caesar paused, then suggested gently, "Perhaps forging peace with these humans might lend meaning to your wife's passing. One group of scavengers wounds us deeply, yet we find it in our hearts to embrace another."

After a few seconds, Brutus nodded. "Of course, Father. I'll do as you ask."

The trek had proved arduous, the summer heat unrelenting for those covered in body hair, not to mention leather armor.

This extended their travel time longer than anticipated, stretching food and water supplies thin—which was a big concern for the travelers, but a bigger issue for the horses carrying the expedition and their belongings.

Finally, they reached the outskirts of the Forbidden City. Brutus called a halt and considered the landscape. The chimp had led his team to the decaying ruins, assured by Virgil that they could withstand the radioactive environment for the limited time the mission would require—provided the mutants didn't kill them outright.

Brutus had discussed with Caesar and his advisors how best to proceed. Unlike past quests to the Forbidden City, they would avoid being stealthy on this one. At best, it would make clear their benign intent. At worst, it left six mostly unarmed targets standing out in the open, waiting to be picked off.

He hoped this would not be a day for worst-case scenarios.

The valley was silent, save for agitated whinnying and the footfalls of travelers unloading their packs. Brutus had assigned a gorilla to monitor each entrance onto the street, reminding them not to take aggressive action without his authorization. He'd suspected it might take a while to grab the inhabitants' notice, and had ordered his team to set up a conspicuously visible camp between the debris lining either side of the cracked road.

Five hours had passed without any indication that anyone was aware of their presence. Brutus felt a headache coming on, and idly wondered how long a chimp could last amid radioactivity without mutating as well. He checked the detector, which showed safe levels in their vicinity.

Finally, one gorilla gave a signal discreetly alerting Brutus that they had company. Four humans in black hooded jackets approached, their faces thin and scarred, their hair missing in patches. A few had visible tumors. Behind them was an unassuming figure wearing similar garb but lighter in color.

The man was slight of frame, his head devoid of eyebrows or other facial hair. He seemed in good health, despite some scarring of his own.

"I am Gorman," he said in a soft tone. "I speak on behalf of Mendez I, leader of the Fellowship. We've been monitoring you since before you reached the city. While our laws no longer condone violence, there are still some among us who would see you eliminated. I'd prefer to avoid that outcome, as it would offend God greatly, but some wounds heal slowly."

Brutus noticed a gorilla edging a hand toward his weapon. "Understood, Gorman," he called out, making eye contact with the soldier, who relaxed. "Our purpose is a peaceful one."

"As is ours. We are God's Children," Gorman said.

"My name is Brutus and I've come from Ape City to invite your leader to meet with ours. My father, Caesar, desires a permanent peace between our domains."

"I see," Gorman said, appraising him. "Do you desire this as well, Brutus?"

"Where my father leads, I follow. He believes we can establish a friendship for the benefit of all. Please convey this message to Mendez on Caesar's behalf."

Gorman studied him for several seconds, saying nothing. The shorn human's unblinking gaze made Brutus uneasy, but he shook it off. "Come with me," the man said, "and you can tell Mendez this yourself."

"Thank you," Brutus replied, rubbing the back of his neck to lessen his headache. He and his team followed the others deeper into the ruins.

Class was still in session when the travelers returned. Teacher did her best to keep the students focused, but once they caught sight of the strangers accompanying the expedition, she knew it was a lost cause. Karne and other children ran toward the window as the riders entered the city. Jeric's twin, Megan, shot a pleading look at Teacher.

"Okay, go ahead," she sighed. "It's just about mealtime anyway. But don't be gone long. We're not finished with the lesson."

The students ran outside. It had rained earlier that day, and the horses' splashing footfalls created a muddy mosaic. Caesar's prince rode alongside an elderly human. He and his people wore liturgical vestments, differentiated by the color of each rider's cloth stole. The old man's stole, like that of a younger man to his other side, was violet. Gorman rode behind them, his stole dark blue. Alongside Gorman was a middle-aged woman, her stole sage green.

The sight was impressive, though Caesar noticed that the scarring and sores on the visitors' faces made some citizens ill at ease. It unnerved him as well.

The riders came to a halt in the common area. Brutus dismounted as Caesar descended from the treehouse he shared with his wife and fourth child, climbing more slowly than he'd once been capable. "My son," he said, adding in a low voice, "How was the expedition?"

"Long and tiring, like an orangutan's sermon," Brutus said. "It's good to be home." More quietly, he warned, "Not all of them favor your proposition, Father. Don't expect miracles today... especially from the son. It's been an interesting trip." He rubbed the back of his head.

Lisa left young Armand with his sister Zoe and her mate, then joined MacDonald and Virgil next to Caesar. Gorillas stood at attention, weapons pointed downward. General Athen had ordered them to avoid appearing belligerent, per Caesar's request, and to their credit, the gorillas were doing as she'd instructed.

"His Holiness, Mendez I," Gorman announced as the young man in purple dismounted and helped Mendez to do the same. Though stooped, the mutant monarch was strong for someone who had lived decades in a radioactive wasteland. So were they all, Caesar noted of his retinue, epidermal damage notwithstanding.

"Welcome," Caesar said. "I'm honored that you have come." He introduced his advisors and family, and the elder human nodded at each in turn, smiling at MacDonald as though in recognition. MacDonald glanced at Virgil, who raised an apprehensive eyebrow.

"Thank you for your gracious invitation, Caesar," Mendez said.

"It's my honor to welcome you to Ape City," Caesar replied.

Mendez indicated his entourage. "My cardinals, Van-Nga Alma and Rod Gorman, and my son Steven, who shall one day succeed me in guiding the Fellowship."

"Then we have something in common. I am grooming Brutus to replace me as well."

"They may come after us," Mendez said, "but I like to think of myself as irreplaceable."

"Yes, of course," Caesar replied with a soft laugh. "It's of replacements that I'd hoped to speak—replacing the conflicts of our past with the promise of a united future. The losses we both suffered have weighed heavily on my mind. It's my hope that together, we can ensure the safety of the world our children will inherit."

"That's my hope as well, Caesar," Mendez said. "We are a people changed by war, but God has shown us a different path. Perhaps, in time, you and I can walk it together."

Caesar smiled. "I would like that." He gestured to a tent nearby. "Please come this way, Mr. Mendez."

"Mendez is fine," he said. "We've met before, though admittedly under less pleasant circumstances. This isn't my first visit to Ape City."

A murmur spread through the crowd as Mendez and his

entourage headed for the tent. Caesar cocked an eyebrow toward Lisa, who shrugged.

"Have we?" He scrunched his nose. "Hmm."

A long, wooden table had been prepared in the tent, with dried fruit, fresh bread, and pitchers of water and sweet juices. Caesar and Mendez I sat at opposite ends. Steven, Alma, and Gorman lined one side, with other members of their party in a second row, near one wall. Across from Mendez's inner circle sat MacDonald, Lisa, Virgil, and Brutus.

General Athen and two gorilla soldiers stood along the wall behind Caesar's cabinet. Lieutenant Kwai noticed Karne and his friends trying to listen in between the tent's folds, and shooed the children away with a stomp.

MacDonald broke the silence. "Mendez, I hope you don't take this the wrong way, but I have to admit to some surprise that this meeting is taking place. When Caesar mentioned what he had in mind, I was skeptical."

"How so, Mr. MacDonald?" Mendez asked.

"MacDonald was concerned that my son's expedition might receive an unfriendly welcome," Caesar explained. "His advice is invaluable, but I'm afraid he sometimes worries too much." MacDonald glanced sideways at the chimp.

Mendez smiled. "Humans do have a tendency to do that."

"Well, I'm glad to have been proven wrong," MacDonald said.

"Of course, those same concerns had crossed my mind," Caesar admitted. "Our cultures haven't interacted in two decades. I had no idea what to expect."

"Yet you sent your son into radioactive territory inhabited by your enemies," Alma noted, her expression unreadable.

"My father didn't ask me to do anything I wasn't willing to do," Brutus said, though he wondered, given his persistent headache, if Virgil had underestimated the health hazard.

"Perhaps apes don't value their children as we do," Steven said.

Brutus rubbed his eyes tiredly. "Here we go…"

Mendez shot his son an angry look. "That's not helpful, Steven. We're guests here."

Lisa's posture straightened. "Of course we value our children. Caesar loves our son. You'll never meet a more devoted father. He values all of his people."

"If that's true," Steven asked, "then why is this village called *Ape* City? Clearly, some here are more valued than others."

"Now, just a minute—" Brutus began.

"Please forgive my son's ill-chosen words," Mendez interrupted. "The trip here was long, and we're all tired. He meant no insult."

"With all due respect, Mendez, I think it's clear to everyone what he meant," Brutus said. "It was clear yesterday."

"Please, everyone, let's remember why we're here," Caesar said calmly. He turned to Alma. "Sending my son to the Forbidden City was not something I did lightly, believe me. I thought the risk worth taking because I'd hoped it would lead to this discussion… such as it is."

"'Forbidden City,'" Steven repeated. "That name denigrates us. Ours is a *Holy* City. It is the home of our God. You speak of peace, yet disrespect us in the next breath."

"I meant no offense, of course," Caesar said hastily. "*My* words were ill-chosen."

"Caesar believes meaningful peace comes from inclusion," Virgil said, "not isolation."

"Whereas I care even less for what a chimpanzee believes than I do an orangutan."

"Steven," Mendez said sharply. "That is enough."

Uncomfortable seconds passed.

"This… may take some time," MacDonald commented.

Virgil offered a subtle grumph of agreement.

"Perhaps, Holiness, it would be best if we were to change the subject," Gorman suggested.

"A good idea," Mendez said.

"Yes," Caesar nodded, grateful for the distraction. "Mendez, you mentioned that we've met. I'm afraid I don't recall that meeting."

"I was curious as well," Virgil said. "Forgive my directness, sir, but… were you among Kolp's survivors?"

"No, I had no part in that action, nor did I agree with it," Mendez said. "I wasn't convinced you meant us harm when our cameras detected you in the Archives, and urged the Governor to let you go peacefully. Kolp attacked anyway. He left me and Alma in charge while he led the assault. He wasn't thinking rationally. Maybe it was the radiation, or just boredom, but many needlessly died as a result. He'd ordered us to level your village if he didn't return, but we chose not to. The killing had to stop. On that day, we came to understand God's plan."

"I'm afraid I don't quite understand," Caesar said. "You're saying we met in the Forb—in your city?"

"No, it was… several years before that."

"Oh?"

"Holiness," Gorman cut in, "are you sure this is the best—"

"It's all right," Mendez said. "It's time for the truth."

"What truth is that?" MacDonald asked.

"There is only one truth," Virgil noted. "It is perception that varies."

"Alma and I lived here long ago," Mendez explained.

"I don't recall either of you," Lisa said.

"Neither do I," Caesar added with a frown.

"You probably wouldn't, unless you'd spent a lot of time among the laborers. Only the gorillas paid us much mind, and they didn't usually bother learning our names."

"You mean..." Caesar said.

"Yes," Mendez nodded. "We helped you build Ape City."

"Not by our own choice," added Alma.

"They were your slaves," Steven said.

"I see." Caesar lowered his head, closing his eyes. "I had no idea. I'm sorry."

"I remember now," MacDonald said quietly. "I didn't recognize you."

During the weeks following the ape rebellion, thermonuclear war devastated the planet, creating unlivable zones in many major cities. As Caesar led his ape followers away from civilization, numerous humans with nowhere else to go joined them, hoping to survive the new world among those innately suited to the wilderness. He allowed them to do so.

However, the death of Malcolm MacDonald, Caesar's first human liaison, changed things. Kolp had deemed the elder MacDonald brother a traitor, and shot him while leading a failed mission to assassinate Caesar. Soon thereafter, General Aldo urged the ape king to let him conscript the humans as slaves, and though it shamed him to admit it now, Caesar had let the brutal gorilla have his way. His fury at Kolp and Breck had clouded his judgment, and so the humans began their Ape City existence as slaves mistreated by Aldo's troops. The military then supplemented the labor force by capturing outsiders.

Bruce MacDonald—the brother of the very friend whose death had caused Caesar to make this mistake—had been among the slaves, and remained so for two years before Caesar, guilt-ridden at having allowed gorillas to do to humans what had been done to them, abolished slavery. The humans learned to forgive and even respect Caesar, and MacDonald honored his brother by taking his place as the chimp's new liaison.

"For two years we toiled and were tortured," Alma said. "Finally, we escaped to the city. The Governor took us back in, sheltered us, and gave us a new purpose: survival."

"That's all in the past now," Mendez said. "God has given us an even greater purpose. But I wanted you to know the truth, Caesar—and that Alma and I hold no ill will against anyone here."

Alma said nothing.

"It was a violent time, before God showed us a better way," Mendez said. "What matters now is that we move forward."

"I agree. Thank you," Caesar said gratefully. Lisa squeezed his hand, knowing the shame he still felt for having allowed it to happen.

"There's… something else you should know," Mendez continued. "The reason we ended up slaves in the first place."

"Mendez," Alma said, her composure dropping. "Oscar, no. We agreed not to do this."

"Holiness," Gorman said, "I suggest we discuss this privately."

"Among allies, secrets have a way of seeking the light of day, and private discussions tend to breed public distrust," Mendez replied. "I feel it's best that they know everything."

"Sir," Gorman tried again, "this is not… this strikes me as a very—"

"Enough," Mendez snapped, silencing his aides. He faced the chimpanzee. "Caesar, when Governor Kolp tried to assassinate you… Alma and I were members of his commando unit."

Caesar's eyes widened. The gorillas shifted uncomfortably.

"What did you say?" Lisa asked.

"You tried to murder my father…" Brutus said, the throbbing in his head intensifying.

"Something I have long regretted. Understand that I was a soldier, and Kolp was my superior. I followed his orders, even those I disagreed with. Thankfully, we failed in the attempt, but Alma and I were captured while retreating. I didn't yet know God's will in those days, but He has since revealed His love to us, alpha and omega, reshaping us in His image. We are no longer the brutalized slaves who resented our masters, nor the desperate, hateful creatures who attacked you. We have peace now, just as you have. It was divine will that led you to us, Brutus, so I could make amends for what I'd done."

All eyes were on the mutant leader.

"I have already sought God's absolution, Caesar," Mendez said. "Now I seek your forgiveness and friendship. Your dream is mine—and, I believe, the Lord's as well."

Caesar didn't entirely understand everything Mendez had said, but the passion and conviction in the man's words moved him.

Brutus pressed a hand against his throbbing head.

"This is getting strange," General Athen muttered low enough for only her soldiers to hear. "Be vigilant," she added.

"I'll never understand humans or chimpanzees," Kwai responded in a low growl.

Caesar regarded Mendez with a tilted smile. "Recently, I told a group of children that when we break rules, those rules may need to change," the chimp told him. "Today, I see there was more truth in that statement than I'd realized at the time. You ignored Kolp's orders to attack Ape City, and you renounced the violence inherent to your species. You broke the rules—not only of a man, but of men—and we benefited as a result."

"Just as you, in fighting for ape freedom, changed the rules for all our species."

"We've each been the hunted and the hunters," Caesar said.

"The enslaved and the slavers," Mendez agreed. "And now the peace seekers."

"I think we understand each other, Mendez—and I forgive you."

"I forgive you as well, Caesar."

Mendez rose and offered Caesar his hand. As Caesar

reached out to take it, Brutus stood abruptly, his face clenched, his arms shaking.

"Brutus?" Lisa asked.

"No," Brutus said. He backed toward Athen and the guards, panting. "No, no… hurts… stop…"

A guard heard the commotion and poked his head into the tent. "Run and get Tanya," MacDonald told him. "Hurry!"

The guard obeyed, leaving the flap slightly open as he ran to fetch the doctor. Karne and Tiptonus, who'd been listening from outside, leaned in for a better look.

"*No!*" Brutus yelled again, diving at the gorillas. Gripping his head with one hand, he made a grab with the other for the pistol in Kwai's holster. He fired twice at Caesar before the gorilla realized what was happening.

"Caesar!" Lisa pushed him out of the way as soon as she saw the weapon in her son's hand. One bullet tore through her chest, propelling her into the side of the tent, which ripped from the force of her momentum. Screams emanated from citizens going about their business outside as Caesar's queen thumped onto the saturated grass, her pooling blood quickly darkening the muddy ground.

Caesar let out a guttural yell, leaping in the direction of his wife as MacDonald and Athen reached for his gun-wielding son. He cradled her frail form, weeping into her hair. She was already dead.

Brutus screamed like a trapped animal and kept firing wildly, the muscles of his chest and arms rigid from strain as he struggled against those holding him. He let go of the weapon once it ran out of ammunition, raging for another moment before falling silent and slack. "Seraphine…" he said, barely a whispered croak, then began seizing. As Athen pinned his twitching body to the ground, rivulets of blood oozed from one nostril and both ears.

At the same time, Alma grabbed a knife from the bread tray

and rushed at Mendez, slashing at Gorman and Steven on the way to her target. Gorman managed to sidestep her without injury. He pushed Steven out of the way, but the blade sliced through the man's arm before ending up embedded in the chest of his father, all the way to the hilt.

Mendez I staggered backwards, tripping over a chair and landing on his side, sputtering up blood that stained his vestments and the tent wall crimson. His guards rushed at Alma, wrestling her to the ground. She thrashed about wildly, but the men were larger and she went down hard, slashing one man's cheek and mouth open before landing on the knife, which plunged into her neck, killing her instantly.

Tiptonus screamed, and Virgil, who'd been knocked off his chair during the chaos, saw what had so terrified the young gorilla. "Karne…" he yelled hoarsely.

Virgil sprang to his feet and ran to his grandson. Karne lay unmoving between the open flaps, a single hole in one side of his head. The stray bullet had found its mark and he was dead by the time Virgil, sobbing, pulled the boy to his chest.

Time slowed for Caesar as he held Lisa's lifeless body. He vaguely registered the additional shots and the screaming from all directions, heard the gorilla child's shriek and Virgil's heartbroken cries. He knew something had happened to Mendez, but had no idea what it was, who had done it, or why. He remained numb to everything around him until he saw Brutus lying bloodied. As he reached his son's side, the shaking stopped and Brutus lay unmoving, his open eyes fixed on some horror only he could see.

"Why?" Caesar demanded, gripping his heir in his arms. No parent should have to endure a child's death, yet here he was going through it a second time, only moments after losing his wife. "What did you do, Brutus? Our most sacred law… you *killed* her, Brutus…"

MacDonald tried to offer a consoling hand, but stopped mid-reach, a startled look contorting his face as his knees buckled and he slipped sideways into a chair. "What...?" he said, then noticed the hole in his abdomen and the scarlet stain spreading across his tunic. He had felt no pain during the scuffle with Brutus, but now he felt a fast-growing coldness.

Caesar watched his friend fall, but could find no words.

Tanya entered the tent, stunned at the carnage that had been the site of peace negotiations only moments prior. She saw her husband slumped in a chair near Caesar and ran to him, repeating "Oh my God" and "Bruce," and she ripped his shirt open and tried to save his life. It was too late. Brutus had taken his third victim from the grave.

Caesar saw the bodies of his friend and family, saw a kneeling Virgil rocking Karne, saw Athen and her gorillas scrambling to maintain order, saw and heard it all from the kaleidoscopic view of someone gazing down an echoing, darkened tunnel.

Then, across the tent, he saw the mutants.

Alma was a limp pile of bloody cloth discarded on the floor. Steven knelt near his father, his expression tear-streaked as he and Gorman held Mendez's hands. The others in their party knelt around them, praying.

"How could this happen?" Steven asked.

Mendez showed no sign of having heard his son. His quick breathing was shallow and raspy.

"Why, in the name of the Bomb, would Alma do this?" Steven stammered. "She was your friend since before I was born. It makes no sense."

"It's this place," Gorman told him. "It is unholy. God is absent here. In bringing us beyond our city, your father unknowingly removed us from grace. We must return home. He and even Alma must be renewed on sacred ground."

Mendez's breathing came more jaggedly now. As Caesar

knelt beside them, Gorman and Steven lowered their heads in prayer.

Can you hear me, Mendez? Gorman asked. But it wasn't words. It was something beyond words, beyond the limits of language. Mendez heard, or rather felt, Gorman's question in his mind, but could neither comprehend nor respond in kind.

I know you're confused, but you are not dreaming, my friend.

"How?" Mendez asked aloud in a dry rasp.

Steven's voice broke at the sound. "We don't know, Father. It all happened so fast."

"Gorman..."

"I am here, Mendez."

I am here, Mendez. God has granted a gift—an inner voice, control of others' thoughts and actions. I was the first to receive this gift, but others will follow. I can feel it. It is the will of the Bomb, and it is good. God forbids us from killing, Mendez, but He protects His Children. Through His gift, our enemies will kill each other for us.

Alma's sacrifice was unavoidable, as was yours. Though she will be called a traitor, her loyalty never wavered. Take comfort in knowing how hard she fought my mind's touch. The chimpanzee's mind was less evolved. His kind is not as open to the gift. The death of his wife provided a trigger, but he resisted with all his will and the effort damaged him.

I take no pleasure in what had to happen this day. You were a great leader, Oscar Mendez, and I shall mourn you. I wish you could have continued to guide us on our path. I wish... but you strayed from that path when you brought us here, to this unconsecrated place of the Devil in ape's clothing. The Fellowship doesn't belong here among blasphemers and beasts. You failed to see that, but a single whispered word, echoed at the edges of your son's mind, helped Steven to recognize God's wisdom: "animals."

Mendez choked up blood as two gorilla orderlies pushed those praying aside so that MacDonald's widow, ignoring her own tears, could reach him. "Animals…" he repeated. The gorillas grunted at each other, but continued trying in vain to save his life.

Steven shall become Mendez II. He shall bring us home to the Holy City, far from those who would turn us away from God, and we shall praise you both in psalm. Goodbye, my friend. We will meet again in the Shadow of the Bomb Everlasting.

It had been a beautiful memorial. That's what many in Ape City had told him, offering their support but no real comfort. He couldn't remember. He'd been too numb to take notice of any beauty save for Lisa's still features.

In one horrifying, inexplicable moment, Caesar had lost his wife, his son, and his friend. Virgil had lost his grandson. Those from the Forbidden City had lost their leader. Ape had killed ape, human had killed human… and his legacy had died with them all.

Mendez II had led his people back to their irradiated land, steadfast in his refusal to continue what his father had begun. "We will not meet again. God has made clear his desire that we remain separate," he'd told Caesar. "Your people are not welcome in our city. Consider it forbidden. Your name for it is finally suitable."

The human doctors had suggested possible causes to explain the bizarre, simultaneous homicides—a rage-inducing virus, or radiation sickness—but it was all just conjecture. Brutus' body showed no signs of illness, and so it remained a mystery, his son forever to be remembered as a crazed killer and not as the good ape Caesar and Lisa had raised him to be.

A month after the tragedy, Virgil and Caesar visited the grave Tanya had arranged for her mate. "BRUCE MACDONALD," it said on one line, with "HUSBAND, FRIEND, LEADER" etched underneath.

"I miss him, Virgil. He was a good man," Caesar said.

"Yes," Virgil agreed. "The best I've known."

The cool breeze felt comforting against their thick pelts.

"I failed him. I failed all of them."

"Caesar…"

"I should have known that what I was after was unattainable. MacDonald knew. I should have listened to his counsel. It was always wise. I didn't, and so many paid the price."

"You had hope. That is no small thing."

"Where did that hope bring us, Virgil? Here, to this stone? Not a place I wish to be."

"Hmm, perhaps," Virgil said. "But without hope, there is little joy."

"My joy died when Brutus did this," Caesar said, waving a hand toward the grave. "When my lack of vision made him try to kill his own father. Their deaths are on me."

"Monkey-feathers."

Caesar stared at his friend. "How can you say that? Your grandson was among those buried."

"Brutus pulled the trigger, not Caesar."

"I'm his father. I should have noticed he needed help, should have realized Seraphine's death still affected him. It was my job to stop him from doing something so unthinkable."

"We all have the capacity to kill, Caesar. We choose as a people not to act on it, but it is there, submerged behind our First Law. We may never know why Brutus did what he did, or why the human woman did the same, but I know this: you have two children who need you, and an entire city that does as well."

"What kind of father am I if I couldn't help my son? What kind of leader if I couldn't protect my own wife, or even a young child?"

"One who cares enough to ask such questions—who understands, beneath the self-pity and recrimination, that life goes on. We still follow your will, Caesar, for you have never led us astray. We need your vision now more than ever."

Caesar closed his eyes. "And what of the Forbidden City, Virgil?"

"It remains forbidden." Virgil grumphed. "But we do have peace. And hope."

Caesar pondered that for a moment, tears glistening his cheeks, then grasped his friend's arm. Perhaps Virgil was right.

Perhaps, for now, that was sufficient.

Finally, never before have orangutan and gorilla joined forces such as they do in Jonathan Maberry's "Banana Republic," a devious political tale with far-reaching ramifications for the future of the planet...

BANANA REPUBLIC

by

JONATHAN MABERRY

"Master Dante!"

The cry roused the orangutan from a light doze and he jerked awake, turning on his stool, spilling scrolls and knocking a wooden cup of fig wine to the floor. Dante snarled as the wine splashed across the papers, and the sound of his fury made the younger ape skid to a halt, one hand on the threshold of the cabin, the other pressed to his mouth. The younger orangutan's hair was windswept and there was rock dust on his face.

"What *is it?*" roared Dante as he stooped to try and slap wine away from the reports he had been reading. "Speak up, Caleb—does a human have your tongue?"

"M-Master," stammered the boy, "it's K-K-K-Krastos, h-h-he f-found s-s-something."

Krastos was the chief engineer of the excavation and a smart and sensible ape. Young Caleb was a second-year seminary student and served as a general assistant at the construction site. There were more than forty students from the School of Holy Law and half again as many manual laborers, all of them working long hours to clear the land and dig the foundation for the planned Shrine of the Tenth Scroll. It was backbreaking work and comforts were few.

Dante considered it an honor for them, however, to be part of something so important. And the way in which each accounted himself would allow the senior clerics to get their measure. Some would be asked to leave and return to secular life. Most would, in the end, because serving the will of God and following the true path of the Lawgiver was not for everyone. Not for most. When the toiling was done and the shrine constructed, only a handful of apes here would live there as clerics or servants. Caleb, young as he was, often showed some promise and aptitude, but at the moment Dante would gladly have sent him to burn ticks off of humans.

"Y-y-you must c-c-come s-s-s-see what he f-f-found," urged the boy, his words juddering out like automatic rifle fire, hard and discordant.

Dante sat back on his heels, a dripping scroll held carefully away from the other documents, and cocked his head to look up at the boy. There was a strange light in Caleb's eyes.

"Exactly *what* did Krastos find?" he asked.

The young assistant ran ahead faster than Dante wanted to walk. The cleric was amused by the boy's enthusiasm, though he was still annoyed about the wine on the scrolls. Dante was also curious. This construction site had been well-planned, but the process had been long, arduous, and frustrating. When Dante had first approached the church elders with his scheme, he was shot down three times, and in each case had to burn away weeks or months in lobbying for support. Then, when the council had finally given their grudging approval to build a shrine such a long way from the metropolis of Ape City, Dante had forwarded fourteen different locations, each in a spot that would draw on commercial trade routes, civilian travelers, itinerant scholars, and pilgrims. The shrine, the elders told him, needed to be anchored by a town that would benefit from the increase in tourism, but which would not be marginalized by the presence of a holy place. Politics. It was always politics. Even more than faith, even more than the evangelical demands of their faith, it was politics.

Or, as he privately saw it, it was chimpanzees.

Sure, all of the apes played politics in their own way, and his kind, the orangutans, played it very well—especially since they were the traditional keepers of the faith. But for years now, it had been the intellectual nitpickers, the politically correct, the let's-find-a-common-ground chimpanzees who had slowed the process to a lame shuffle. Even here in Big Rock, which everyone in the world regarded as the mole on the left buttock of civilization, the chimpanzees were delighting themselves by cluttering up what should have been an easy process. And the town's energetic young mayor, Cato, was no friend of the orangutans. Dante suspected that the brash upstart was probably a closet heretic, though proving it would be virtually impossible. Cato was no fool.

Dante frowned at how empty the worksite was. Where was everyone? It was still only late morning and there were enough clouds to keep the day cool even in mid-summer; surely, the lazy louts were not taking a midday rest.

No, he thought as he saw that there were tools scattered around as if dropped during startled flight. *What could be happening?* Caleb had sputtered so badly he hadn't been able to say much more than Krastos had found something and everyone was terribly excited. Thoughts of what that "something" could be made Dante slow his pace for a few strides, and he cast a quick, uneasy glance toward the east. Big Rock was bordered on one side by a rain-swollen river, on another by impassible marshlands, but rich with fertile grove lands everywhere else. Pecan and peach trees grew in abundance, and the lush woods were heavy with game.

But there was a darkness here, too, and a big part of

the reason this site was ultimately chosen was to fight that darkness. The lands allotted to the shrine butted up against a series of low, broken hills through which narrow rivers ran. The first of those rivers was known as Boundary Run, and everything beyond it was left unnamed. Not a brook, not a hill, not a grove, not a lagoon was given a name because they were all already labeled. They formed the tip of a longer finger of land into which no sane ape would travel.

The Forbidden Zone. Or, Dante privately conceded, one of them—because, in truth, there were several areas collectively known as the Forbidden Zone. Never *Zones*. Singular, because they represented a single, shared thing.

Evil.

Nothing that went into the Forbidden Zone did so because it was drawn by anything save sin, madness, or darkness. And nothing came out of there that was not an abomination in the eyes of God.

The shrine was to be built here as a statement, and one day the church's greatest stoneworkers would erect a monolith on the banks of Boundary Run. It would say these words: "HERE AND NO FARTHER."

And it would say that on both sides, the one that faced the people of the town and the one that looked out across the river. It was a bold statement, and one of Dante's devising. As much as he appreciated subtlety, this was not a time for metaphor. The chimpanzees, of course, spent days debating whether it should read "farther" or "further." Dante wanted to brain the lot of them.

Up ahead, he saw that all of the workers—the laborers, the assistants, the monks and priests and novices—were clustered around the edge of the broad pit that was being dug so they could lay the shrine's foundation. Caleb was so excited he actually grabbed Dante's hand and tried to pull him, like a child tugging his father along to watch the humans cavorting in the circus. Dante nearly snatched his hand back, but did not, and allowed himself to be pulled toward the throng. As he closed on them, the cleric could hear snatches of the questions they threw at one another in tones of whispered excitement.

"...what is it... what's it for... who put it there... what's it mean...?"

Only when he was within a few feet of the massed people did Dante pull his hand free and call out in a ringing tone, "What's all this nonsense?"

Everyone whirled at the sound of his voice, from the smallest assistant to the largest of the burly gorilla laborers. And every single one of them backed away, bowing in deference. Unlike chimpanzees, the apes here knew their place and they understood respect. Even so, Dante had a certain reputation to uphold, so he glared at them and watched every set of eyes briefly meet his own and then fall away. Even young Caleb suddenly remembered himself and stood to one side, head down, hands clasped in front of him. Dante gave it all a moment, allowing their silence to be the substance of any lesson this required.

"Step aside," he said quietly, and the crowd parted like a curtain to reveal the great pit beyond. Dante walked to the edge and looked down to see a lone figure standing in the deepest corner of the foundation hole. Dante recognized the lumpy, sturdy shape of Krastos, senior engineer for the shrine project—a steady ape upon whom Dante thoroughly relied. The engineer stood facing a section of dirt wall, leaning on a long-handled spade whose blade was buried in the hard, dark soil. The distance was too great for Dante to see what the engineer had found, but there was both tension and defeat in Krastos' posture. A chill swept up Dante's back and made the hairs on his neck stand out straight as needles.

A single word escaped his lips.

"No..."

•

Dante ordered everyone to leave the dig site and return to their tents for meditation and prayer. They obeyed, but not without throwing lingering looks back at the pit. Their eyes were filled with thousands of questions, and Dante knew that he would have to concoct some kind of answers.

For now, he needed answers of his own. His guess, though, as he climbed down the ladder to the floor of the pit, was that his answers were not going to satisfy their curiosity. No. He knew that this was going to be a problem. Possibly a fatal one for the shrine project. Perhaps even fatal for Big Rock.

Young Caleb lingered, shifting from one foot to the other in his nervous agitation. "Sh-sh-should I-I c-c-come w-w-w—?"

Dante patted him on the arm and then gave him a gentle shove. "No, my boy, this is not for you. Go on, now, and make sure no one else comes down here. Mind me, and see that I am obeyed in this."

Caleb straightened as if he'd suddenly been tasked with saving all of apedom from the hordes of Hell.

"Yes!" he said without a trace of a stutter.

Dante watched him go, amused and touched by the young ape's dedication. But as he turned back toward the excavation, his smile melted away and the coldness was there again. The chill. The fear.

He stepped to the ladder, swung around and climbed down into the pit.

Krastos came hurrying over, his spade still clutched in one hand. The old engineer had massive shoulders covered in graying orange hair, but had lost most of the whiskers around his face. It made him look even older than he was. He nodded to the cleric, then fell into step with Dante as they began walking toward the far wall.

"We thought we'd hit a layer of rock," said Krastos,

jumping right in, "and I ordered the diggers to clear it off. I figured that if it was big enough and solid, then maybe we could level it and use it as the under-floor for the shrine."

"But…?"

"But it was already level. See there?" Krastos pointed to a cleared section of the ground. At close range, Dante was able to see that there was, indeed, a hard layer beneath the dirt, but it wasn't raw stone. He went over, bent, and ran his fingertips over the exposed gray-white surface. "It's concrete."

Dante snatched his hand back.

"*Poured* concrete," elaborated Krastos. "Very good quality, too. Industrial. Whoever laid it knew what they were about. I had my people drive rods down through the dirt to establish its size, and it covers nearly half the pit we've dug. Flat and nearly square, too. Call it forty yards per side, though it might be bigger because some of it goes under the ground we haven't dug."

Dante did not comment on that. Instead, he rose and walked slowly over to the wall. Krastos kept pace with him, and when they reached it the old orangutan sighed heavily. "And… then there's that," said the engineer.

The flat concrete pad ran up to the side of the pit, but it was evident the pit itself had been excavated within a few yards of another wall. A concrete wall. "When we found this I cleared everyone else out," said Krastos quietly.

Dante saw that Krastos had dug out a section of wall fifteen feet wide and ten high. It was all the same dull gray-white. Except where it wasn't. Except where there were words painted on it in blocky black letters. Dante did not dare speak. Not at first. He turned slowly, looking at the cleared section of wall. At the letters. At the words they formed, running left to right. Dangerous words. Terrifying.

Most of the others at the construction site would not understand what this meant, or what horrors they implied, but Dante knew. Every senior initiate in the sacred order of the Guardians of the Scroll would be able to read those words and understand what they meant. That understanding, and any actions that might be taken as a consequence, were a heavy responsibility. It's why apes like Seneca, Pliny, Abraham, and even Zaius himself had sworn oaths to die rather than let this kind of evil endure or spread. Seeing it here, on *this* side of Boundary Run, right at the spot where the shrine was to be built, felt like a dagger in his heart. He stared at the words and felt the dagger turn.

Naval Air Station Joint Reserve Base New Orleans

Dante snaked out a hand and caught Krastos by the elbow, pulling him close to whisper in the old engineer's ear. "Did anyone else see this?"

"No," said Krastos, moving up to stand very close. "I made them all wait on the far side of the excavation because they can't read it from there."

"Good."

Krastos rested the point of his spade against the concrete pad. "I can bring tent poles and sheeting if you want, and build a screen."

Dante nodded. He felt faint and sick and had to brace his feet to keep from swaying. *Here? Of all places, here?*

Krastos cut a nervous look at the cleric. "What does it mean?"

Dante licked his thin lips.

"It means that God is testing us," said Dante in a cold little whisper. "It means that God is watching us."

"I…"

Dante turned to him. "Erect the screen. Do it yourself. No one else is to see this. And send for Captain Maximus. Do it now."

Krastos nodded, took his spade and trudged away. Once he was alone, Dante placed both of his hands against the wall beneath the words.

"The one and only God is watching us very closely," he murmured.

Dante saw him arrive.

Captain Maximus was very hard to miss. He was not the biggest silverback Dante had ever met, but he was easily the broadest, with massive shoulders, arms that were packed with muscle, and a brutish face that even scared horses. An old human male had once died from sheer fright when Maximus roared at him. That had been on a market day and everyone in Big Rock laughed about it for weeks. Except the chimpanzees, of course, who managed to find something wrong with anything any ape did who wasn't part of their cabal of snobs.

The big captain did not bother with the ladder but instead dropped from the edge of the foundation wall, landed on all fours, punched the ground once as if to teach it its place, then straightened and strode over to meet the cleric. He wore a black leather tunic but no cap. Studded gauntlets were buckled around his forearms, and he had a pistol and dagger on his broad belt. As he approached, Maximus looked slowly around, surveying the site. He nodded as if satisfied that it was empty. Far above, the clouds had thickened to cover the sky and a false night was already falling. Lanterns cast the whole scene in shades of flickering orange and midnight black.

"Dante," said the gorilla, his voice a deep rumble.

"Captain," replied Dante. They nodded to each other. They were not exactly close friends, but their politics and religious views coincided on every important point, and that made them allies.

The gorilla glanced at the screens. "Krastos found something?"

"Yes."

"What is it? A fault in the foundation? Are we going to lose this site?"

"We may lose the site," said Dante, "or we may not. You tell me."

Dante turned and gestured to the screens. Maximus frowned for a moment, then slapped aside the edge of a curtain and stepped inside. After a moment Dante followed, and he nearly bumped into the captain, who had stopped in his tracks and stood staring at the wall. Although literacy was lowest among gorillas, no one could rise to the rank of captain without being able to read and write. Maximus was well read and shrewd.

Maximus read the words and then wheeled on Dante. "What heresy is this?"

"Again, you tell me," said Dante.

Maximus walked over to the wall, touching it in much the same way Dante had done. He traced several of the letters and then stopped, but left his thick fingers there. "How is this here?" he asked. "How is it on this side of Boundary Run?"

Dante said nothing.

"The Run is the outside edge of the Forbidden Zone," continued the gorilla. "There isn't supposed to be *anything* like this here."

Dante said nothing.

"We were *told*," insisted Maximus. "It's written in all of the books that no evil has set foot in this part of the world."

"And yet," said Dante quietly.

Maximus turned quickly and there were dangerous lights in his black eyes. His voice, though, was calm. "And yet," he agreed.

They were silent for a long time, but much was said in the looks they exchanged. Dante followed the big ape's eyes as he worked it through. Maximus flicked his eyes toward the screens, beyond which was the excavation for the shrine, and beyond that the small village of tents for the workers. Maximus shifted his gaze toward Big Rock, and then another shift in the direction where, many hundreds of miles from there, was the sprawling metropolis of Ape City.

Then the gorilla's eyes shifted to two items that stood leaning against the wall: a sledgehammer and a pickaxe. Without saying a word, the gorilla began unbuttoning his leather vest. He handed it to Dante, then took the handle of the pickaxe, hefted its weight in his hands, set himself and swung with all of his considerable strength. The cold steel point of the pick bit deep into the concrete between the words "Naval" and "Air." Chips of stone flew.

Dante, smiling, stepped aside and watched with great interest as the captain attacked the wall. The grunt of the big ape, the whistle of the tool as it whipped through the air, and the heavy *tink* of impact were the only sounds in the world.

It took Maximus nearly two hours to smash the wall.

He never once stopped, never paused, and instead worked like a machine, his huge muscles bunching and flexing beneath the rubbery hide and dense black hair. Fissures whipsawed out from the impact points as concrete chipped away to reveal cinderblocks. Once he was at that level, the destruction became easier as the lighter composite building blocks crumbled beneath the savage impacts. A cloud of white dust hung in the air around the ape, gradually coating him so that he looked like a ghost from a midnight horror tale. Like the ghost of "Hector and the Five Demon Men" that was told to children to make them eat their greens.

Then Maximus tossed the pickaxe aside, chest heaving, and snatched up the sledgehammer. He gave Dante a strange and almost manic look and then attacked the edges of the hole, breaking out spikes of rock the way he would knock out an enemy's teeth in combat. Even though this was only stone, there was a joyful brutality about it that Dante admired. A true soldier of the faith.

Finally, Dante said, "That is enough, Captain."

The big ape swung the sledge a last time, assessed the damage, and let the tool drop with a ringing clang. The hole was now ten feet high and seven wide. Dust swirled into it and vanished into deep shadows. The gorilla had chopped out all of the letters, though, so that lines of destruction spread out like wings from the hole.

The captain and the cleric moved to the very edge of the hole. The air from inside was cold and surprisingly dry, as if tightly sealed from the moisture of the rich dirt around it. Dante doubted any rain had even seeped inside; there was no smell of mold or rot.

"Who knows about this?" asked Maximus.

"Who knows that we found something?" said Dante. "Everyone in camp. But if you're asking about what was written on the wall, then it's the two of us and Krastos, and he knows when to hold his tongue. He's a good ape, and his loyalties are to the church."

"This will get out, though."

"Only if we're sloppy," said Dante. "Only if we're foolish."

Maximus cut a look at him. "Surely, Cato will find out. His spies are everywhere, and I'm not just talking about the chimpanzees. There are orangutans on his payroll and maybe even some of my lads."

Dante nodded. "Sad, but all too true. Trust is hard to come by in these troubled times."

"And Cato is smart, damn him," growled Maximus. "He'll know something is happening out here. If he comes out here for an inspection…"

"This is church ground," Dante reminded him. "Even the mayor has to get permission from the council first, and that's a bureaucratic process that can take an alarming amount of time… if managed correctly. No, Cato won't find out about anything specific right away. We may have as much as a week or two before—"

Maximus laughed. "Two weeks? Ha! I bet he already knows something is going on out here. All it takes is for one ape to come in here while we're sleeping…"

He trailed off, leaving the obvious unsaid.

Dante nodded. "Then we need guards. You say that you can't trust all of your people, but surely there are *some* who are reliable. Can you pick four or, better yet, six to stand watch?"

Maximus thought about it for a moment, then nodded. "My sister's husband would walk through hellfire for me, I know that. And his brother. And there are the three river gorilla brothers. You know the ones. They were offered prison or the army, and they've been with me for years now. And they're no friends of Cato and the chimpanzee courts. They'll do, and maybe one other." He nodded again. "Yes, I think they're all trustworthy. And tough, too. They know that you're my friend, so they think you're the right hand of the Lawgiver."

"Useful," said Dante.

They studied the darkness.

"Mayor Cato could jail us for even breaking down this wall," said the gorilla.

"A bit late to point that out," said Dante.

"My point is that we may be playing into his hands," said Maximus. "We gorillas are strong and you orangutans are devious, but here in Big Rock the chimpanzees outnumber us six to one. Weak as they are, there are enough of them to force us to turn this site over to them. And they have the legal right to demand it. Cato wants all of this land to expand the farms—farms that are almost entirely owned by his lot. Most of the gorillas have moved out of here because there's no one to fight, no way for a decent ape to make his mark on the world. By the Lawgiver, there are ten gorilla families who are already planting beans. *Beans,* for all that's holy." He gave Dante a curt nod. "You wouldn't even be here if you hadn't somehow convinced the church elders that this was a good spot to build a shrine. You think Cato doesn't resent you for that? And he knows where my loyalties lie, so he lumps us all in together."

"And your point?"

"My point is that we're already playing a dangerous game, Dante. Not only can Cato arrest both of us, but he'll snatch all of this land. Then anyone who was ever close to us—those who aren't breaking rocks along with us—will be planting beans and banana trees all throughout this region. There won't be a shrine."

Dante considered. "If he becomes aware of what we've found."

"We don't even know what we've found."

"Don't we?" asked Dante. "Besides… had these lands been left to Cato and his farmers, they would have found this place in time. And where would we all be?"

"We'd be standing on the same cracked tree limb ready to fall."

"Would we, captain?" Dante slowly shook his head. "I rather think not. Because Mayor Cato would not react to this place as we are reacting—with reasoned thought and self-control. He would abandon this entire region, even at the expense of his people's financial welfare. He would run screaming like a monkey."

"Or he'd go inside and see what he could use to really overthrow us. Cato is ambitious, Dante. If he had real power—not just numbers, but something more—do you think gorillas or orangutans would have any of the freedoms we currently have? Not a chance of that. The chimpanzees would love to turn us into slaves no better than humans."

Dante shook his head. "Maybe. And although Cato is smart, I think you overestimate him as much as he overestimates himself. He has numbers, yes, and he certainly has ambitions, but would he go so far as that? I don't know."

"I do. And as much as it causes me physical pain to say it, I fear the little bastard. You should, too. You think the church would remain in power if the chimpanzees took control? They're closet atheists, all of them."

Dante shrugged. It was a topic often discussed among his fellow orangutans, but he'd never before heard a gorilla say it.

"Cato is dangerous," Maximus said flatly. "And he will find out about this place, mark me on that."

"Perhaps he will, but not as quickly as you believe," soothed Dante. "Cato *thinks* he has the best spy network in town, but believe me when I tell you this, Captain Maximus, *no one* has a better network than the church. No one ever has, and no one ever will."

The gorilla snorted and slapped the edge of the wall hard enough to knock a big chunk of concrete and cinderblock down. "How can they *not* know? We can't just bury this and pretend it doesn't exist. The whole camp knows that something is here."

"Yes, they do," said Dante, "but that is all they know."

"Meaning what?"

"Meaning, that we've found something of great importance on a site that has been sanctified and consecrated. Surely, anything found in so holy a place must be of great spiritual importance."

The gorilla looked at him. "And you think they'll buy that?"

Dante held up a hand the way clerics often did when quoting the scriptures. "'And when the savages had set his field alight with yellow flames and pursued the pilgrim, Josiah and his wife and their children out into the wastelands. They beheld a thing like unto a tower of flame that spoke in the voice of the Lawgiver, and the Lawgiver said to them, 'Take heart and do not fear, for I have planted the seeds of your salvation in the very ground.'"

"Oh, very nice," said Maximus with a harsh laugh. "That's a quote about finding potatoes to feed them on their flight from the edge of the Forbidden Zone to the valleys near Ape City. How does that...?"

The gorilla's voice trailed off and a look of understanding came slowly into his eyes. The big ape turned and looked back once more to the wall of screens and then nodded. "Ah," he said.

"Ah," agreed Dante. He gave Maximus a long and calculating appraisal. "Many people underestimate gorillas."

Maximus smiled. "And you?"

"There are wise apes and fools of every stripe, my friend. I've learned long ago not to judge but rather to observe and evaluate. And though we have never had an explicit conversation on the subject, it's my belief that we are of a mind when it comes to what makes the territories beyond Boundary Run 'forbidden.'"

Maximus grunted.

"Just as I believe we are both adult enough to understand *why* it's forbidden," continued Dante, "and why it needs to remain forbidden. The nature of what *makes* it forbidden does, by extension, make this place forbidden as well."

"Yes," agreed the captain.

Dante bent and picked up a lantern. "Once we step inside, we are breaking the laws of our own faith."

The gorilla straightened. "Maybe. But aren't all things done in the service of the Lawgiver, and to protect his people, sanctified as necessary?"

"Cato would not agree."

Maximus showed his white teeth in a killer's grin. "No. I don't suppose he would."

Together, they stepped into the darkness.

The place was massive, cold, dark. Alien.

But familiar, too, at least to Dante. He had never *been* in a place like this before, but the tales told by the older members of the Guardians of the Scrolls had carried him there. Those stories had lifted him and brought him across the borders of the Forbidden Zone, into strange tunnels and through doorways, down flights of dusty stairs, into chambers built by hands that did not belong to any of the great apes.

The very fact of their existence, the undeniable truth of what it all meant, was the very reason the Guardians had been formed in the first place. It was the truth that held their brotherhood together and had shaped their resolve over many hundreds of years. It was a truth they rarely spoke aloud, even among themselves, even when they were behind their own strong, locked doors. It was a truth they did not dare share with the chimpanzees, and only in the rarest of cases with the most trusted of the gorillas.

It was a truth that should have shaken their faith to its core and made a liar of the Lawgiver. And yet...

It did not.

In very real point of fact, the knowledge that human hands had built those places became the strongest possible reinforcement of their faith. There was no doubt at all about the unrelenting savagery of humankind. There was no doubt that they had been warlike, destructive and, worst of all, self-destructive. They had built weapons that were designed to kill their own kind in staggering numbers. They had built appalling machines that could lay waste to vast tracts of land and poison the soil so that nothing would ever grow again.

They had darkened their skies and turned the very weather against their own. Even the wisest of the Guardians could not understand why. How could a species that, despite popular belief, had been capable of advanced thought not have the compassion to provide for their own children by handing over a safer, cleaner, and less dangerous world?

As the two apes stood together in a room that was stacked floor to ceiling with crates of rifles and grenades—enough in that one chamber to slaughter fifty thousand apes—Maximus seemed to catch the thread of Dante's dark musings. And although neither had spoken more than a dozen words since entering the complex, Maximus touched his hand to his heart and murmured old words he had no doubt learned in church as a young ape.

"'And when the human child reached out his hands to beg for bread from its father, he was instead given a scorpion.'"

Dante nodded. "The Eighth Scroll, fifteenth chapter, ninth verse."

Maximus cleared his throat and walked over to one of the metal racks that lined the walls. He curled his fingers around the barrel of a rifle of strange design. Unlike the smooth and elegant designs of the rifles he had always used, this one was all hard edges and ugly lines. He pulled the weapon from the rack and weighed it in his hands.

"It's light," he said. "Feels like a toy."

Dante said nothing and watched as Maximus turned the gun over, making sense of its functions, experimenting with the action. Then the gorilla prowled the room until he found a stack of empty magazines beside an even taller stack of boxed cartridges. In the quiet darkness, there was the harsh, metallic click and rasp as Maximus fed one bullet after another into a magazine... the jolting slap of the magazine as the gorilla rammed it into the body of the gun. The captain glanced at Dante and then walked out of the room, and the cleric followed.

They went into an adjoining chamber whose function was unclear to either of them. There were row upon row of tables on which sat boxes of metal, plastic, and glass, with boards of small squares with letters and numbers on them. Maximus raised the weapon, seating the stock against his hip. He glanced again at Dante, who nodded.

The gorilla's finger was almost too thick to fit inside the trigger guard.

He pulled the trigger and held the weapon as it roared. Flame and smoke erupted from the barrel and bullets filled the air, punching into the small boxes, exploding them, scattering pieces everywhere. Dante cried out and clapped his hands over his ears, wincing and backing away from the thunder. It took only seconds to empty the entire magazine and silence crashed down at once.

The gorilla stood panting, staring down at the weapon in his hands. His eyes were filled with strange lights. Fear and excitement.

"By the tears of the Lawgiver..." gasped Maximus. "The *power* of this thing. Our best rifles are six-shot. I put *thirty* bullets in that and they all fired. Even after all this time, they fired. A dozen apes with guns like this could... could..."

He swallowed and didn't finish. Dante came and took the weapon from him, turning it over in his hands. Then he went back into the armory with the gorilla close at his heels. Dante placed the gun carefully atop a case marked "HIGH-CAPACITY MAGAZINES" and stood with one hand resting on it.

"Tell me, my friend," he began slowly, "what is the greatest danger to apes today? Is it man or is it something else?"

The gorilla walked the length of the room, turned, and walked back before answering. "Man is nothing," he said. "Not anymore."

"Is that what you believe?"

The captain nodded. "Man isn't man anymore." He gestured to the room. "What man alive today could build this? No, point out any man you've ever met who could pick up a gun and know which end to point at an ape? If he pulled the trigger, it would be by accident and he'd likely blow his own foot off. No… man fell, and he fell all the way down to ruin and simplicity and stupidity."

Dante nodded encouragement. He liked this gorilla.

"If man were to ever reclaim what he had," continued Maximus, "it would take too long and we are always watching. Always."

"Yes we are," agreed Dante. "So where is the real danger?"

Maximus pointed the way they'd come. "It's there," he said. "It's back home. It's in Rock City and in Towering Tree and it's in Simian Shores and Ape City and everywhere else. It's us."

"'Us?'" echoed Dante.

"Us. Not you and me. Not the gorillas or the orangutans. It's the chimpanzees and everything they believe."

Dante gestured for him to elaborate.

"Cato wants us to farm this region. He has plans to extend the farmlands down south and out west. He wants to cut the hunting woods down to plant grasslands for cattle and sheep. He wants to build dams to flood the swamps so he can stock them with fish. And where will the labor come for all of this? I'll tell you where." He slapped his hand down on a crate with a sound like a gunshot. "*Us*. Gorillas. Cato will take the guns from our hands—as he's always done—and turn us all into farmers. Not just a few, but every last one of us. He might as well geld us while he's at it… the effect would be the same. Cato thinks the world is conquered, that there are no real threats out there and no need for an army, a militia, or even a police force. Oh, sure, he may let a few of us walk around in uniform as tokens, but that's all we'd be."

"Do you think that is likely to happen?" asked Dante.

"Of course I do. So do you. The chimpanzees breed like lice, and the more of them there are, the fewer of us get into any positions of real power. Mark me, Dante: Ape City may be different, Zaius and the elder orangutans may still be in power there, but that won't last. It won't. The intellectuals may be weak as individuals, but there are already too damn many of them." He pointed a finger at Dante. "And be warned. If the military and police numbers go down, if the chimpanzees crowd us out, how long do you think you orangutans will hold power?"

"Even though we are the guardians of the faith?" asked Dante, smiling.

"Ha. You know that Cato doesn't care about any of that. Atheist scum. Leave it up to him and every church would be razed and the land given over to pig farmers. He would tear down the statues of the Lawgiver and replace them with corn silos and then we would all have to pray to a new god—progress. Tell me I'm just being an alarmist, Dante. Tell me I'm wrong."

Dante sat on the edge of a crate of grenades. "God is God. He is jealous and He is harsh in His justice. That is the law. That is the only law, and it has kept our people safe through the darkest of times."

Maximus nodded.

"This place was consecrated in the name of the Lawgiver," continued the cleric. "Everything between the hunting woods and Boundary Run belongs to the church. Every stick, every stone, every blade of grass. All of it is holy ground. And we have been told that the evil lies beyond the water, in the Forbidden Zone. Evil is there and righteousness is here. That is what the elders say, and that is what the law says."

Maximus was watching, nodding, saying nothing.

"To find such a place," said Dante, "filled with all of this…

a weak mind and a weak spirit would see it and say that the law is wrong, that the church is wrong, that what we believe in is wrong because here is proof to the contrary. Here is proof that evil is everywhere. But I trust in the law, Maximus. I trust in the elders and in the writings of the Lawgiver and in all that is holy. If this is here, it is because God *put* it here. And if it was put here for us to find, God wants us to have it."

"Why? Why put *this* kind of temptation in our path?"

"Do you see it as temptation, my friend? Or can you open your heart to see that God has revealed to us a way of purifying His flock and bringing His people back to the path of righteousness? Consider the scrolls of the Lawgiver and the passages that talk about separating the chaff from the wheat, of culling the sickly cattle from the herd so that disease does not flourish and our kind diminish. We have been taught to eschew the tainted meat of the deer that wander from the Forbidden Zone. Those are stories that run deeper than what is obvious. We have been taught to protect apekind by cutting away at the impure, just as a surgeon removes a gangrenous leg."

He ran his hand along the top of the crate.

"Cato and his kind will bring us to ruin. He will weaken the apes and allow mankind to become strong." He looked around the room. "Strong again. We will fall and the human will rise again. Or the great apes will become scattered and only those of superior number will survive. And, as you have observed, we orangutans and gorillas are few and the chimpanzees are many. So many."

"No," growled Maximus.

"No," agreed Dante. They sat in silence for a long time, then Dante rose and crossed to the rifle and picked it up. "Tell me, Maximus, how many of the righteous would it take to change the course of history? How many true believers would it take to save Big Rock from itself? From the heresy that is Cato's plans for this region?"

Maximus took the rifle from him and studied it for a long, long time. "With God and the Lawgiver on our side?" he asked. "Not many. No... not many at all."

They stood in the lamplight, surrounded by the sacred objects provided for them by a jealous God, and they smiled.

A QUESTION OF SIMIAN SURVIVAL
AN AFTERWORD

by

JIM BEARD

I don't want to get too heavy here, especially after you've just finished reading sixteen mind-blowing stories, but let's talk about the future.

The future, you see, is *bright*.

Yeah, I get it; that's a funny thing to say in a book based on a fictional, dark, dystopian prediction of things to come for the human race, but I promise you I know what I'm talking about. How? Well, a few things…

One, the past.

I knew the strength of the *Apes* property at a very young age, just from looking at the newspaper. To my young self growing up in the late 1960s and early 1970s, it seemed like every day I checked the "Now Playing" section of the local paper's movie page, another *Planet of the Apes* film had hit town. In my perception, there was a new one, like, every other month. Now, *that's* a strong franchise right there! Add in the TV series and the Mego figures and the bubblegum cards, and I just *knew* in my tiny human heart that apes were sure to rule the planet by the time I was twelve.

(They actually took over when I was twenty-six in 1991, but that's another story.)

So, two, the present.

When you're putting together an original anthology of *Planet of the Apes* stories and you're swept away, every single time one of your authors hands in work, by that person's unbridled enthusiasm as he or she tells you how much *fun* it was to write (I don't exaggerate here), that tells you something. And what does it tell you?

It tells you that a) Such a book was long overdue, and b) People really, really love *Planet of the Apes*. Even writers.

Especially writers.

This is a healthy, vibrant, *living* franchise. When a writer joyfully exclaims a word that I cannot type here after being invited to join an *Apes* anthology, you pause a moment and reflect (and maybe cock an eyebrow in arch amusement). When that same writer delivers his tale and tells you it challenged and engaged him, enthusing him to write it, you wonder why you hadn't thought to put together such a book years earlier.

(For my own part in this, I couldn't choose just one spot in the property's two-thousand-year-plus storytelling potential for my own tale. Nope, I had to have them *all*, and jumped through time like an ANSA spacecraft on a Hasslein bender. The moment I'd finished writing, I was thinking of the next story I wanted to do. And the next. And the next…)

My co-editor Rich Handley and I began to look forward to that email from each of our writers, because there would not only be a new *Apes* story attached to it (cause enough for celebration, yes), but also a message of hope and prosperity. To paraphrase a 1970 Fox executive:

"Apes exist, anthology needed."

That brings us back to the future.

Planet of the Apes is all about the future, dark as it may be. Far more than just a planet of possibilities, it is an entire *universe* of them. I knew this as a kid, and I was reminded of it as an adult working alongside some of the biggest *Apes* fans on *this* planet. It's a property that can encompass nearly any storytelling genre and can take us on journeys far beyond the constraints of our own so-called real world. It inspires excitement in its admirers, and it elevates professional writers to even greater heights of creativity... or maybe it devolves them into kids again, staring at a grainy black-and-white announcement of what looks like the ninety-fifth film in the franchise.

Rich and I had a nuclear blast putting this book together, and I hope it shows on every page. It was a series of thrills to have our pitch accepted by Titan and Fox, to build our murderer's row of writers, and to read and edit each tale as it flew up and over the transom. Every editor should be as lucky as we were and are.

Because the future of an ape-dominated planet is so bright, we want to keep the dream (or nightmare) of talking chimps and gorillas and orangutans alive and well for years to come. You can help in that by fanning that flame in your own heart—and asking for more anthologies like this one.

It's a question of simian survival, you know.

JIM BEARD
March 2016

ACKNOWLEDGMENTS

The editors of this anthology wish to thank every individual who helped to build the *Planet of the Apes* film and literature franchise—all of the writers, directors, producers, actors, makeup artists, effects teams, composers, and everyone else involved along the way. Without them, this book would not exist.

In addition, we are profoundly grateful to Twentieth Century Fox, Titan Books, and editor Steve Saffel for allowing us to stake our claim on this corner of the mythos, and to the immensely talented writers who joined us on this journey.

We thank the following individuals for their support: Joseph Berenato, Joe Bongiorno, Steve Czarnecki (beyondthemarquee.com), Joseph Dilworth, Paul Giachetti (hassleinbooks.com), Hunter Goatley (pota.goatley.com), Joni Handley, Neil Moxham (planetoftheapes.wikia.com), and *Simian Scrolls* editors Dave Ballard, Dean Preston, and John Roche. Special thanks to novelist Robert J. Sawyer for providing a cover quote, and to Pierre Boulle for giving us all a planet on which to monkey around.

Finally, we dedicate this book to our wonderful and supportive wives, Becky Beard and Jill Handley, who keep us both sane when the world around us goes ape.

ABOUT THE CONTRIBUTORS

Dan Abnett is a seven-time *New York Times* bestselling author and an award-winning comic book writer. He has written more than fifty novels, including the acclaimed *Gaunt's Ghosts* series, the *Eisenhorn* and *Ravenor* trilogies, volumes of the million-selling *Horus Heresy* series, *The Silent Stars Go By* (*Doctor Who*), *Rocket Raccoon and Groot: Steal the Galaxy*, *The Avengers: Everybody Wants to Rule the World*, *The Wield*, *Triumff: Her Majesty's Hero*, and *Embedded*. In comics, he is known for his work on *The Legion of Super-Heroes*, *Aquaman*, *The Teen Titans*, *Nova*, *Wild's End*, and *The New Deadwardians*, and he also helped to craft Dark Horse's *Planet of the Apes* comic line. Dan's 2008 run on *The Guardians of the Galaxy* for Marvel formed the inspiration for the blockbuster movie. A regular contributor to the United Kingdom's long-running *2000AD*, he is the creator of series including *Grey Area*, *Lawless*, *Kingdom*, and the classic *Sinister Dexter*. He has also written extensively for the games industry, including *Shadow of Mordor* and *Alien: Isolation*. Dan lives and works in the United Kingdom. Follow him on Twitter: @VincentAbnett.

Kevin J. Anderson is the author of more than 130 books, 54 of which have appeared on national or international bestseller lists. He has won or been nominated for the Hugo, Nebula, Bram

Stoker, Shamus, Scribe, and Colorado Book Awards. Kevin has written numerous *Star Wars* projects, three *X-Files* novels, and fifteen bestselling *Dune* novels with Brian Herbert, and also collaborated with Dean Koontz on *Frankenstein: Prodigal Son*, which sold a million copies during the first year of its release. He has written the epic science-fiction series *The Saga of Seven Suns* and a steampunk fantasy adventure novel with legendary Rush drummer Neil Peart, based on the concept CD *Clockwork Angels*. In addition, he has written a humorous horror series featuring Dan Shamble, Zombie PI. As the publishers of WordFire Press, Kevin and his wife, Rebecca Moesta, have released more than 300 titles from Alan Dean Foster, Frank Herbert, Jody Lynn Nye, Allen Drury, Mike Resnick, Tracy Hickman, Jay Lake, Brian Herbert, Ken Scholes, and their own backlist. Kevin climbs mountains. He and his wife have been married for twenty-five years and live in a castle in the Rocky Mountains of Colorado.

Co-editor **Jim Beard** became a published writer when he sold a story to DC Comics in 2002. Since that time, he's written official *Star Wars* and *Ghostbusters* comic stories and contributed articles and essays to several volumes of comic book history. His work includes *X-Files: Secret Agendas*; *Gotham City 14 Miles*, a book of essays on the 1966 *Batman* TV series; *Sgt. Janus, Spirit-Breaker*, a collection of pulp ghost stories featuring an Edwardian occult detective; *Monster Earth*, a shared-world giant monster anthology; *Captain Action: Riddle of the Glowing Men*, the first pulp prose novel based on the classic 1960s action figure; and an essay for Sequart's *The Sacred Scrolls: Comics on the Planet of the Apes* anthology. Jim currently provides regular content for Marvel.com, the official Marvel Comics website.

Nancy A. Collins is the author of numerous novels, short stories, and comic books. A recipient of the Horror Writers Association's Bram Stoker Award and The British Fantasy Society's Icarus

Award, she has also been nominated for the International Horror Guild Award, the John W. Campbell Award, the James Tiptree Award, the Eisner Award, the Horror Comics Award, and the World Fantasy Award. Her published novels and collections include *Sunglasses After Dark*, *Lynch: A Gothik Western*, *Knuckles and Tales*, and *Absalom's Wake*. Her critically acclaimed *Golgotham* urban fantasy series—*Right Hand Magic*, *Left Hand Magic*, and *Magic and Loss*—has been optioned by Fox Studios for series development at NBC. She is currently the writer on Dynamite Comics' *Army of Darkness: Damned If You Do*, and her previous work in the comics industry includes a two-year run on DC Comics' *Swamp Thing*, a year-long run on *Vampirella*, a *Sunglasses After Dark* graphic novel from IDW, and the current *Army of Darkness: Furious Road* limited series. Nancy, along with her Boston terrier, is a recent transplant to the Tidewater area of Virginia.

Greg Cox was eleven years old when his parents dropped him off at a triple-feature of the first three *Planet of the Apes* movies. Some say he has never been the same since... Nowadays, he is the *New York Times* bestselling author of numerous novels and short stories, including the official movie novelizations of *War for the Planet of the Apes*, *Godzilla*, *Man of Steel*, *The Dark Knight Rises*, *Ghost Rider*, *Daredevil*, *Death Defying Acts*, and the first three *Underworld* movies. In addition, he has written books and stories based on such popular series as *Alias*, *Buffy the Vampire Slayer*, *CSI: Crime Scene Investigation*, *The Green Hornet*, *Farscape*, *The 4400*, *Leverage*, *Riese: Kingdom Falling*, *Roswell*, *Star Trek*, *Terminator*, *Warehouse 13*, *Xena: Warrior Princess*, *The X-Files*, *Zorro*, and assorted Marvel and DC superheroes. He has received three Scribe Awards from the International Association of Media Tie-in Writers, and lives in Oxford, Pennsylvania. Visit him online at gregcox-author.com.

Andrew "Drew" E.C. Gaska is the founder and creative director of BLAM! Ventures, a guerrilla design studio that produces integrated media for the entertainment industry. Drew's graphic novel and prose work includes *Critical Millennium: The Dark Frontier*, *Hawken: Melee*, *Space:1999—Aftershock and Awe*, *Classic Space:1999—To Everything That Was*, *Conspiracy of the Planet of the Apes* (with Christian Berntsen, Erik Matthews, and Rich Handley), and the *Buck Rogers in the 25th Century: Draconian Fire* novella series. His upcoming releases include the graphic novels *Charger* and *Madness*, as well as a new classic *Planet of the Apes* prose novel series from Titan Books. For fifteen years, he has served as a visual consultant to Rockstar Games, and he is now also a franchise consultant to Twentieth Century Fox. Drew resides beneath a mountain of action figures in New York with his gluttonous feline, Adrien, who often perches atop this pinnacle of plastic, proclaiming himself "Lord of the Figs." Drew humors him.

Robert Greenberger has been a teacher, writer, editor, and historian, working mainly in the media tie-in field. His many credits include visits to the worlds of *Star Trek*, *Hellboy*, Zorro, Captain Midnight, the Green Hornet, and DC Comics' universe of characters. He spent twenty years on staff at DC and one as a publishing executive at Marvel Comics, in addition to serving as managing editor of *Weekly World News*. Bob is a co-founder of Crazy 8 Press, a digital press where he is working on creating new worlds to explore. He continues to write, living in Maryland where he makes his home with his wife Deb.

Co-editor **Rich Handley** is a co-founder of Hasslein Books, the managing editor of *RFID Journal* and *IOT Journal* magazines, and the author or co-author of *Timeline of the Planet of the Apes*, *Lexicon of the Planet of the Apes*, *Back in Time: The Back to the Future Chronology*, and *A Matter of Time: The Back to the Future Lexicon*. He has written licensed *Star Wars* fiction and non-fiction, and helped to craft the novel *Conspiracy of the Planet of the Apes*. Rich has co-edited five Sequart essay anthologies to date—*The Sacred Scrolls: Comics on the Planet of the Apes*; *Bright Eyes, Ape City: Examining the Planet of the Apes Mythos*; and a trio of books covering the *Star Wars* mythos. He has penned essays for IDWs five *Star Trek* comic strip reprint hardcovers and Sequart's *New Life and New Civilizations: Exploring Star Trek Comics*, and has contributed to StarTrek.com, StarWars.com, *Star Trek Communicator*, *Star Trek Magazine*, *Cinefantastique*, *Cinescape*, *Movie Magic*, *Dungeon/Polyhedron*, and more. In 2015, Rich became a character in the comic book miniseries *Star Trek/Planet of the Apes: The Primate Directive*, by Scott and David Tipton; he can now die happy.

Greg Keyes was born on April 11, 1963, in Meridian, Mississippi. When his father took a job on the Navajo Reservation in Arizona, Greg was exposed at an early age to the cultures and stories of the Native Southwest, which would continue to inform him for years to come. He earned a bachelor's degree in anthropology at Mississippi State University and a master's degree at the University of Georgia. While pursuing his Ph.D. at UGA, he wrote several novels, one of which—*The Waterborn*—was published, along with its sequel, *The Blackgod*. He followed this with *The Age of Unreason* books, the epic fantasy series *Kingdoms of Thorn and Bone*, and numerous franchises, including *Star Wars*, *Babylon Five*, and *The Elder Scrolls*. In 2014, he wrote the novel *Dawn of the Planet of the Apes: Firestorm* and in 2017 the prequel novel for *War for the Planet of the Apes*. He now lives and works in Savannah, Georgia, with his wife Nell, son Archer, and daughter Nellah.

A Colorado native, **Sam Knight** spent ten years in California's wine country before returning to the Rockies. When asked if he misses California, he gets a wistful look in his eyes and replies that he misses the green mountains in the winter, but he is glad to be back home. As well as being the distribution manager for WordFire Press, he is a senior editor for Villainous Press and the author of four children's books, three short-story collections, two novels, and more than two dozen short stories. A stay-at-home father, Sam attempts to be a full-time writer, but there are only so many hours left in a day after kids. Once upon a time, he was known to quote books the way some people quote movies, but now he claims having a family has made him forgetful, as a survival adaptation. He can be found at samknight.com.

Paul Kupperberg is the author of *The Same Old Story*, the short story collection *In My Shorts: Hitler's Bellhop and Other Stories* (both from Crazy8Press.com), and more than two dozen books of fiction and non-fiction for all ages, including the humor book *Jew-Jitsu: The Hebrew Hands of Fury* (Kensington Books). He has contributed stories to many anthologies, including those featuring such characters and franchises as Batman, *Doctor Who*, *Star Trek*, The Lone Ranger, The Green Hornet, and others, published by Pocket Books, Ace, Kensington, Warner, Bantam, DAWS, and Moonstone. Paul is also a prolific writer of more than 1,000 comic book stories to date for DC Comics, Marvel, Bongo, and others, including the controversial 2014 Archie Comics "Death of Archie" storyline. His credits include *Superman*, *Supergirl*, *Masters of the Universe*, *Captain America*, *Conan*, *The Simpsons*, and dozens more. He created the DC series *Arion Lord of Atlantis*, *Checkmate*, and *Takion*, and has written online web animation, the syndicated *Superman* and *Tom & Jerry* newspaper strips, the feature "Trash" for England's *2000 A.D.* magazine, and humor and parody for Marvel's *Crazy Magazine*. Paul has been an editor for DC Comics, *Weekly World News*, and *WWE Magazine*, and is currently the executive editor and writer for indie comics publisher Charlton Neo (morttodd.com/charlton). He can be found online at paulkupperberg.com.

Jonathan Maberry is a *New York Times* bestselling novelist, five-time Bram Stoker Award winner, and comic book writer. He writes the *Joe Ledger* thrillers, the *Rot & Ruin* series, the *Nightsiders* series, and the *Dead of Night* series, as well as standalone novels in multiple genres. His new and upcoming novels include *Kill Switch*, the eighth in his best-selling *Joe Ledger* thriller series; *Vault of Shadows*, a middle-grade science fiction/fantasy mash-up; and *Mars One*, a standalone teen space-travel novel. He is the editor of many anthologies, including *The X-Files*, *Scary Out There*, *Out of Tune*, and *V-Wars*. His comic book works include, among others, *Captain America*, the Bram Stoker Award-winning *Bad Blood*, *Rot & Ruin*, *V-Wars*, the *New York Times* bestselling *Marvel Zombies Return*, and others. His books *Extinction Machine* and *V-Wars* are in development for TV. A board game version of *V-Wars* was released in early 2016. He is the founder of the Writers Coffeehouse and a co-founder of The Liars Club. Prior to becoming a full-time novelist, Jonathan spent twenty-five years as a magazine feature writer, martial arts instructor, and playwright. He was a featured expert on The History Channel's documentary *Zombies: A Living History*, and a regular expert on the TV series *True Monsters*. He is one third of the very popular and mildly weird *Three Guys With Beards* pop-culture podcast. Jonathan lives in Del Mar, California, with his wife, Sara Jo. Visit him online at jonathanmaberry.com.

Bob Mayer is a *New York Times* bestselling author, graduate of West Point, former Green Beret, and feeder of two yellow labs, most famously Cool Gus. He has had more than sixty books published to date, including the number-one series *Time Patrol*, *The Green Berets*, *Area 51*, and *Atlantis*. Born in the Bronx and having traveled the world (usually not to tourist spots), he now lives peacefully with his wife (who collaborates with him), and said labs, at Write on the River, in Tennessee.

John Jackson Miller is the *New York Times* bestselling author of several *Star Wars* prose novels from Del Rey, including *Kenobi*, *Knight Errant*, *Lost Tribe of the Sith*, and *A New Dawn*; *Star Trek: The Next Generation—Takedown* and the 2016 *Star Trek: Prey* trilogy from Pocket Books; and *Overdraft: The Orion Offensive* from 47North. His comics work includes writing for *Star Wars*, *Iron Man*, *Mass Effect*, *The Simpsons*, and *Conan*. John's website is farawaypress.com.

Will Murray is the author of more than sixty novels, including several posthumous *Doc Savage* collaborations with Lester Dent under the name Kenneth Robeson, as well as forty in the long-running *Destroyer* series. He has pitted the Man of Bronze against King Kong in *Skull Island* and teamed him up with The Shadow in *The Sinister Shadow*. Will's first Tarzan novel is titled *Return to Pal-ul-don*. His second is *King Kong vs. Tarzan*, a project first envisioned by Merian C. Cooper back in 1935. Other Murray novels star Nick Fury, Agent of S.H.I.E.L.D.; Mack Bolan; and the Martians of the *Mars Attacks* franchise. For various anthologies, Will has written the adventures of such classic characters as Superman, Batman, Wonder Woman, Spider-Man, Ant-Man, The Hulk, The Spider, The Avenger, The Green Hornet, Sherlock Holmes, Cthulhu, Herbert West, Honey West, Sky Captain, and Lee Falk's immortal Ghost Who Walks, The Phantom—and he now contributes to the celebrated *Planet of the Apes* franchise. For Marvel Comics, he created Squirrel Girl.

Ty Templeton was born in Toronto, Canada, into a show-business family. His mother was a pop singer and his father a TV personality, so a future in the entertainment industry was a foregone conclusion. After spending his misspent youth as an actor and musician, Ty settled down to write and draw comic books for a living, working on *Superman*, *Spider-Man*, *Batman*, *The Simpsons*, *MAD Magazine*, *The National Lampoon*, *The*

Avengers, *The Justice League*, *Howard the Duck*, and *The Evil Dead*, as well as serving as the editor and co-author of the *Revolution on the Planet of the Apes* comic book series. When he was five years old, the first movie Ty ever saw in a theatre was *Beneath the Planet of the Apes*, and it clearly left a mark on him. He still lives in Toronto with his wife, four children, and three cats. One of his sons is named Taylor, but his other children are not named Brent, Zira, and Nova, so it wasn't an ongoing thing.

Dayton Ward is the *New York Times* bestselling author or co-author of numerous novels and short stories, including a whole bunch of stuff set in the *Star Trek* universe, often written with his best friend and co-writer, Kevin Dilmore. He has also written (or co-written) for *Star Trek Communicator*, *Star Trek Magazine*, *Syfy.com*, StarTrek.com, and *Tor.com*, and is a monthly contributor to the Novel Spaces writers blog (novelspaces.blogspot.com). Dayton is known to wax nostalgic about all manner of geek and sundry topics over on his own blog, *The Fog of Ward* (daytonward.com).

PLANET OF THE APES

OMNIBUS 2

Collecting together the novelizations of the iconic sci-fi films:

CONQUEST OF THE PLANET OF THE APES
by John Jakes

BATTLE FOR THE PLANET OF THE APES
by David Gerrold

PLANET OF THE APES (2001)
by William T. Quick

AVAILABLE APRIL 2017

TITANBOOKS.COM

For more fantastic fiction, author events, competitions, limited editions and more

VISIT OUR WEBSITE
titanbooks.com

LIKE US ON FACEBOOK
facebook.com/titanbooks

FOLLOW US ON TWITTER
@TitanBooks

EMAIL US
readerfeedback@titanemail.com